W9-BPM-560

My Name Is Falon

My Name Is Falon

a novel

One Woman's Saga from Scotland to the Texas Frontier

Kim Wiese

Brown Books Publishing Group
Dallas, Texas

My Name Is Falon

One Woman's Saga from Scotland to the Texas Frontier

Cover map obtained from Texas General Land Office.

This is a work of fiction. All characters, names, and scenarios are ficticious and do not represent any actual persons or events.

Manufactured in the United States of America.

For information, please contact:
Brown Books Publishing Group
16200 North Dallas Parkway, Suite 170
Dallas, Texas 75248
www.brownbooks.com
972-381-0009

A New Era in Publishing™

Hardbound ISBN-13: 978-1-934812-28-0
Hardbound ISBN-10: 1-934812-28-5
Paperback ISBN-13: 978-1-934812-29-7
Paperback ISBN-10: 1-934812-29-3

LCCN: 2008943087
1 2 3 4 5 6 7 8 9 10

In loving memory of my great-grandfather,
Hiram Alexandra Tumlison,
who first told me the story about his great uncle,
George Tumlison.

★Acknowledgments

Writing is often a solitary job, however it is not a lonely pursuit. I have been blessed to be surrounded by knowledgeable and helpful people. Kudos to the folks at Brown Books who put this project through its final paces: to Kathryn Grant who managed the project, to Dr. Janet Harris, who oversaw the editing process, to Joy Tipping, who did the final editing and untangled my knottier sentences, to Bill Young for designing such a wonderful cover, to Jessica Kinkel for making the book interior beautiful, and to all the rest of the team who made this book a reality.

A big thank you to the Colorado County Historical Society for their timely and thorough information regarding the development of Columbus, Texas from a raw settlement into a fully-established, thriving town. Special thanks to Bernice, the docent at the Water Tower Museum who showed me around and answered my many questions. Thanks also to the Texas State Historical Association and their wonderful Web site.

Love and kisses to Vera Forteson Taylor, childhood friend and partner in crime, who ran all over town with me and showed me a side of Columbus I never knew existed. Write on, Vera!

And the first shall be last . . . My greatest debt of thanks to my husband, Bob. You have always been my number one cheerleader. And to my long-suffering children, thanks for your patience and your great input. I'm a better writer, thanks to you guys.

★Prologue

Columbus, Republic of Texas, May 1836

It was a miracle the little book survived the burning. Everything else was destroyed beyond recovery. Falon used a corner of her apron to scrub the clinging gray ash from the leather cover. *This was my first journal, the first book I made.* She raised her eyes and took in the ruin all around her. *So long ago. Seems like it was another lifetime.* Holding the book lightly in one hand, as if her touch might frighten it and cause it to fly away, she opened the carefully stitched front cover.

The first light-gold page was undamaged—the first entry was dated nearly thirteen years earlier, but the ink wasn't even smeared. She might have written the words yesterday.

January 20, 1823—My name is Ellen (Falon) Carson. I made this book with my own hands, and I have decided to keep a record of our life here on the Colorado River. Whether anyone will ever find my thoughts of interest is doubtful. Our journey here began just last year, less than twelve months ago, in fact. How can that be? How could it all have happened in such a short time?

We came from Scotland, but it was not our choice to leave. . . .

★1

Sgall, Sutherlandshire, Scotland, 1822

Falon knew something was wrong the moment her father came in from the fields that bleak spring afternoon. He wasn't singing or whistling as he normally did, and he didn't meet her eyes.

Camran Macvail took off his battered cap and tossed it onto the table. "Where's your mother?"

"She's down the lane visiting with Maire Morgan." Falon set a mug down for him and filled it with steaming tea from the kettle. Though she hardly dared to ask, she knew she had to. "What is it, then, Dad?"

He wrapped one hand around the mug, and heedless of the liquid's heat, took a long swallow. Still without meeting her eyes, he said, "Eviction notice. They nailed it to the oak."

Falon felt her knees go weak. Her village, like so many others in the Highlands, was about to be destroyed and abandoned. It was the only place she'd ever known as home in all of her going-on fifteen years. She steadied herself against the table with one hand. "How long do we have?"

"One week." Her father sighed and took another gulp of tea. "It's criminal, that's what—forcing people out this time of year." He looked over to where little Robbie napped on the bed. "Going to be hardest on the wee ones and the old ones."

"Dad," Falon asked as she set the kettle back on the hearth, "don't you think I should put a few things together—just in case?"

He glanced in her direction with a wan smile. "Nay, lass. We Macvails won't be evicted. We're kin to Her Ladyship on my mother's side. I expect we'll be tending her sheep. But the others . . ." He sighed again and shook his head.

She had heard him say the same thing every time the question of eviction came up. They would stay put. She wanted to believe him, but after Father left, Falon found an old feed sack she could stow away in a corner. She slowly turned on her heel, surveying the contents of their single-room house. She felt a twinge of guilt, disobeying her father. He said they wouldn't have to go. He sounded so certain. But still . . . what could she gather up that no one would notice?

The agents came midmorning, when the menfolk were out in the fields. They came the day before the leases were up, and caught everyone off guard. They came shouting and banging on the doors of Sgall's houses with their truncheons. "Git out wi' ye now! Come on, out!"

Falon heard the commotion before the agents reached them. A piercing scream ripped the air as one of the women was dragged out of her home. Falon glanced at her mother, who had gone white around the mouth. "We won't be evicted," she murmured over and over. "We won't be evicted." She held a dishcloth, which she twisted in her hands until her knuckles stood out, sharp and hard, like glass.

But we will. Falon didn't know how she knew, but against all her father's insistence that they'd be spared, she knew. They were going to be forced out. Her heart hammering in her chest, Falon set Robbie down on Will's bed, then ran her hand under the mattress. When she found what she was looking for, she pulled it out and stuffed it inside the waistband of her skirt. Then she hurried to her own bed and pulled the half-filled feed sack from beneath it.

Even as she did, a thunderous pounding shook the door frame and sent dust falling from the overhead beams. Mother opened the door. "My husband's not home . . ." Whatever else she meant to say ended in a scream as the agent grabbed her arm and flung her to the ground just outside. His raucous laugh echoed through their little stone house, sounding like a terror from the Pit. Falon snatched up her baby brother from where he sat on Will's bed and shouldered her way past the agent just as he lifted his torch and lit the thatched roof.

Her father must have heard the screams; seconds later, Falon spotted him running toward them with her older brother, Will, at his heels. The agents, having done their devilish work, backed off to watch and laugh as the two men hurried to save what they could from the inferno.

Falon retreated to the far side of the big oak, putting its broad trunk between her and those agents, peeking around and keeping her eye on them as best she could. If one of them came after her, she'd have to run. She chewed on her lower lip, praying she'd be invisible to them. *Lord, help me protect the baby. If anything happens to him . . .* Shifting her stance to ease the ache in her back, she hiked Robbie higher on her hip. She looked over once at her mother, who was still collapsed in a wailing heap on the ground. Falon wanted to help her, to pull her to her feet and bring her to the relative safety of the tree's shadow. But Mother would refuse, would fight her off, just as she always did. Falon had the baby to think of, so she shifted him again as he whimpered. She kissed his cheek. "Dinna' cry, laddie. Tha's all right. I have thee."

Driven by a capricious wind, the fire caught the thatch roof with a roar. The supporting beams, now fully ablaze, snapped and groaned and threatened to collapse at any second. "No, Will!" Her father's alarmed cry startled her. "No more, lad. That's all we can do."

"But Dad . . ." Will protested. "Just one more run."

Father grabbed Will's arm and cuffed the side of his head. "Ye'll obey me, ye hear?" As he released his son, Father rubbed at his eyes with both hands. "It's over. Let it go."

Falon patted at the front of her dress to reassure herself of her one treasure. Uncle James had carved a beautiful wooden flute for her the year before, and it now hung securely around her neck on a leather cord. This past week she had worn the flute constantly, even to bed, keeping it secreted under her shift. Though Mother often scolded her for wearing it, today she was glad she had. *Mother will say it was sinful for me to keep my flute safe.* But Falon thought it would probably be a while before her mother even noticed.

So much for being the marchioness's relatives. Her agents are forcing us out, just like the others. Kin or no kin, it doesn't matter. Falon had been paying attention to the men's talk. The lairds who owned the land had discovered they could make far more money by grazing sheep on it than they could by keeping crofters, who farmed the land and paid rent. *Dad says blood is thicker than water. Someone should tell that to Her Ladyship.* All of the half dozen houses that teetered on the edge of the blue Loch Naver were now engulfed in flames.

She could barely make out the forms of her neighbors as they scurried to and fro in the dense smoke between the houses, desperate to salvage what they could. But when her baby brother whimpered again, she realized he'd had nothing to eat that morning. "Oh no!" she gasped aloud with horrified realization. "The byre's on fire, and the nanny is still in her pen." Grabbing a cup from among their possessions that littered the ground, she trotted around to the back of the smoking byre. She feared the worst: that the goat had been burned, or that one of the agents had clubbed her out of spite. But the nanny was still in one piece, and greeted Falon with a plaintive, fearful bleat. Falon exclaimed, "Oh, what luck!" Then—remembering what the reverend said, that luck was sinful—she quickly amended her words, hoping heaven hadn't yet noticed her error. "Thank you, Lord, for providing for Robbie."

Falon set the baby down inside the pen where he could safely toddle about. Keeping one eye on the hungry flames licking up the sides of the byre, she squatted at the nanny's flanks and crooned, "It's breakfast time, lassie. Just you give us a little, and I'll have you out of here." Holding the cup with one hand, she milked with the other. Somewhere in the back of her mind she heard Mother calling, but was so intent on her task that she didn't take heed. When the cup was full, she took it to the baby and held it for him so he could sip at the rich milk.

"Oh, you wicked, wicked girl!" Mother rounded the corner. "What do you think you're about, making me search for you?" She barreled into the pen; Falon had the presence of mind to set the precious cup of milk on the ground just before Mother hauled her up by one arm. Mother shook her till her teeth rattled, railing, "You wicked, selfish thing! Getting food for yersel' when the rest of us has got none. Shame!"

Falon bit her lip. *Why can't you ever understand?* Tears gathered in her eyes, and she turned away so Mother wouldn't see.

"That's enough, Esme." Father appeared at the pen just in time, dabbing at a scarlet trickle running from his forehead down the generous plane of his cheek. "Dinna' ye see she's feeding the lad? Leave her be. Falon, put a lead on that nanny. We're going to need her. Quick now, the fire won't wait."

"Aye, Dad." Sobered by the sight of her father's blood, and impelled by the snapping flames at her back, she disengaged her arm from Mother's grip as gently as she could, then pulled a coiled hank of rope from a nail on the fence post.

By the time Falon turned around again, Mother had picked up the baby, and was giving him the milk that remained in the cup. "And what's to become of thee, little mite?" she was saying. "No more home to grow in. Tha's cast out onto the world's mercy, and thin enough it is."

Falon slipped the rope around the goat's neck. Once Mother was out of sight, she squatted down again. Turning the nanny's teat up and out, she squirted herself a few warm mouthfuls. She wiped her face with a corner of her apron to do away with any incriminating evidence. "Thanks, old lass." Spying a battered tin bucket in one corner of the pen, she picked it up to take along. *When you're cast out onto the world's mercy, there's no knowing what might come in handy.*

Father loaded up the few items he and Will had managed to rescue from the fire into their small hay wagon. "Well, then," he said, looking around with a sigh of resignation, "that's that. Let's go." He clucked his tongue to the pony in the wagon's traces, and started off. Mother rode in the wagon amid their meager possessions, clutching a pillow—now singed on one end—that had belonged to her mother. Falon stopped to rub at her smarting eyes before she tied the nanny's lead to the rear of the wagon. She walked beside it, with Robbie perched once again on her hip. Will followed behind, driving their half dozen head of cattle, their lowing anxious and fearful in Falon's ears.

They moved up the lane through dense, black smoke, the last of Sgall's families, in a weird funereal procession, silent now but for the cattle. The cries of alarm and wailing of loss had ceased for the moment, muted by the roaring inferno. The only other sounds, small and pitiful in the fire's din, were the creaking of wagons, and the final footfalls of a people leaving home for the last time.

The fierce heat fairly drove the breath out of Falon, as if the smoke alone weren't bad enough. Robbie started wailing; he coughed and spluttered in the choking air. Falon pulled her shawl up over her head, tucking her little brother inside its folds, where he rubbed his face furiously against her dress. Now she couldn't see, so she rested her right hand on the sideboard of the wagon and walked blindly, trusting Father to lead them all out to safety. The smoke thickened, swirled up underneath her shawl. She coughed with wrenching, hacking barks that rose from deep in her lungs. Brilliant lights flashed inside her eyes, and the effort to clear her chest left her staggering.

Grinding her teeth and gasping for air, she remembered the picture of hell she had once seen in the reverend's Bible, with the leaping tongues of fire and agonizing torments. Fear gripped her heart. *So this is what it's like. I'm not going to make it through this.* Her head started to swim, and she almost lost her grip on Robbie when she dimly heard Father's shout, "Hang on, lass! We're nearly out of it." His voice gave her the strength she needed to keep walking, and after several long moments, the air around them began to clear. A cool wind out of the west kicked up and blew the smoke away. She took in great gulps of clean air, and when she finally lowered her shawl again, the burning village was behind them.

Just before they crested the first hill, Falon swatted flying embers and ash away from her face and paused to look back. All that was left of their village were burning bowls of rock walls and thick columns of black smoke pointing at the sky like evil omens. The houses were gone, the byres were in flames, and the agents had even set fire to the vegetable patches and the fields of crops beyond. By nightfall, their tiny township would be nothing but blackened rock sitting atop heaps of ashes and embers. The acrid smoke clotted in her nose; every time she swallowed, bitterness coated the back of her throat. *No matter where we go*, she told herself, *no matter how far, I'll always taste the smoke.*

She faced forward again. Father's bowed shoulders and steady plodding gait made him look like just another beast of burden. For the first time that morning, Falon's eyes filled with tears. *Where are we going, Dad? Where are you taking us?*

Her heart turned back where her eyes couldn't see, to her secret place in the hills. Midsummer two years before, she had found a shelter in the tumbled heath with a tiny rivulet sparkling and chuckling alongside. It was about the time of her twelfth birthday, and it seemed as though the hills had given her the perfect present. It was not quite a cave, more an indentation of white rock—just deep enough for shelter from a passing shower. Clumps of purple heather cloaked the ground all around, and in high summer there was no finer place, none better for sorting out the thoughts that seemed hopelessly tangled at home.

No one in her family knew about her sanctuary. She held onto the secret from everyone—everyone, that is, but her best friend, Betsy. Falon had taken her to the spot one time. "'Tis a bonny place," Betsy murmured over the little river's music. The two of them had gathered wildflowers, and were plaiting them into crowns. "'Tis perfect for thee, just perfect." She finished her crown and set it carefully, almost reverently, onto Falon's head. "Dinna' worry. I'll keep it secret. I won't tell a soul."

Betsy had been as good as her word, and Falon had run to her refuge as often as she could, her quiet place. And now, though she hadn't shed a tear over the loss of her house, she found herself sniffing with sorrow at the thought of never seeing her special place again.

The travelers turned westward and followed the road between the folds of the hills. To their left lay the loch, sparkling carelessly under the pale spring sun. To the right, a dozen agents and policemen traveled with them, herding them as though they were sheepdogs. With the threat of their truncheons, and with no more place to call home, the families of Sgall didn't stop until dusk. Shelter was naught but a tumbledown shed, abandoned long ago and huddling next to the road like a beggar. The cows and the goat, glad for a respite from walking, were turned loose with the rest of Sgall's livestock to graze on the sparse vegetation, while Will and the other young men went to the loch for water and began scouring the byway for fire fuel.

Falon put the baby down. Her arms and back felt as if they'd caught fire; she had carried Robbie most of the day. Mother allowed him to be up in the wagon only for about an hour in the afternoon—and that because Father intervened. "Have a thought for the lass,

Esme," he had said. "She's borne him all day, and she's nobbut a wee one herself."

So Mother took Robbie. But she was so busy, so occupied bemoaning her own fate, that she didn't have the energy to spare for him. "What are we to do?" she cried. "Where are we to go? I was born in that house, as was my mother, and her mother before her. Our little Annie was born there. Who will tend her grave? And who'll give a thought for my bones when I'm gone?"

Even now, when they had stopped, Esme Macvail continued her litany of woe. The neighbor women eyed her, shook their heads, and turned away. A few of them cast sympathetic glances at Falon. She felt her cheeks go hot—she'd seen those looks too often—and busied herself with Robbie. Not for the first time, she found herself wishing she had died of the fever instead of her little sister. *Annie made Mother happy.* After she had changed Robbie she milked the goat again, taking a few sips for herself before passing the cup to her brother. About a half cup remained when he was done, and she carried the still-warm milk to Father. "Here, Dad, this bit's for thee."

He shook his great, shaggy head. The firelight cast uncertain shadows across his face. "Nay, lass. I've no stomach for it." He raised his faded blue eyes to hers. "Drink it yourself. You've need of it. You worked hard carrying your brother all the way."

"There's plenty more where this came from," she lied. "And I've already had all I want."

"Then give it to Will, or to your mother." He drew a pipe and pouch from his coat pocket. "A bit of leaf and a good sleep will do for me."

Will returned with a skin full of water, and a sack. "Here's some oats. 'Tis the only bag we have, so be sparing." Falon thought about the bit of food she'd managed to stow in her feed sack, two solitary turnips and a handful of potatoes. *They won't get us far.* She added a fistful of grain and some water to the milk and cooked it over the fire. "Do we have any bowls?"

"We do. I'll go find them."

But when Will started rummaging in the wagon, Mother raised an outcry. "What are you doing? Stay out of my things!"

"Mother," came Will's weary protest, "Falon's made porridge. I only want the bowls so I can bring you some." How he managed to keep his voice gentle mystified Falon. "Just let me look in this corner. Ye see? Here they are."

"Well, just see to it that you bring them back, you hear? And don't think I'm not watching."

"Aye, Mother."

After Falon had filled a bowl for Mother, Will came to sit beside her again at the fire. He slowly stirred the thin porridge and cleared his throat. "Those agents . . . they . . . they didn't hurt you, did they?"

She felt her face go hot. "Nay," her voice was scarcely a whisper. "They hardly gave me a second look."

He nodded, the muscles in his jaw bunched. "'Tis well tha' art but a wee thing." He gave her a sideways glance with a hint of a mischievous smile. "Scrawny."

She bumped her shoulder against his at the old taunt and sniffed, "Missus says I'm *petite*."

He chuckled at that, but his humor quickly faded as he glanced in the agents' direction. "I just wanted to know. Canna' help thinking about those poor Macneil sisters."

Falon's breath caught in her throat. The girls, barely older than she was now, had hanged themselves the year before when they were evicted. "Well," she ventured, "with their mother and father gone, they had no one to look out for them."

He nodded. "Aye, and they couldn't live with the shame."

"The shame belongs to those agents for what they did to them."

When her brother's face darkened with embarrassment, Falon decided to change the subject. "I've a surprise for thee, Will."

"What is it?" he murmured without much interest. "Did tha' put honey in my bowl?"

"Better." Looking round to make sure the agents were all out of earshot, she tugged at the waistband of her woolen skirt, and from inside it she pulled an old *sporran,* a pouch of goat hide. "I saved this for you." She opened the pouch and pulled out Will's hunting knife, still in its leather sheath. "Tuck it inside tha' boot."

"Ah, lass," he breathed, setting his bowl down between his feet, "you never did. What a clever girl!" He took the knife and turned it over and over in his hands, as if he expected it to disappear. "How did you think of it?"

"I took it from under the mattress when I picked up Robbie to get him out of the house. I waited till now to give it to you because those agents were watching, and I was afraid they'd take it if they saw. I saved my flute, too." She patted the front of her dress. "Just don't tell Mother."

"D'ye think I'm daft? Your secret's mine." He hid his treasure inside his left boot.

She smiled. "Eat your dinner before it gets cold."

There may be naught but stars for a roof, but my name is my own. Falon had been named for her grandmother on her father's side, and her grandmother had been named for her mother before her. "The firstborn daughter has always been called Falon," Father had told her. "I dinna' know how many generations back. Of course," he added, "in my generation there was only James and meself, so the name skipped over to thee." Falon prepared to bed down, telling herself, *But my name is my own. My name goes with me wherever I go.*

On that first night away from home, Father spread an old cow hide under the wagon, while Falon stood, gazing about, trying to spot Betsy among her other neighbors. But it was full dark, and the Mackays were on the far side of their little camp. "Well," Falon told herself, "I'll see her tomorrow for sure." Gathering Robbie in her arms, she lay down on the hide, but there was no keeping out the cold spring night. She curled around her baby brother, her teeth chattering. She opened out her shawl to cover them, wrinkling her nose at the stench of smoke in her clothing, and pulled Robbie in closer.

Overhead, Mother continued to moan and wail, until at last Father's heavy tread sounded beside the wagon. "Hush, woman," he growled. "D'ye think you're the only one hurting? Remember what the reverend said Sunday last? We dasn't complain. 'Tis judgment for our sins."

"For your sins, more like," she hissed. "Haven't I darkened the doors of the church house every time 'twas open? Haven't I given alms?"

Father's sigh came from a bottomless well of patience and pain. "My sins, then. Have it your way. Only be quiet now, or those agents will be on us. Go to sleep."

To Falon's surprise, Mother obeyed, and now that her wailing was done, other, quieter sounds of sorrow reached her cold bed. Their neighbors all around sobbed and murmured entreaties to each other and to Heaven. "Who'll tend the graves . . . ? Dad built the place with his own hands . . . And where will we go now . . . ? Ah, Lord, what'll we do . . . ?"

We're going down to the coast. That much she gleaned from listening to the men, who were now discussing their fate around the fire. All the families she knew in Sutherland County who had been forced out had headed either north or west. She raised up on one elbow and rested her head in her hand so she could watch as well as listen. George Morgan said, "If it comes to it, I'm taking my family to America. I've cousins there. No point in trying to settle on the coast. I'm no fisherman. I'm a farmer. Can't farm on the shore, can't raise cattle."

"But how'll tha' get to America?" Father asked him. "How'll tha' pay the ship's fare?"

"I've a wee bit put aside, see? And if needs be, we'll sell what we can for the rest. Canna' take most of it with us, anyhow."

Donald Morgan, George's brother said, "We should all go, or all stay." His black eyes gleamed in the firelight. "We've helped each other through bad times before, the Lord knows. How will any of us make it if we split apart?" This idea started a quiet, if spirited, argument.

Angus Magee cleared his throat, and the rest fell silent. "I've seen plenty of bad times, lads," he said. "More than eighty years—good times and bad. But this is no' just bad times." He shook his head, his wispy gray beard trembled in the light. "This is the worst, and for some of us, there'll be no redeeming." He held up a crooked, bony finger and pointed at each man in turn. "Tha' has to decide, Camran, and George, Robert, Donald, William, each of thee, and once tha' does, there's no going back. We canna' stay all together this time, Donald. There's a parting coming, sadder than the last, when we'll have to say goodbye." He wiped at his shining eyes with the back of his hand. "I just thank the Lord my Maire didn't live to see this."

The circle went silent, each man a picture of the others: shoulders hunched over, heads bowed, hands clasped uselessly together. For the first time, Falon saw how heavy his world weighed on her father. She put her head down again, blinking back her gathering tears.

Later that night, she had the nightmare again about her sister. Annie, alive, knelt on her hands and knees on a rock hanging over the loch's edge. They were looking for eels. Annie pointed to a flash under the surface and bent forward. As she did, she lost her balance and fell into the water. Falon cried out just as Annie's copper curls disappeared below the dark ripples. She dove into the frigid water, dove in again and again. But Annie was gone. The loch had swallowed her.

Tears were streaming from Falon's eyes as she awakened to a movement behind her. When she started up in alarm, Will whispered, "Whisht, little sister. It's only me. Lie still now." He curled in behind her and put a protective arm over her and Robbie. Grateful to be rescued from the dream and for the warmth of him at her back, she drifted into deep sleep.

The next day they passed through the blackened ruins of another village. Weeds had sprung up next to the crumbling walls, and the acrid smell of smoke was all but gone. This township had been burned long before Sgall, maybe as much as a year before. Falon walked with her neighbors in light-footed silence, as if through a graveyard. *What did they do? The wrath of the Lord is surely on us, but why? What did any of us do that was so terrible to deserve this?* The reverend had said last Sunday that their Heavenly Father was punishing them.

She shook her head. Camran Macvail never punished his children without telling them why. She kissed Robbie's cheek—not so rosy as it should be. "Poor little lad," she murmured, "Tha's not even had a chance to be naughty yet." *But I've not always obeyed my parents. Maybe I do deserve it.* She sighed and wiped her eyes with a corner of her shawl.

Late in the afternoon they left Loch Naver behind. She wasn't aware of the change at first, the loch gradually narrowing until it was but a river. Falon marched on a while; then, realizing the loch was gone, halted in her tracks, dismayed and confused, until Will caught up with her. "Go on then, Falon. What's the matter with thee?"

"I . . . I thought the loch was bigger," she stammered. "I thought it went all the way to the sea."

"Nay, lass." Her brother shook his head and took her arm, leading her forward again. "'Tis not so big as that. We're following the river, though. There'll be plenty of water, no fear."

A possible lack of water had not occurred to her. All Falon knew was that the loch that had always bordered her life was behind her now, along with the farms and the familiar mountains ringing the village. *Will there be a loch where we're going? How can any place be home without one?* She walked alongside Will for a while longer, and then, since Robbie was napping in the wagon, she trotted to the front where Father held the pony's lead. Without a word, she took his free hand, finding comfort in his rough skin and hardened fingers. "Where are we going, Dad?"

"To the coast, lass. We're going to the sea."

"Aye, to the sea. But what then? Will we live there?"

He clucked his tongue at the pony. "I've been thinking on that. America sounds like a fine place. Maybe we'll go there. What d'ye think?"

"America," she murmured. "I don't know, Dad. What is it like?"

"It's big. Bigger than all of Scotland, with lots and lots of farm land. I hear they want good, honest farmers there."

They don't want them here, do they Dad? Falon was careful to keep that bitter thought to herself. She didn't want to poison her father's hopeful mood. Instead, she asked, "Is it far—America?"

He nodded. "'Tis a long, long way, lass. We'd have to go there on a ship."

She tried to imagine a ship. She knew it was a big boat with sails that caught the wind. *But how big? And how fast does it go?* She turned her head to check on Mother. She and the baby were still asleep. "Dad?"

"Aye, Falon, what is it?"

"Will we ever have a home again?"

He went on in silence for a while, and Falon wondered if she'd angered him. Finally he said, "We'll be together, lass. You and me, and Will, and your mother and the baby—we'll all be together." He squeezed her hand. "Comes down to it, that's what home really is. It's family, no matter where they are."

She leaned her head briefly against his arm. "That's fine, then."

Camran Macvail gifted her with a rare smile. "Tha' art a good lass, even if tha' art but a wee sparrow."

"How long d'ye guess it'll take us to reach the sea?"

"At this rate, at least two more days, maybe three."

Falon left off her questioning, sensing her father had no answers to the ones that remained. She contented herself with walking beside him for a time, letting her eyes wander over the neighbors who traveled ahead of them. *There's Mr. Magee almost at the front of the line. He's still a strong one, for all his age. And that's his youngest son William with him, and William's Ann following with their children. I hear she's carrying another baby. Donald's and George's lads are herding their cattle ahead of their families. And aren't the cows thin this spring? I hope the grazing's good down by the sea. Donald's Janet has that big load on her back. I don't see how she does it, but their cart lost a wheel yesterday, so she's had no choice. And there's George's wife, herding her children and Janet's, too. So many little ones. How will they feed them all?*

She glanced uneasily toward the agents who still accompanied them, then turned her eyes forward again, afraid just looking at them might draw their attention. They had kept to themselves for most of the journey, but their very presence made it clear they would brook no disrespect, no outbursts. And pleading would only fall on deaf ears. *They care nothing for us, whether we live or we die. Once they get us out of Her Ladyship's way, they'll be done with us, and they can go home to their families.* Her next thought came bitter as gall. *I'll bet their children never go hungry at night.*

Falon chewed at the edge of one fingernail, ignoring her growling stomach. *They'll go home, and we'll go—where?* Her thoughts went back to her neighbors. *There's Robert Mackay and Missus with their cart. But where is Betsy?* She searched the whole line, but couldn't find her best friend. *I don't see her with them. I didn't see her this morning, either. And who is that with their cattle? It can't be Patrick. He went off to London, and that lad's too big to be John. No, there's John behind us with Will. What's happened to Betsy?*

Full of curiosity, she released Father's hand and trotted up to Mrs. Mackay. "Good morning, Missus."

Mrs. Mackay, whose given name was a mystery to the whole village, answered, "Falon, good morning, lass. I see tha's holding up."

"Aye, Missus, and thank ya'. I was just wondering, where is Betsy?"

Missus' face was solemn as her answer. "Our Betsy is gone for now." She lowered her voice. Her eyes canted toward the agents. "You'll see her again when we get to the sea."

In confusion, Falon blurted out, "Is she already at the coast, then?"

"Nay, lass, but you'll see her there, never fear." Missus pulled her close to her side. "How is thy mother today? Any better?"

Failing to notice how seamlessly Missus had changed the subject, Falon shrugged. "She sleeps." Glancing at Missus, she added, "And that's a blessing—for Dad, at least."

"For all of you," Missus nodded, "and not the least for herself." A tense knot that had ridden at the base of Falon's neck for the last two days came loose, and her shoulders eased. Missus understood, somehow she always seemed to understand. Sometimes, in unguarded moments, she wondered why her own mother couldn't be like Missus. Or worse, why Missus wasn't her mother, instead of Esme Macvail.

They passed a patch of thistles, and Falon paused to pluck two. One she handed to Missus, who thanked her as prettily as if Falon had given her a full-blown rose. As Falon absently brushed her cheek with the prickly tips of the purple blossom, Missus remarked, "They're early this year." A few steps later, she added, "Tha' knows, thy mother is like a thistle."

"How d'ye mean? That she's prickly?"

Missus smiled. "Well, for sure." Falon colored with embarrassment, and Missus added, "It only means that ye have to grasp her firmly, so ye aren't stung. And look . . ." With one arm, she gestured to a hillside cloaked in waves of purple. "See how beautiful, how graceful they are?"

Beautiful? My mother, graceful? Falon tried to dismiss Missus' comment as nonsense, but before long, her heart whispered confirmation. Mother was a comely woman. *Especially when she's happy. But it's been so long since I've seen her that way or heard her sing.* At one time, people in Sgall asked her to sing for them whenever they were all together. *They don't ask anymore,* she thought sadly. *There hasn't been much music in our house in more than a year. Dad hung his fiddle on the wall, and Mother put her voice away.*

"I wonder if Dad got his fiddle out of the fire," she murmured aloud. Just then she caught the sound of Robbie's after-nap whimper. She stopped in the road and waited for the wagon to catch up with her.

"Where has tha' been?" Mother demanded like a petulant child. "The lad's crying for thee."

Robbie held out his arms, and she plucked him from the wagon and swung him onto her hip. As she did, her lack of nourishment for the past two days caught up with her. Her head swam with the sudden movement, and she stumbled and went down on one knee.

"Whoa," Father ordered the pony. He stopped and pulled her up. "Let me have the lad." He took the baby from her and set Robbie on his shoulders while Falon struggled to her feet. "All right now?"

"Aye, Dad." *If only the hills would stop swimming.* "I'm all right." Falon held onto his arm for another few steps to steady herself.

Father cast a worried glance toward the agents. Two of them had broken off from the pack and were heading their way. "We best keep moving," he told her.

Once they started up again, one of the two broke off his approach and continued downriver. The other, however, a broad-chested oaf with thick, black brows that met in the middle, kept coming. When he reached the wagon, he laid one grimy hand on the sideboard and leered at Mother. "Well, well," he announced in a loud voice, "what have we here? A fine lady riding to town in her carriage?" Snickers from the other agents encouraged him, and he leaned in with a wink. "Is there room for me in your conveyance, my lady? We could have a bit of fun, you and I."

Falon glanced at Father, whose face had gone scarlet and tight as a fist. If he interfered, if he dared to defend his wife, he might be shot on the spot. At the very least, the agents would descend on him with their clubs and beat him senseless. It had happened to others. But she knew Father couldn't take much more. Fortunately for Camran Macvail, his wife cringed away from the agent's attentions and the oaf sneered, "Just as well. Who'd want a woman as ugly and skinny as you? Look at you—nothing but a bag of bones." With another uproarious laugh at his own cleverness, the agent left the wagon and rejoined his cronies.

Moments later, Falon heard a strangled noise, and looked back to see Mother quietly sobbing into her hands. Seized with compassion—this was her mother, after all—Falon paused for the few seconds it took for the wagon to catch up. She walked alongside, gathering her thoughts, then offered her mother the thistle. "That agent is blind as well as daft."

Sniffing, Esme Macvail accepted the prickly blossom with shaking hands. "What d'ye mean?"

"Tha' art the bonniest mother in the whole village," her daughter answered. When Mother started to shake her head, Falon insisted, "Everyone knows tha' art." She nodded toward the agent. "His mother must have dropped him on his head when he was a babe."

Father chose that moment to put in his bit: "Eh, too bad he bounced."

Mother clapped a hand over her mouth to stifle her laughter, though her eyes still streamed with tears. Falon nodded to herself. *Missus is right. Grasp the thistle firmly.*

That evening, after the people of Sgall settled in around their campfires for yet another meager meal, her curiosity about the lad driving the Mackays' cows drew her to the circle of near-grown boys. She sat down just behind the right shoulder of the new boy, hoping at least to learn his name. But the lads were unusually quiet that evening, and the firelight cast them in an eerie pall, as if the light itself were afraid of the dark. She noticed hollows around Will's eyes—shadows that gave him a haunted, haggard look. With a start, she thought, *Why, he looks just like Dad!* She brushed away a stray tear. *He's too young to look so old.*

At that moment, the boy she had wondered about turned his head, giving her a good view of his profile in the firelight. Falon bit back a gasp of shock. *Betsy! She's dressed like a lad. And, oh—she's cut her beautiful, beautiful hair. Ah, so that's why she wore a scarf all last week, to hide it. Why in the world?* But as soon as the question formed in her mind, she knew the answer. Betsy was two years older than

Falon, and she wasn't the least bit scrawny. Missus had cut Betsy's hair off, had bound her breasts and dressed her in boys' clothes—probably Patrick's old things—to save her daughter from the agents' attentions.

They must have planned it ever since the evictions were tacked up on Sgall's doors. Falon wondered how many people in their little village had noticed? How many knew the identity of the "lad" following along with the Mackays? She pressed her lips together. There would be no speaking of it to anyone; certainly not to Mother, who was ever envious of Missus, and in an even more unstable frame of mind than usual. Falon cringed at the thought of Mother screaming pronouncements of sin and eternal punishment on Betsy and her family for dressing her as a boy. That would be sure to get the agents' attention. A secret place was one thing—Betsy's honor, her life, were something else altogether. No, there'd be no speaking of it, not one whisper, until they were safely to the coast and the agents were gone.

Still, Betsy was her best friend, and Falon wanted her to know that she knew. As she got up to lie down with Robbie for the night, she rested one hand lightly on her shoulder. Betsy didn't look up, and Falon said nothing. The touch was enough.

The next two days passed without incident, and on the evening of the fourth day of their journey they topped the last hill and found themselves looking out over a vast, blue expanse. "The sea," Falon murmured to Robbie. "We're here at last."

"Well, almost." Will came up behind her. "It's still a good long way. We'll do well to reach it before nightfall."

Apparently the men thought so, too, and they rounded up their families to prepare to camp where they were for the night. But the agents would have none of it. "What d'ye think ye're doing?" one of them shouted, waving his club. "Ye cannot stop here. Get on with ya! Move!"

So they moved. Aching with hunger, bone-weary from their journey, Sgall's families started the trek down the final hill to the sea. Just when it was getting almost too dark to see their feet, they passed a cluster of houses, and the women all came out to stand in their yellow-lit doorways and watch them file by. One, stooped and white-haired, reminded Falon of her grandmother. This old one wept openly and waved a corner of her apron at them. Her gaze touched Falon's; for no good reason, the sight of the old woman's tears sliced through her heart like a hot knife, and she broke down and started to cry.

"What's the matter with thee?" her mother hissed. "Tha' had no tears for the leaving, but now that we're here, tha' wants to weep?"

Growling low in his throat, Father turned, his eyes swollen and red-rimmed. "Not another word, wife." He took Robbie from Falon's arms. "I'll bear him a bit, lass. Hang onto my coat." For the second time on their awful journey, she found herself walking blind behind her father. Her right hand grasped a handful of his worn wool jacket, while she held her shawl to her face with her left and sobbed into it.

★2

. . . To this day I don't understand it. How could they force us to leave our home? How could they send us to such a horrible place? Did they really expect us to live there? Did anyone care what we did, where we went . . . ?

They camped out on the rocky beach that night, Sgall's families ringed in a tight circle around each other. They moved, sat, and slept within a breath of each other, as if their proximity might crowd out the dark. Tired as she was, sleep fled from Falon's eyes, chased away by the roaring, churning sea. *How can anyone rest with all the noise? We can't live here. It'll never be home.* She shifted on her stony bed, finding no relief from the rocks under the old hide. They gouged into her ribs and hips. They crunched and grated in her ears each time she moved. *There's no grass here, no heather—only stones. And it smells wrong.* She wrinkled her nose. *It smells like dead things.* She heaved a deep sigh, one of countless sighs that long night. *Maybe tomorrow will be better. Maybe we'll find a place to live.*

She briefly fantasized about running away, slipping off into the night and making her way back into the hills, back to Loch Naver and her secret place in the moors. *I could hide there. No one would find me for ages and ages. I could catch fish and eels from the loch to eat.* But she quickly dismissed her wayward thoughts. *There'll be sheep on that land soon, and dogs to herd them. They'd find me.* She sighed again. *And who'll look after Robbie if I leave? Not Mother, that's for sure.* A new thought, black and dreadful in its surety, closed in and pinned her down until she could scarcely breathe. *My mother is going to die from this. Maybe not tomorrow or the next day, but soon.*

Falon bit her lip and squeezed her eyes shut tight. *'Twill be my fault. The Lord will punish me for wishing I had a different mother.* Her heart thudded dully in her chest. *Reverend says the Lord God knows my thoughts. There's no escaping it—no escaping Him.* She pulled Robbie in closer, all the while wanting to push her baby brother away, to save him from being sullied by her touch. *They'd be better off if I did go.*

In the end, the courage to run away failed, crushed as it was under her guilt and shame. And there was nothing to run to. She would end up lost, wandering the moors. Those ghost stories told in the half-light of an evening's fire, ancient tales of specters haunting the hills, those tales would end with her—she would become one of them. Falon shivered on the old hide. She owed it to her father, at least, to stay and help with Robbie, and with the cooking and all.

She smelled the dawn just before it came, felt the air lighten and prickle against her skin. With it came the thinnest thread of hope. *Maybe today we'll find a place to stay, a place out of the wind, at least until Father decides what to do.* With no clear plan for the day in her head, Falon got up, aching in every joint and bone, feeling a hundred years old instead of going-on fifteen. She gathered Robbie and settled him in the cart with Mother. Neither of them stirred, except that the baby stuck a grimy finger in his mouth to suck on.

Falon turned at the sound of footsteps. A figure approached in the dark with a knapsack in one hand. It was Will, and he put a finger to his lips and beckoned her to follow. They slipped away as quietly as they could on the crunching rocks. When they had rounded the corner of an old boat shed, she whispered, "What is it, Will? What has tha' got in the bag?"

"Mussels." He opened the bag to let her see.

She took a peek at the gray shells heaped in the bottom of the sack. "Why there must be more than a dozen of them!"

"Two dozen, more like. I gathered them this morning before anyone else was awake."

Falon's head swam at the prospect of meat. "But how did tha' do it, Will? How did tha' know where to look for them?"

"One of the lads who lives here showed me last night." His face lowered like a coming storm. "The Poor Laws forbid them to give us any help, but they don't say anything about telling us how to help ourselves." He glanced at her. "We'll have to cook these right away. They won't keep."

"How do we cook them?" she wondered aloud.

Will shrugged his shoulders. "Perhaps like eels? You could make a soup."

With nothing in it but mussels and water? Still, it was meat, and they had eaten the last of the potatoes the night before. "I'll get the cook pot and see what I can do."

"I'll start shelling them." Will drew his knife from his boot, hunkered down and pulled the first mussel from the bag.

Falon left him and crept back to the wagon for the smaller of their two cook pots, which she retrieved without waking anyone. From there she headed to the village well for fresh water, just as the leading sliver of sun had peeked over the eastern ridges. She had filled the pot when a woman appeared at her shoulder. "Tha'rt with the group that came last night," she said. The woman looked cautiously about her. When she saw that no one appeared to be watching, she said, "Tha' can eat the seaweed."

"Seaweed?"

Falon wrinkled her nose at the thought, but the woman nodded. "'Tisn't tasty, and that's a fact, but it's nourishing. Keeps body and soul together when there's nothing else. And there's always plenty."

Falon thanked her and moved away quickly so they wouldn't be seen together. The woman had already risked enough. The Poor Laws forbade offers of food or shelter, or any other material help to those who were forced out. If anyone defied the laws and was caught, he or she could lose everything and be evicted, too. No one was sure if passing useful information was also against the laws, and a few risked it. The least Falon and her neighbors could do in gratitude was to minimize the risk by talking to the locals as little as possible.

"Seaweed," she muttered on her way back to Will. "I suppose I can put it in the soup with the mussels." She shook her head. "And we can pinch our noses and gulp it down."

By the time she found her brother again, Will had shucked all the mussels and was cutting the meat into smaller pieces. "Here," She held out the pot. "Put them in."

He gathered up two double handfuls of the glistening morsels and lowered them into the water. "We'll need a fire." He glanced around. "And where will I find wood for it?"

"A lady told me we could eat seaweed." Ignoring Will's dubious snort, Falon said, "I'll take this to Father for safekeeping. You go find wood, and I'll gather the weed." She lugged the now-full pot back to the wagon. Father was just getting up. When she whispered to him what they had done, and what they planned, he shook his head. "I'll go after the seaweed, lass. I dinna' want thee wandering off."

After another half hour or so, during which time their neighbors began to get up and stir about, Falon spotted Father coming toward the wagon with a green, dripping mass in his hands. He stopped and talked to Missus and to Ann Magee. They looked at him—and at each other—as if he'd told them a wild tale, then promptly headed to the water's edge.

"Tha' told them about the seaweed?" Falon asked when her father squatted near her pot.

"I did." He shook his head. "I hope it tastes better than it smells." He glanced at her and raised his eyebrows. "We'll learn to like it soon enough if it keeps us alive, eh, lass?"

"That we will, Dad. Just dump it in the pot. I'll break it up with the spoon as I stir. And here's Will with the wood."

"Good lad," Father murmured, taking an armload of twisted driftwood and stacking it for a fire. "You need to find a place to graze the cattle. I'll bring some of this soup out to thee when it's done."

Will sat on his heels next to Falon and peered into the pot. "I've already asked about grazing, Dad. There isn't any." To Father's exclamation of disbelief, Will explained, "There aren't any free lands about, and we aren't allowed to use the commons unless we're renters. I might be able to gather enough here and there to feed the nanny and the pony, but not the cows. We'll have to butcher or sell them."

Father's faded blue eyes, ringed harsh with red, gazed off westward. "Get what grass ye can, then. I'll go see what I can find out." He heaved himself to his feet, and moved away as if every bone hurt.

Falon turned to her brother, her eyes stinging with tears. "What are we going to do, Will?"

"We have to go away."

"Go away?" Her throat closed up in sudden consternation and sorrow.

"I've had a look at the renters' houses. They're falling down and filthy. We can't make any kind of life here. The agents and magistrates will drain it all out of us. We'll end up with nothing."

"But what do you mean, go away? Go away where?"

Will never answered, because Mother woke up at that moment, complaining that the baby was kicking her. Will and Falon exchanged a look—their conversation was over for the time being. Suppressing a sigh, she got up from stirring the pot and lifted Robbie out of the wagon.

"Tha' knows," Will said when she came back to the fire, "we'll have to share out the mussels."

Though she knew he was right, she groaned inside. *That lovely meat!* "Bring me a bowl," she told him.

Falon dipped the ladle into the soup again and again, catching most of the pieces of mussel, and dropped them into the bowl Will held out for her. "There's only a bit or two for each of us now," she finally said. Will stood, walking away to give most of his hard-earned meat around to their neighbors. "Just as well," Falon murmured to Robbie. "We can get more tomorrow."

Father came back after about an hour, looking even more haggard and discouraged than before. His face had a pained, pinched look, and he didn't bother to speak to any of the others on his way to the wagon; he just trudged up the hill to their fire, where he lowered himself onto the rocks and sat, his hands hanging loosely over his knees. Falon didn't have to ask him about the grazing. The answer was etched in the lines around his eyes. Searching for some way to distract him, she said, "Soup's almost done. Will took a lot of the meat to share around."

He nodded in wordless approval, and taking off his hat, ran his fingers through his graying hair. *We have to go away,* Will had said. He was right. There wasn't going to be any kind of life for them on this rocky coast, this dead-smelling place.

The next morning, Will came back from hunting mussels with nothing but a blackened eye and an empty sack. When Father saw him, his face lowered like a storm. "What happened to thee, Will? Who did this?"

The muscles in Will's bruised face bunched with suppressed fury. "Agents," he muttered. "There'll be no mussels today, Dad."

"That tears it," Father growled. "Do they expect us to squat here on this rotted beach till we starve?"

Mother, who till then had remained silent said, "We'll butcher one of the cows. Keep us alive till . . ."

Father crossed his arms tight against his chest. "Until what, Esme? And how do we keep the meat from spoiling? I dinna' think the agents will leave us be long enough to dry it all." He glanced around, his eyes narrow with distaste. "That is, if anything can be dried here. The air's so damp, I think the meat would just rot."

"What are we to do then?" Will asked.

"We have to sell the cows, lad. And we have to get out of here while we can."

Will hung his head. The cows had been his responsibility for years, his job and contribution to the family. Presently he nodded, and with that gesture, Falon saw her brother become a man. "We'll get a better price today while they still have a bit of flesh on them. If we wait, they'll only go thinner."

"What of us?" Mother cried. "How will we keep body and soul together? And where do you think we can go, Camran Macvail, where the agents won't follow and plague us?"

"America, or Ireland maybe," Father answered, standing. "I'll see what I can find out."

Falon glanced at her mother, then away. Esme's face had gone pale but for the dark rings around her eyes. Bad enough to leave her home. Bad enough to abandon the graves of her parents and child. Bad enough to live like a vagabond in a strange place. But to leave Scotland, to leave her homeland altogether . . .

"I'll go get seaweed," Falon said, standing up.

"Not alone, tha' doesn't," Will answered. "I'll go with thee." The agents kept an eye on them and ridiculed them as they waded into the cold, crashing surf for sustenance. Otherwise, they let them gather seaweed unmolested.

Father was away most of that day. When he came back late in the afternoon, his bent shoulders told them things hadn't gone well. He dropped down next to the fire and heaved a sigh. Falon had seen him look less tired after a long day plowing fallow ground. In heavy silence, he watched Robbie, who had busied himself trying to build a tower of rocks. Her little brother, by this time, was as grubby a child as Falon had ever seen. His hands were grimed black with dirt, his nose was running, and his hair hadn't been tended to since they left home. He tried and tried to stack the rocks, but never really succeeded because the smooth stones kept rolling around and collapsing. They looked more like a burial mound than a tower.

Careful to contain her dread of what her father would eventually say, Falon ladled a bowl of watery green soup and handed it to him. He sniffed at it, his expression impassive, and she realized he was trying to spare her feelings as much as she wanted to spare his. "Try it," she urged. "It's fine stuff."

He gave the broth another dubious sniff. "Is it?"

"Aye, Dad—the tastiest seaweed stew in seven counties."

He snorted, and she heard the faint glimmer of humor when he answered, "In seven counties, you say?" Blowing on the hot broth, he put the bowl to his lips, took a swallow, and tried not to grimace. "Powerful stuff," he murmured.

"It'll make thee grow big and strong."

"Will it make my hair turn black?" he wondered, attempting another swallow.

"Oh, aye. And thy teeth, too."

Now he did smile, if only briefly. When he had finished, he said. "It's not terrible. Goes down all right, so long as it's hot."

Will had been off talking to his friends. When he returned to the fire, Father glanced at each of them. "Cows didn't bring much," he said. "The price of beef is down. We have enough to get to Ireland if we leave on the next ship." He sighed. "Still and all, I'd rather go on to America." His eyes touched Mother's, and Falon recognized the look. He was willing her to be reasonable, to understand him. "You children will have a better chance there."

Somehow, Mother held herself together. "But we don't have enough to make the trip?" she asked.

"Nearly do," Father replied. "There's a ship headed there in three days. I saved my fiddle from the fire. If I sell it, we should have enough."

Falon heard the uncertainty in his voice. Something was bothering him. Whatever it was hung in the air for several heartbeats until he added, "Problem is, we'd not be able to go to a settled area. The next ship is sailing for a place called Texas. It's a wilderness, more like. And it's part of Spain."

"Papists," Mother spat.

He nodded. "True, but we'd be able to get land. And if we needed to, if things didn't work out, it's not so far to the border. We'd just have to cross a little river, and we'd be in America."

"But it's not safe in America, Camran," Mother whimpered. "I've heard things. There are wild savages there."

Father nodded toward an agent sauntering up from the water's edge, his truncheon ready in his hand. "No more savage than what we have here, I think." Silent and docile as the sheep they had become, they bowed their heads as the agent passed by, hoping he wouldn't take notice of them.

That afternoon, from the sale of the cows, Father bought one bag of oats and a handful of potatoes. "These will have to keep us till we leave," he told his family.

Falon wanted to ask what they would eat once they were aboard ship, but she bit her tongue. *Other people have made the trip,* she reasoned. *So will we.*

That evening, she spotted Betsy threading her way through their makeshift camp to her parents' place. She still wore boys' clothing, and had learned to walk with a masculine swagger. Falon wanted to go and talk to her, but she didn't dare. Betsy wasn't safe yet from the agents' attentions. They were going to remain, truncheons ready in their hands, until every evicted family had either rented a shack or gone away.

But I can't leave Betsy without saying goodbye. Falon's throat closed at the thought of never seeing her friend again. *There's a parting coming,* old man Magee had warned. That thought pounded at her, relentless as the sea scrubbing the shore, scrubbing as a woman might scrub a filthy floor, scrubbing at the awful dead smell.

Father sold his fiddle the next morning. No one in the village wanted it, but one of the sailors on the ship bound for Ireland took it, and Father traded the silver for their passage to America. "We leave day after tomorrow, if the weather holds," he said. "We can take the small things with us, but we'll have to sell the wagon and the pony, and the nanny, too."

"But Dad," Falon protested, "she's a wee thing. Don't ye think we could take her? Her milk would help feed us. I'll look after her, I promise."

As Mother clucked her tongue in reproach, Father laid a heavy hand on Falon's shoulder. "I know tha' would, lass, but what would tha' feed her?" His hand dropped, and he shook his head. "I'd like to take her, and that's sure, but we can't. We can't gather enough grass to keep her alive for the whole trip."

His gentle refusal shamed Falon, and she hung her head. She had dared argue with her father. She deserved to be punished, but he didn't even reprove her for it. "Ah well," she managed in a shaky voice, "she'll be better off here anyway. She can learn to be a shore goat."

Her father actually chuckled. "Mayhap she'll end up liking the seaweed."

The following morning, Missus beckoned to Falon after a spare breakfast of thin oatmeal. "I hear you're leaving for the Americas."

"Aye, Missus," she answered. "Our ship is supposed to sail tomorrow."

Missus nodded, her manner solemn and careful. "I know tha' wants to have some time with our Betsy before tha' goes . . ."

"But 'tisn't safe," Falon finished for her.

Missus heaved a deep sigh and murmured, "When will it ever be, I wonder?" She glanced around, her eyes searching and wary. "I think 'twill be all right, lass, if tha' wants to come by at dinnertime. 'Twill be near dark then, and the agents won't think anything of the two of you talking quietly together."

In gratitude, Falon circled Missus' waist with her arms. Missus held her close, and Falon laid her head against her, listening to the steady rhythm of her heart. She closed her eyes briefly, allowing herself to feel safe and warm, until a teardrop splashed atop her hair. Unwilling to cause further pain, Falon released her and stepped back. "Thank you, Missus." She wasn't quite able to meet her eyes. "I'll be back around sundown."

By that time, Father had sold all he could. The wagon they were allowed to keep another night, but the pony was gone, and a girl about eight or nine years old came to claim the nanny. Falon had just milked the goat for the last time, saving the rich liquid for their dinner. She wordlessly handed the lead over, rubbing the goat's nubby head. She turned her back as the child led the nanny away.

Falon added water to the milk. As the liquid heated, she tossed in cuttings of two of the potatoes Father had bought from the sale of the pony and wagon. *I wish we had some salt.* She thought briefly of adding seaweed to the mix—it would stretch the soup, and make it more nourishing—but in the end, she couldn't bring herself to ruin the taste of the potatoes and milk. After they ate, Falon excused herself and went to the Mackays' fire.

Betsy stood up when she saw Falon coming. "Let's walk a bit," she suggested.

"Are you sure? Agents are about."

"They're always about," Betsy answered, her voice hardly more than a whisper. "I told Father we wouldn't stray. We'll just go down to the water's edge and come right back. We won't be out of sight." She nodded behind Falon, "And there's your Will to look after us."

Falon turned to see Will standing about ten paces back, his hands jammed in his pockets, pretending not to take any notice. "He's coming, too?"

"I asked him to come," Betsy answered. "I trust him." Even as she said it, her face reddened in the twilight, and Falon suddenly understood. Betsy and her brother fancied each other. If they had been allowed to remain in Sgall, her best friend would probably have become her sister.

"Let's walk, then," Falon said, and they turned toward the water. After the first few silent steps, she asked, "What will your family do? Will you stay here?"

"No," Betsy answered. "Mother has relatives in Ireland. We're going to them."

"I see." In truth, she could hardly see at all. The stones at her feet had become a blur. "When will you leave?"

"Tomorrow." Falon's friend gestured toward the ships that lay at anchor on the far side of the village. "Our ship will sail about the same time yours does."

That brought them to the tide's edge where they halted. Will's footfalls behind them also ceased. A stone's throw off to their right, three agents sat around a fire, taking turns pulling at a bottle of some kind of liquor. They laughed among themselves, and so far had taken no notice of them. All the same, Falon felt glad for her brother's stout presence at her back.

"You'll be safe once you get to Ireland, won't you?" she asked.

"As safe as I'll be anywhere," Betsy replied. "I can be a girl again."

"You'll be glad of that."

The corner of her mouth turned up. "Aye, but I have to tell thee . . ." She gestured at the breeches. "These are awfully easy to wear. They don't drag and get caught on things. They don't trip you up."

A twinge of envy caught Falon then, and she had to shake herself—to remind herself why Betsy was dressed as she was. This wasn't some game she had been left out of. Betsy wearing her brother's old things was deadly serious. And the masquerade had to continue until she was safe away to Ireland. In a low voice, and keeping one eye on the agents, Falon said, "Well, at least you'll get to grow your hair again."

Betsy nodded, and tugged at the shorn ends with one hand. "I have missed that part. I wonder how long it'll take to grow back?"

Falon thought about Will, and how often Father had to cut his hair. "It'll probably be long again in about a year. Long enough to pull back, that is."

Betsy bent down and picked up a stone. "That sounds about right." She hurled the stone out into the rolling waves. She turned to her friend, eyes brimming. "Play your flute, Falon. Play one last time for me."

Falon's fingers strayed to the front of her dress, and she pressed the smooth wooden cylinder against her heart. She wanted to play for Betsy—oh, how she wanted to! But how could she possibly manage it when tomorrow would be goodbye, when she knew they would never see each other again? How could she make her fingers move? Where would the breath come from? "I'll try," she answered lamely. "But let's go back. I don't want them . . ." She nodded toward the agents.

"I understand." They turned away from the water.

None of them saw what caused Betsy to trip, whether she caught her shoe in a hole, or one of the rocks gave way, or whether her ankle simply turned. She fell to the ground with a sharp cry—a distinctly feminine cry. The agents looked up, and in that moment, but half a heartbeat, Falon knew Betsy would be caught. She fell on top of her friend, making it look like Betsy had pulled her down, hoping the darkness would help the impromptu charade. Will had started up ahead of them, and as he turned back, Falon jumped back to her feet, yelling in an indignant voice, "What d'ye think you're about, Will? Ye had no right to hit him!" Grabbing Will by the arm, she added, "You just leave us alone!"

Bless him, Will caught her intent immediately. "Here, you!" he shouted at Betsy. "Stay away from my sister!" He yanked her to her feet and gave her a rough shove. "Get on with thee, then. My dad'll whip you for the cur you are."

Two of the agents were upon them before they could get away. "Here now," one of them growled. "What's all this?"

Will gave Betsy another shove, this time toward camp, and put himself—with Falon in tow—between her and the agents. "My sister here has been sneaking off with him, with that lad." He nodded toward Betsy, who was now trotting up toward the camp. He gave Falon's arm a shake. "Dad's going to tan your hide for this. You'll wish you'd never laid eyes on him."

Her stomach churned with anxiety. One of the agents leaned in with a leer. "Looking for some fun, missy?" Beneath the liquor fumes, his breath reeked of rot. His lips stretched over his crooked yellow teeth in a hideous grin. "You can do better than a raw boy." He tried to touch her face, but she ducked away from his hand. Not knowing what else to do, she fled down the beach, following the water's edge.

"Hey! Come back here!" She heard one agent bellow as they started after her.

Falon's feet had always been quick, and now fear drove them as she gathered up her skirts and flew. Even on the rocky beach, where the going was rough, she ran faster than she ever had before. The agents' footsteps pummeled the ground behind her, but after about a half mile they gradually grew fainter, until the only sound left was the breath rasping in her throat. She paused to listen and look back, peering through the darkness for some sign of her pursuers. The agents were nowhere in sight. She was alone, bent over and gasping for air in front of a row of one-room shacks. *These are the rent houses Will told me about. They expect us to live in these?* Even the darkness couldn't hide the squalid disrepair, the hopelessness of those empty, gaping windows and falling-off doors.

Falon turned away with a shudder, wiping sweat from her brow. A cluster of ragged boulders loomed black against the night. She hiked up her skirts and climbed atop them. Even from that vantage, she saw no one on the beach. Worn out from the run, she sat down on the topmost rock to catch her breath.

Will is all right, she told herself. *The agents followed me, so he'd have made it back up to the camp. Betsy is safe with her parents. I doubt the agents ever really got a good look at her.* She hugged her knees and rested her head against them. *Now, how am I going to get back without being seen?*

Soon a more sobering thought pressed in, and she lifted her head and looked out to sea. *Tomorrow. Tomorrow we'll be in the ship on that water. We'll be going away. Father said home was family.* She sniffed and lowered her head again. *But it has to be more than that. Family, yes, but a place, as well. Our place in the world is gone. And home is friends, people who are dear as family. Tomorrow we lose them, too.* "Ah, Lord," she whispered, "how will we live without a home? The reverend says You give and You take away. What will You give to replace what we've lost?"

Falon let more than an hour pass before she tried to get back to camp. By that time, everyone had settled down for the night, and the fires burned low. She saw but one agent up and about, and easily dodged him by hiding behind an old shed until he passed by. When she found the wagon, Will was underneath on the hide, his arms around Robbie. Thinking him asleep, she crawled in as quietly as the rocks would allow, but when she lay down, Will's eyes were open. He'd been waiting for her.

"Art tha' all right?" he whispered. "Did tha' get away clean?"

"Aye," she answered, resting her head on her arm. "Is everything all right here?"

Will's lips pressed together in a tight line. "I wish I could say so, lass. Tha' art in trouble with our mother."

Falon shrugged. "When am I not?" He didn't answer, so she asked, "What is it, then?"

"I had to lie to her. 'Twas the only way to protect Betsy."

She nodded. "What did ye say?"

"I told her the agents caught you fooling around with Angus Magee."

Falon came up on one elbow. "Why in heaven's name did you tell her that?"

"When I came back up after Betsy, one of the agents followed. He hadn't seen her, but he grabbed me and demanded to know what the ruckus was about. Angus caught on—all the lads have helped protect Betsy—and he stepped in and said the whole thing was his fault, that he fancied you." Will stopped, swallowing. "I'm sorry, Falon. Father knows the truth, but I had to keep it from Mother." He reached over and touched her shoulder. "So some of our neighbors think . . ."

He didn't finish. He didn't have to. Unless they were told otherwise, they now thought she had shamed her parents. Mother thought so for sure, and Falon might never be able to tell her the truth. She turned onto her back and stared at the bottom of the wagon. *I guess I didn't get clean away after all. At least Father knows. And Betsy is safe.* She sighed. *After tomorrow it won't matter so much. We'll be going where no one knows us.*

Falon didn't think she would be able to sleep, but sometime during the dark hours, she had harrowing dreams. She was alone, running along a seashore, someone chasing her. She had to get away, but there was no end to the shore, no end of running. And the running carried her away, away from her family, away from her home, away and away . . .

The next morning, the family rose early and ate a hurried breakfast. Mother refused to look at Falon, or to speak to her. Father said little, but he paused once to lay his hand on her head; that was all the reassurance she needed from him. She caught Janet Morgan staring, and when Falon met her eyes, Janet shook her head and turned away. Missus looked up once from her preparations to leave and gave her a solemn nod. Falon's shoulders loosened a notch. As always, Missus understood.

Within an hour of rising, they were on their way to the dock where the ship waited. Father and Mother said hasty goodbyes to everyone but George and Maire Morgan, who were the only other family from Sgall sailing with them. Falon couldn't watch. She held Robbie, putting her forehead against his, whispering little rhymes to keep her thoughts busy.

Presently old Mr. Magee approached her and chucked Robbie under his chin with one bony finger. "Give us a kiss then, lass." He turned his leathery cheek to her, and Falon gave him his kiss, noting that the seams running down his face had become tiny riverbeds. He kissed her in return, and nodding, moved away, taking a swipe at his eyes.

Moments later, Betsy and Missus sought her out. "We canna' let thee go without our love, lass," Missus said. Betsy took Robbie, and Missus held Falon close. "Blessings on thee," she murmured. "Tha' has been a true friend to our girl." She raised Falon's face with one hand until their eyes met. "Now listen—we'll be in the town of Armaugh," she spelled it, "and my cousin's name is Ian Machone. Can ye remember that? I taught you your letters. You write to us when you're settled. Let us know how you're getting along."

Falon nodded. "I will." Her eyes started to sting. "I love thee, Missus."

The older woman pulled the girl to her again. "Ah, lass," she crooned. She kissed her head. "Tha' will always be a daughter in my heart."

Then it was Betsy's turn. She handed Robbie over to Missus, then pulled something out of her pocket. "I saved this for thee when we cut it." She pressed a braided lock of her hair into Falon's hand. "It'll help you remember me."

"How could I forget thee?" Falon tucked the braid into her sporran and threw her arms around Betsy's neck. "Tha' art my friend forever."

They held each other but for a moment, and then Mother was hissing in Falon's ear, "What are you about?" She yanked her away from Betsy. "Are ye daft?" She gave her a rough shake. "First the Magee boy, and now this one? Will ye shame us to an early grave?"

Betsy backed away. Without answering her mother, Falon took Robbie from Missus' arms and started down the path to the dock. *White Arrow* was blazoned on one end of the hull, the name that would bear them away. Mother hounded her steps, muttering shame and the doleful judgments Falon was going to face for her sins. Just before she boarded, Falon heard someone call her name. There to her left was Angus Magee, standing at attention. As she stepped onto the gangplank, he gave her a military salute. She nodded once, then turned her gaze to the ramp leading up to the ship.

"Well!" Mother exclaimed, loudly enough for everyone to hear. "I never saw such brazen behavior in my life!"

Keeping her eyes on her feet, Falon trudged up the ramp and onto the ship. She had little interest in her surroundings at first, her heart ached so with the leaving. But when Robbie pointed upward and cried out, "Ah!" she looked up at the pair of masts rising to the sky like church spires, with the heavy canvas sails furled and lashed down to their arms. "Ship," she told her baby brother. "We're on a ship, laddie."

"Sip," he confirmed with a nod. He pointed up again. "Sip."

"That's right." She had to smile. "Tha' aren't sad to be leaving, hey? 'Tis a game to thee." She brushed his black curls away from his face. "America will be thy home, and tha' won't even remember Scotland." Before she could grieve over this new thought, she realized that Robbie would also have no memory of the past week, of being rooted out of his home and sent away. "Good for thee," she murmured. "We'll make a happy place for thee in America so tha' can grow up strong and brave."

She walked with him to the rail and looked down at the village. "At least we're leaving this awful place. This is no kind of home for thee, nor for any of us." In the distance she could just make out the row of mean shacks huddled in a despairing line along the shore. *Anything will be better than that,* she decided. *Living here would sooner or later kill us all.*

She turned toward the other ship that lay at anchor next to theirs. Her eyes roamed what she could see of its deck, then down its gangplank, and there she found them. Betsy and Missus were gathering the few things they had and getting ready to board. Falon kept her eyes on them as they mounted the ramp, until a grating noise behind her made her jump. When she turned around, the gangplank was being hauled into the ship. "Weigh anchor!" came the order, and a mighty rattling of chains followed as the anchor was hoisted out of the water and their ship began to move.

"This is it." Will stood at her left elbow. "No turning back now."

"There's never been any turning back. Not since they fired our house."

And there was Betsy, standing at the rail of the other ship, watching them as they began to drift away from the dock. She lifted a hand in farewell. Suddenly, Falon remembered. "I never played for her last night," she told Will. "Here, you take the baby." She handed Robbie over and fished her flute out from beneath her bodice. "Think she'll hear it?" she wondered aloud.

"She'll hear," Will assured her. "The water'll carry the music over."

Taking a deep breath and willing steadiness to her fingers, Falon put the flute to her lips and played a lament. The notes, high and piercing, sailed out across the waves. The seamen had been busy shouting to each other as they went about their tasks. Now they fell silent, and the only sounds behind the music were the slap of the waves against the hull and the creak and groan of the ponderous ship. Even those milling about on shore stopped to listen. The liquid notes cried out, cried for a loved land, for the hills and the moors, for the lochs and rivers, the heather and thistle. They cried for friends and family left behind, both living and dead. They cried for home.

When she finished, her last note played out, she turned and looked at her father. He'd pulled his cap down over his face, and his shoulders were shaking. Several of the sailors wiped at their eyes. Maire Morgan had her face buried in George's chest as he patted her back with one hand. Only Falon's own mother seemed unaffected; she remained stone-faced, her lips tight with disapproval. Will wiped his nose against his sleeve and whispered, "Don't leave it like that, lass. Play us a dance."

He was right, of course, but Falon couldn't quite manage a reel. So she played a ballad instead, a lively enough tune. By the time she was done, their ship's sails were unfurled, and they were truly underway. She could barely make out Betsy's form, but she saw when Betsy took off her cap and waved goodbye.

★3

. . . The voyage on the White Arrow was both better, and far worse, than anything I expected . . .

The Macvails had a spot in the hold just large enough for them to all stretch out and sleep. Seven other families had also taken passage on the *White Arrow*, four from Ireland, three from Scotland, and they were packed into the hold cheek by jowl. *It's a good thing we don't have much to take with us,* Falon told herself after her first look around.

Mother dropped their bits of baggage onto the floor of the hold and dusted her hands as though throwing out the garbage. She turned to Falon with a glare, her hands on her hips. "That was really something up there, wasn't it?"

"What was?" Falon asked, confused.

"Thy little concert. Tha' really made an impression."

Falon bit her tongue and started to turn away, but Mother grabbed her arm and yanked her back. "Is it not enough that you shame us with those boys? D'ye have to parade and flaunt yourself, too? Here we are, leaving our home, and ye have to go and make a party of it." She shook Falon until the girl's teeth rattled. "I'll not stand it. Give me that flute. Ye'll have no more need of it where you're going."

Falon wasn't sure whether Mother meant she was going to America, or to hell, but she wasn't about to give her the flute.

She tried to pull away, but Mother clutched her all the harder. "Give it to me!" she rasped, trying to dig it out of Falon's dress.

"Mother, stop it." Will had come down into the hold, and now he put himself between his mother and sister. "Leave her alone. She's done nothing wrong."

Esme Macvail had had all she could take. She hauled back and slapped Will square in the face. "How dare ye speak to me that way!"

Will didn't flinch or back down. Instead, he took his mother's hand, and gently pried it from Falon's arm. Then, with a tenderness Falon would never fathom, he raised Mother's hand to his lips and kissed it.

Mother's eyes widened, filling with tears. "Why, lad? Why are ye all against me?"

"We aren't against ye. Ye just don't know the whole story."

"What whole story?" she demanded. "What are ye talking about?"

He put an arm around her shoulders. "What happened with our Falon isn't what ye think. She didn't do anything wrong."

Mother crossed her arms, regarding Falon with suspicion. "I don't know what ye're driving at, Will, but I saw her with my own eyes—she practically threw herself on that lad on the beach just before we came aboard. I know what I saw."

"Ye saw what ye saw," Will agreed with a nod, "but still, it's not what ye think. Dad will have to explain it to ye."

"Does Dad have Robbie?" Falon clenched herself to keep her voice steady. Will nodded. "I'll just go and get him then." With that, she climbed back up the steep steps onto the main deck. Whatever else

Will and Mother had to say to each other, they could say without her. She found Father standing at the stern rail with Robbie perched on his shoulders, watching the greening hills disappear over the horizon. She stood beside him, and after a while leaned her head against his arm. "Well, we're on our way," he murmured.

"It's America for us," she answered, putting her arm around his waist.

"So it is. I think you children will do all right there."

"We all will. We'll find our place and make it home."

His arm went around her shoulders. "My brave lass." He cleared his throat. "Just so ye know, I told the Morgans about last night, about what ye did for Betsy."

"Thanks, Dad." She took in a long breath and let it out. "D'ye think ye could explain it to Mother? She's awfully pained."

He nodded. "I will do that. There's no need to tiptoe around it anymore, now that your little friend is safe away." His arm around her tightened. "I'm glad tha' saved thy flute from the fire. Ye gave us a fine send-off."

She thanked him again. "But it's too bad tha' had to sell thy fiddle. We could have played together."

"The fiddle served its purpose," he answered, his voice harsh with emotion. "It made music for a time, and it bought us passage to America."

At that moment, Falon made herself a promise. Somehow, when they got to their new home, she would find a way to get another fiddle for her father. *Mother will sing, and we'll make music together again, just like we used to.*

Father was true to his word. Before nightfall, he took Mother aside, as well as he could do on a crowded ship, and explained the whole situation concerning Betsy. If Falon thought his explaining would make things better, she was in for a sorry surprise.

"So ye see, Esme, our lass was only helping her friend," Father finished. "She did what she had to do to keep Betsy safe from the agents."

Splotches of high color flared in Mother's cheeks. "And ye never spoke a word to me of this."

"I'm telling ye now."

"Why couldn't ye have told me before, when it mattered?"

Father bowed his head, contemplating his rough hands as if they held an answer. "We had to keep it as secret as we might."

"Yet everyone in the village knew but me." Mother crossed her arms tight against her chest.

"Not everyone. The Morgans didn't know." He sighed, "In the leaving, everyone was thinking only of themselves and their own. Hardly anyone noticed the lass was gone, or that we had a new lad with us."

"But you noticed," Mother pointed out.

He didn't try to deny it. "I did, but it took me a bit to sort it out."

Mother nodded at Will and Falon. "The children knew."

Will answered her: "All the lads knew. The Mackays gave us the secret to keep."

"And Falon?" Mother's eyes were hard with hurt.

"I didn't know until the third or fourth day." Falon couldn't stop the pleading in her voice as she added, "She was . . . she is my best friend. I recognized her, that's all."

Esme's accusing gaze raked each of them in turn. "But none of ye could tell me." There was the rub. None of them had dared spill the secret to Mother for fear of what she might do or say. But there was no good way, no kind way to tell her that. In the guilty silence that followed, she said, "Oh, I see. Ye didn't trust me to keep it quiet."

"It wasn't that, love," Father protested. "No one spoke of it to anyone. None of us talked about it among ourselves."

That wasn't good enough. Mother's eyes filled with angry tears. "Ye didn't trust me to keep my own counsel." She turned away then, muttering, "Well, we'll see whether I can or not."

Falon looked at Will, who just shook his head. Taking Robbie with him, he climbed back up the stairs to the deck. Father looked as if he would say something else, but he changed his mind, clenching his jaw and shaking his head just as Will had done. What more, after all, could he say? Mother had gotten to the truth, and there was no softening it. From then on she refused to speak to any of them.

The sailing was smooth their first night out. The ship rocked gently enough to lull Falon into a deep, dreamless sleep—the first good sleep she'd had since they left home. She woke the next morning, staring at the wooden deck above that was now their ceiling in the hold, feeling hopeful for the first time since their house was burned. They had crossed an invisible line sometime in the night; they were going toward a place now, not just away from home.

She took the time to look around at her fellow passengers. She noticed that the Scottish families seemed to be on one side of the hold, while the Irish passengers were on the other side. One of the Irish passengers was a girl about her own age, with curly red hair and a generous sprinkling of freckles. She sat with her parents and a younger sister, all of them sporting the same fiery hair, and with a grandfather who looked as gnarled as the single old oak that had shaded the house in Sgall.

As Falon stirred their breakfast of thin oatmeal, she nodded toward the girl and asked Will, "Do ye think it'll be all right if I talked to her?"

"I wouldn't, if I were you," he answered in a near whisper. "We've problems enough as it is."

"Problems? What d'ye mean?"

He gestured toward Mother, whose back was turned.

Falon leaned toward him. "Why would my talking to another girl be a problem? It's the boys Mother was angry about."

"Those people are Irish," he answered, as if that explained everything.

"Irish, aye."

"They're Catholic, Falon. Papists."

"Oh." Falon's heart sank. Neither of her parents would tolerate her talking to a Catholic, much less making friends with one. When the red-haired girl looked her way and smiled, Falon turned her back, feeling disappointed and lonely.

After breakfast, she climbed the steps to the deck, struggling to keep her unsteady feet firmly planted on the rocking boards. She shivered in the bracing sea breeze. It was colder than the stuffy air in the hold, but smelled like a garden in comparison. Several people had gotten sick in the night, and though they had tried to clean it up, the sour smell of sickness lingered below.

Will was ahead of her, already at the stern of the ship, looking out at the sea they had left behind. "Can't see land anymore," he murmured as she came up beside him.

She followed his gaze. Nothing but water, stretching all the way to the horizon. "Will we see Ireland, I wonder?"

"I don't think so. I heard them saying we'd sail around north of Ireland, and then west and south to America. We won't be seeing land for a long time."

She glanced around at the busy deck of the ship. "Seems so small now. In the dock it looked bigger."

One corner of Will's mouth curled up. "Aye, and that's the truth. 'Tis but a tiny thing in the middle of the sea."

"You there, girl!" The shout made Falon jump and spin around, heart in her throat. *Oh no, please don't make me go back down into the hold!*

One of the sailors gestured at her. "You the little girl who has the music?"

Her hand felt for the reassuring length of her flute. Unable to answer him, she nodded.

"Play us a tune, won't you?" He grinned, showing a row of crooked, overlapping teeth. "Makes the work go better."

She glanced at Will, who answered with a shrug. "All right, then." She licked at her lips, and put the flute to her mouth, considering. *I should play something lively.* After a moment, she launched into a shanty her uncle had taught her, a tune called "The Fish of the Sea." A couple of the sailors knew it, and they took turns singing the verses as they worked.

Up jumps the eel with his slippery tail,
Climbs aloft and reefs the top sail.
Windy weather, boys, stormy weather, boys,
When the wind blows we're all together, boys.
Blow ye winds westerly, blow ye winds, blow.
Jolly sou'westerly, boys, steady she goes.

When the song was done, one of the other seamen called out, "Bring the lass amidships, so's we can all hear!"

The sailor who had first called to her bowed low, sweeping his arm in the direction of the ship's midsection. "This way, if you please."

She had started that way, one step ahead of him, when the ship took an unexpected pitch. Just as she lost her balance, he grabbed her shoulders from behind and steadied her. "Whoa there, little bird! We wouldn't want to lose you." He released her. "Step careful now. You haven't got your sea legs yet."

"Sea . . . sea legs?" The idea of falling overboard had her badly shaken.

"That's right. Takes a while for your limbs to learn the ways of the sea, so that you don't fall. It'll come. Another day or two, you'll be walking like you were born on a ship."

Falon decided she would have to take his word for it. Her legs suddenly felt like water; only a fierce desire not to fall in front of everyone kept her upright and moving. Another sailor indicated a small keg. "Plant yourself here, young'un." She sank gratefully down.

Bracing her feet on either side of the keg, she let out a long breath. *Another song. They want me to play another song.* From somewhere in her memory she pulled another tune, and then another. The sailors sang along, joked and laughed among themselves, and walked the deck in rhythm, a fine drumbeat for her melodies.

"Play us 'The Mermaid,'" one of them shouted.

Falon didn't know that one, but the sailor who had steered her to her barrel seat saved her. "Watch yourself, man!" he roared. "That ain't no proper tune for the young lady here!" Leaning toward her, he asked, "Do you know 'We're All Bound to Go'?"

Falon nodded and started in on the tune. After the fourth song, she had to stop to catch her breath. 'Her' sailor handed her a dipper of water. "Good work, Little Bird," he grinned.

She gulped down the cool liquid and handed the dipper back. "Thank ye, sir."

He chuckled. "Oh, no need to be so formal as all that. You can call me Shaddie."

"Shaddie?"

He pulled off his cap and ran his fingers through the damp curls that plastered his pate. "My mama, God rest her, named me for Shadrach in the Bible. You know, that fella' that walked in the fiery furnace." He fished around in a pocket and drew out a copper penny, which he handed to Falon. "Thankee for the music, Little Bird. Maybe tomorrow you'll play for us again?"

She stood, just managing a curtsy on the rocking deck. "If I may." Will took her arm and helped her below deck. She took the coin to her father. "Here, Dad. Maybe this will help us in America."

Will explained what had happened, and Father accepted the penny with a nod. His eyes glistened with unshed tears. "You children are going to have a good life there." He tightened his fist on the penny. "I just know it. I can feel it down in ma' bones."

Mother turned away without comment and busied herself re-folding the one piece of good linen she still had—a small tablecloth. Ever since she had told them she could keep her own counsel, Mother had guarded her silence as if her life depended on it. Not one word, not a sigh, not an exclamation had escaped the seal of her lips. Father didn't comment on her silence. He'd learned long ago not to butt his head against Mother's iron stubbornness. Will and Falon followed his lead. They continued to talk among themselves as though nothing were amiss.

George Morgan came down from the deck later that morning, high-stepping over children, bundles of food, and household goods. He hunkered down next to Father. "I've been talking to one of the sailors."

"Aye?" Father drew his pipe from his pocket and stuffed a small wad of leaf in the bowl. Falon couldn't help noticing how flattened his pouch had gone. He'd be out of tobacco soon.

"He told me about the land there. You can get an acre for twelve cents."

Father's eyebrows shot up. "Twelve cents? Are ye sure?"

George nodded vigorously. "Sounds almost too good, I know. So I asked him, 'Is the land so poor, then?' and here's what he said." They all leaned closer to catch every word. "He said the land is good enough. We'll have no problem making a crop. It's cheap because there's so much of it, do y' see. Texas is bigger than all of Scotland; they need good people to settle it."

Dad took a puff on his pipe. The sweet, white smoke circled up and away, wreathing itself around his head. He squinted at George through the haze. "Even at that price, we'll be starting small. We have to buy seed and food to tide us over till harvest."

"Nay, nay." George laid a hand on Father's arm. "Tha's the other thing. You go ahead and take the acres you want, and they give you up to three years to pay for it."

Father's eyes went wide with disbelief. "On top of rents, then?"

"No rents."

"Are ye' crazy, man? What d' ye mean, no rents?"

"I'm telling you, Camran." George now stabbed at Dad's forearm with one finger. "Ye don't pay rents at all. Ye raise the crops and sell them to pay for the land, and then it's yours. You own it."

Father took another long drag. "Hm-m-m. Well, there has to be a catch. It just sounds too good."

George cleared his throat. "Ye'd be right about that, but 'tis a small thing. Ye understand that this Texas is part of Mexico, aye? And Mexico is part of Spain."

Father glanced at Mother, who was smoothing imaginary wrinkles out of her tablecloth. "Aye, I understand."

"Well, the catch is, ye have to become citizens of Spain."

Father's eyes narrowed. "Citizens of Spain." When George nodded, he growled, "I'm a Scot, no' a Spaniard."

George's eyes went hard as he stood. "Aye, well, Scotland doesn't want us, now does it?" He left them then, crossing the hold to where his wife waited.

Father continued to suck at the stem of his pipe, considering. Young as Falon was, she clearly understood his dilemma. They had to have land—and quickly—or they would starve. But it was still too soon and too painful for her father to completely turn his back on the country that had spat him out. He needed time—time to think on it, time to make it right in his mind. He would have things figured out by the time they got there.

The first two weeks out were much the same: Father lost in thought, Mother in silence. Will and Falon spent most of each morning on deck. She piped for the seamen while her brother stood by. One morning, Shaddie took Will in hand and began teaching him the rudiments of ship craft. Will went at it as if he'd been born to sail, and the next day, Shaddie took him aloft into the rigging. Falon sat on her barrel perch amidships and watched him climb and clamber above her until her neck ached.

At one point, Will laughed at something. It was a good, clean sound she had not heard in months. His joy rang out over the water from above her head, and hope for the future stirred in her. Maybe, just maybe . . .

When Will was down again, when they were ready to go below, he told her, "I could do this, Falon. If need be, I'll hire myself to a ship and send the money home to Dad."

But now that it was out, now that he'd spoken his desire, fear closed in on Falon like a hardened fist. The thought of him being gone for months on end, the thought of her family breaking up—she could not bear it. "But Will, Dad'll need thee on the farm. We're going to have land, and you'll have to help."

As soon as the words left her lips, she wanted to recall them. The light went out of her brother's eyes, and an angry flush reddened his face. "I shouldn't have told thee. Tha' art but a child, and a lass at that." He took her arm to steer her toward the hold.

"I'm sorry, Will."

"Nay," he answered roughly, "'tis nothing after all."

Every day that she played for the sailors, one or the other of them rewarded her with a penny. She passed them all to Father, counting as she did, hoping her contribution would in the end be enough at least for seed, or maybe even to buy an acre of land. That day, though, she had no pleasure in the coin she earned, and nothing she could say would amend for her thoughtless words. Miserable, she picked Robbie up and held him close to her hurting heart. The agents' burning their place had set a huge wheel turning, and she couldn't help but wonder if it would grind them all to dust.

Two days later, Mother woke with a fever.

Shaddie told Will that Mother had typhus. "I've seen it many times, boy." He shook his head sadly after Will described her symptoms. "Just you hope and pray that the Little Bird doesn't come down with it, or your baby brother."

There was no more going up on deck for Falon. She now had double duty, caring for Robbie and nursing her mother. She bathed Mother's flaming face with a rag dipped in cool sea water, and tried to feed her a thin oat porridge. Lost in the haze of fever, Mother couldn't respond, and most of the food dribbled from the corners of her mouth.

Father kept silent vigil, stolidly sucking at the stem of his now-empty pipe. He might as well have been carved of granite, for all he moved or spoke. There had been many times when the weight of his presence had been a comfort. Now it angered Falon. *He sits here, thinking and figuring,* she told herself. *Thinking about the land he wants to buy, figuring how he can pay for it from the sweat of his brow and how he can become a Spaniard and still be a good Scot. Meanwhile, my mother . . .* She couldn't finish the thought without bursting into tears, and so she didn't finish it. She let it hang, and biting her lip she dipped the rag into the water again.

It was the fever that finally broke Mother's silence. In her delirium, she muttered to the stinking air, to people only she could see. On the fourth day of her sickness, she rose up suddenly on one elbow and peered at Falon with bloodshot eyes. "Annie?"

Annie had died of the fever more than five years before. "No, Mum," Falon answered. "It's me. It's your Falon."

"Falon," her mother rasped. She lay back again, repeating, "Falon," as if the name had some significance she had forgotten.

It was this—more than her mother's scolding, more than her threats and warnings—this being locked out of her memory, being shut out of her head, and maybe her heart, too, that broke Falon's dam of grief. She bowed her head and wept into the damp rag.

"Ah, lass," she heard her father sigh. He laid a heavy hand on her shoulder. "Come here to me." He gathered her and held her in his lap, as he had not done since she was a tiny child. His clothing reeked of sweat and stale smoke and the sickness in the hold, but she buried her face in his chest, for all that. "This has been too much for thee," he murmured.

They sat in silence, but for Falon's quiet weeping. Father didn't offer empty words of consolation. Life had beaten them hard; he held her, and she held on. Before long, Robbie was there, trying to climb into Father's lap, too, so Falon pulled him up. He wrapped his thin little arms around her neck and laid his head on her shoulder.

On the tenth day of her sickness, Mother succumbed. Falon, assured by her father that he would keep watch, had been asleep. When she woke in the morning, Mother's body was already wrapped in the sheet she had been lying on, and Father was nowhere in sight.

Falon stood up, blinking the sleep from her eyes, staring in horror at the white-shrouded form on the hold's floor, gooseflesh rising on her arms and running down her back. *I knew this would happen. I knew when we left Sgall that Mother was going to die.* She sank to her knees. *And there was nothing I could do to stop it.*

She nearly screamed when a hand touched her lightly on the shoulder. She jumped up and whirled around. "Whisht, lass." It was Maire Morgan. "'Tis only me. Thy mother died in the night, and thy dad and I took care of her body for thee."

Until that moment, Falon had given no thought about what she'd have to do if Mother died, how she'd have to wash the body for burial. Now she had been spared that awful task. "I thank thee, Maire. And where is Dad?"

Maire nodded toward the stairs. "He went above. You go on up. I'll watch little Robbie for a while."

Falon thanked her again and went looking for her father. The wind had picked up, and a thick, chill mist soaked the deck. She wiped the glaze of water from her face with the edge of her shawl, and ventured out across the slick boards toward the stern, where her father was standing with one arm around Will, staring out at the cold waves and the misty curtain separating them from home. When she joined them, Father sighed. "Well, children, this is a hard thing, and no mistake."

That was all he said. Falon leaned her head against his arm, and they remained there for the better part of an hour, moving only to wipe the mist from their faces and their eyes. *Mother would have wanted to be buried in Scotland,* Falon told herself, *but we can't go back now. I suppose we'll have to bury her in Texas.* She closed her eyes and imagined the place she would choose for her mother's grave—something on a green hill, under a spreading shade tree, the kind of tree where birds nested and sang. *Maybe with a loch or a river nearby,* she thought, *and flowers on the hill in the summertime.*

Aloud she asked, "How much longer will it take us to get to Texas, Dad?"

He brushed his sleeve against his face and shook his head. "Don't know for sure. Maybe another two weeks?"

"At least that," Will answered. "If the wind holds, and we don't run into foul weather, it'll be about two weeks, maybe two and a half."

"Where will we keep her all that time?" Falon wondered.

Father's voice sounded choked and harsh. "What d'ye mean, lass?"

"Where will we keep . . ." Falon struggled with the awful words. "Where will we keep her body until we can bury her?"

Father groaned, covering his eyes. Will said, "We cannot keep her, Falon."

"Then what . . . ?" Even before the question was fully formed, she knew the answer. "No," she said, horrified, "we can't do that. We can't just throw her in the water."

At that, Father turned abruptly, and trudging across the slick deck, disappeared down the stairs to the hold. "Will?" Falon whispered. Her brother wouldn't look at her. He stared out over the empty water, his jaw clenched tight, his hands gripping the rail, his breath rasping out of him in ragged gusts. Frightened, she tried again. "Will, please . . ."

"What would ye have me say? What's happened has happened. And we have to do what we have to do, that's all."

"I didn't mean to make you angry." His face blurred and swam before her eyes. "I didn't mean to."

"It's not thee, Falon." Will tucked his chin against his chest and drew a deep breath. "None of us wants . . ." His throat worked as he swallowed. "None of us wants to do this, but we must. We have no choice." He turned his eyes to meet hers. "We have to do it now. Today." He lifted his cap and ran his fingers through his damp curls. "And we have to be strong, to help Father through it."

Falon nodded, her heart thudding miserably in her chest. "Aye, I understand."

As if he had heard her, Father climbed back up onto the deck, cradling his wife's shrouded body. Maire and George Morgan followed close behind, with Robbie perched in Maire's arms.

The ship's captain joined them at the stern, a little black book clutched in one hand. Falon knew who the captain was; she had seen him every day that she had been on deck, but he had never acknowledged her presence. Now she studied his face so she wouldn't have to look at her father's burden. Captain Ferguson's eyes were the color of the mist and the sea, his hair a darker gray, like iron. A long scar ran down the right side of his face, from the corner of his eye to his jaw, a permanent tear streak. When Father approached the stern railing, the captain cleared his throat. "On this day, the twenty-first of March, year of our Lord 1823, we consign our sister to the arms of her Heavenly Father." He opened his book, found the page he wanted. "Our Father which art in heaven, Hallowed be Thy name. Thy kingdom come, Thy will be done in earth as it is in heaven . . ."

"Give us this day our daily bread," Falon murmured the well-worn prayer along with the others. "And forgive us our trespasses as we forgive those who trespass against us . . ."

Trespass. Reverend had told them that was another word for sin, but it still made Falon think of the time, three years before, when someone had gotten into their oat field and trampled about half of the crop. Father had gone out the next several nights and sat watch over what was left, trying to catch whoever had done it. The trespassers never came back, but their destruction made for a lean winter.

"Lead us not into temptation, but deliver us from evil . . ." *Well, at least we're away from those agents. And Betsy's away from them.* Falon touched that last thought lightly; then shied away from it. This day's pain was enough.

"For Thine is the kingdom, and the power, and the glory forever. Amen."

"Amen," a voice murmured a beat after the others. Falon looked up and saw Shaddie standing just behind the captain's left shoulder, his cap in his hands.

The captain gave a nod, and Father stepped up to the rail. He held Mother's body close to his chest for a moment. "She was a bonny lass," he said. George and Maire both nodded in agreement. "And she was a good wife."

She was, Falon thought. *I remember the happy times. I remember how it was before Annie died.*

Father heaved a great sigh, lifted the shrouded bundle up and over, and let go. It slipped into the waves with hardly a splash, leaving only a faint glimmer of white as it sank below the surface.

Will leaned toward Falon, whispering, "Can thee manage to play a hymn?"

Falon shook her head. "Mother wouldn't have wanted it."

"But would tha' do it for me and for Dad?"

She wanted to cry out, *You ask too much!* She wanted to slap and kick at him, to make him go away and leave her alone. Instead, she pulled out her flute, but she couldn't think of a hymn. Her mind had gone completely blank. The only song she could remember was "On the Banks of the Roses," a love song, and that was what came. Maire looked shocked, but the men nodded to the music, and a few murmured the words along with the tune.

On the banks of the roses my love and I sat down,
And I took out my violin to play my love a tune.
In the middle of the tune, oh she sighed and she said,
O-ro Johnny, lovely Johnny, would you leave me?

Father's eyes closed as he turned his face up, toward the falling mist.

When she was done, Falon tucked her flute away and walked to the barrel amidships that she had always sat on to play for the sailors. But instead of facing the deck, she turned around to watch the water rush by beneath the ship. No one bothered her there or told her to move, and she propped her arms on the railing and sat with her chin on her hands. She knew without looking when everyone else in her family had gone below, and still she sat unmoving in the mist. Her face felt hot, and her head was starting to ache. The water had a soothing, hypnotic effect. She didn't have to think, only to watch and listen. She gave herself over to the mesmerizing rush, to the foamy wake, to the hiss and splash against the hull.

After a time, she felt a light tap on her shoulder. She looked up to find Shaddie standing over her. He pulled respectfully on the bill of his cap. "Here's a bit for you, Little Bird." He held out two dried apples. When she accepted them and thanked him, he added, "I'm real sorry about your mother." With that, he moved away again.

Falon sniffed at the apples. The musky, autumnal scent reminded her of home. She bit into the leathery skin of one and rolled the piece around in her mouth, savoring its sweetness. *I hope we have apple trees where we're going,* she thought, taking another bite, *and if we don't, I'll plant them myself. And we'll have pies and cider, and dried apples in the winter.* Falon pocketed the second apple in her sporran, and pried the first apart with her thumbs. When she found the core, she coaxed the pips out with a fingernail, and slipped them into the pouch. Saving the seeds, at least, was something practical, something her mother would have approved of.

Her thoughts strayed again to her flute. Mother had not approved of her music. Falon clutched at the familiar length of the instrument beneath her dress. "Honor thy father and thy mother," Reverend had told them. *Would Mother have been happy if I had rid myself of it? Would that be honoring her now?* Falon pulled it out, studied its fipple and holes, ran her finger along the grain of the wood. She looked out into the water. *I should have let her have it when we came aboard. She might still be alive if I had.* Falon harbored no illusion that a mere fever had killed her mother. No, she had died of a broken heart, and though the flute was but a little thing, giving it over might have been enough to save her. Falon pulled the leather thong from around her neck, and looked out again at the foaming waves.

"Don't do it."

Startled, she turned to see Captain Ferguson standing there. He didn't meet her eyes, but looked out at the sea, as if searching for whatever had caught her attention. "Don't do it," he repeated. "Your mother has died. It's up to you to live."

She started to answer, but he had already walked off. Swallowing, she donned the flute again, and sat with her hand holding it against her heart.

★4

. . . and what strange dreams I had . . .

It's quiet here in her little hiding place, quiet and warm and sunny. Falon has a roasted potato in her pocket and a flask of clear water. And her flute, of course. Annie is here with her, humming a little tune under her breath. Falon stretches her legs out, lets the coarse grass tickle her bare toes. A purple haze of heather cloaks the hills all around. "We could bundle some of that to take home to Mother," she says. Leaping to their feet, she and Annie wade out into the knee-high heather, where Falon snaps off a double handful of fragrant stems. She hasn't gone far when she hears someone calling her name. "Falon . . . Falon . . ."

Betsy? No, that's Will's voice. Why is he out here, and how did he know where to come looking? For a moment, she thinks of ducking under her overhanging rock and hiding. But if she does, he might find her anyway, and then her secret will be spoiled. With a groan of resignation she hurries away toward the sound of his voice . . .

. . . and into darkness. What in the world? It's no' so late, is it? And where has Annie gone? No longer able to see where she is going, Falon stumbles in the dark and cries out. "Will?"

"Falon!" came his answer, from far away now.

"Will!" she cries, "Where are you? I can't see you!"

All of a sudden, someone grabs her shoulders, and she screams in fright. "Falon." Will's voice is in her ear now. "Falon, it's me. It's your Will. Wake up. Please wake up."

She opened her eyes. Wood planking stretched above her. Falon blinked in confusion. *Where am I?* As Will bent over her, she remembered. *The ship's hold.* A sob of bitter disappointment tore through her.

Will pulled at her until she sat up, and he held her. "Tha's all right now, lass. 'Twill be all right."

"No!" she cried, pounding feebly at his shoulders with her fists. "I was home. D'ye hear? Annie was with me, and I was *home*!"

Will ignored the pounding and kept repeating, " 'Twill be all right." Finally she stopped, resigned again to reality, relaxed in his arms. When she did, he told her, "I thought we might lose ye, Falon." He pulled back from her and held her face in his hands.

A buzzing like a swarm of bees filled Falon's ears. Her vision went foggy, and as it darkened she felt him shake her again. "No, lass! Come back! Come back to us. Falon, please . . ." It was this last that pulled her into the light again. Her brother's sea green eyes, full of worry and fatigue, searched hers.

"I was home," she murmured. "Full summer. So beautiful . . ." She closed her eyes.

When she opened them again, it was out of a chilled darkness with no dreaming, and her father was leaning over her. "Heaven be praised," she heard him mutter. "Stay wi' us, lass." He bathed her face with a cool, wet rag. "Stay wi' us, now."

"Dad," she whispered through chattering teeth as a shiver wracked her body.

"Let me sit you up, and just you drink a sip of this. I've kept it nice and warm for thee."

She had no strength to resist, even when she caught the astringent odor of whatever was in the beaker he held to her lips. She took one obedient sip and choked as the dark liquid flamed down her throat.

"Try again, sweeting," he urged. "'Twill give thee strength."

When she had caught her breath she sipped again, bracing herself for the hot rush. This time she didn't choke, and the heat actually did seem to fortify her. Swallow by tentative swallow she emptied the cup. "What is this stuff?"

Her father sighed and swiped at his forehead with the back of one hand. "'Tis rum, lass. One of the sailors sent it down for if . . . for when ye woke up."

The alcohol went right to work and right to her head. "'Tis nice." Her own voice sounded dreamy and far away in her ears. She was already on her way back into the darkness, but this time it was warm there, warm as a womb.

Some time later, Falon woke again. Her father sat at her left, softly snoring with his chin resting on his chest. Will lay to her right, cradling Robbie in his arms. Over the now familiar creaking of the ship she heard a new sound—high-pitched cries coming from above. *Birds! We must be near land now.* Falon tried to push herself to a sitting position and found that she lacked the strength even for that. A shaft of gray penetrated the hold from the stairway, more an absence of darkness than a suggestion of light. *Must be nearly dawn,* she reasoned. *If we're so close to the land that there are birds, we got here quicker than Will thought we would.*

The events of the day before settled in on her. Mother. *If only she could have held on another day or two.* She was close. So close. Falon brushed away the tears that streaked down her face. *When we get to Texas I'm going to find that place, that hill with a shade tree, and flowers, and . . .*

And what? What would she do with a hill and a tree? There was no bringing her mother back, no final chance to make things right. She let out a long, shuddering sigh.

Later that morning, Will, who had gone on deck, came below again to confirm what Falon had suspected. "We're just off the coast of America," he told them. "The sailors say we should dock in Texas in three or four more days if this wind holds, and if we don't run aground on an island."

"Wisht, Will." Dad scowled at him, gesturing toward Falon. "Mind your tongue."

"Sorry, Falon." Will's face went scarlet. "I dinna' mean to frighten ye." He plunked himself down on the floor. "I guess I was carried away a bit at the sight of land." He took off his cap and ran his fingers through his hair. "The Captain's landed in Texas lots of times—dozens. He knows how to get round the islands all right."

"How did we get here so fast?" Falon asked.

"What d'ye mean, lass?" Her father stroked a stray lock of hair from her face.

"Well," she gingerly licked her lips, now cracked and dry. "Ye said it'd be another two weeks, but it's only been a day."

"A day? Ah, lass," her father moaned. "It's been two weeks and more. Ye've been out for a long time."

"I . . . I've been out for two weeks?" Dad and Will nodded in tandem.

Falon closed her eyes so she wouldn't have to watch the hold spin slowly around her. *I've been gone all this time and didn't know it. Gone from home. Gone from Mother. And now we're nearly there.* She whispered, "Has . . . has anything else happened?"

Her father cleared his throat. "Others have died."

Who? She turned her head as far as she could, searched all around her. "The Morgans? Where are they?" She took a shuddering breath.

The hold wasn't nearly as crowded as it had been. Maire Morgan sat alone in one corner, her back to them, her head bowed. A sick feeling hit Falon in the pit of her stomach. Where was George? And their children? The red-haired girl's grandfather was gone, and so was her little sister. "Dad?" Falon's voice shook. She didn't want to ask, but . . . "Where's Mr. Morgan? Is he up on deck? With the children?"

Father tightened his grip on her. "They're not on deck, lass."

What her father didn't say spoke volumes. "How many?" she whispered. "How many have died?"

"Don't know exactly," the awful words rumbled in her ear. "Your mother was the first, and then . . ." He cleared his throat. "George Morgan is gone, and both of their little ones. Young George will have to look after his mother now."

"Shaddie says this happens all the time," Will said. "Nearly every passage, some get sick of one thing or another."

A sudden surge of fear gripped her heart. "D'ye think Betsy . . . ?"

"Nay, nay," her father reassured her. "They had but a day's voyage to Ireland. Just a skip and a hop. Nay, the Mackays will have landed fine, and they're probably settled in their new home by now."

"Armaugh," she murmured, faintly surprised when the town's name came so readily to her memory.

"What did ye say, lass?"

"Armaugh," she repeated. "That's the town where the Mackays were going."

"I see." Her father laid her down again on her pallet and stroked her head with one callused hand. Falon moaned and rubbed at her burning eyes. She wanted to cry, needed to cry, but she had no tears. Her tongue felt like sandpaper in her mouth, and her eyes like wooden marbles rolling around in her head. "Was it the typhus?"

"Aye. We were afraid we'd lose you, too," Will told her, his own voice thick with tears, "but Shaddie took a look at ye and told us ye were stronger than ye seemed. The sickness came on because ye were worn out, and not eating enough."

Falon stopped rubbing at her eyes and peered at her father as he swam in and out of focus. He pulled her into his lap and cradled her with one arm. "Let me help thee eat a bite of this." With the other hand he picked up a steaming bowl and put it to her lips. "I made thee some porridge. Try to eat it all."

Falon wanted to refuse. But there was the bowl at her lips. She took a tentative swallow. The salty soup was nice and hot. After a few sips, something odd hit her tongue, something she had to chew. "What's in this, Dad?"

"Well, there's bits of salt pork," he told her.

"Salt pork?" Aside from the mussels, she hadn't tasted meat in weeks. "Where did ye get it?"

"From one of the other families. Dinna' worry about it. Just eat."

Falon took another sip. No meat in that one, but the next had a good-sized chunk. She knew the Morgans didn't have the luxury of meat. And as she puzzled it out, she couldn't imagine that any of the Scottish families had boarded with something so precious. Her gaze wandered across the hold to the group from Ireland. The girl with the red hair caught her eye and gave a solemn nod, as if to say, "We're separated by many things, you and I, but we're both alive. We made it."

Falon glanced at her brother, caught his warning look and the almost imperceptible shake of his head, and she understood. Father got the meat from them, from the Irish. A flush of shame rose to her cheeks as she realized how it must have wounded his pride to beg for meat from people he scorned. *He had to do that for me. They probably didn't give it to him, either,* she told herself. *I bet they made him pay for it with my pennies.* Something in her turned over, and she hated them, the Irish, hated the very sight of them. With one shaking hand she pushed the bowl away. "No more," she muttered.

"Ah now, just a bit to go, lass," Father coaxed. "Two more swallows for your old Dad, eh?"

Falon couldn't resist the plea in his voice. She allowed him to give her another sip, and though her stomach protested, she managed to get that bit down. But when he tried to get her to take the final swallow, she was certain she'd had enough. "I . . . I can't," she stammered.

"All right, then." He put the bowl down and rested his chin atop her head, letting out a long sigh. "It's been a hard trip, sure enough."

Falon's hand strayed to her flute—and found nothing. Captain Ferguson's words came back to her. *"It's up to you to live." I kept it, didn't I? Or did I throw it in the water after all?* Falon felt the blood drain from her face. She couldn't remember. "Dad, my flute. Where is it?"

He reached into his coat pocket. "Ye were so hot with the fever, I took it off ye. Didn't want it ruined." He held out the short length of wood on its cord. "D'ye want it?"

Falon touched the flute with the tip of one finger. "You keep it for now, Dad." She managed a brief smile before she fell asleep again. "I know tha' will keep it safe."

Falon was stronger the next day, and her father carried up to the deck so she could see the land as it flowed by. Her eyes widened in awe as she tried to take it all in. "It's so big," she murmured.

"Aye. And we've already gone by miles and miles of it. Look at the trees, lass. Never in my life have I seen forests go on and on like that." He shook his head. "I would never have even dreamed it."

Falon followed the tree line with her eyes, followed it where the trees seemed to march down almost to the water's edge, and followed it back where they receded. Such a mighty, unbroken line! "Is all of this America?"

"Aye. Every bit of it. We're not to Texas yet."

She drank in the everlasting green with her eyes, and before long, caught movement. Tiny with the distance, two deer had stepped out of the forest's cover and were grazing in plain sight. They lifted their heads as the ship sailed by. Wordlessly, Falon pointed them out.

"I see them," Father said. "That's good. There'll be wild game to feed us until we can get a crop in."

Wild game. Falon hadn't thought of that, hadn't thought of the deer that way. Her throat thickened with grief at the thought of killing and eating something so graceful, so beautiful. But deep down she knew that when it came to it, she would eat. They all would.

Will came to stand beside them. He held Robbie, and the little boy stared at Falon as if she were a stranger. "We should arrive at port sometime tomorrow," Will told them, "and depending on the tide, we'll land either tomorrow or the next day."

"We go in with the tide?" Father asked.

"Aye. The bay isn't very deep. In some places, it's hardly as deep as the height of a man. The ship has somewhat of a shallow draft, but even so, she still has to sail around the barriers and sandbars."

Falon shook her head. Will might as well have been speaking Chinese, for all she understood what he meant. But he did say tomorrow or the next day. That much she grasped. "We're nearly there," she murmured. *We're nearly home.* "Set me down, Dad."

"Are tha' sure, lass? Tha's still weak."

"I can stand," she assured him. "I want to stand."

"All right, then, but I'm holding onto thee, all the same."

Her father gently lowered her to the deck. Immediately, her legs tried to give way under her, and she wondered if she'd made a mistake, but she gritted her teeth and willed her limbs to hold her up, and with her father's firm grip on her arms she was able to stand. She grasped the ship's rail and held on as though weathering the fiercest storm, though the sea was calm and the day fair, with a light, following wind.

Young George Morgan came to stand beside Will. Though two years younger than Falon, shadows of worry and grief around his eyes aged him well beyond his youth. "I see tha' art up again, Falon." His words were clipped, full of sharp edges.

She swallowed. Her mother's death had been the first on the ship, but not the last. Never that. "Thank you, George. I am sorry about your dad and the little ones."

His cheeks went scarlet. He nodded and hung his head, the muscles in his face bunched and tightened. Father said, "George and I had a talk. We're going to be neighbors, help each other out." He put one arm around George's shoulders. "'Twill be all right, lad. We'll look after each other, same as our families have always done."

George nodded again. "I'd better go see to my mother." His shoulders stooped as he walked away, as though he carried the world on them.

Falon's legs trembled; she knew she wouldn't be able to stand much longer. She looked around for a barrel or a crate to sit on, but saw nothing close at hand. She reached up and touched one of the hands that held her shoulders. "You'll have to pick me up again, Dad."

He scooped her up in his arms as easily as if she'd been a babe, holding her close. "Tha' will see, lass. We'll get some land, build us a fine little house and raise our crops. We'll live free."

Free. Falon let out a long breath. She was old enough to know that troubles of one kind or another would follow them. But today, watching the endless forest glide by, living free sounded good. It sounded like it might be enough.

Early the next morning, Falon woke to the shrill of the bosun's whistle. Moments later she heard the shouted order, "Weigh anchor!"

"Weigh anchor, aye!" came the reply, followed by the clank and rattle of the huge chain. Moments later, a splash, and Falon felt the ship give a gentle buck as its momentum stopped and it strained against the anchor.

She tugged on her father's sleeve to wake him. "Dad," she whispered. "We're here. We've stopped."

He opened his eyes, looked around him. The surprise in his face told her he'd been dreaming. He'd been somewhere else. Then, rubbing his face with both hands, "We've stopped?"

"They just let down the anchor. That means we've arrived, doesn't it?"

"I believe it does," he answered as Will, who had wakened to their whispered conversation, scrambled to his feet. "Go have a look, lad. We'll be right up after ye."

Will went at the stairs with an eager clatter that woke everyone else in the hold. "Is this it, then?" someone murmured. "We've made it," came a reply, and somewhere in the dim hold a woman sobbed, "At last!"

Falon wiped at her own tears. The terrible voyage was nearly done.

"Art tha' ready to go up?" her father asked, his voice husky with emotion. Falon nodded, and he picked her up again and carried her to the stairs, where they had to stop and wait. Everyone in the hold, it seemed, was straining to go out on deck.

Her father finally mounted the steps, and the new day's light filled her eyes, making her wince and blink at the brightness. *This must be the way a newborn babe feels, coming out of the dark.* By the time Falon's eyes cleared, her father had squeezed in at the rail, and she got her first look at her new home.

The ship's prow pointed at a gap between two islands off the Texas shore. They were ready to sail into the gap as soon as the tide turned and brought them in.

Texas. The name sounded funny and foreign in her ears, and she wondered if it was Spanish. Will had told her there were islands off the shore, but she didn't expect what she saw. The islands off Scotland rose high and hilly above the waves. The islands she saw now were wide, flat swaths of sand and grass. "Dad, what's that?" She pointed to a large blackened area a few miles off to her left.

"Looks like a town burned," he answered grimly, and Falon knew he was thinking of Sgall. Had the troubles that plagued them there run ahead to greet them here?

Will pushed up beside them. "The port is just through there." He pointed to the narrow inlet between the two islands. "Shaddie says the tide's turning now, so we'll be heading in shortly."

"Did he say anything about that?" Dad nodded toward the burned town.

Will shook his head. "I'll ask him." And he took off again.

So this was going to be their new home. Falon glanced down at her dress, spotted and pocked with tiny burn holes from Sgall's falling embers. The dress hung on her thin frame like a scarecrow's rags. The others around her fared no better, all of them haggard with worry and want, a few still aching with the sickness. *What a ragtag lot we are!*

A little later, Will was back. "That town belonged to a pirate named Lafitte."

Every head around them swung in his direction. "A pirate?" echoed the man next to him.

"That's what Shaddie told me," he answered. "Story goes, this Lafitte attacked the wrong ship sometime last year. It was an American ship, and he was forced to leave these waters. He burned his town so no one else could have it."

"Well, that's all right then," Father said. "We don't need the likes of him around here anyway." Several nodded assent and murmured approval.

But Falon shivered in her father's arms. If there were pirates, what else might there be?

About an hour later, the sailors shooed them all into the hold again. "We're going to be a mite busy," Shaddie explained to Will. "We've caught the tide just right, but we still have to bring her through." He held up one hand, palm out. "But never worry, we'll have you on solid ground before the day's out."

It was hard, so hard to go below again now that they were in sight of land. But go below they did, and Father cooked a fresh batch of porridge to celebrate. No salt pork this time. The bit he had was long gone. Falon couldn't help but notice that the oats were nearly gone as well. They maybe had enough left in the sack for one more meager meal. But that's tomorrow's worry, she told herself. *They probably have seaweed here. We can live on that if we have to.*

She took off her shawl. "It's hot down here," she remarked to no one in particular.

"'Tis," agreed one of the other passengers, a Scot named Maccready, as he stepped past her, "and it isn't even summer yet."

Falon looked at her father, who shrugged. "If it's hot, it's hot. We'll learn to like it, aye?"

Will interrupted. "Dad, there's something I need to tell thee." He glanced once at Falon, then turned his eyes back on his father.

Falon thought, *Here it comes. He's going to leave us.*

"Shaddie says they'll be losing a couple of hands when we put into port. He said he talked to the captain about hiring me on." When the muscles bunched up in his father's face, Will added, "I wouldn't be gone long, only for a season, till winter." He took a deep breath and continued. "They'd give you a scrip for my wages. That way you will have money to get started proper."

"A scrip, you say?"

"Aye, Dad. You can trade it for seed, animals, tools, whatever you need."

"Tha' art a farmer, Will, no' a sailor." Before Will could reply, Father held up one hand. "Let me think on it. How soon do you need to give an answer?"

"The ship will be in port for a week."

Father nodded. "You'll have my answer before we leave the town."

Will nodded and leaned back against a crate, studiously avoiding Falon's gaze. *This is it, then.* She had no doubt what the answer would be.

A little later, Father asked, "D'ye think ye could pipe us a tune, lass? Sort of a homecoming?"

Falon shook her head. "I haven't the wind for it, Dad."

His face fell. "Oh, aye. Tha's still weak."

She had been reclining on the floor. Now she struggled to sit up. "Well, maybe I can try."

"Nay, nay." He pushed her gently down again. "Dinna' fash yerself. Save thy strength for the landing, hey?"

Falon stretched out, pillowing her head on her folded shawl. The heat, combined with the warm porridge in her stomach, made her drowsy enough to fall asleep. She closed her eyes one minute, and the next, it seemed, her father was shaking her awake. "We're here, lass," he told her. "Time to go have a look at our new home." He handed Robbie and their few possessions to Will, and scooped his daughter into his arms.

When they were finally on deck and standing at the rail, Falon saw the *White Arrow*'s bow nosing the end of a short pier. On the other end of the pier stood a town bristling with new buildings, and off behind them stood a fortress. She could just make out the figure of a man pacing the top of the wall.

"Perry's Point," Will murmured.

"Say again?" Falon asked.

"The name of the town is Perry's Point."

Falon glanced upward. The ship's sails were furled and lashed to the giant masts for the first time since they had come aboard. Tears stung her eyes. *I wish tha' were here with us, Mum. Surely this place would have made you happy again.*

The bosun's whistle sounded, and the gangplank was lowered with a resounding thud onto the end of the pier. Shortly, a thin stream of passengers began to disembark. "Well," Father said, giving Falon a quick squeeze, "let's go."

"Put me down, Dad. I want to walk."

After a moment's hesitation, he set her on her feet. She straightened her skirts and ran her hands over her unruly, tangled mess of hair. With Will and Robbie leading the way and her father following close behind, they approached the top of the gangplank.

Shaddie was waiting there. He took off his cap and nodded at Falon. "Fare thee well, Little Bird."

"And you, Shaddie," she answered with a little curtsy. "Thank you for everything."

Captain Ferguson approached them, hands clasped behind his back. "Your son has the makings of a seaman, Mr. Macvail."

Father doffed his cap. "So I hear, sir."

"If you decide to sign him on for a season, I'll need to know within three days."

"Three days, aye. Soon as we figure out what's what."

The captain turned to Falon, holding out a hand. "Goodbye, miss. The best of luck to you."

Falon felt the flame of a blush rise in her face as she took his hand and gave it a shake. "Thank you, sir." With a final nod, the captain turned away, and Falon followed her father and brothers down the gangplank, across the pier, and onto solid ground.

★5

. . . So this was Texas. On the one hand, it was confusing, and the prospect of building a home here seemed impossible. On the other hand, anything was possible in such a wild, young place . . .

As it turned out, the Macvail family found out they had been misinformed.

"No, Mr. Macvail," the government official—a Mr. Stephen Austin—told them, pulling himself up to his full height. "Mexico is no longer under the rule of Spain. We officially received the treaty from Cordoba last summer. The gentleman who gave you that information was incorrect."

Though the Macvails were last off the ship, they were first to find the land office, and now their neighbors from the voyage crowded into the doorway, passing the word to those who waited outside.

"So then, we don't have to become Spanish citizens?"

Falon thought that Mr. Austin would look more at home in an elegant drawing room than in the rough-and-tumble of Perry's Point. His thick, black hair was combed neatly back from his high forehead, and his spotless frock coat sported brass buttons. His dark eyes crinkled with a smile. "You will be Mexican citizens instead."

"I see." Father ran his fingers through his hair. "What do I need to do?"

"It's simple. There are three requirements." He held up one hand and ticked off three fingers as he spoke. "First, you must obey the laws of Mexico. These laws are reasonable. If you are an upright man, you will not find them odious. Second, you must be prepared to defend yourself against the Indians. The Mexican government does not have the resources to patrol the entire region of Texas. And third, you must become a member of the Catholic Church, if you are not one already." He spread his hands. "You see? Simple."

Falon glanced behind her at the crowd in the doorway. *Simple enough if you're Irish.*

"I heard the land was about twelve cents an acre. Is that right?"

Mr. Austin chuckled and shook his head. "I am an empresario, and I've made a deal with the government. So, because you are dealing directly with me, I can make you a better offer." He stabbed at a map on his desk with the tip of his finger. "Since you are the head of a household, Governor Martinez has authorized me to offer you a sitio and a labor of land."

"A sitio and a labor?" Father seemed to be having some trouble wrapping his tongue around the unfamiliar words. Falon noticed that he didn't even bother to ask what an empresario was.

"A sitio is nearly four and a half thousand acres." A collective gasp sounded from the others in the doorway. Mr. Austin went on as if he hadn't heard—or as if he'd heard it many times. "That's for grazing your livestock. The labor is about one hundred eighty acres, which is for you to grow your crops."

"And how much does all this land cost?"

"Thirty dollars." Before Father could protest that he didn't have that kind of money, that he had never had that much money at one time in his life, Austin added, "Which you may take up to six years to pay."

Father twisted his cap in his hands, and Falon noticed tears standing in his eyes. *This is his chance*, she thought, *his chance to have something he can call his own.*

"I suppose the land around here is already spoken for?"

Austin nodded. "Oh, yes. But as I said, Texas is a big region." He turned the map so that Father could study it. "Here is where you are now. These blue lines, of course, are rivers, and you'll want part of your land on a river so you can irrigate, but only the smallest side of your land can touch the water." He pointed to a series of elongated rectangles along one snaking blue line. "You see how it is done?"

Father nodded in return. "But how will I know which land I can claim?"

Austin looked toward the crowd. "Once you've all been baptized by Father Santiago, you will come back here, find the parcel you want, and I will mark it on a map. My agent will go with you to your settlement, and when he returns with the map, I will record it permanently. We will put as many of you in one area as possible." He gave Father a warm smile. "The more of you there are, the safer you are. I think," he pointed to one river, "along here. This is the Colorado. Good farmland, plenty of trees, and of course, you have water."

Less than an hour later, Falon and her family stood in the spring sunshine. Father shook his head in disbelief. "So much land," he murmured. "Who would ha' believed it?"

"So what do we do now?" Will asked.

Father ran a hand over his beard. "We had better see about finding food, and about getting seed to plant. And then, I suppose we'll have to look up this Father Santiago."

"I wouldn't do that." They all turned to see a lanky man with an impressive mustache sitting on a barrel outside the general store across the way.

"Were ye talking to us?" Father asked.

The stranger nodded once, tipping his broad brimmed hat toward Falon. "Father Santiago, well—he's a man of God and all, but he's just a little zealous, if you ask me." He had been whittling on a stick, and he took another couple of strokes. "Now Father Vincente, he can put you in the Catholic Church without a fuss. Donate a penny or two to his orphans, and he's a happy man." The stranger stopped carving and blew on the stick. "You get the paper you need, he gets what he needs."

"Where do we find this Father Vincente?" Father asked.

The stranger nodded toward the direction of the fort. "His mission house is just this side of the presidio. Has a wooden cross over the door. And I saw him head that direction not ten minutes ago, so I know he's there."

Holding out his hand, Father approached the stranger. "My thanks for the help. I'm Camran Macvail."

"Ed Blaloch," the other replied. "And don't mention it. I was in your shoes myself not so long ago."

"Blaloch?" Father's face brightened. "Now that's a good Scots name."

With a ghost of a smile, Ed Blaloch nodded. "My great-grandparents came over and settled in Tennessee."

"Did you came into Texas on a ship?" Will asked.

"No, son, overland from the United States. Walked down the Natchez Trace." Blaloch gestured with his stick toward the land office. "The Mexican government may mean well, but church isn't something you force on someone. Father Vincente makes it easy for a man to comply with the law and follow his own conscience at the same time."

Father thanked him again, and they started toward the mission. Falon's legs seemed to get weaker and shakier by the minute. Though the day was warm, she clutched her shawl tighter around her shoulders. She'd never been in a Catholic church, had no idea what they were like, and she certainly didn't want to be baptized by a priest.

Across the way from the mission was a trim little house, and in front of it near the street sat a tree stump. Seizing the opportunity, Falon called out, "Dad, I need to sit a while." And she sank down gratefully on the makeshift seat.

Will and her father turned back. "Are tha' all right, lass?" Father's brow furrowed with concern. "I forgot all about thee, so I did."

"Can I carry thee?" Will asked. "We need to go see this man."

Falon answered, "Why don't you go on without me? I'm sure I'll be all right, and I'll stay till you come back."

"But you have to go, too, lass," her father reminded her.

"D' ye really think they'd miss me?" she asked. "I mean, who would notice one little girl, more or less, or care whether she was baptized? You can leave Robbie with me while you go inside."

Her father studied her a long moment, then nodded. "I'd be glad to spare thee the fuss. But stay right here, lass. I'll keep the laddie with me. If tha' has a problem, come and find us."

"Aye, Dad." The smile she turned on him was genuine enough. She wouldn't have to go into that papist church after all.

"We shan't be long," he promised, and he and Will trotted across to the mission. Falon watched as they knocked on the massive wooden door. A black-haired boy about ten years old let them in. Falon breathed a heavy sigh of relief generously mixed with weariness. A light breeze played with the stray curls around her face, and with it she caught the sweet scent of flowers. Turning around, she noticed that the house behind her was practically surrounded by roses, just coming into bloom.

The bush nearest her was covered with crimson buds. A few had blossomed, and their heady fragrance stirred in the wind. The aroma and the color drew Falon like a moth to a flame. She stood and wandered close enough to peek into one of the blossom's fiery depths.

"Like my roses, do you?"

Falon jumped and wheeled around to find an older woman, shopping basket looped over one arm, peering at her through a pair of wire-rimmed spectacles. "I . . . I'm sorry, Missus," she stammered. "I didn't mean to trespass."

The woman's eyes narrowed. "You're new here, aren't you?"

Falon managed to drop a curtsy. "Aye, Missus. I . . . that is, my father and brothers and I came in on a ship just this morning."

"What is your name, child?"

"Falon. Falon Macvail."

"Well, Falon Macvail, you have the look of someone who could use some tea. My name is Matilda Logan. People around here call me Miss Mattie." She turned toward the house. "I was just about to brew myself a cup. I hope you'll join me."

Falon curtsied again. "It's kind you are to offer, but I promised my father I'd stay there on the stump and wait for him."

Miss Mattie's eyebrows went up a notch. "Then I'd say you've already broken your promise."

Falon blushed to the roots of her hair. "You're right, Missus . . . Miss Mattie. The roses were so pretty they made me forget."

"Where is your father?"

"He's gone into the mission there to see Father Vincente."

"Ah, another dutiful citizen for Mexico."

Falon caught a note of irony in Miss Mattie's tone, but suddenly feeling out of her element, she backed away toward the stump. "I really must wait there for him."

"You will be waiting awhile," Miss Mattie informed her. "Father Vincente is a good man, but he loves to tell stories about his work." The corners of her mouth turned up. "And he has hundreds of stories." She started toward the house. "I'll tell you what—it's a nice enough day. We can bring a couple of chairs outside and have tea under the shade tree. You can see the mission from there."

Falon was painfully aware of the sorry state of her appearance, with her dirty dress pocked with burn marks, and her hair a hopeless tangle, but though she could hear her mother's voice chiding her, a cup of tea sounded so good, so *normal.* "It's kind of you to ask, and I gladly accept."

"Good," Mattie answered with a brisk nod. "You come and get the chairs while I put the water on."

With another glance toward the mission, Falon followed her hostess into the single-room house, marveling at its refinements, from the metal latch on the front door to the wide plank floor that shone from a recent waxing. Immaculate white muslin curtains stirred at the windows, and a larger panel of the same fabric draped off one end of the room. Falon guessed Miss Mattie's bed was tucked behind the drape.

"Why don't you take three of the chairs outside?" the older woman suggested. "We can set the tray on the third chair."

"Yes, Miss Mattie." Falon hefted one of the cane-bottomed chairs up and carried it out. Fortunately, the chair was light enough that she wasn't completely out of breath when she set it down beneath a tall tree between the house and Father Vincente's mission. She paused before going in again, smoothed her hands against her skirt. But there was no improving her appearance. It felt wrong, somehow, to be sitting down to tea when she was so filthy.

Stepping in again, she picked up the second chair. "You have a lovely house, Miss Mattie."

"Thank you, child. It's a little easier getting nice things here. Ships bring in all kinds of useful things from the United States, and from your part of the world."

My part of the world? What is my part of the world? Falon went out and set the second chair opposite the first. By the time she came in again, Miss Mattie had the tea kettle heating on the fire.

"I'm fresh out of flour," the older woman said without turning around. "We'll have to settle for corn pone. I do have a couple of boiled eggs to go with it."

"That sounds wonderful," Falon answered, though she had no idea what corn pone was.

"Go wash your hands at the pump, and when you come back in, you can help me make the pone."

"Where . . . where is the pump?"

"Just out the back door," she answered with a nod. "There's a towel hanging on the handle."

Falon found the pump just a step from the back door, along with a clean towel. A cake of lye soap sat in a dish on the window ledge. Stepping back, she took a quick look toward the mission. Still no sign of her father, or of Will. Falon worked the pump handle a few times until water spilled out. Then she washed her hands with the soap, scrubbing at her nails, picking at the dirt beneath them until it was gone. With a quick glance at the back door—was she being presumptuous?—she took the soap, lathered her face, and pumped again, splashing her cheeks and forehead with the fresh water.

How wonderful it must be, she thought, *to live here, to not have to draw water or live on a dirt floor. I wonder what our house will be like.* Falon harbored no illusions that the house her father built for them would be as fine. She took the towel and dried her face and hands. *Where we're going, shelter will have to be enough. But we're here, and we'll have land. It'll be ours, and no one will ever tell us we have to leave it.* Another quick look toward the mission, and she went back inside.

"You need to know how to make pone," Mattie told her when she came in. She held up an ear of corn. "Make sure your father gets plenty of seed corn to take with you, and sow it as soon as you get to your land. The plants will grow quickly, and they'll be taller than you are. When you pick the ears, either boil them to eat right away, or leave them like this and store them to dry. When they've dried, you can grind the kernels to make meal. Then all you have to do is mix in water and a little salt, and make it into cakes. You can fry them in lard or bake them." Mattie showed Falon how to shape the cakes. The sizzle of them frying made her mouth water.

About half an hour later, Falon sat back in her chair with a happy sigh. Tea under the shade tree had been perfect. She hadn't had a cup of tea since she left Sgall, and this was piping hot and sweetened with a touch of honey. *I could drink gallons, if I only had room.* A boiled egg and two pieces of corn pone had filled her up nicely.

"So your father and brothers are with Father Vincente?" Mattie's question brought her back to the present.

"They are, yes." Another glance at the mission, but no sign of them. "And they've been in there a long time now."

Mattie chuckled over her teacup. "Not so long, child. Father Vincente has a way about him. He has them trapped in there, and they probably don't even realize it."

"Trapped?" The word made Falon start to rise from her chair in alarm.

"Oh, goodness, child! Nothing like that!" Mattie smiled. "Father Vincente is harmless. Your father and brother are having a wonderful time, I promise you. For the moment, they've forgotten everything else. And when they leave, Vincente will have them believing they're his best friends."

Falon swallowed. She couldn't imagine her father having a friendship with a papist—not ever. Nor her brother. She shook her head in bewilderment.

"What is it, Falon?"

Miss Mattie's friendly gaze emboldened her to say, "It's crazy here—in Texas, that is."

Mattie laughed. "So it is. But it's usually a good kind of crazy. You'll get used to it."

Just then, Falon caught a movement at the mission. The door swung open, and her father and Will emerged, both of them laughing. A youngish priest with a shock of red-blond hair followed them out. He embraced them both, chucked Robbie under the chin, then waved after them as they walked away.

"What did I tell you?" Mattie chuckled.

They were halfway across the open space between the mission and Mattie's house before Will looked toward the stump and stopped in his tracks. Falon stood and called out, "Over here, Will!"

The two men trotted over, then slowed to a walk as they neared the shade tree. Her father took off his cap. "Well, and aren't you ladies a picture?" His smile was genuine. Falon's eyes blurred with sudden tears. She hadn't seen him really smile in ever so long. She cleared her throat and managed to make polite introductions.

"Your daughter has been keeping me company," Mattie told them. "Did you get what you needed from Father Vincente?"

"Oh, aye. That and more." Camran Macvail beamed. "He was good to tell us all the ins and outs of choosing our land and getting provisions."

"He was," Will affirmed. "We'd never have known the half of it but for him." He eyed the leftover corn pone on the plate.

"Did he feed you?" Mattie asked.

Father nodded. "Gave us each a bowl of beans and corn."

"Are you too full to finish off the rest of this? It doesn't keep well."

"Well, I suppose we could . . ." Will began as she handed him the plate. "Thank you, Missus." He broke off a piece and handed it to Robbie.

Falon held out her hands to take her little brother, but he paid her no attention. *Ah well,* she told herself, *he's just interested in the food, as well he should be, poor laddie.*

"Do you all have a place to sleep tonight?" Mattie asked.

Father shook his head. "I figured we would sleep out." He looked up at the cloudless blue above them. "'Twill be a fine night."

"The house behind mine is a boarding house. You can stay there for a penny, if you wish, or you can bed down in the yard between." She nodded toward Falon. "But I would feel better if you would allow your daughter to stay with me tonight. Safer for a young woman to be inside."

Falon was about to protest. Nice as Mattie's house was, she didn't want to be separated from her family, but Father nodded. "I canna' turn down an offer like that." He turned to Falon. "We'll be just outside tonight, lass. You stay with the nice lady. Your brother and I have business to attend to." And with a nod and another word of thanks to Miss Mattie, they took off toward the land office.

"Why don't we take everything back inside and wash up?" Mattie suggested.

With reluctance, Falon turned away from the retreating backs of her father and brothers. She stood and picked up her chair. "You needn't worry about them, child," Mattie reassured her. "They're only relishing the feel of the earth under their feet after being on a ship for so long."

Falon understood. Solid ground felt good to her, too, though her legs seemed unusually heavy, as if she had been walking on stumps all day.

Once the chairs were inside, Mattie said, "I imagine you'd like to have a clean dress."

Falon bit her lower lip and nodded. "This one is a bit dirty."

Mattie smiled at the understatement. "A bit, yes. I'll loan you my other dress to wear while we wash and dry yours. But first, if you're going to share my bed tonight, you'll need a bath. Take this bucket out to the pump and fill it up. I'll heat the water for you."

Less than an hour later, Falon sat waist-deep in a washtub, scrubbing herself with a rag that had been generously lathered with Mattie's soap. Falon sniffed at the soap's sweet scent and closed her eyes. Her hostess had apparently used roses to perfume it. And who could have ever guessed such a simple thing as hot water could feel so good?

Mattie had taken her dress, shift, and shawl outside to launder them, and Falon, as much as she was enjoying the bath, hurried along with it, wanting to be finished and into Mattie's borrowed dress before the older woman came in again. She looked down at herself and clucked her tongue in dismay. Her rib cage rippled under her glistening skin like a washboard. "I'm naught but skin and bones," she muttered, running the rag in and out between her toes.

Shortly after that, as she was attempting—without much success—to wash her own back, Mattie came in. "Oh, child, let me help you." The older woman took the rag, lathered it, and scrubbed Falon's back. "Your things are clean and drying on the porch rail. Warm as it is today, they won't take long."

Falon was glad her back was turned, glad Mattie couldn't see the blush she felt rising to her face, a blush that deepened when Mattie said, "Bless your heart, you haven't had much to eat lately, have you?"

"I've always been little," Falon answered, feeling that to admit otherwise would deny her father's care for her. "And I was sick a while on the ship."

"I see." Mattie poured rinse water on her shoulders and back. "We need to do something about your hair. I have some softened rainwater here, and I've added a bit of soda to it, but it's not hot. Think you can stand it?"

"If it will get the smell out, I can." The lingering odor of the ship had embedded itself in her hair, and had trailed her all day.

"You'll be nice and clean after this," Mattie assured her. "Tilt your head back."

The water, though not cold, was far cooler than the water in the tub, and Falon gasped as it washed down her scalp and neck. Mattie worked her fingers through Falon's hair, then rinsed it with what was left of the hot water. "Here's a towel," she said, wringing the excess water from Falon's hair. "Dry yourself off, and you can get dressed."

Falon scrubbed vigorously with the towel, working some heat back into her chilled arms and legs. When she was done, Mattie lowered the dress over her head. "It's a mite big, but we'll pin it up so you aren't tripping over it."

When Falon had buttoned the bodice, Mattie stood back, her hands on her hips. "Feel better?"

"Oh, aye. Ever so much better, thank you."

"Good." Mattie pulled a comb from her pocket. "Why don't you sit down and work on those tangles while I clean up?"

Mattie hauled the tub to the door and emptied the contents onto a pair of rosebushes that blossomed on the other side of the pump.

That done, she turned the tub upside down on the grass, and coming in again, wiped up the droplets of water that spattered the floor. Falon watched her all the while as she tried to work the comb through the mass of tangles her hair had become.

"Miss Mattie," Falon started, then realized she hardly knew how to frame the question that had almost formed itself on her lips.

"What is it, child?"

"Why . . . why are you doing this for me?"

Mattie had been on her knees on the floor. Now she rocked back, pushed her spectacles up on her nose and met Falon's gaze. "Because you don't have a mother."

Without warning, Falon burst into tears. Mattie pressed a handkerchief into her hand and pulled Falon toward her until the girl's face was buried in her apron. "I am sorry, child."

The grief Falon had pent up inside now spilled out, and as each fresh sob tore out of her, another girl, another Falon, seemed to be watching, amazed that she could cry so hard. And it wasn't just her mother, was it? She wept for all she had lost, for her home, for Betsy, for her secret place, for the security she had known as a child. Even for Annie.

When the tears at last began to subside, Mattie asked, "It was recent, then?" Falon nodded. "Do you want to tell me about it?"

Falon nodded again, hiccupped, and cleared her throat. "It all started when they fired our house."

A light vertical crease between Mattie's brows deepened. She pulled a chair opposite Falon's and sat down. "Fired your house? Who did this?"

"Agents." Falon told her the whole sorry tale.

When she was done, Mattie stroked a stray curl back from Falon's face. "I lost my mother when I was about your age. I'm sorry you have to go through this." She sighed and added, "It's so hard sometimes—living is. We women need to do what we can to help each other along."

Falon found her voice again. "I . . . I don't know how I can ever repay you."

Mattie's fingers gently lifted her chin until their eyes met. "Someday you'll have the chance to help someone. When you do, that will be payment enough."

Falon woke sometime in the deepest part of the night. Her father had come back at twilight and told her that tomorrow, or the next day at the latest, they would leave Perry's Point and start out for their piece of land, the sitio and labor, their homestead. And Will would not be going with them.

"We have to buy seed to get started," he explained, "and an axe, and a plow blade. All those things. Will is going to finish this season with Captain Ferguson, and then he'll come and find us on our new farm."

Mattie, who had been listening, said, "Mr. Macvail, if I may be so bold, there are a number of items that Falon will need, especially if she's going to be the woman of the house."

Father scratched his head. "Well now, I expect that's true. What kinds of things?"

"A skillet and a pot, for starters, if you don't have them, scissors, and needles for sewing and darning, and thread for mending. You will want a washtub, and a kettle for coffee or tea. Best to get a few hens to take along for eggs. Are you planning to plant cotton, Mr. Macvail?"

"Aye. Father Vincente recommended it."

"Then you'll need a set of cotton combs to pull out the seeds and twigs. One more thing: your daughter simply must have a bonnet. Summers here are fierce, much hotter than you're used to. If she doesn't shade her face, she'll burn."

"We have a pot," Falon interjected, "and I think there was a package of needles somewhere in our things." Needles had been one of the last things she had stowed in her feed bag before the agents came.

"Let's have a look." Her father brought in the two small canvas bags and emptied their contents out on Mattie's table. "Pot and bowls . . . spoons . . . cups . . . Esme's tablecloth." He glanced at Falon. "That'll dress up our place for sure. The one pillow, a couple of blankets. Ah, here they are." He opened a square of embroidered muslin to reveal a half dozen needles of various lengths. The delicate bit of fabric looked misplaced in his rough, calloused hands. He gave the needles to Falon and rummaged through the rest. "I thought she had scissors, but it looks like those didn't make the journey."

He straightened and pulled at his forelock in a gesture of respect. "I'm obliged to ye, Missus. I wouldn't have thought of those other things. We'll stop in at the general store tomorrow for seed, and food, and we'll get the rest at the same time. Will's scrip should cover it."

Now as Falon lay in Mattie's bed, listening to the older woman's deep, steady breathing, she thought, *I'd rather have Will than a pair of scissors or a washtub.* She toyed with the things she could say to change her father's mind about letting him go—that they'd need his strong arms working for them on the farm, that two men were better than one in the case of Indians. But she knew she'd never be able to bring herself to say the real reason Will shouldn't go: that they'd had enough losses, and that they would lose Will, too, whether to sickness or accident or the call of the sea. She didn't believe her brother would settle for only one season on the ship. He'd want more. He might come and find them at the end of the season, but as soon as the weather warmed, he would be off again.

Falon took in a deep breath and let it out slowly. *I'll never sleep if I think on this all night.* Closing her eyes, she imagined herself in her secret place. She had stems of pink primroses in her lap, and was plaiting them into a crown. Falon lay quiet and watched herself weave the stems until quiet and fatigue overtook anxiety, and she fell asleep again.

The next morning, after Will and Father had doused their heads under Mattie's pump, they presented themselves at the back door. "We'll be leaving town this afternoon," Father said. "Apparently, Mr. Austin is eager to have us on our land as soon as possible." One corner of his mouth quirked up. "Or maybe he's eager to have us out of here. Either way, we're obligated to go if we're going to travel with the others."

"Would you like a quick cup of coffee before you go, Mr. Macvail?"

"Thank ye, Missus. That would be welcome."

Falon had just finished drying the breakfast dishes. She took a pair of clean cups from the shelf and put them on the table. It was then she noticed her little brother wasn't with them. Her heart twisted. "Dad, where's Robbie?"

"Dinna' worry about the lad," he reassured her. "Maire Morgan is looking after him." Her eyes met her father's, and it seemed he was really seeing her for the first time since they had arrived in Perry's Point. "You look better this morning, lass. Look like you're well on the mend."

Falon knew she did look better now that she was clean. Her dress, although still pocked with burn holes, had been freshly pressed, and her hair was combed and neatly braided in a single plait down her back. Though some lingering weakness troubled her, and would for a while, she had a full stomach and had gotten a decent night's sleep. "I do feel better, Dad."

He and Will drank their coffee as quickly as manners allowed, then stood to go. "I don't know how to thank ye, Missus," Father said to Mattie. "Tha' has taken good care of our girl."

Mattie waved him off with one hand. "I didn't do anything special. Falon has been good company." To Falon she said, "I have something you can take with you." She reached in her pocket and pulled out a handful of brown nuts. "When you find your land, plant these near your house. They are a kind of hickory nut, and the trees grow quickly." She poured the nuts into Falon's hand. "One other thing. Would you like to take a cutting from one of my roses with you?"

Roses. Now wouldn't that make our place look like home! "I would, Miss Mattie."

Mattie began rummaging through the dishes on the shelf. "I hoped you would. I give as many cuttings away as I can. Now where's that bottle?" When she had found it, a slim green glass bottle, she said, "Take this and fill it with water, and we'll decide which rose to cut." Once they were outside, she said, "I would recommend either that red one there," pointing to a thick, squatty bush to the left of the pump, "or there's a yellow one on the side of the house." She led Falon to a taller shrub, covered with fat buds. "It hasn't bloomed yet, but these smell the best, I think."

"This one, then." Falon touched a bud with the tip of one finger.

"Well, really," Mattie murmured, studying the green bottle, "I think there's room enough for both. That would be better. If one doesn't take, maybe the other will." She cut a stem from each shrub and pinched the buds off. "Make sure you keep water in the bottle all the way to your new home," she instructed. "Check it every day. Once you get there, plant these cuttings where they'll get plenty of sun, and water them every morning. By next spring, you should have flowers."

"Mattie!" A man's voice called out, and they turned around. The young priest Falon had seen the day before came over to Mattie and kissed her cheek. "Lovely day, yes?" He turned to Falon. "And who is this young lady?"

"Vincente, this is Falon Macvail, my guest. Falon, I'd like you to meet Father Vincente."

Falon curtsied, but could hardly bring herself to look at him. He said, "Ah, you must be Camran Macvail's daughter."

"Yes . . . yes, sir," she stammered, wishing at the moment that she could be somewhere else, anywhere else. *If he says I have to be baptized . . .*

Fortunately, he turned his attention to Miss Mattie. "I wondered if you would check in on Maria Vargas sometime today. She's close to delivering, and her sister is sick."

"I will. Have you heard anything from her husband?"

The priest shook his head. "Not a word." The two of them sighed and shook their heads at the same time. "I have to get back," he said. "Nice to have met you, Falon Macvail. I wish you well on your journey." He kissed Mattie again and with purposeful stride went back to his mission.

"You know Father Vincente well?" Falon asked as she watched him go.

Mattie nodded. "He's my brother."

Falon nearly lost her grip on the bottle. She clutched it around its slim neck and said, "If he's your brother, that makes you . . ."

"His sister?" Mattie took a leisurely snip at a dead leaf.

"Well, yes . . . I mean, no." Falon closed her eyes against a sudden image of the red-haired girl from the ship. Only now did it occur to her to wonder what had happened to her and her family.

Mattie arched one eyebrow. "Are you trying to say it makes me Catholic?"

With a gulp, Falon nodded. "Not meaning to be rude . . ."

"Of course you aren't. Yes, I am Catholic." She smiled. "Who around here isn't?"

I'm not. Falon didn't dare speak this aloud. The fear of Catholics that had been drummed into her since earliest childhood, all the reverend's pronouncements against them, that they were Christ killers and devil worshippers, even her own hatred rising from the bit of salt pork in her porridge—none of that could make her be rude to the woman who had fed and sheltered her and dried her tears. With a pang, Falon remembered telling Mattie about the Irish on the ship, how Father had had to beg from them. Her face now flaming with shame, she said, "Last night, what I said . . ."

"Don't give it another thought, child." They started toward the house, and then Mattie stopped. "Except perhaps for this." She laid one hand on Falon's shoulder. "Remember that the things people do speak more loudly than what they say."

She steered Falon back into the house, where Father and Will waited. There she stopped and drew the girl close, one arm around her shoulder. "If you ever find yourself in Perry's Point again, please come and see me."

"I will. Thank you, Miss Mattie." Falon returned the embrace. The night before, a part of her wanted to stay with Mattie, to offer to clean, to fetch water, to do whatever was needed to earn her keep. If only she could stay. But there was Robbie. And now there was the insurmountable problem of Mattie's religion. Falon stepped out of the circle of her arms and gave her a wan smile. Even if she could remain with Mattie in Perry's Point, if that were possible, living with a papist would surely result in damnation. Who knew how deeply she had already compromised her soul's destiny with one overnight stay?

"Are tha' ready then, lass?" Her father and brother stood halfway between the house and street.

"Aye, Dad." Clutching the bottle, she turned away with them. She couldn't bring herself to look back, not even for a final wave. *No tears,* she told herself, *not today.*

★6

. . . Having got a little help and plenty of advice, having spent one year of my brother's life and work, we prepared to go inland, to find out what kind of home we were going to have . . .

On their way back toward the main part of town, Falon tucked her free hand into her father's, taking comfort in its callused ridges. He said, "I'm glad ye had a woman's company for a bit. It did ye good."

"Aye, Dad."

"I'm hoping . . ." He fell silent for a few steps.

"What, Dad? What are ye hoping?"

"Well, lass, I'm hoping you and your new mother will get along, as well."

The ground seemed to suddenly drop out from under her feet. She stopped in her tracks. "New mother?"

"Aye, Falon." Her father gestured up the street to where Maire Morgan and Young George waited for them just outside the land office. "I talked to Maire yesterday, and we decided it might be a good idea to marry—to join forces, so to speak."

Maire held Robbie in her arms. Falon wanted to run and snatch him away from her. "So that was your 'business' yesterday?"

"Part of it, aye." He squeezed her hand. "It'll be better this way. Easier for all of us, don't ye see?" Falon didn't miss the pleading note in his voice. "You lasses can do the cooking and whatnot, and George and I can manage the farming, now that our Will here is off sailing."

Falon glanced at her brother, who kept his expression carefully blank.

Her father went on, "And tha' won't lack for a mother."

She's not my mother. Falon lifted her chin and held her hurt close. *But what's done is done. No changing it now.* She bit her lip and started forward again.

"There's my girl," she heard her father murmur.

"Good morning, Falon," Maire said, handing Robbie over to Will. "What has tha' got there?"

"Morning, Missus . . . er . . ." she faltered.

"'Tis all right, lass," Maire assured her. "Tha' can call me by my given name, since tha' art nearly grown. I hope we can be friends."

Falon stammered. "I . . . I hope so, too." Remembering Maire's question, she held out the bottle. "I've rose cuttings. A red and a yellow."

Maire took the bottle. "Ah now, that'll be nice. We'll have to be careful to keep water in." She handed it back.

Falon nodded and let out a breath she hadn't known she was holding. She turned to Young George, who refused to meet her gaze. When he started to turn away, Maire scolded, "George! That's no way to greet your new stepsister."

He narrowed his eyes at his mother, and Falon saw that they were red and swollen, as if he'd been crying—or trying not to. He held out a reluctant hand. "Good morning."

Falon shook his hand, clammy and limp in her own. "Good day to you, Young George." His social obligation met, the boy stepped back.

Falon surreptitiously slid her hand under her shawl to wipe off the fishy feel of him.

She held out her hands to Robbie. "Come here, laddie. I've missed thee." But Robbie turned away with a whimper and laid his head on Maire's shoulder. Falon swallowed hard. She hadn't held him since she had fallen ill on the ship. Had he forgotten who she was?

"He just woke up," Maire told her, and Falon knew she was trying to spare her feelings. "He'll want thee soon enough."

"We'd better get on to the store and find what we need," Father said. "The others will be waiting." The store was a short walk from the land office. He held the door open for Maire and Young George, but stopped Falon. "Wait a bit." When they were alone outside, Father dug into his pocket and pulled out a handful of pennies. "I want you to have them, lass. 'Twas thee who earned them."

Falon backed away a step. "No, Dad. Those are to help us get started."

"So they are," he agreed. Taking her hand, he poured the coins into her palm. "Remember what Miss Mattie told us? Use this money to find the things you need."

Falon stared at the coins—the most money she'd ever held in her life. "Aye, Dad."

He opened the door, and she stepped in.

Any mental list Falon might have had went flying away the moment she walked in. Only at the annual county fair at home had she ever seen so many things for sale in one place. A window at the front of the store—with real glass in it!—let in a generous splash of sunshine. Long display counters ran along two walls, both of them jumbled with every manner of merchandise, from knives and axe heads to tea kettles, salt, paper, and tiny black bottles of ink. The middle of the floor was dominated by stacks of seed bags and wooden barrels.

In a daze, Falon set her glass bottle down, and counted her pennies. Fourteen of them. She poured the pennies into her sporran and, gazing all around her, tried to think.

"Salt," she murmured. "We'll need that. And soap and candles, until we can make some. What else?" As she turned a full circle, she spotted a half dozen bonnets in one corner hanging by their ribbons on a nail on the wall. She found a pale blue one and separated it from its companions. As she did, she noticed a green one, just the color of Maire's eyes. On impulse, she took it off the nail too and went looking for salt.

Maire stood at the other end of the store with Father, deciding about seed. Falon had started that way when she spied a stack of salt boxes. She picked one up. Next to them were the paper and ink. Her eyes lingered longingly on the white pages and the chubby black bottles. "Armaugh," she murmured. "Ian Machone in the town of Armaugh. But how can I get a letter to them?" Then she remembered. *Will.* He would be sailing soon, maybe sailing to Ireland.

She wanted to ask him, but she didn't see him in the store. Where had he gone?

Falon approached the storekeeper. "How much are these, sir?" She held up the bonnets and the salt.

"A penny each," he answered.

"And the paper and ink?"

"A bottle of ink is two cents. Paper's a penny for five, but I'll throw one piece in free if you buy the ink."

"Do you have scissors?"

"I have one pair." He took a slim wooden box from a shelf and opened it to show her. The steel blades gleamed in the light. "Ten cents. They were made in Germany."

Falon swallowed. Scissors would take most of her money. Just then, Maire appeared at her shoulder. "I have scissors, Falon." To the storekeeper she said, "Thank ye, but we won't be needing those."

"Maybe you had better help me shop," Falon told her stepmother. "I don't know what ye have, and it'd be a shame to buy what we don't need."

"Well, we need candles and soap. I think I saw those over here." Maire paused to ponder aloud, "How many candles, I wonder? It'll be a while before we can make them."

"Aye, but the days are getting longer, so we won't have to burn them so much."

Maire cocked her head. "Thy mother did a good job training thee." A sudden lump closed Falon's throat, and she ducked her head. "The candles are a penny for twenty." She picked one up and clucked her tongue. "And that's all they should be. They're summat thin. But I think that'll be enough to hold us."

In about half an hour, they had finished purchasing the essentials, and Falon had four pennies left. She picked up a bottle of ink and shook it. Satisfied that it was full enough, she chose a sheet of paper and returned to the shopkeeper. "I'll be wanting these as well."

"Two cents, miss." Reaching behind the counter, he pulled out a stout brown feather. "And here's a quill for you."

Falon made a curtsy. "My thanks." She gently gathered her treasures into the cloth sack that held her mother's tablecloth and needles, picked up Mattie's rose cuttings, and went outside.

Will sat on a bench just outside the door, leaning forward with his elbows on his knees. "Did tha' find everything?"

Falon nodded and sat beside him, feeling shy and strange. "Dad and Maire should be finished soon." Her heart began to throb with hurt. This was it—her time with him to say goodbye. She cleared her throat. "I have paper and ink to write a letter to Betsy."

"That's a good idea. I know she'd like to hear from you."

"Will your ship be sailing back to Ireland?"

He nodded. "The *White Arrow* runs back and forth between here and there."

"D'ye think ye could take the letter for me, then? I want to make sure it gets to her."

"You'll have to write it quick." When she pulled the quill out of the bag, he asked, "Want me to sharpen it?"

"Aye, if you please. But let me have your knife first—just for a bit."

He hesitated, then pulled the blade from his boot. Separating a lock of curling brown hair from her braid, she cut it, then handed him the knife. While he whittled the end of the quill, she worked a thread free from her shawl and used it to tie the lock at both ends. This she handed to her brother. "Keep this with thee. Something to remember me by."

He accepted the keepsake and turned his face away, but not before she saw the tears gathering in his eyes. What could she say to him to make the parting easier? She tried to put herself in his place. "Is it scary," she finally asked, "when you're up in the rigging? Are you ever afraid you'll fall?"

He nodded, gave the quill a final shave, and handed it to her. "'Tis scary. Shaddie says it should be a little, all the time. Never know when the ship's going to pitch." He turned to her, his eyes bright with unshed tears and something else. "But there's pleasure in it, too. When I'm up there, I feel like I was born to it. One thing I think I've figured out is that here, in this country, a man can do whatever he feels strongest to do, never mind what his father and grandfather did before him."

"You'll come to us this winter?"

He put an arm around her. "I promise."

Falon leaned her head into the curve of her big brother's neck. Unable to hold them back any longer, she let her tears fall freely. Will's tears mingled with her own, though neither of them made any sound other than sniffing. Finally, Falon squeezed her eyes shut to stem the flow, and bit the inside of her cheek until she tasted blood.

After a few minutes, Will, his voice harsh and gravelly, said, "Tha' had better be quick with that letter."

She sat up. "Aye. D'ye think ye'll see Betsy?"

Will sheathed his knife with a shrug. "Who can say? I hope so."

Falon wiped her eyes on her sleeve and turned her attention to the paper. She took the ink out of the bag. "Here, hold the bottle for me." Using a bit of the bench between them, she wrote,

Dear Betsy,

Father and Will and Robbie and I have made it to Texas. Mother got sick on the ship, and has passed from us.

Texas is nothing like Scotland. It's very warm here, and there are more trees than you could ever look at. We are about to set out to our land claim. It's supposed to be on a river, but I looked at the map, and didn't see any lochs. Isn't that odd?

Will is working on the ship that brought us here, and I hope he will be able to bring this letter to you himself. I will give him a kiss to give you. Give your family my love, especially Missus.

Your friend always, Falon

As she was finishing up, Father and Maire emerged from the store. Maire carried Robbie with one arm, and had a small crate under the other. Father toted a sack and a long-barreled gun. Falon sucked in a breath. She had never seen a gun in her father's hands. At home it wasn't allowed. Young George followed close behind them, lugging a plow blade. "Will," Father said, "I need you to get the rest of it. It's in a washtub just inside the door. Bring it around back. Falon, art tha' ready to go?"

"Aye, Dad." Falon tore her eyes away from the rifle, folding the letter as Will stood. Without another glance at her, he went inside, while she followed the others around to the back where several bags of seed had been stacked on the ground near a pair of empty carts.

"He said I could take my pick," her father muttered, squatting down to inspect the wooden wheels on one of them. After several minutes, during which Will joined them with the tub full of provisions, Father chose one cart over the other, though Falon could discern no difference between them. "All right," he announced, "let's load everything up. George, that plow blade should go in first, and then the seed bags."

When all their possessions were loaded, Father stepped between the handles and gave a tug. The cart rolled smoothly behind him.

"The rest of the families are gathering at the northern end of town," he called back over his shoulder. He paused once to adjust his grip, then set off with long strides.

"How long d'ye think he'll be able to pull that cart?" Maire wondered aloud.

"All day, if he has to," Will answered.

By the time they reached the designated meeting place, four other families were already there, and the land agent's man was with them, holding the reins of his horse. The short-haired American horses were taller and more muscular than the shaggy highland ponies Falon remembered. This one was predominately brown, but with large white patches of white scattered over its back, withers, and rump. It turned its face toward them, revealing a blaze of white that ran the length of its nose. *Too bad we couldn't get one of those,* she mused. *An animal like that could take us all the way there, no problem.*

She had been so interested in the horse that she didn't at first notice who held its reins. As he turned to greet them, she recognized the man who had directed Father and Will to see Father Vincente. So he was Mr. Austin's agent.

"Mr. Blaloch." Her father settled the cart and held out his hand. "'Tis good to see thee again."

"Please call me Ed. I guess you found Father Vince all right?"

"You mean Father Vincente? We did, and he was a great help."

Ed Blaloch nodded, tipping his hat to Falon and Maire. "Well, yours is the last family I'm waiting for. We'd better get underway while there's still daylight." He swung onto his horse. "We're going to skirt the northern end of the bay and head west. Hasn't rained much this last week, so the trail's passable."

"How long d'ye think it'll take us?" one of the other men asked.

Ed shrugged. "Depends. If we keep a good steady pace, ten days. If we run into weather or Indians, maybe longer."

Camran Macvail paused, turning toward his older son. "Will, come to us when tha's done, lad."

Will stepped into his father's embrace. Falon looked down, blinking back bright tears. "Aye, Dad," she heard him say. "Tha' knows I will."

The next thing she knew, Will's arms were around her, and she pressed her face against his rough shirt. He held her wordlessly a minute, until by unspoken agreement they let go of each other. She started to turn away, then remembered the folded bit of paper she still held. "Here, Will." She pressed it into his hand. "You know where to find them, aye? You know what town they're in?"

"Armaugh." Will turned the folded paper in his hands, turned it and turned it.

Rising on tiptoe, Falon gave him a peck on one cheek—"That's for Betsy"—a kiss on his other cheek, "and that's for Missus," and a quick kiss on his lips, "and that's for thee." Unable to endure another embrace, she backed away. "Come soon as ye can."

She watched him gather Robbie for a quick kiss. He said his goodbyes to George and their new stepmother and, with a final wave, started back toward town. Seized by a sudden idea, Falon turned to Maire. "Here, hold this." She handed her rose bottle and fumbled in her bodice for her flute. Wetting her lips, she thought, *A reel. Something lively.*

When the first piping notes reached Will's retreating back, his head snapped up and his footsteps quickened. The song followed him for but a minute, and at the end of it he did a quick dance step, causing the waiting travelers to laugh. He twirled around, swept his cap from his head and bowed low. Then, with a jaunty wave, he took off into town at a trot.

Ed Blaloch murmured, "Very good." Raising his voice, he called, "Let's be away." He swung his horse's head to the north.

The next thing Falon knew, she'd been hefted into the air and deposited in one corner of the cart. "I want thee to ride this morning, lass," her father instructed. "Tha's been sick. Tha' needs time to get stronger."

"No, Dad," she protested, "I can walk . . ."

"Tha' will ride this morning and watch thy brother." He bundled Robbie into the cart with her, and turning his back, spat on the palms of his hands and rubbed them together. "Aye, then. Here we go." He took up the cart handles and fell into line with the others. Young George glared at her for one heartbeat before turning his back to her as well.

Yes, here we go—again. Falon tried to ignore the heat that was rising to her face. *Here we go, taking everything we own and setting off for who knows where.* She glanced at the gun nestled in the wagon just behind her father's back. *But it's different this time. We're going to our home, not away from it. Father will be able to hunt for food.* She twisted one end of her shawl around her fingers. *He can protect us.* She wondered about the Indians, if they would actually see them. *Well, they can't be worse than Her Ladyship's agents.* She allowed herself a smile. *No agents here except for Mr. Blaloch, and he seems decent enough.*

There were the other differences, too, but Falon didn't dwell on them. *Time enough later to mourn and be sad. Maybe when they were on their claim and settled. Plenty of time later.*

She took quick note of the other families. The red-haired girl and her parents were part of the group. The grandfather and the little sister were gone—died on the ship, Falon supposed. *Nor do I care.* The other girl's dress was still stained and filthy from the voyage, as was her mother's. Falon felt a surge of smug satisfaction, which she quickly tamped down. Pride, after all, went before destruction, or so the reverend had expounded to them again and again. *Poor thing,* she said to herself, smoothing a nonexistent speck from her skirt, s*he hasn't had a chance to properly wash.* The girl didn't look Falon's way anymore, didn't smile. Her family walked near the back of the group, all of them looking thin and worn, twisted, like old rags. Falon tore her eyes away, told herself she was glad the girl had ceased trying to make friendly overtures.

She took stock of the others. One, a Mr. Garrett, was a single man who looked four or five years older than Will. Reed-thin he was, with a pockmarked face only partially veiled behind a scraggly mustache and beard. Sitting astride a gray horse, he rode in the rear. There was a younger couple with two small girls in tow, and from the looks of it, the mother was expecting another baby. A middle-aged couple walked behind them, and with them was the most extraordinary person Falon had ever seen. He was a young man, probably no older than Will, and about Will's height and build—but his skin . . .

Falon tried not to stare, but she had never seen anyone with skin so dark. *He can't be their son, nor any kin at all,* she told herself. *He must be a servant.* She cast curious glances his way now and again, though, owing to the man's broad-brimmed hat, she couldn't make out much of his face.

They set out on a trail that only Mr. Blaloch could see. Keeping the bay's edge on their left, the travelers followed the tall horse through knee-high shore grasses. Seagulls wheeled and cried overhead.

"'Tis a fine day," Falon finally remarked to George. Without a glance at her, he bit his lip, quickening his pace until he was abreast with her father.

"Never mind him," she heard Maire say. "He's been that way since . . . since . . ." Her voice trailed off.

"I understand," Falon quickly answered. "'Tis all right." She swatted at a cloud of midges with the end of her shawl and turned for one last look at Perry's Point. Will was no longer in sight, but she could still make out the *White Arrow* anchored in the bay. Suddenly aware that she was getting hot, she shrugged off her woolen shawl.

"'Tis warm," Maire murmured in agreement.

The bonnets. Falon had forgotten all about them. She opened her canvas sack and pulled them out. "Here, Maire, this is for thee." Falon handed her the green bonnet and put the blue one on herself.

Maire stopped just long enough to make a quick curtsy. "Why, thankee, lass! What a pretty bonnet." She tied the strings under her chin. "So light and airy."

Falon nodded. The bonnet's brim gave her eyes a welcome shade from the sun.

"Have ye seen the chicks?" Maire asked. She lifted the slatted lid on a small crate in the wagon. Inside were a half dozen cheeping balls of fluff, floundering on a bed of straw. Robbie let out a delighted squeal when he saw the baby birds, and reached to grab one. "We're going to have to keep an eye on the lad," Maire noted, plucking him out of the wagon where he couldn't reach the chicks. "The tradesman promised me that at least half are hens," Maire said.

Falon lifted a brown-and-white chick from the crate and held it up. "So what are thee, then, little mite? A crower or a layer?" Maire laughed, and Father looked back at them with a grin.

Young George, however, continued to stare straight ahead. He held his shoulders stiff, his gait matched his shoulders—stiff and stilted. It almost pained Falon just to watch him walk. *Well, and of course,* she told herself, *he misses his father and the little ones. But at least he doesn't have to be the man of the house for his mother.* Since he was her stepbrother now, Falon knew she was going to have to find a way to be friendly with him, whether he wanted it or not.

Less than half an hour later, Mr. Blaloch reined in and dismounted. He plucked a flowering plant from the ground at his feet. "Everyone gather around." Falon seized the opportunity to escape the cart. When they had arranged themselves in a half circle around Mr. Blaloch, he held the plant up. "Take a good look at this." He broke the stem in two and passed the pieces to those nearest him. "It's called poke salet. It's a wild plant you can cook and eat."

Poke salet. What a funny name. Falon took the stem, studying its broad leaves and tiny white flowers. She passed it on and looked around her feet until she found another plant just like it. She pulled off a leaf, and was just about to sample it when Mr. Blaloch added, "Do not eat any part of poke salet raw. It's poisonous until it's cooked."

Falon snatched the leaf from her lips and threw it to the ground. *Poisonous!*

"It won't kill you," he was saying, "but it will make you plenty sick. To cook it, you can boil it or fry it in lard."

With a wink at Falon, Father asked, "Is it as tasty as seaweed?"

Mr. Blaloch tipped his hat back and scratched at his forehead. "Seaweed? I wouldn't know, Mr. Macvail. I've never had the pleasure of eating seaweed." Everyone chuckled at that; everyone that is, except Falon.

When they were underway again—Falon walking now, after a solemn promise to return to the cart as soon as she got tired—Maire said, "Let's look for the plant as we go. Maybe we can find enough to cook for our dinner." All the rest of that day, whenever she saw the treacherous plants near the trail, Falon plucked them and passed them to Maire, who dropped them in the vacated corner of the cart. All that day, Falon kept a close eye on Robbie, to make sure he went nowhere near them.

By the end of the day, Perry's Point was far behind, and they had skirted most of the northern end of the bay. Mr. Blaloch stopped at a freshwater spring as the sun sank over the tops of the trees ahead. "We'll make camp here tonight."

Each family drew water, and Falon helped Maire strip the leaves of the poke salet and put them into a pot of water. Father started a small fire, and soon the greens were cooking. As Maire stirred them, Mr. Blaloch came and squatted on his haunches by the fire. "I see you have some salet cooking."

"How can a plant that's poisonous when it's raw be all right to eat when it's cooked?" Falon asked.

The agent shrugged. "I've wondered that myself. But I've eaten enough of it to know it'll keep you alive." He smiled. "And if you fry it with a few wild onions and a little salt, it's good eating."

"Wild onions?" Maire asked.

"Oh yes, ma'am. You'll be able to find them a little further along the trail." He grinned. "Just follow your nose."

"What else might we find growing wild? Berries? Seeds?"

"You can look for dewberries. They're a type of small blackberry. And if you're lucky, you may run into wild grapes."

"Wild grapes!" Maire turned to Falon. "Imagine that!"

"The juice is awful hard on your skin, though," he warned her. "It'll make your hands itch and burn. So remember that if you are planning to preserve them. You also want to look for hickory nuts late in the summer and early autumn. Lots of hickory trees in these parts. The nuts—some folks call them pecans—are small, not much bigger than your thumbnail. It's worth the work to get the meat out of the shell, though; it's that sweet."

Falon dug Miss Mattie's nuts out of her sporran and held them out. "Like these?"

Mr. Blaloch nodded. "The very ones." He turned to Father. "Mr. Macvail, can I prevail upon you to take the second watch tonight?"

"Oh, aye. Just shake me awake."

When the agent had excused himself and walked away, Father turned to Maire, his eyebrows raised. "Well, I guess we won't starve, hey?"

Maire nodded, but Falon knew what she was thinking. It was going to be a lot of work to hunt for and gather enough food to keep them going until they could get a crop in. And it would be up to the women; the men would have their hands full getting seed into the ground.

Speaking of hands, Falon's father had left the campfire and was squatting by the spring, bathing his hands. She went to him. "Let me see, Dad."

He shook his head. "'Tis nothing, lass. Dinna' worry yourself."

But she insisted until he finally gave in and showed her.

"Ah, Dad," she moaned. His palms, once hardened from farmer's work, were now lined with angry red blisters.

"Not so much work the past few weeks," he murmured. "Ma' hands have gone soft."

"We're going to have to do something about this."

"Nay, nay." He curled his fingers, then stretched them out again. "'Twill be all right."

"And if the blisters open up and go bad?" She put her hands on her hips in her best imitation of her mother. "Who will pull the cart then?"

He ducked his head, and she saw him fighting back a grin. "Well then, lass. What did ye have in mind?"

"Let's wrap them, at least for a day or two. 'Twill cover them and give ye a bit of cushion on those wooden handles—just until your hands are hardened up again."

He nodded. "I won't argue wi' ye."

Falon borrowed Maire's scissors and cut two strips from the top of her canvas sack.

"What are ye doing?" Maire asked her.

"Making bandages for Dad's hands."

Her stepmother clucked her tongue and turned away, leaving Falon to wonder what she had said to upset her. *Well, no matter*, she told herself. *This has to be done.* She filled a pot with water, glad at least that they now had two, and set it on the fire to heat once the greens were cooked. By the time they finished eating, the water was boiling, and she lowered the canvas strips into the pot.

Later that evening, his hands wrapped with clean bandages, her father flexed his fingers. "Tha's done a good job, lass. This'll be on the mend in no time."

When Falon had bedded down and was nearly asleep, she overheard her father asking Maire, "What's the matter, then?"

She couldn't hear the whispered reply, but her father answered: "She knows me better, Maire, and so she saw what tha' didn't. 'Tis no crime or shortcoming of yours." Another muffled reply, and her father chuckled. "In no time, she'll be married off, and it'll be thee who's taking care of me."

Falon squeezed her eyes shut tight. So that was the problem. Falon had seen to her father's hands, and it upset Maire because she hadn't noticed it first. Falon gathered in a long breath, and let it out slowly, silently. She had tried to be friendly toward George, and he had rebuffed her. No one had understood the incident with Betsy until Father explained it. And then there was her music, which had set Mother off. She rubbed at a tight spot between her brows with the tip of one finger. It seemed she could hardly put one foot in front of the other without upsetting someone. *Even Robbie—he wants to be with Maire all the time now, and not with me.*

Falon woke deep in the night to her father's soft footsteps. She followed his dark form with her eyes as he crept past, rifle cradled in his arms. He stopped at camp's edge and hunkered down, facing away from her, looking out into the wild darkness. The only sounds were the singing of little frogs at the spring and a gentle sighing in the tree branches overhead. Falon turned her gaze heavenward. No moon tonight, just an arching blackness studded with countless stars. *Not so very different from home,* she told herself. And then—*but this is home now.*

Her eyes shifted back to her father. She stared at his still form until he was just another deep shadow among many. She wanted to lie awake, to watch with him as long as he was up. She briefly considered going and sitting beside him, but knew he would send her back, telling her she needed to sleep.

And so she did. She had walked all afternoon, but though they'd gone a long way, the bay was still close at hand, not much more than a stone's throw south of their camp. The journey from Sgall to the sea had taken less than a week. But Mr. Blaloch had told them this journey would take ten days—if they didn't run into problems.

Texas must be a big place. Falon yawned, turned on her back and fell asleep.

★7

. . . Back home in Sgall, I knew everyone. I knew what people would say, what they would do in any given situation. Now we were thrown in among strangers, and there was no telling. In some ways, I even felt like I was a stranger to myself . . .

Her name was Kathleen. Falon knew that now. Aboard the *White Arrow,* Falon had been strongly warned by her brother to avoid the Irish, and once the sickness came, she'd been so wrapped in her own troubles that she had never learned the red-haired girl's name. But that first morning on the trail, Falon heard the mother call to her, "Kathleen, run fetch us one more pot of water."

Kathleen hurried by, a small cast-iron pot swinging from her hand, her freckled cheeks and chin reddened from a recent scrubbing. Her flaming hair, hanging in wet ringlets, was gathered at the nape of her neck with a bit of string. She didn't so much as glance in Falon's direction.

Falon adjusted the bow of her sunbonnet and finished rinsing the bowls they'd used for breakfast. *Will we be neighbors when we get there?* She figured that there wouldn't be a village like they'd had in Scotland. Each house would be separated from the others. *It's going to be strange, us living off by ourselves.*

She sighed and rocked back on her heels. She missed Sgall, missed the stone house she'd grown up in, the wide loch, her secret place. She refused to think about the people she had lost, choosing for the moment, for today, to think on other things. "The nanny," she murmured. "I miss her naughtiness, the times she got into the garden. I miss her milk."

They walked all that day. Falon rode in the cart with Robbie for the first two hours, but when they topped a low rise, she scrambled out, exclaiming, "Would you look at that!" They had come upon a meadow cloaked with all manner of wildflowers. She and Maire waded into the knee-high grass a little away from the group. Tiny daisies, yellow as sun's fire, nodded next to sky-blue lupines. "Look at these pink primroses," Falon told Maire. "Just like at home, but paler."

"I never saw so many different colors," Maire answered. "All the colors of the rainbow."

"And then some," Falon agreed with a laugh.

"Did you see these orange . . . ?" Maire halted in mid-sentence, reached out and grabbed Falon's arm. "Let's go." She turned on her heel and headed back toward the cart, pulling Falon along with her. Maire's face had gone pale, and her lips were set, tight and grim.

"What is it?" Falon asked.

"Snake."

Falon glanced back over her shoulder, but saw nothing in the high grass. "Was it a viper?"

Maire shot her a look. "I didn't get close enough to see."

Pirates on the coast, poisonous plants to eat, and now snakes. Subdued, and more than a little shaken, Falon climbed back into the cart.

The group stopped only for a noon meal. Toward dusk, when they had entered a clearing, Mr. Blaloch held up one hand to signal them to stop, but instead of dismounting as he ordinarily did, he urged his horse forward a few more paces. The woods around them suddenly seemed eerily quiet. No one in the group made a sound. Father eased the cart's handles down and picked up his rifle. Gooseflesh prickled Falon's arms and neck. *What's out there? Indians? Wild animals?*

Mr. Blaloch turned in the saddle. "Men, circle up." Each man in the group took up a weapon of some sort—though for Young George and for the Eversons' Negro servant, the weapons were only stout sticks—and arranged their provisions and families into a loose circle. The head of each family stood on the outside, forming a protective shield against danger. They did this so quickly that Falon guessed the agent had already privately instructed the men. She glanced at Maire, who had gone white around the mouth.

Birdsong called out from the silent trees ahead. Mr. Blaloch put his hands to his mouth and answered with a series of chirping whistles. Moments later, a dark figure stepped out from the trees, eliciting gasps and soft exclamations of dismay from the travelers.

The Indian was strongly built, though not tall. His head was mostly shaved, but for one patch on top, and from it flowed a long tail of hair, black as ravens' wings. His breeches and shirt were of some kind of animal skin, unadorned but for a beaded belt at his waist. Over his shoulder hung a bow and a quiver full of feathered arrows. He seemed utterly alien, with his square face, high cheekbones and dark complexion, but what caught Falon's attention were the marks on his face. Four black lines ran vertically from his jaw on each side more than halfway to his eyes, giving him the feral look of a tiger.

With shaking hands, Falon pulled Robbie close to her. The Indian's coal-black eyes ranged over the group, resting a bare moment on her before passing on. But even with no more notice than that, she wanted to crawl under the cart and hide. She remembered thinking the Indians couldn't be worse than agents. How could she have been so foolish? *Mother was right to be afraid of savages.* Falon briefly wondered what else her mother might have been right about.

The Indian spoke a few short words to Mr. Blaloch in a low, gravelly voice. The agent answered, waving his hand back toward the group. Moments later, he dismounted and approached the visitor on foot. Falon couldn't hear their words, only the murmur of them, but the Indian pointed off to the North. Mr. Blaloch shook his head. The Indian held up two fingers and pointed to the sky. The agent shook his head again. The two of them argued quietly for a while before the Indian grunted, then sat on a fallen log. Mr. Blaloch turned to the others. "We make camp here." With that, he sat beside the Indian and they continued to talk.

Mr. Blaloch offered no further explanation, and no one approached him with questions. Maire's mouth settled into a grim line as she ordered her family: "George, we'll need wood. Camran, that creek we passed a little while ago . . ."

Father nodded. "Aye, Missus. Falon, come wi' me, lass."

She picked up a pot and followed him back down the trail. Soon she heard footsteps behind her. The Eversons' servant and Kathleen were both behind her, and Mr. Garrett, the single man, took up the rear. He came on foot, his rifle in one hand and his horse's reins in the other. They must have made some noise in the darkening woods, but to Falon they seemed quiet as ghosts, and as somber.

When they got to the creek, Mr. Garrett went downstream to water his horse and stand watch. Father stationed himself upstream, rifle at the ready. Falon knelt to take a quick drink. Kathleen was just to her left. As the Irish girl began to fill her pot, she suddenly pulled back with a gasp, clutching her arm. She turned toward Falon, her eyes wide with hurt.

Falon's curiosity won out over her pride. "What is it?"

"I've been stung." Kathleen looked around. "I brushed against that." She pointed to a plant between them.

Falon inched closer for a better look. The stems and broad leaves of the bushy plant were covered with fine, white hairs. "Must be a nettle. Let me see your arm."

All she could make out in the twilight was a red patch near Kathleen's elbow where she had been holding it. "Dip your shawl in the water and see if it'll wash off."

Kathleen nodded and took off her shawl, careful to avoid the offending plant. Dipping one end of her wrap in the stream, she proceeded to scrub at the sore spot. Falon took Kathleen's kettle from her and filled it along with her own. "'Tisn't any better," Kathleen hissed between her teeth.

"What's going on, ladies?" Falon jumped a little and looked up to find Mr. Garrett standing over them.

"Kathleen's been stung," she told him. "'Twas likely that plant."

He stooped to look. "Bull nettle." He pulled a handkerchief from his back pocket and soaked it in the stream. "Here, miss. Wrap this around your arm to keep it cool. It's going to sting awhile." His deep bass voice startled Falon, coming out of such a slight chest.

Even in the twilight, Falon could see the flush that rose to Kathleen's cheeks as she accepted the dripping cloth from Mr. Garrett. "Thank you, sir. You are very kind."

She fumbled briefly with the cloth. "Here, allow me." He wrapped the handkerchief around her arm and tied a loose knot. "That should do." He stood again and tipped his broad-brimmed hat. "We'd best be going. We have lingered here long enough."

Kathleen stood and took her kettle from Falon with a nod of thanks. They walked single file back to the clearing, where they discovered that Mr. Blaloch and the Indian were gone. "They took off together," Maire said. "Never a word to the rest of us where they were going or for how long."

"I'm sure he had good reason," Father said. He sat on the ground, tugging off his shoe to shake a pebble out of it. "He'll be back, no worry."

"We've naught for dinner but salet," Maire went on, "unless we use a bit of the corn or the oats we bought."

"The corn's for seed. We canna' eat it. We'll make do with greens tonight, and maybe tomorrow we can hunt for some game to feed us."

Maire nodded and started stripping the salet leaves from their stems. Before the water had started boiling, the agent and his Indian companion returned, each carrying a large, limp bird by its feet. Mr. Blaloch held his up. "Wild turkey," he announced.

Turkey! Falon could hardly believe her eyes. They were going to have a meal—a real meal with meat. The men constructed spits for the birds while the women plucked and cleaned them, chatting as they worked. The presence of meat had suddenly lent their camp an almost festive air. When the birds were spitted and roasting, Falon thought she had never smelled anything so lovely, and when they were done she ate her fill, relishing the savory meat.

Mr. Everson, an older man whose perpetually sour expression made him look as though he'd been weaned on a pickle, paused between mouthfuls. "How did you kill these birds, Mr. Blaloch?" he asked. "I never did hear your gun go off."

The agent nodded toward the Indian. "This is John." The Indian nodded and grinned as Mr. Blaloch continued, "At least, that's what I call him. His real name's impossible for me to say. Kind of wraps around my tongue and won't let go. John shot the turkeys with arrows. He knew where they were roosting."

That's clever, Falon thought, but apparently not everyone shared her sentiment.

"I heard the Indians around here were hostile," Mr. Everson said. The frown lines around his mouth and eyes deepened.

Falon's next bite wavered uncertainly near her mouth. Her eyes darted toward Mr. Blaloch, who stretched his legs out and grimaced as though they pained him. "Some are hostile, Mr. Everson. The Comanche are for sure, and the Karankawa. John here is Tonkawa, and his people are pretty much at peace with us."

"So you trust this savage? Is that what you're saying?"

Mr. Blaloch was silent for a long moment. "This turkey he shot tastes mighty good, wouldn't you say so, Mr. Everson?" The other didn't answer, but his face flushed dark with anger. "I've known John a lot longer than I've known you, sir," Mr. Blaloch added. "In a pinch, if I had to choose, I'd pick the savage."

Mr. Everson made a strangled sound of disgust as he stood and stalked off to the other side of the camp. Mrs. Everson and their servant watched him go, but neither made a move to follow. Mr. Blaloch leaned over and spoke to the Indian, who responded with a chuckle and a shake of his head.

Startled by the sound of the Indian's laughter, Falon found herself admiring John's painted face rather than fearing it. *His stripes are not so different from the woad streaks our clansmen used to wear to battle.* Idly, she wondered if the stripes could be washed off or if they were permanent.

"Miss Macvail." Falon nearly choked on her last bit of turkey when Mr. Blaloch addressed her. "Would you be so good as to give us a bit of music tonight?"

She glanced at her father, who nodded and smiled. "All right, then." But what was appropriate for a night like this? She pulled her flute out and put it to her lips. Remembering the way the Indian and Mr. Blaloch had first signaled to each other, she started with a thrush's call, repeating it several times. "Song thrush," she heard Kathleen say, and Maire nodded. She changed the call. "Why, that's a robin," Mrs. Everson exclaimed softly.

The Indian spoke, and Mr. Blaloch chuckled. "My friend here says that if you can imitate a mockingbird, you'll be busy all night."

She paused. "Mockingbird?"

"Mockingbirds don't have a song of their own," he told her, "so they imitate the songs of other birds. And unlike most birds, mockingbirds love to sing at night." He smiled. "One mockingbird can make it mighty difficult for a man to get his sleep."

Not knowing what to say to that, Falon played a dance tune. No one seemed to want to dance, but they all clapped to the music. "I need to rest just for a bit, Mr. Blaloch," she said as she finished the tune. "It's a little hard to catch my breath, my stomach's that full."

"Whenever you're ready," the agent replied. He translated for the Indian, who laughed and saluted her with a turkey bone.

A little later, Falon launched into a second tune, a reel, and John stood up and started shuffling his feet. It took Falon a few beats to realize that he was dancing. He spread his arms and turned round and round in one place, a big smile lighting his painted face. Mr. Blaloch was grinning, too, and he kept rhythm by slapping the log he sat on. Mesmerized, Falon stared at the Indian's feet as she played, watched as he ground last year's leaves into the earth. One and two, up and down on the balls of his feet, though he barely moved them. One and two. One and two in the darkening night. Falon lost herself in the flickering firelight, in the dance's movement and flow. And then the song was done, the flute came away from her lips, and still she stared, until the people around her started applauding. When she came to herself, John turned to her and gave her as courtly a bow as ever a good Scot did.

She played two more tunes, and then finished with a quiet hymn. It was nighttime, after all. When she was done, Mr. Blaloch gave the men their watch assignments, and the rest of the group got ready for bed. As he kissed her goodnight, Falon's father remarked, "Well, and that was something."

"What was, Dad?" though she knew what he meant.

"That Indian. Who'd have thought he'd like our tunes so much, hey?"

That he might not have liked them had never occurred to her. "I wonder what their music is like—the Indians' music, I mean."

Father shook his head. "No telling. Maybe no' so different than ours."

The next few days passed without much to mark them. They continued west and a little north, seeing no one but themselves. On the afternoon of their seventh day on the road, the sky turned dark with gray-bottomed clouds. "We're in for a storm," Mr. Blaloch called out to them. "We're going to have to find a good spot to camp and call it quits for the day."

In the end, there were no good spots. Falon pulled her shawl up over her head as the first fat drops fell, but the spattering rain soon became a downpour and the wool soaked through, as did her dress until the fabric clung to her legs. They had an oilcloth in the cart, and Father spread it out over the bags of seed to keep them dry. If the corn got wet and rotted, he explained, it would be a misery for them in the year to come. They finally came to a stand of trees and huddled underneath to keep off the worst of the rain. And that's where they stayed all that cold, wet evening and night.

Falon hunkered down with her back to the glistening trunk of one tree and wiped at her wet face with her dripping shawl. For the first time since they left Perry's Point, she began to doubt that she would make it to their homestead. A chilly drop slid down the center of her back, and she shivered. *Ah, Mother, what would you say if you could see us now?*

The rain let up just before dawn, and the travelers set out at once, not bothering with a meal. No one wanted to stay in that sodden spot another minute. "We'll have our place soon," Father reassured them, "a cozy little place with a good, strong roof, never fear."

Falon smiled in spite of herself. *That's my Dad. Never a worry.* She turned her face to the early sun. *Now we'll have a chance to dry out.* But the drying out didn't come that day. The air steamed with the night's rain, and vapor rose from the swampy earth as it warmed. Her dress and shawl weren't dripping anymore, but they didn't quite dry out, either. And it was near impossible to draw a good, deep breath. She looked around to see her father struggling to pull the cart across the sodden ground. The wheels stuck in the mud, and mud stuck to the wheels. They all looked bedraggled, at the point of exhaustion.

She glanced at Maire, who shook her head. "Is it always like this, I wonder?"

"I hope not," Falon murmured.

There was precious little conversation that day. For the most part, Falon felt like she was walking alone. All that kept her going was her feet. They seemed to have a mind of their own, and they carried her along, whether she willed it or not.

They stopped at midday to eat. John left them briefly and returned with a brace of rabbits. It wasn't enough meat for them to have their fill, but Falon welcomed the bit she got—part of a leg, still on the bone.

She noticed that Mr. Garrett had settled himself down next to Kathleen. "And how did ye come to Texas, sir?" the Irish girl was asking him.

"Well, Miss, I was pretty much forced to come when my brother cheated me out of my inheritance," he answered. From there, he launched into a story about how he had to leave his home place—he called it Kentucky—and find somewhere new to settle.

Falon hardly heard the rest of the story. In her opinion, Mr. Garrett was sitting much too close to Kathleen. *'Tisn't proper.* She sniffed and tried not to stare, but she couldn't help herself. Mr. Garrett kept his eyes on his food most of the time, but when he looked at Kathleen, his admiration for her lit up his eyes, making him almost handsome. For her part, the red-haired girl looked better than Falon had ever seen her. She had managed to keep her face and hands clean, and her fiery hair was braided, coiled around her head like a copper crown. And she had some color in her cheeks, color that heightened every time Mr. Garrett looked her way.

They're courting. And her parents must approve, because they're allowing it. Kathleen's mother and father kept a watchful distance; as Falon watched, the mother leaned over and whispered something into her husband's ear. He smiled and nodded.

Would my father allow a man to sit and talk with me like that? Falon shook her head and swallowed her last bite of rabbit. *'Tis no use thinking that way,* she scolded herself. *Tha' art plain as plain can be, and no' a woman. 'Twill be a cold day in the Pit before any man looks at thee that way.* She tossed the bone into the bushes.

When they were on their way again, Kathleen passed close by, nodding once as she went. Falon said nothing. She still couldn't quite get over her mental image of her father having to beg a bit of pork from Kathleen's family to keep his own daughter alive. *We can never be friends.* She briefly tried to imagine Kathleen in Betsy's place, talking and laughing with her, playing girlish games. It didn't work. Kathleen was not, and never could be, Betsy. Not ever.

The next morning, her father had words with Young George. There had been another spate of rain the night before—a short shower this time, heaven be thanked — but it made the trail even muddier. The hems of the women's dresses were soaked and filthy, and mud clung to everyone's shoes. Father continued to wrestle with the cart, and often as not, when it was stuck, Maire or Falon had to come behind and push while he pulled. It made for hard, slow going.

Young George ignored them all, walking off to one side, his stick in hand in a pretense of warding off any lurking dangers. Finally fed up, Father called, "George, I need you over here, lad. Come help push the cart." George looked the other way, as if he hadn't heard. "George! Come give us a hand."

The boy jutted his chin out. "Nay."

"What?" Father dropped the cart's handles and turned around. "What did ye say?"

Young George bristled, but there was a quaver of uncertainty in his voice. "I said nay. Let the women do it."

"George . . ." Maire started.

Father held up a hand. "Leave this to me, Maire." He strode—as well as he could in mud-clotted shoes—to where the boy waited. "What d'ye mean by this?"

George's chin lifted another notch. "I meant nothing. The women can do the pushing. Someone has to keep watch as we go."

"Keep watch is it? Ye're doing naught but swinging that stick of yours at the bushes. Dinna' think I don't see you."

George's face mottled red with anger. He gripped the stick in both hands. Father took another step forward. "Like it or no, lad, ye'll do as I say."

The other travelers by this time had stopped to watch. Falon chewed at the corner of one fingernail. Will had had his moments of disobedience, but he'd never been defiant. She had no idea what her father would do next.

"You canna' tell me what to do!" George shouted. "You are not my father!" He raised the stick and struck.

The blow hit Camran Macvail on the shoulder with a resounding thump. It was the only blow that landed. Camran caught the next swing with his hand, and with one jerk, he wrenched the stick away and raised it.

"I'll thrash you within an inch of your life, boy."

George backed away. "It's your fault!" he cried.

The older man stopped and blinked. The hand that held the stick wavered. "My fault? What are ye on about?"

"It's your fault my father died." George spat out the words as if they tasted foul. "If it weren't for you," he gestured toward Falon, "and for her, he'd still be alive. You had to get on the ship with us. You had to make my father and the little ones sick." He backed away another step, angry tears pouring down his face. "Your fault."

Falon's gaze flickered over to Kathleen, who had suddenly found her own shoes very interesting. She would not raise her eyes to meet Falon's. *Does she blame us, too?*

Of course the accusation made no sense. People got sick; no one could help it. Apparently, George realized it, too, as soon as the pent-up words were out of his mouth. He turned away and pulled his cap over his face.

Father let out a groaning sigh. He started to toss the stick away, then thought the better of it and dropped it into the cart instead. He took a step toward the boy, jammed his bandaged hands into his pockets, and said, "Come and help with the cart." Without looking back to see if George would obey, he turned away, took up the handles and pulled. Moments later, Young George was at the back of the wagon, his shoulder and arms bunched with the effort of pushing. The rest of that day, he labored to move them down the trail, and wouldn't let Maire or Falon take a turn.

Well now, there's a change, Falon said to herself. But when evening came, her stepbrother still refused to speak to her.

Falon kept hoping they'd see a town along the way, some sign of civilization to break the never-ending wildness of the trail. A few days after the incident with George, Falon asked Mr. Blaloch about other settlers. He shook his head in answer. "The only towns are north of us—not including Perry's Point, of course. San Antonio de Bejar is west and a little north of where we're going." When he saw the girl's crestfallen expression, he added, "There are families ahead of you who have settled in the Colorado River area. Not anything you'd call a town, just farms."

"How much longer do you think it'll be?" she asked. "How much longer till we get there?"

He sighed. "Well, Miss Macvail, the rain slowed us down some, but we did make it through the bayou. We should be at the Brazos River today or tomorrow. When we've crossed that, we'll be nearly there."

A river. Maybe we'll have a chance to wash. The bath she'd had at Miss Mattie's was a distant memory. She clucked her tongue with dismay over her skirts, crusted knee-high with mud. The skin around her nails had gone black with grime. *And I need to put fresh water in the rose bottle.* "At least no one's gotten sick," she murmured, hardly realizing she'd spoken aloud.

"Heaven be praised for that," came a soft reply just over her shoulder. Kathleen caught up with her. "I want to thank you for your help at the river the other day," she ventured.

Falon felt her face go hot. "It was nothing." She couldn't think of anything else to say.

"You must be missing your brother," Kathleen continued. "I have a brother, too. He's still in Ireland. We hope he'll come to us next year." When Falon still didn't answer, she added,

"I am sorry for you—about your mother."

A sudden rush of grief closed up Falon's throat, and the bright day went blurry. She swallowed. She swallowed again. *And I am sorry for your grandfather and little sister.* The words formed in her mind and waited there, unspoken. In the end, she couldn't work them out from behind the aching knot in her chest. If Kathleen took offense at Falon's inability to reciprocate, she didn't show it. She laid one hand briefly on Falon's shoulder before dropping back to where her mother walked.

★8

. . . Just before we got to our homestead, Texas finally showed its teeth. It is, after all, untamed . . .

It was nearly dusk when the travelers stopped at the edge of a broad river. "El Rio de los Brazos de Dios," Mr. Blaloch announced as he dismounted. "The River of the Arms of God. Those Spanish," he explained with a smile, "they do love to put fancy names on things."

"How do we get across?" Father asked.

Mr. Blaloch tipped his hat back. "We came in a little north of where I wanted. There's a ford, probably about a half-hour's walk south." He took a glance at the westering sun. "We camp here tonight and find the ford tomorrow."

Mr. Everson's scowl deepened—if that were possible. "We have had enough of your delays. I say we find the ford tonight, go ahead and cross over."

The agent bent down and loosened the girth on his horse's saddle. "I might consider that, Mr. Everson, if it were midsummer, or if there were just the two of us, but the river's swollen with spring rain. The current's swifter than it looks."

The older man growled. "You don't think we can get across the ford?"

Mr. Blaloch sighed, the muscles in his face bunching and tightening. "I am loath, sir, to cross this river in near dark with women and children." He straightened and faced the other. "If I am concerned for the safety of your good wife, you certainly must be." To the rest he repeated, "We make camp here. Get whatever water you need for this evening before the sun goes down. I don't want any of you approaching the river after dark." That said, he turned his back on Mr. Everson, dismissing him.

"Why, I ought to . . ." The older man raised his rifle.

Ignoring the gasps around him, and without turning around, Mr. Blaloch said mildly, "You don't want to cross me, sir."

After a few anxious heartbeats, Mr. Everson lowered his weapon and stalked away.

Falon sucked in her lower lip and picked up the larger of the two cooking pots. Noting the tightness that still lingered at the corners of the agent's eyes, she stepped gingerly past him and went to the river's edge.

The surface of the water glimmered in the waning light, soothing her frayed nerves. *We're nearly home,* she told herself as she filled the pot. She lifted her eyes to the far side of the Brazos, and held her mother's face in her memory. *Such a beautiful place, too. So many trees. I wish you were here to see it.* A movement on the other side caught her attention, and an Indian stepped out from among the trees. It wasn't John. This one was younger, naked to the waist; his unbound hair caught and lifted in a passing breeze.

Falon froze, and she heard Mr. Blaloch swear softly behind her. A moment later, the Indian was gone, swallowed up in the shadows of the tree line. Falon glanced back over her shoulder. Mr. Blaloch and Mr. Garrett were both there, staring across the water. Mr. Garrett murmured, "He meant for us to see him."

"He did."

"Wonder why?"

Mr. Blaloch grunted. "I can think of a half dozen reasons." His eyes shifted to Falon. "Miss Macvail, I'd appreciate it if you wouldn't mention what you have seen to the others."

Falon hesitated. Only the night before, she had heard her father remark to Maire, "That Edward Blaloch is a man of uncommon good sense." High praise from Camran Macvail. She asked, "You will be telling them, won't you?"

"If it's necessary. But please allow me to choose the time and place of the telling."

Just then, Kathleen edged around them and knelt at the river. Falon nodded acquiescence to the agent. As he touched the brim of his hat in thanks and moved away, she heard Maire call out, "Falon—the water?"

When Mr. Blaloch didn't say anything about the Indian at dinner, Falon guessed he would privately tell the men when he assigned night watch. But though she hardly let him out of her sight all evening, she didn't notice him speaking to anyone except Mr. Garrett. Just before she bedded down, she asked her father, "When will tha' be sitting up tonight?"

He tossed another stick on the fire. "I have fourth watch." With a weary roll of his shoulders he added, "'Tis a good thing, too. I had third last night, and I'm beat."

Falon nodded. Third watch was hardest. Not only did a man have to wake in the dead of night, but when his watch was over, he'd get only a couple hours of sleep before he had to be up and off again. Fourth watch was better—at least a man could get his sleep "all in one swat," as Father put it. "Time for thee to turn in, lass," he told her.

"Aye, Dad." She started to get up. "Maybe George could sleep in the wagon tonight." She had slept atop the seed bags the entire trip; they make a much better bed than the hard ground. She'd heard George grumble about her favored position more than once, and would have been happy to take turns in the wagon with him, if her father had permitted it.

Tonight was no exception. "Nay, Falon. I want thee in the wagon with Robbie. We men will sleep on the ground." Behind his back, George sneered at her and rolled his eyes.

Falon didn't bother to point out that Maire also slept on the ground. And arguing with her father . . . well, she might as well beat her head against a stone wall. She reluctantly climbed into the wagon. *If Indians come, this will be the first place they look.* She gazed all around, peering into an inky dark lit only by restless firelight. *There's a goodish-sized bush by that tree. If they come I can jump out and duck under that.* It wasn't much of a plan, she knew, but she went over and over it in her mind, just how she would roll out, grabbing Robbie as she went, how many steps it would take to get there. She rehearsed it mentally, feeling her muscles tense each time, until she was certain she could do it.

Why hasn't he told them? Mr. Blaloch and Mr. Garrett sat deep in conversation over a small fire. No one else was in earshot. *He's going to pretend nothing happened.* The seed bags beneath her bunched into hard lumps. She shifted, trying to find a more comfortable position. *So he's just going to go to sleep tonight, knowing we're not alone out here? How can he do that?* Her stomach twisted into anxious, angry knots.

Should I tell Father? She turned to look in his direction. He was still sitting at their fire, with George right beside him. There was no way she would be able to speak to him privately. She wanted to tell him, but more than that, she didn't want George hear what she would say. Falon sighed and turned on her back. *Mr. Blaloch is a smart man,* she reasoned. *Just because he hasn't told anyone yet, doesn't mean he won't.* She rested one arm on her forehead and stared at the stars. *Too bad*

Will isn't here. I could tell him, and he'd believe me. He'd know what to do. He must be halfway back to Scotland by now. She imagined him landing in Ireland, giving Betsy her letter. *We should have gone to Ireland.* No *Indians there.* Her thoughts returned to the deep darkness all around. *There will be no sleep for you tonight, Falon Macvail.*

But sleep did come, fitfully, like the campfire's light. Falon dozed, only to be jerked awake by the smallest noise—the snapping of a twig, the rustling of someone turning over in their sleep. Sometime in the dead of night, a branch on the fire popped like a gunshot, and before she knew it, Falon was out of the wagon with her baby brother, crouching behind a bush. Her sudden movement was so swift and stealthy she woke no one, and the only sound that followed was the hammering of her own heart and a low whimper from Robbie. Scolding herself for her foolishness, Falon started back to the wagon, but her father's light snore, a home sound, drew her, and she turned and lay down at his back instead, cuddling Robbie close. By degrees, the warmth of them and her father's steady breathing coaxed her back to sleep. She didn't wake again, even when he got up to take his turn watching.

After a hasty breakfast the next morning under gray, grumbling skies, the group started south along the river's edge. Falon, bleary-eyed and stiff from sleeping on the ground, stumbled along behind the cart, pausing every so often to scan the tree line on the far side. It was impossible to shake the feeling that they were being watched. The trees, once a source of wonder and delight, now held secrets. They hid things. They had eyes. But that morning, whatever secrets the trees knew, they kept. Falon saw no one, not even a hint of movement.

The day had dawned sunny and clear. Falon didn't even bother with her shawl. It had gotten far too warm. *What's it going to be like when summer comes?* She eyed the river gliding alongside them. *I guess we'll be cooling off soon enough.*

It took a little less than an hour to reach the place Mr. Blaloch was looking for; just where the river veered eastward, a rocky shoal jutted about a third of the way across the water. Beyond that, the river tumbled and foamed over larger rocks that huddled just below the surface.

Mr. Blaloch waded his horse out about midway into the stream. The horse, apparently not happy about the water that came up to his chest, laid his ears back and shook his head against the reins. With some effort, Mr. Blaloch turned him and called out, "This is where we cross. Mr. Garrett, you will join me and position your horse about there. Everyone else will cross upstream of us." He surveyed the group. "I believe I want your family to go first, Mr. Macvail. You can hand your little son up to Mr. Garrett. He will hold the boy while the rest of you cross. Mr. Everson, you and your wife and man will follow once the Macvails are on the other side. Mr. O'Connor, your family next and then the Thompsons." He nodded toward the Thompsons' two little girls. "Mr. and Mrs. Thompson, your children will also go safer on horseback either with me, or with Mr. Garrett."

Father turned to Maire. "How will we keep our seed dry?" When she shook her head, he stared at the tumbling current with narrowed eyes. "Well, we do our best, and if it gets wet, we'll just have to put it in the ground all the faster, hey?" He turned to George. "I'll need you behind, lad, to push and help balance. Maire, you'll be on the upstream side of the wagon. Falon, you'll ride."

She knew it was coming. Father would want her to ride in the wagon while the others struggled across, but she was weary of being a burden, wearier still of Young George sneering at her because of the preferential treatment. She prayed the speech she had rehearsed in her mind would work, that Father would listen. "Father, it frights me to think of riding across in the wagon. What if the current bears it away? Please let me walk with Maire. I'll hold onto the side, I promise."

He rubbed the bridge of his nose with one finger and sighed. "All right, lass. I can see tha' art stronger than tha' wert. Just follow close behind thy mother."

She's not my mother. Unable to control her wayward thoughts, Falon bit her lip. She had known Maire most of her life, and had always liked her well enough. She edged away from the next thought, even as it came. *It's easier now, isn't it? Easier without Mother.* She felt her face go hot with shame.

But there was no more time to dwell on it. Mr. Blaloch and Mr. Garrett had already taken up their positions in the rushing water, with Mr. Garrett holding Robbie astride his horse. Maire grasped the side of the cart, and Father took up the handles. There was George behind, getting ready to help shoulder the thing across. She barely had time to get her own grip on the cart's edge before they started forward. The rocky stream bed made moving the cart into the water fairly easy, so for the first few steps Falon imagined she'd be able to help push from her position.

She gasped once when the first rush of water found her toes inside her shoes. Cold! So cold! Just a few steps later, the water swirled around her knees, dragging at her skirts, and she understood it was going to take all her strength just to hang on. She clenched her teeth. This reminded her far too much of that awful dream, the dream where Annie drowned. *Don't think about that. Keep walking.* One foot in front of the other, the current constantly pushing her, trying to force her underneath the wagon. Her shoes slipped, twisted and turned on the mossy rocks beneath as she struggled for a foothold.

She looked up once at Maire laboring just in front of her, and in that moment felt her feet lift from the riverbed entirely. With a small cry of alarm, barely audible above the rushing water, she faced the cart and tried to pull herself up against it, but with each second the water tugged her lower. She heard Mr. Blaloch give a shout of warning, then felt herself being lifted up and over the edge of the cart. Young George grabbed her just as she was about to go under, hauling her out of the water. For all his youth, he tossed her into the cart like a sack of potatoes, where she lay atop the seed bags, gasping and panting.

Heat flooded her face. She couldn't move from where she had initially landed in the swaying cart. She could only lie there and drip. *Well, if the seed bags aren't wet from the river, they'll be wet from me, and that's sure.* She glanced at her father, noting the cords and veins in his neck standing out with the effort of pulling the loaded cart through the rushing stream. *I've done nothing but add to Father's burden.*

"Falon," she heard Maire gasp, "The chicks!" Falon sat up and looked around her. The slatted crate had settled in one back corner, which was rapidly filling with water. She struggled against the lurching movement of the cart, reached down and pulled the crate toward her. A forlorn cheeping came from the box, not nearly as vigorous as at the beginning of the trip, a pitiful sound against the rushing water.

Father lost his footing moments later and went down in the water almost to his neck. Falon cried out in horror, but Mr. Blaloch was there, leaning down from his horse, offering his hand. Father grasped it and pulled himself back up, took the handles again, and another eternal minute later they were across and on dry land.

Falon scrambled out and lifted the lid on the crate. Four chicks remained of the six they had started with. One had died on the second or third day out; another now lay motionless in a heap of damp feathers on the straw. "Four left," she told Maire, holding out the crate for her to see.

Maire plucked the dead chick out and tossed it into the bushes. "Well, let's hope at least one of these left is a hen."

Falon turned to see where the dead chick landed, then remembered the Indian from the night before. She scanned the wooded area nearby, but saw no movement, no misplaced shadow. *We're the only family across.* The Eversons were still struggling midstream, and all Mr. Blaloch's attention was on them. *What will we do if we're attacked? Run back into the water?* She couldn't understand why the land agent had kept the Indian a secret. It made no sense. *Shouldn't we be prepared, just in case?* Even if Mr. Blaloch was a man of uncommon sense, he could still make a mistake, couldn't he?

The Eversons were nearly across now, and Falon felt better for it. She didn't much care for the dour Mr. Everson, but the more of them there were on this side of the river, the safer they'd all be. Father and Maire were busy unloading their possessions, shaking as much water out as they could. Falon grasped the hem of her dripping skirt, wrung it out, and went to join them.

Suddenly, there was a shout from the Eversons' servant. Falon turned just in time to see him grab Robbie by one arm and haul him behind him. Mr. Blaloch shouted, "Watch it! That one's poisonous!" and the slave leapt out of the way just before the snake at the river's edge struck. Falon screamed, but the sound was lost in the general commotion. The slave picked up a large rock, and with a sure aim, hurled it at the serpent's flattened, triangular head and crushed it. The rest of the snake's black body writhed in a death agony for several minutes. It took much longer for Falon's heart to slow down.

Poisonous plants, and now poisonous snakes, she thought. *What's next? A poisonous bird?*

Father approached the slave. "What is thy name, lad?"

He took off his hat and held it in both hands. "Joe, sir."

Falon heard unshed tears in her father's voice. "Joe, this family owes you a debt we can never repay." He stuck out his hand.

Joe didn't take it, but sent a sidelong glance toward Mr. Everson. "You don't owe me, Mr. Macvail. I'm just happy the boy's all right."

Father's hand faltered and fell to his side. His blue eyes studied Joe's black ones for several heartbeats. Finally, he nodded. "All the same, I won't forget this."

Not long after that, the last family had crossed over safely. The only thing lost was a cook pot belonging to Kathleen's family. It had worked itself loose from their possessions and bobbed merrily downriver. Mr. Garrett leaned out and tried to catch it as it floated by, but the pot evaded his grasp, hit a rock and almost tipped over before righting itself and sweeping out of sight around the bend. Mr. O'Connor clucked his tongue. "Well, and if that's all our loss, it's lucky we are," he said, in his broad brogue.

Mr. Blaloch addressed the group, now assembled on the Brazos' western bank. "This is as good a place as any to stop for the noon meal. We'll continue to your claims after we've eaten." Falon stole a glance at Mr. Everson, but though he glowered, he kept quiet.

While they were eating, Mr. Blaloch dismounted and walked a little way into the trees, his rifle at the ready. But if he found anything, or anyone, he said nothing when he returned.

After the noon meal, he pulled a map from his saddlebag and motioned to Father. "I will be settling your family first." He pointed to a long rectangle on the map marked "CMV." "Your claim is about a half-hour's walk south. The others here are south of you."

When he'd taken his look, Father straightened up with a nod, his throat working vigorously, his blue eyes rimmed with unshed tears. As he walked off, Falon heard him murmur. "So close . . . so close."

True to his word, after a short walk southward, the agent halted them and consulted his map again. "This is it. Beginning here, Mr. Macvail, all the way down to where the Brazos breaks off to the left." Then he smiled. "You can take your claim now."

Father walked gingerly onto his land, stepping lightly as if he was afraid his presence might frighten the ground beneath his feet. He gazed around him, broke a branch from a nearby tree, and stuck it into the earth. He pulled off his worn, woolen cap, and in a voice thick with emotion said, "By the grace of the good Lord, this is ma' land. I thank Thee, Father, for Thy provision, for getting us safely here." He looked up at Mr. Blaloch. "Will that do?"

The agent nodded, "That will do, sir." He held out a hand for Father to shake. "I will be back tomorrow to check in on you before I head home." With that, he mounted his horse.

The other men in the party lined up to shake Father's hand and wish him well, and to doff their hats and nod at Maire. One by one they filed away, and at the very last, Falon felt a warm tug at her hand. *Kathleen.* "I wish thee well."

Falon swallowed. She had hardly exchanged a dozen sentences with the Irish girl all the far way from Scotland to this place. And she hated her, didn't she? All of a sudden, her reasons seemed dim, confused, and she wasn't sure she wanted to see Kathleen go. "I wish thee well, too . . . Kathleen." The red-haired girl's face lit with a smile as she gave Falon's hand a final squeeze before turning away.

After everyone had gone, Father ran one hand through his hair and donned his cap. "Well . . . well, now." He gazed around, transfixed, as if now that they had stopped, he didn't know what to do with himself. Maire touched his elbow and pointed to the gray sky above. "Shelter, Camran. We need a roof over our heads."

"Shelter, aye." He kicked at the ground. "No' so many rocks. They told me in town we'd have to use the trees." He rubbed his hands together and pulled the axe from the cart. "Best get busy, then."

Before the sky went fully dark, Camran Macvail had managed to construct a passable lean-to from small timbers and branches. There was just enough room for them all to get under. The precious seed bags remained in the cart, covered with the oilcloth. Falon and Maire found a good stand of poke salet, and Young George proved his mettle as a fisherman when he came up from the river with three perch, each about the length of Falon's hand.

While the fish roasted, Falon asked, "Where will our house be, Dad?"

Father sucked at his teeth and considered. "I'm thinking we'll put it somewhere nearby, so we'll be close to the water." He sighed. "But we've got to get that seed into the ground first thing." He tried a smile of reassurance. "Summer's coming. The weather will be mild."

Falon glanced at Maire, who was staring into the fire. The older woman seemed to be trying to hold herself still. *She'll have words with him later,* Falon told herself. *But Father is right. 'Tis rough, but the crop has to come first.* She gazed up at the leafy canopy. *Surely we women can make this a better shelter, find some way to improve it.*

She thought about Miss Mattie's snug little house. What a far cry from that this lean-to was! And then she remembered the roses. *I'll pick a spot for them tomorrow.* Her eyes grew heavy and she yawned. *And we need to build a pen for the chicks and start a vegetable garden . . .*

Whatever rain might have lurked in the gray clouds the day before moved off overnight and fell elsewhere. The morning dawned clear and warm. After a quick breakfast of thin oatmeal, Father and George set off, high-stepping through the tall grass and brush to look for a place to start planting. They were back before Falon finished washing the dishes. "We found a likely spot just on the other side of that tree line," Father explained. "Close by, and no' so many trees and shrubs." He hummed under his breath as he loaded the axe, shovel and plow into the cart. "We'll be back before ye know it!"

When they were gone, Maire looked at Falon, one brow arched. "Ye would think he was off to the fair." She lifted the lid on the chicks' crate. "Still the four left." One at a time, she plucked them out and set them on the ground. "They've grown a bit."

"They have." Falon chuckled at the birds' flapping as they stumbled on unfamiliar ground. When Robbie spied them, he squealed with delight and chased after the nearest one. Falon scooped him up. "Nay, laddie," she laughed, "leave the wee ones be. They'll peck thee."

Robbie cried out in wordless protest, pulling away from her. When she set him down, he ran to Maire and hid behind her skirts. Falon chewed on her lip as she turned away. *Robbie will come back to me. He still needs time. And at least he's alive. I got him here alive.* She remembered the day before and let out a long breath. *With Joe Everson's help, of course.*

She had left the bottle with the rose cuttings leaning against a rock. Falon pulled the stems out. No sign of roots yet, but the leaves, though wilting, were still green. She looked around her. *Where to put them? They need a sunny spot.* She found a likely place about thirty paces up from the river, where the grass hadn't grown so high. *This will do. 'Tis nice and sunny and not too far from the water.* She found a short, stout stick and dug a pair of holes, tenderly setting the stems in and patting dirt around them. When she went to get the kettle to water them, she nearly stepped on one of the stems and realized how hard they were to see, even with fresh earth turned around them. "Well, and they're only wee sticks, aren't they?" she remarked aloud. "I need some way to mark them so they aren't trampled."

As she was filling the pot, she spotted smooth stones at the water's edge. After she watered the roses, she returned to the river and gathered stones in her shawl, then placed them in a protective ring around each stem. On her second trip up from the river, she saw that Robbie had followed her and was playing with the rocks she had already placed. "Come here, laddie. Help me with these."

She showed him how to make a circle of rocks around each stem, but he quickly tired of the chore and wanted to stack the rocks instead. Falon had an idea. "Come, Robbie, I know where there are lots of rocks." She took him to the water's edge—and instantly regretted it. When he bent down to pick a stone out of the river, she had a sudden vision of that awful dream about Annie drowning. *She died of a fever,* Falon told herself, *and I'm right here for Robbie.* Still, it felt like a goose went walking across her grave. Seizing another idea, she plucked a handful of stones from the stream. "Robbie, watch this!" She backed up a few steps and threw a stone into the river. Robbie laughed and clapped his hands at the plop and splash. When Falon held out a stone for him, he ran up to her, snatched the rock and hurled it toward the water. His throw was wild, but he did manage to just hit the water. So Falon made a game of throwing the stones, and she kept Robbie back from the river's edge, at least for a few minutes.

"Falon!" Maire was calling her. "Fill that pot and bring it to me."

"Aye," she responded, but realized she had a new problem. How to get the water up to Maire and watch Robbie at the same time?

The chicks! She snapped her fingers. "Laddie, let's get some rocks. Let's build a pen for the chicks!" Robbie wasn't excited about leaving his rock throwing, but he complied, a stone in each grubby hand. Stacking stones seemed to be his specialty, and when he understood what Falon wanted, he went to the task, trotting to and fro from the river, his big sister keeping a close eye.

She added a second ring around each rose stem for good measure, and had just finished when she detected a movement off to her left. She looked up and froze. It was the same Indian she'd seen before they crossed, and he wasn't twenty feet away. He was so close that, for the first time, she noticed two blue circles that had been painted or tattooed on his face and a long, dark scar zigzagging across his right forearm like a lightning bolt. His black eyes shifted back and forth between her and Robbie.

Falon stood, her heart hammering in her throat. What did he want? Was he going to try to take Robbie? She took three measured steps, just enough to place herself between the stranger and her brother. Thinking to appease the Indian, Falon drew her flute from beneath her tunic and played a few notes, just a bit of a dance tune. What the Indian made of her playing, she never found out, for in that moment came a splash behind her. Before she could respond, Maire screamed, "Falon! The baby!"

She whirled around and bolted to the river where Robbie had fallen in and was now on his hands and knees trying to regain his feet. Falon scooped him up, and he let out an explosive sneeze, spraying water all over her. She looked back. The Indian was gone, disappeared like a shadow in the noon sun.

But here was Maire charging toward her, fear and indignation pulled her normally pleasant features into a scowl. She snatched Robbie from Falon's arms. "What art tha' about? Playing thy music while thy brother drowns?"

"Nay, I . . ."

"Tha' has no excuse for this, ye hear? No excuse at all. After what happened to thy Annie . . ." Maire stopped and bit her lip.

"I was taking care of him," Falon insisted.

"Aye, well, we'll see what thy father has to say about it."

Falon squatted where she was, her face in her hands, not caring that her skirts trailed in the water. *I was watching him. It was that Indian made me look away. I've taken care of the lad—at least while I wasn't sick—got him here safe and all.* She sighed and splashed her face, wiping away the river water and some tears of angry frustration. *And Annie died of the fever. It wasn't my fault. Dad has said so over and over.*

As she sat there, a new thought struck her. *And just why is it he's had to say it over and over?*

★9

. . . Ah, Annie, I miss you still. Could I have done anything differently . . . ?

Father wasn't speaking to her. Maire got to him first, when he came in from clearing the land for planting. Falon couldn't hear what she said, but could imagine it well enough, judging from the disappointed look Father sent her way. If only Will were here . . . He was the one person in her family who always understood her and always believed the best of her.

To make things worse, Maire wouldn't let Robbie come near her for the remainder of the afternoon, even when he wanted to come. She pulled him away, her lips set in a tight line. "Nay, laddie, tha' must stay over here wi' me." To hide her hurt and shame, Falon concentrated on finishing the chicks' pen, not bothering to try to defend herself to her stepmother or father.

What should I have done differently? Falon replayed the incident with the Indian over and over in her head. At the time, everything she had done—putting herself between the Indian and Robbie, playing her flute to distract him from her brother—had seemed logical, sensible. But was it? It happened so quickly. And now, sensible or no, there was no going back. Robbie had fallen in the water, and Falon was going to have to bear the blame.

Young George's reaction to Maire's telling of the incident was even harsher than Father's, more condemning. He stared at her for an eternal minute, his face red, as if he'd been slapped, as if what she had done was a personal affront. Then he shook his head and turned away without a word.

I'll have to tell Dad about the Indian, Falon reasoned. Not that it was an excuse for turning her back on Robbie, but Dad needed to know what was going on. *I'll tell him after we've eaten.* But her plans were interrupted at dusk, when Mr. Blaloch arrived. "Just stopping by to see how your family is getting along," he announced as he dismounted his horse. He nodded to Maire and Falon and shook hands with Father and George. "You've made a shelter."

"We've already cleared for the planting." Father couldn't keep the pride from his voice. "Found a likely spot. We should be able to start plowing tomorrow."

"That is excellent." Mr. Blaloch clapped a hand on Father's shoulder. "You're making a good start." He gave Father more advice and information about how to irrigate, how to mark his boundaries, how to build a cabin. All the while Father nodded and murmured agreement, as if everything Mr. Blaloch said was self-evident, as if working just the one day on his land had given Father the wisdom he needed to proceed.

The agent had brought a haunch of a small deer with him. "I shot it this morning and passed the pieces around to your neighbors," he explained. "This is the last of it."

"We're obliged to you," Father answered. "Ye've been a big help to us, getting us here and settled and all."

"It was my pleasure." Ed Blaloch squatted, resting his back against a tree trunk and taking off his hat. "This site will be a fine home for your family." He accepted a cup of coffee from Maire and blew on it before taking a sip. "Thank you, ma'am."

He might be sitting in someone's parlor—he looks that at home. Falon sat a little outside the circle of her family. The agent glanced her way from time to time, his normally controlled expression curious, quizzical. She hoped he wouldn't say anything, wouldn't ask questions.

While they were eating, George asked, "Have ye seen any more Indians?"

Indians. Falon had just taken a bite of her meat, and though she kept chewing—slowly— the meat seemed to get bigger in her mouth. Did George know something, or was this just an innocent question? She had to swallow hard to force the meat down.

"I see them all the time, son."

"Did you ever kill one?"

"George!" Maire scolded, "What kind of question is that to ask our guest?"

The boy muttered an apology, but though Mr. Blaloch's eyes were narrowed in a pained expression, he answered, "It's all right, Mrs. Macvail. Boys want to know these things." To George he said, "I never have killed any man, and I have no ambition to do so."

"Are there Indians in this area?" Maire asked.

"There are, and your family needs to have a plan—a way of protecting yourselves, a way of escape if you're attacked." He set his cup down. "But you all have more neighbors than just the few who came with you, and their numbers will help."

"More neighbors?" Father asked.

"Stephen Austin has brought and settled some three hundred families, mostly over around the Colorado, but some parcels back up to your own."

"Three hundred families," Maire echoed. "Imagine that, Camran! We'll have a full-grown city out here, for sure."

"You may," Mr. Blaloch nodded. "Each family has land, but people do tend to cluster, so I wouldn't be surprised to see a town or two spring up."

He ended up staying the night. The next morning, Falon hoped for an opportunity to have a private word with him. But just after breakfast, he announced, "Well, I have to be getting back. I told my Janie I'd be gone about a fortnight, and it will just come to that." He smiled, "She's an understanding woman, but I don't want to worry her needlessly."

Until then, Falon hadn't given much thought to Mr. Blaloch having a life apart. Apparently, Maire hadn't either. "And do ye have children, sir?"

He grinned. "We have three sons, all just about grown." He untied his horse's tether and to Falon's surprise asked, "I wonder if I might borrow your daughter? I want to show her something down at the river."

Father nodded his permission, his expression more eased than the day before. Falon followed the agent to the river's edge—and out of earshot of her family. Mr. Blaloch paused to look out over the water. "Something troubling you, Miss Macvail?"

"I saw that Indian again yesterday, the same one we saw just before we crossed."

To her relief, he didn't ask if she was sure what she'd seen, or whether she was certain it had been the same Indian. He just nodded. "I don't know him, but he's a Coco."

"A Coco?"

"The Cocos wear those blue circles. Men and women both. I don't think he'll bother you, though you may spot him from time to time."

"Should I tell my father?"

He sighed, "If you keep seeing him, you should. But don't let that brother of yours hear about it."

Falon couldn't help herself. "He's my stepbrother."

"Yes, well, brother or stepbrother, his blood runs a little too hot. Boy like that can make trouble where there is none. Understand?"

"Oh, aye. I do understand."

He glanced at her. "Anything else?"

"Only my own troubles. Nothing you can do aught about."

He stood silent awhile, watching the rushing water, combing his mustache with his fingers. "You know, when I first saw you, Miss Macvail, I thought you were a goner."

"A what?"

"You looked so weak and frail, I thought that you'd succumb of one thing or another. I have seen it happen to people who looked hardier than you." His features relaxed until he was almost smiling. "But you proved me wrong. You're made of stern stuff, young lady." He lifted his hat briefly. "Whatever your troubles are, you'll manage them. I have full confidence in you." He swung up onto his horse, and with a final nod, rode upriver toward the ford.

That afternoon, when Father and George had come in from their day's plowing, Falon waited until the others were occupied, and while Maire was tending to Robbie and George was down at the river, she pulled up her courage. "Dad, can I talk to thee?"

He laid one rough paw atop her head. "'Tis all right, lass. I know what tha' wants to say."

"You do?" *How does he know about the Indian?*

"Aye. That business wi' Robbie. I know thee. Tha' has always taken good care of our laddie."

"Aye, but . . ."

"Dinna' worry, sweeting. Our Maire will be occupied with other things. She'll soon forget that she was ever upset wi' thee." He smiled. "I expect to be able to start building us a little house in a few days. That'll be nice, aye?"

"Aye, Dad." Falon gave up—for the moment. "That'll be wonderful."

"That's my good lass." He patted her head and moved off toward the river.

Father was as good as his word. After about a week, he and Young George had finished planting and they started felling trees to make a cabin. Maire and Falon stripped the small limbs from the logs and gathered stones to build a fireplace and chimney. Log by log, the walls rose from the ground. After two more weeks—during which time Falon saw no sign of Indians—they had a snug little house built, with window openings at each end and a tight-built fireplace centered on the back wall.

Falon was so busy, they were all so busy, that the incident with Robbie was not mentioned again. Once the walls went up, Falon began hauling mud from the river, one kettle full at a time, to fill in the chinks. And there was the tending to the chicks and planting the vegetable garden, along with the daily hunt for food. *It'll get easier,* she told herself, *once we have the garden producing.* And she had to give George his due. He had proven himself handy at trapping small animals and catching fish.

The Indians left them alone, and Falon didn't see them, though one day she thought she'd caught sight of something across the river out of the corner of her eye. But when she turned to look, there was nothing. *Deer, most likely,* she told herself.

By this time, summer was truly on them. Falon hadn't guessed that it could ever be so hot. *Thank heaven Dad thought to leave the trees standing near the house,* she told herself one sticky afternoon. *Otherwise, it'd be unbearable.* Robbie had taken to running around in nothing but a shirt. Falon watched him with envy. Her own wool dress seemed to get heavier and hotter with each passing day.

"I'm done," Father announced one sultry afternoon. He wiped the sweat dripping from his brow, took a long drink of water, and lay down with a groan on shaded grass. It wasn't long before the rest of the family joined him. Falon lay on her back, listening to the insects buzzing in the trees above. Their pulsing drone made her eyelids grow heavy. *I wish they'd hush,* she thought. *All that noise just makes it hotter.*

I wonder what Mother would have thought of all this? With a stab of guilt, she realized she hadn't thought about her mother in weeks.

She would have liked the house, for sure. Just before Falon dozed off, she realized she had passed a milestone. *It's midsummer. I'm fifteen now.*

The hot months droned on, and just as summer reached its zenith, their first cash crop was ready for harvest. They had built a house by hand, had gathered and cooked their food, had planted and tended and harvested vegetables, but Falon decided that picking cotton was the worst—the hardest, hottest job. Day after day, up and down the rows they worked, bent in the glaring sun with sweat dripping from their brows, pulling fat bolls off the drying plants and stuffing them into the now-empty seed bags.

"We'll be keeping some of this, won't we, Camran?" Maire asked on the first day of the harvest.

"We can keep maybe a third. I have to sell the rest to pay this year's due for the land. The tobacco doesn't look sa' good. I'm thinking the cotton will make us the most money."

By the end of the third day of picking, Falon decided that Father could sell it all. She never wanted to look at another boll. *I could go on wearing this dress till it falls off me, as long as I never have to do this again.* But of course, she knew she would have to—they all would. Even little Robbie was expected to pitch in and help.

Maire seemed to be having the hardest time. She frequently stopped to stand and stretch, one hand clutching the small of her back. On the fourth day, Falon heard her groan, and when Maire straightened, she noticed an unmistakable thickness around her middle. Falon felt her heart drop. *So Maire is going to have a baby. Father's baby. We have no near neighbors, either. It'll be up to me to help with the birthing.* Falon swallowed and bent again to her task. She had never even witnessed a birth, much less helped with one.

It took the entire week, but they finally got the cotton picked. Mr. Everson came to call two days later. "We're heading out to San Antonio the day after tomorrow," he said. "Do you have your cotton picked?"

"We just finished," Father told him, adding with a rueful smile, "It about did us in."

"You should get a slave. At harvest time my Joe is worth every penny I paid for him."

"I canna' see owing another man. Doesn't seem right."

Everson smirked. "Another couple of years of picking cotton will change your mind. I tell you, darkies were made for this work. You have to stay on top of them—they can be lazy, but with a firm hand they sure make the job easier."

"But owning slaves is against the law in Mexico," Father pointed out.

Another smirk. "That's what I hear, but no one has ever interfered with me or mine. And they'd better not."

Father elected to change the subject. "We're leaving day after tomorrow, you said?"

"The plan is to have everyone meet up at the ford. It should take a week to make San Antonio from here, and we can sell the cotton there and make payments to the land agent, too."

After Mr. Everson was gone, Young George began a heated campaign to be allowed to go with Camran to San Antonio. "Tha' will need me wi' thee," he insisted. "The load will be too much for thee to handle alone."

"I need thee to stay here," Camran retorted. "The women will look to thee for protection while I'm gone. Tha' will have to be the man of the house."

George held his peace, for the moment, but at every opportunity he pointed out how difficult the journey to San Antonio would be for Camran without him. "And what if the cart loses a wheel? Who'll be there to help thee fix it?"

"George," Camran growled, "that's enough. Tha' art staying here, and that's that."

So George sulked. And Falon marveled. *Will would never have defied his father so. If he had, Dad would have shown him the end of his belt. Why was Father so easy with George? Did he really feel guilt over the Morgan's losses? Or was it because he wasn't George's father after all?* Neither did Maire make much of an attempt to discipline the boy; as a result, he pouted and sulked for two days, until Falon wanted to slap him.

She even thought about encouraging Father to take George with him. Better that he was gone, better that they'd have some peace, than having to endure his "protection." But in the end, she decided to stay out of it. For once, George wasn't getting his way, and for her, that made his whining more bearable.

More than a dozen men from the surrounding area were going together to sell their cotton and tobacco in San Antonio. *Father will be in good company,* Falon told herself. *The men will help and protect each other.* Still, it was hard to say goodbye. "Be careful," she whispered in Father's ear as she kissed him farewell.

"Dinna' worry about a thing, lass," he told her, smiling. "Take care of Maire and Robbie for me, aye?"

"Aye, Dad. You know I will."

"I'll be back before tha' can turn around." He hugged Maire, picked up the handles of the cart, now loaded with crudely tied bundles of cotton, and set off north along the river.

Maire sighed, and shaded her eyes as she watched him go. "'Twill be a long fortnight, I think, before he's back again."

Three days later, Falon saw not one, but two Indians.

She had all but forgotten them, and when she caught movement in the trees across the river, she first assumed it was one of their neighbors. They regularly saw people passing by their place en route to the ford. She had started to lift a hand and call out a greeting when she realized that she was seeing Indians.

One of them was the Indian with the scarred arm she had seen twice before; the other looked a little older, and he was taller and heavier. She stared at them, her heart in her throat, for several long seconds before she realized the younger Indian was gesturing to her. He held his hands in front of his mouth and wiggled his fingers. The meaning was unmistakable. He wanted her to play her flute.

She glanced back over her shoulder. Neither Maire nor George was in sight. Before she could decide whether this was a good thing or not, her hand went to the front of her dress, and she dragged out the wooden flute. Her mouth had gone so dry she wasn't sure she'd be able to squeeze out a single note, but her shaking fingers did a quick dance over the holes, and she played three bird calls in quick succession. Then, without waiting for a reaction from the two men, she turned and fled to the house. Robbie was inside, napping on the rope-frame bed, and Falon could hear Maire out in the back, probably hoeing weeds in the vegetable patch. Falon gulped down a dipper of water, glad that she was alone, and edged over to the door to see if the Indians were still there. She wasn't much surprised to find they'd vanished.

Whatever the reason they had come, the Indians stayed away for a while, though Falon did have a strange dream that the younger Indian was there in the house with her. They sat down at the table and had a talk over coffee, just as if they were old friends. He spoke English, and told her about his family. When she woke, she couldn't remember what he had said, and she found this oddly disappointing.

After a fortnight, Father came home from San Antonio astride a black-and-white horse, driving a half dozen head of strange-looking cattle. "Look what I brought thee from the city!" he called out.

"Those are ours?" Maire asked.

"Aye." He grinned broadly, dismounting. "Cotton brought a good price, and I even sold the tobacco—for more than I expected. Paid this year's price on the land and had enough left over for these beauties."

Beauties? Falon covered her mouth to stifle a laugh. She had never seen rangier animals—piebald white and brown—and those horns! They stood out from the long, bovine faces in the oddest twists and turns. Some horns curled one way, some the other. There was no rhyme or reason to them. And the ends of those horns were as sharp as if they'd been ground on a whetstone.

Maire, too, eyed the cattle dubiously. "Are tha' expecting me to milk those?"

Now Father laughed. "The horns look wicked, but these animals are gentle as lambs."

His wife cocked one hand on her hip. "I'll be taking thy word for it."

George was beside himself with excitement. "A horse! You got us a horse!"

"Aye, and that means you and I are going to have to build a byre to put her in."

"Can I ride her?" The boy ran his hands over the mare's neck.

"Not tonight," Camran answered. "She has a few years on her, and she's worked hard today. Time to give her a rest."

"What happened to the cart?" Maire asked as she accepted his kiss on the cheek.

"Sold it and bought the horse," he answered. "I'll build us a bigger wagon this winter."

They gathered brush for a makeshift livestock pen against one side of the house. "This'll have to do for the night," Father announced. "We'll make a better one tomorrow." With that, they went inside for dinner, and Father regaled them with stories about his trip to San Antonio, the big city. "There were almost as many Americans there as Mexicans," he said. "Some hotheads have been trying to stir up trouble with the government in Mexico City, but I think it'll come to naught. If a man works hard, he can build himself a good life." He smiled at each of them in turn. "All I ever need is right here."

He's on top of the world. With a pang, Falon remembered how it had been when they were driven out of Sgall, how her father had been beaten down, almost hopeless. Her heart ached for Will and for her mother. *But Father did the right thing coming here. This is our place now, and no one can take it away.*

★ ★ ★

The cattle went missing the same day Falon discovered the first bud on her roses. She got up that morning and went down to the river to fetch water. As she passed the little rose plants—fully leafed out now, no longer just sticks in the ground—she noticed a swelling at the end of one of the canes. When she stopped to investigate, she realized it was a bud. One of the roses was about to bloom. *Is this the red one, or the yellow?* she wondered. The bud was still a tiny closed fist, and there was no way to tell what color the flower would be. *Ah well, I'll find out soon enough.* She wished for some way to let Miss Mattie know her cuttings had survived—and to thank her again.

Less than an hour later, George came tearing up to the house from the newly constructed barn yelling, "They're gone! They're gone!"

Father tugged on his shoes. "What's all this, lad? Who's gone?"

Young George leaned over and put his hands on his knees, panting heavily. Falon rolled her eyes. It wasn't that far from the barn to the house. "They're gone," he repeated. "Three of the cows. They were in the byre last night, and now they're gone."

Father charged out of the house, Falon and George on his heels. He shouldered open the door of the barn and went inside. Falon followed, then stopped. The big bull was there, and two of the cows. And in her pen in the corner, the horse stood quiet and patient, as if nothing were amiss.

"Three cows gone," Father muttered. "They can't have gotten out by themselves." He turned to George. "Tha' did secure the door last night, aye?"

"I swear I did."

Father gave him a not-too-gentle cuff on his ear. "Dinna' swear. Ye say 'aye' or 'nay' and be done wi' it."

George glanced at Falon and away as he rubbed the side of his scarlet face. "Aye. I did shut the door last night."

"All right, then. So what happened to the cows? If they didn't get out, someone took them. Indians, maybe?"

"But Dad," Falon wondered, "why would anyone take just the three? If they were going to steal, why not take the whole lot?"

"Only a girl would ask such a stupid question," George muttered.

Father turned and regarded him mildly. Falon recognized the look—he was standing on the last edge of his patience. "And what was stupid about it? I was wondering the same."

George shot his stepsister a look of pure venom, but he held his tongue.

"Was the door shut this morning?" Father asked.

The boy had to think about that one. He squinted up toward the ceiling. "Aye?"

"Well, which is it, aye or nay?"

George made his decision. "Aye. The door was shut."

Father heaved a heavy sigh and shook his head. "We'll have to go looking for them."

"Can I ride the horse?"

Father didn't answer George this time; he merely looked at him. After a few seconds, the boy realized the gravity of his own situation, if not of the missing cattle. Falon actually felt sorry for him. *The lad's having a very bad day.* She understood what that was like.

She tugged at her father's sleeve. "Dad, can I talk to thee?"

"Can it wait, lass? We've got a job to do."

"I know, Dad, but I need to tell thee something." She glanced at George, who was making a show of ignoring her, and pulled her father out of the barn and out of earshot. "I've seen Indians." She told him the whole story, beginning with the day they crossed the river, including Mr. Blaloch's warning about George. "I saw them again when tha' was away," she concluded. "But apart from that one time, they've been on the other side of the river."

"I'm thinking it was them that probably took the cows."

"I suppose that's possible, but why only the three? It doesn't make sense."

Father sighed and shook his head. "I wish tha' had told me sooner, lass."

"Stupid!" Falon jumped and turned. George had followed them, and Falon had little doubt he had heard every word. "You've seen Indians, and you didn't tell us? What's the matter with thee? Are tha' not right in the head?"

"George, that's enough." But Father's stern words didn't stop him.

"Something's wrong with her," the boy insisted. "She's cursed. Bad luck follows her everywhere. All those people got sick on the ship, and my father and the little ones died, and she almost drowned Robbie the way she drowned your Annie. And now the cows are gone." Falon gasped.

"George, go to the house and wait for me," Father told him.

"Aye. Aye, I'll go to the house. I'll wait for thee, and tha' can strop me, if that makes thee feel better, but it doesn't change the truth. She killed her sister, she killed her mother, and she tried to kill the baby. And now she's in with those savages. I tell thee, she's out to kill us all!" With that, George whirled around and marched toward the house.

Falon's knees gave way and she sank to the ground. "Dad?" Her voice sounded harsh and strange in her ears. "Annie died of a fever. Didn't she?" All those nightmares of Annie drowning rose up to mock her.

When her father didn't answer right away, she knew George had spoken the truth. "Tha' didn't kill thy sister." Father's quiet words were like hammer blows. "She did drown, and tha' nearly did, too. She fell in the loch, and tha' fell in when tha' tried to pull her out. By the time we had thee out of the water, tha' was half dead." His throat worked convulsively. "Thy sister was gone. There was no saving her."

"But you said she had a fever."

"Ah, lass. By the time tha' was better, tha' had no memory of what happened, and it seemed good to us to spare thee."

"So the whole village knew."

"Aye, and Young George was there when it happened. He was the one who came running to tell us you'd both fallen in."

Tears spilled down Falon's face. "I didn't kill her," she sobbed. "I loved Annie."

Father groaned as he gathered her in his arms. "We all loved her, lass. And no one blamed thee. 'Twas an accident."

But that wasn't quite true. *Mother blamed me.* Suddenly, so much of what Mother had said and done now made sense. Annie, the golden child in the Macvail family, had died. Falon had not only been unable to save her, she had had the great gall to survive in Annie's stead.

Slowly, Falon pulled away from her father and stood. "Don't punish him, Dad." With shaking hands, she gathered her shawl close around her. "He's only told the truth."

"Nay. He's told the devil's version, and it's no truth at all." He cupped her chin in his hand, compelled her to look at him. "There is no blame on thee for anything he's accused thee of." Unconvinced, she nevertheless nodded as she turned away. With a deep sigh, Father added, "I should have told thee sooner."

She tried to give him a smile. "Tha' did what tha' thought was best." As she started toward the house, it occurred to her that was what everyone around her was doing, even George. *What a shame that our best puts us at odds with each other.*

★10

. . . It was a hard six months, no mistake, but it ended with the best surprise . . .

The missing cows were recovered that same afternoon. They had gotten out and were grazing on the stubble in what was left of the cotton field. When Father figured out that George had lied about shutting the barn door, he took his belt to him. "Those cows are part of our living, boy. We canna' afford to lose them—not even one of them. Your carelessness could have cost us dear."

On top of that, he made George apologize to Falon, something the boy didn't want to do, and Falon didn't want to hear. But Father said, "Like it or no, tha' art brother and sister now. Tha' must get along."

Falon made do by avoiding her stepbrother as much as she could, and since he seemed eager to do the same, they spent little time in each other's company. George even took to sleeping in the barn—to "watch over the cattle"—as he put it, but Falon understood that he stayed out there so he wouldn't have to see or speak to her. She really didn't care what he did or why. His absence suited her.

She kept herself busy. Between harvesting and preserving the vegetables, Falon helped get meals every day and frequently went hunting on their land for herbs to add variety to their diet. One fall day while she was wandering, she stepped on something hard underfoot that snapped, and discovered she had crushed a hickory nut. Falon looked up. The trees all around her were loaded with nuts. Only a few littered the ground, but she knew there would soon be many more. She stooped and started gathering the little brown nuts into the basket she carried. She didn't hear or see anything to make her look up from her task, but look up she did, and there was the young Indian again.

His sudden presence startled her, but for some reason—perhaps because she had told her father—she had ceased to fear him. She stood and said quietly, "You do make my life complicated, you know."

He nodded as if he understood her then motioned a request for her to play. *Well, I might as well play for him as for anyone.* She pulled out her flute and played a short hymn and a dance tune. He grinned as she finished and tucked the flute back into her dress. He motioned toward her basket with a questioning look, his scar flashing in the sunlight. When Falon showed him the contents, he nodded. Bending down, he proceeded to gather nuts into the basket. *Why, he's helping me!* When the basket was nearly full, Falon said, "I should go now," and waved goodbye. He held up one hand, and turning away, disappeared back into the trees and brush.

Daylight was fading fast by the time Falon reached the cabin. "Where has tha' been, lass?" Maire asked. "I've needed thee to help with dinner." Falon showed her the nuts. "I'm sorry to take so long, but these may be worth the time. I'll start shelling them tonight."

After they had eaten, she sat at the table with her father's mallet and cracked and shelled until Father said, "It's time for bed, lass. Blow out thy candle." She was relieved to stop for a while. Miss Mattie had been right. The meat in the nuts was wonderful, but getting at it left her fingertips blistered and sore. Falon fell asleep thinking about the Indian. *I wish I could talk to him.*

Aside from growing and gathering food, the cotton needed to be carded and spun. Father had built a spinning wheel, and bit by fluffy bit, she and Maire turned the piles of cotton into skeins of thread. "I'll build thee a loom this winter," he promised them.

"Maybe by summer we'll be wearing cotton instead of wool," Maire said.

Autumn gave way to winter, and Falon welcomed the cooler weather. She gathered fallen leaves and piled them around the bases of her roses to keep them from freezing, but when November came and went, she began to think she had wasted her time. It was nearly Christmas, but they'd still not seen more than a light frost.

Three days after Christmas, she heard a shout from the river, and jumped up, nearly overturning her chair. She knew that voice! No sooner had she opened the door when Will strode into the house. Another young man followed him in, but Falon hardly noticed him. "Here's my little sister!" Will exclaimed, catching her in his arms and whirling her around till she squealed. He set her down, hugged his father and stepmother, and shook hands with George.

"This is James Carson," he indicated the man with him. "He was coming this way from the coast, so we traveled together." James Carson was about Will's height and build, but where Will was dark, James was fair, with hair the color of straw, and pale gray eyes under nearly white eyebrows.

"Pleased to meet you." Falon curtsied when he tipped his hat in her direction, but she could hardly spare a thought for him. Her brother was home.

"It's a little late for Christmas," Will told them, "but I brought you a few things." He had a bag of wheat flour, a box of coffee, and pieces of sugar cane. He gave ribbons to Falon and Maire, a new pipe to Father, and a small knife to George. For Robbie there was a set of painted blocks to stack.

Father inspected his pipe. "Well, this is a merry Christmas, and no mistake."

"What about Betsy?" Falon asked. "Did tha' get to see her? Did tha' give her my letter?"

Will grinned. "I knew tha' would ask." His chest puffed out. "I'm a married man. Betsy and I are wed these six months." Falon jumped up and threw her arms around his neck. "I knew it—I just knew tha' would marry her! I am so happy for thee, and for her, too."

As Will filled them in on the details of his marriage, Falon began to realize what it meant for her. Betsy was staying in Ireland. She wouldn't be coming to Texas, and that meant Will would be leaving again before long. He would go back there to live. *We won't see much more of him after this—if at all.* She went all tight inside and swallowed hard. *I'm not going to be sad, not at Christmas, not while Will is here.*

"And what is it that ye do, Mr. Carson?" Father was asking.

"I buy and sell slaves, Mr. Macvail."

The room went suddenly quiet. "Well now," Father ventured after a pause, "that's something different. Ye do know, don't ye, that slave trading is illegal in Texas?"

"That it is, Mr. Macvail. However, sometimes necessity forces us to bend the law. Not many farms will make it without the labor I can provide." His pale eyes shifted to Falon. "It takes many strong backs to build a life in this wilderness. I am sure you discovered that for yourselves at harvest time."

"It was hard work," Father admitted, "but between us we managed it."

"I admire your diligence. All I am offering is assistance—another pair of hands, or maybe a few more, to make the work go smoother."

Maire stepped in and changed the subject. "Will, did you see anyone we know besides the Magees? Is old Angus still alive? Did ye see Janet?"

"Angus Magee is alive and kicking. Missus and Robert have a little house, and he lives with them. Your sister and brother-in-law came for a visit while I was there. Donald found work managing sheep on an estate near Armaugh. He and Janet and the children are well."

"Ah, that is good news," Maire smiled. "Ye'll give them my love when you see them again, aye?"

"Of course."

"Are tha' going back on the same ship that brought us?" George wanted to know.

"That I am. The *White Arrow* sails in March, and I'll be on it and back to my bonny lass." He reached into his coat pocket. That reminds me, Falon. Here's a letter for you."

"Betsy wrote to me?" Falon accepted the folded paper as tenderly as she might a newborn kitten.

"She did, and Missus wrote a line or two as well."

Falon opened the letter:

Dear Falon,

By the time you read this, you will know that your brother and I are married. We wed midsummer in the prettiest little church on the western edge of town. The fields all around were full of wildflowers, even the graveyard in the back was covered with them. I wish you could have been here. I miss your music.

I am sorry to hear about your mother, and Will told us about the Morgans' losses, too. But it's good news that your two families are together. I hope to hear from you again. Kiss the wee boy for me.

Your sister, Betsy

Below that, Missus had written:

I just wanted to say that we miss you. We're all doing well. We've found a little house and Robert is working. We are so happy to have Will in our family. He is another bit of Sgall for us. Give our love to your father and to Maire.

With love, Sudia

Sudia? Missus' name is Sudia? Falon almost laughed. No wonder she never told anyone her given name! Falon re-read the letter, aching with longing to see Betsy. There was so much she wanted to tell her. She thought about writing her another letter, but though she still had ink, where would she get a piece of paper?

When she said as much to Will, James broke in. "Sorry, but I couldn't help overhearing. I know how to make paper, and I'd be happy to teach you."

"Make paper?" Falon regarded him with new appreciation. "Ye aren't pulling my leg, are ye, Mr. Carson?"

"I wouldn't dream of it, Miss Macvail. If you'll permit me, tomorrow we'll make a project of it."

So that is how Falon found herself with James Carson, wandering her father's pastures the next morning with a basket on her arm, looking for stands of dry grass that hadn't already been trampled or grazed by the cattle. A bitter wind had blown through the night before, and Falon's breath steamed around her as she searched the ground.

"Here's a good patch," James called out. He cut handfuls of golden-brown grass with his hunting knife and loaded them into her basket.

"How much of this will we need?"she asked.

"More than you'd think. When we're through mashing this stuff, it won't look like much. And," he added, "it is a bit of work, so if you're going to make paper, you might as well plan to make several sheets at one time."

While they searched and cut grass, she asked him about his family. "I'm from the state of Georgia, a long way east of Texas. My mother and father both live there, and I have an older sister and two brothers. Your basket is full. You'll be able to make several sheets of paper with that."

Falon dubiously eyed the dead grass in her basket. "If ye say so."

James laughed. "I am not leading you astray, Miss Macvail." He took her arm to escort her back to the house, and though the day was frigid, her face flushed warm.

When they were inside, he instructed her: "All you want to use of this grass are the blades. Clean off any roots, and if there are seed heads, get rid of those. Then you'll need a knife or scissors to chop the grass into short pieces. I'm going to go see what I can find to build a frame." He headed back out.

A frame. Falon shook her head. She didn't understand how grass was going to be paper, or what a frame had to do with it, but she would go along—to be polite—and on the off chance that this Carson fellow really knew how to transform common pasture grass into something useful.

He returned just as she was cutting up the last handful of stems. "That looks perfect. Now you'll need to put that in a pot and soak it overnight."

"Ye can use the smaller kettle," Maire told her. When James was occupied talking to Will, Maire whispered to Falon, "D'ye think this will really make paper?"

The girl shrugged. "Your guess is as good as mine. He acts like he knows what he's doing."

The following day, James asked, "Mrs. Macvail, could I prevail upon you to loan me a piece of cloth? If you have cheesecloth, that would be perfect."

"I have just the one piece," she told him, "and I need it when we've had a lot of milk from the cows."

"I only need it for two days, ma'am, and you'll be able to use it again when I'm finished, I promise." Maire snorted and shook her head, but she did give him the cheesecloth. "You're an angel, Mrs. Macvail."

She laughed. "Just don't you ruin that cheesecloth, young man, or you'll be thinking otherwise!"

He smiled and turned to Falon. "Do you have a bucket we can use?"

"Aye, out in the barn." The little tin bucket she had once used to feed the nanny goat was hanging on a nail just inside the barn door. As she went to fetch it, she remembered picking it up that day they were turned out. *Plain little bucket, but it made it all this way.*

James filled the bucket halfway with water, then took ashes from the fireplace and added them in, stirring the solution with a stick. "This will turn your grass into pulp, a kind of mash," he told her. When it had soaked, he had her transfer her grass into a bowl, straining the ashy water through the cheesecloth into the kettle. "Be careful," he warned her, "you don't want to get this ash water on you. It'll burn your skin."

"And my cheesecloth?" Maire asked pointedly.

"I'm rinsing it out right now, Mrs. Macvail." He grinned at Falon, and for the first time she noticed a cleft in his chin. "Put your grass in the water and set it on the fire to cook. I'll be right back."

James returned from the river a few minutes later, blowing and stamping with the cold. "It's starting to sleet out there." He held up the cheesecloth. "All clean, and good as new." He winked at Falon. "Just as I promised."

Father came in soon after the grass in the pot began to boil. "Is someone making a pudding?" he asked hopefully. Falon had noticed it, too, a sugary smell coming from the boiling pot.

"No, Camran," Maire answered. "They're making paper. It does smell like a pudding, though."

"It smells delicious." He bent over the pot and inhaled the steaming fragrance. "Paper, ye say, and no' a pudding?"

"Paper, yes, sir." James accepted a cup of coffee from Maire. "Once Miss Macvail knows how this is done, she'll never want for paper again." To Falon he said, "I noticed a couple of little rose shrubs between here and the river. This spring or summer you can collect rose petals and use them in your paper."

"Ah now, wouldn't that be pretty," Maire said.

But Falon was thinking, *He noticed my rosebushes?*

Two days later, Falon had her paper. James showed her how to pound the pulp and to screen it using the cheesecloth attached to a frame he had built. When the damp pages had rested on the tabletop for about an hour, he heated a flatiron on the fire just enough to press the paper and finish drying it. The resulting pages were a beautiful light gold color, curled a bit at the edges. "How can I ever thank you, Mr. Carson?" she asked, holding one of the pages up to the firelight.

"Your pleasure is all the thanks I need." He smiled and added, "Now you can send a letter to your sister-in-law."

James left the next morning, saying he had some calls to make at the newly forming town of Beason's Crossing on the Colorado River. Will went with him. "The two of us agreed to travel together. Besides, I want to have a look at this new town."

When they were gone, Maire commented, "James Carson's quite the gentleman, isn't he?"

"Aye, he is," Father agreed from where he sat in the middle of the floor, assembling a cradle for the coming baby.

Falon saw the looks Maire had been giving her and James, and she knew Maire wasn't just making conversation. She had a pile of nuts in a cloth in her lap and was busy breaking them with Father's mallet and shelling them into a bowl. Her face had gone hot; she didn't want to comment, or even to look up.

"He said he'd be coming back this way," Maire added.

"Can't imagine why. He knows I'm not going to buy a slave from him."

Falon still didn't look up, but she knew what was coming. Sure enough, Maire said, "I think he fancies our Falon."

"What?" Father stared at Maire for a moment as if she'd suddenly turned green or sprouted a third arm. Then he turned to his daughter. "Is this true?"

"I . . . I don't know. That is, I don't think so. I haven't given it much thought." Falon bit her lip to stop herself from babbling.

Maire chuckled. "Ah, ye have been thinking on it, and I'm not blind. I can see what's going on."

"I'm only fifteen."

"That's right," Father slapped his thigh, as if something had been settled. "She's only fifteen."

"I was just fifteen when I married George," Maire pointed out. "And if memory serves, you were barely sixteen when you and Esme wed."

Father had just popped a nut into his mouth, and from the corner of her eye, Falon saw him stop chewing. "Well . . ."

Maire was relentless. "Well?"

"Hm-m-m." He tapped at the edge of the cradle rocker with his fingertips. "Ye know, one of the cows has been acting like she feels poorly. I need to see about her." He stood, took a gulp of coffee from his mug on the table, and headed out the door. Neither Falon nor Maire bothered to point out that George was already in the barn looking after the ailing cow.

Ah, Dad, don't leave me alone with her! Falon was sorely tempted to follow him out, but knew she'd only be delaying the inevitable. So she stayed put and waited.

She didn't have to wait long. "What d'ye think of him, then?"

Falon sighed. "I'm not ready to think of him at all."

"Ye know, sometimes things happen whether we're ready for them or not."

Angry at being prodded, Falon got her dig in: "Like death," she said, and instantly regretted it, for Maire went silent. After a couple of painful heartbeats, Falon whispered, "I'm sorry. I didn't mean it that way."

She marveled that Maire managed to hold on to herself. "I know ye didn't. And I'm sorry, too. I shouldn't press you." She sighed and put a hand to her back. Her baby was due in a few weeks. "But Falon, he's coming here again, and I'm certain he means to court you. You need to think on that and decide what you'll do." She waddled back to the bed and sat down with a groan. "I'll say no more about it unless you want to talk."

Falon could only nod. Her stepmother was doing her best to be a mother to her, and in her heart, Falon knew Maire was right. *What do I think about him? Well, he's helpful and clever.* She warmed as she remembered his comment about the roses. *And observant. He and Will get along, which is no small matter. I wonder what Father thinks of him? He certainly doesn't seem to care much for James' occupation. I'll ask him later, hear what he has to say. If he doesn't like James, I'll have my answer.*

Falon half hoped that James Carson wouldn't be back or that if he did come, he would ignore her, stay a few days, and move on. But she also knew she needed to be prepared in case Maire was right. So one evening she went out to the barn to talk to her father. She found him cleaning one of the horses' hooves. "Dad, I need to talk to thee."

He didn't stop to look at her. "Talk away."

She squatted beside him. "What's wrong with the horse?"

"Ah, the old girl's got a bit of stone lodged in here. It's put her off her gait all afternoon." He grimaced. "But ye didn't come out here to talk to me about her."

Falon took a deep breath. "I need to know what ye think of James Carson."

"What do I think of him? Ah, there it goes." He held up a ragged pebble. "That was her trouble. What do I think of James Carson? Well, I like the man all right, but no' so much what he does."

Falon nodded. "I thought you'd say so. I just needed to be sure."

"What do you think of him, lass?"

Falon sank back against the wall and pulled her knees up to her chest. "I don't know." Her stomach ached, and she felt miserable. "He seems nice enough. And he did spend a lot of time and work to show me how to make the paper. He didn't have to do that."

"So why d'ye think he did?"

She shrugged. "I dinna' think he was showing off. If he wanted to show off, he wouldn't have taught me, he would have just made the paper himself. He acted like he really wanted to teach me how, like he wanted to share what he knew."

"It may be he cares about you."

"But, Dad, he's only just met me."

"Sometimes that's all it takes, Falon." He smiled at her, but his eyes were serious, almost pained. "Sometimes a man catches sight of a lass, and his heart is gone to her."

"Is that how it was with you and Mother?"

Now his eyes did smile. "I teased her for years that she chased me down, but she and I both knew that I was after her. I caught sight of her at a wedding. She had flowers in her hair, and she sang . . ."

Falon's heart ached for the softness in his face. "I wish I could have seen that."

"She was so bonny, and her voice was like an angel from Heaven." He sighed, wiping at his eyes. "I couldn't believe it when she accepted me. I was naught but a poor crofter. Never had much hope of anything more."

And they were happy before things went wrong, before Annie.

"Tha' has the bonny look of her. Especially around the eyes." He cleared his throat. "I'll not say yea or nay about Mr. Carson. The final decision will have to be yours."

"Dad . . ."

He held up one hand. "If I had objections beyond just the one, I'd tell thee. The slave trading worries me, but if ye like him, we'll overlook it."

Falon rested her forehead on her knees. "I don't know how I'm supposed to feel about him." She raised her head again. "How do I know he's the one for me?"

His answering look pierced her, though his mouth played with a smile. "He's the one for you if you marry him." When Falon groaned, he added, "I know that's not what ye were asking, lass, but it's God's truth. Once ye've decided, it's done. So if ye need to take some time, I'll support your decision."

She sighed. "All right. All right, then." She gathered her feet under her and stood up. "Thanks, Dad." She bent over and kissed the top of his head.

He leaned into the kiss. "My wee lass. It's hard to believe we're having this talk already. Seems like just a little time ago you were riding on my shoulders."

As she left, she thought, *Maybe I've ridden on your shoulders long enough.*

★11

. . . I am sometimes still amazed how quickly a person's life can take a turn . . .

Early one morning the following week, Maire asked, "Camran, didn't you say you were planning to go over to the Eversons' sometime soon?"

"Aye, I did. Maybe tomorrow or the next day. Why?"

She took a deep breath and let it out slowly. "I want ye to go today. And take Robbie with ye."

Falon turned from where she stood at the fireplace. Maire's face had gone pale, and she had a look of intense concentration in her eyes.

He frowned. "Why the hurry? I . . ."

"Dad," Falon interrupted, "it's time."

"Time?" Understanding hit him as he looked at Maire and really saw his wife's distress. "Ah, time—I see." He started tugging on his shoes. "What about George? Take him or leave him?"

"I don't know." Maire sat down on the bed.

"Leave him here, Dad," Falon said. "He can stay close by, in the barn maybe. And if I need you I can send him."

Father hesitated. "I'm no' so sure about this. Maybe he should take Robbie and go over there, and I should stay here."

"Camran, we've already talked about this. I'll be fine." Maire stood up again. "You have business there anyway. Kill two birds with one stone. And if George goes, he'll only worry you to death. But I need you to take Robbie."

"Whatever you say, lass." Father picked up the toddler. "D'ye want me to send Mrs. Everson?"

"I'd rather you didn't—at least for now. She's a bit nervous for me. Falon and I can manage." She smiled. "I have done this before."

Falon swallowed hard. She hoped Maire's confidence in her wasn't misplaced.

When Father had gone, Falon took breakfast out to the barn and told her stepbrother what was happening. "I'll call for you if she needs you, so stay close by." She knew better than to say, "if I need you." The boy would run off for sure.

"Will Mother be all right?" His dark eyes looked larger than usual in the dim light of the barn.

Falon decided to be truthful. "She's having a baby, George. It's a hard thing, but your mother's a strong woman."

She hurried back to the house. She didn't want to leave Maire alone any longer than she had to. When she came in, her stepmother was making circuits of the little house. Around and around the room she went for the better part of an hour, pausing occasionally, rubbing her swollen belly. During one pause she said, "I'm thinking this one's a girl."

"Really? What makes ye think so?"

Maire smiled. "No reason really. I have known women who've claimed to know each time whether they were having a boy or girl. I think they were just lucky—or lying." Her smile faded and she sat on the bed. Falon heard her take a long breath between her teeth. "One thing I do know, my babies come quick, and I've been having pains since before light. This won't take long." She nodded toward the table. "The scissors and twine are right there." A long silence followed. Maire sat still, one hand on her belly. Finally she said, "I think I'll get in the bed now." She pulled her legs up. The corn-shuck mattress rustled as she shifted her ungainly weight into the middle of it.

Falon tucked the pillows behind her. "Is that comfortable?"

"Aye. Hand me one of those rags. I'm going to put it under me."

Falon helped Maire arrange herself in the bed. *I've seen lambs born, and kittens, and a litter of pups. This isn't really any different.* She did wish that her mother had allowed her to stay when Robbie was born. She might have felt better prepared for this.

Less than an hour later, Maire started pushing. Falon knotted the ends of her shawl, and passing the middle part around her waist, gave the ends to Maire to hold on to. When Maire pulled, Falon braced herself against the frame of the bed. It wasn't long before the chilly cabin felt hot, and she felt a trickle down one side of her face. *No wonder they call this 'labor.'*

In the middle of one of Maire's pains, Falon heard a scream coming from the barn.

Maire gasped. "George. Go see about him." But when Falon stood, she groaned. "Don't leave me."

"Maire . . ."

"Go!" she moaned through gritted teeth. "Go . . . see what's the matter."

"I'll be right back," Falon promised, tearing out of the house and down the path to the barn. She found Young George lying on the dirt floor, clutching his arm and crying. She rushed to him. "What happened?"

"Cow kicked me," he whimpered. "I think my arm's broken."

"Let me see." She bent over him.

"No, don't touch it! Don't touch it!"

"You'll have to get up and come into the house. I can't leave you injured out here."

"Can't go in," he panted. "Just get that hide I sleep on and cover me. I'll be warm enough with that."

"No, you get up and go to the hide. There's hay over there, and you'll be warmer than out here in the middle of the floor."

Trembling, groaning, George let Falon pull him to his feet. He stumbled to the hide and lay down. Falon covered him the best she could. "I'm going back in to your mother. I'll come see about you as soon as I'm able."

He nodded wordlessly, and she ran out of the barn and back to the house.

Maire was sitting up, her face red, the veins standing out in her neck. Moments later, she panted, "I think . . . almost there."

Falon decided to take a look. She gasped with delight. "I see your baby, Maire. Just the crown of its wee head."

Maire nodded, took a deep breath, and pushed again. Falon had the baby's head in her hands, and when it squawked, she said, "Hello to you, too!" One more push, and the baby was out and squalling. Falon caught it and held it up. "Ye were right, Maire. This is a bonny little lassie."

She handed the baby to her stepmother and got another rag from the table to clean the baby. "What's her name?"

"I'm going to call her Janet—for my sister."

Falon smiled. "Ah, she looks like a Janet."

When Maire had expelled the afterbirth, Falon cleaned her up and covered her and the baby. "If you're all right without me for a few minutes, I'll run out to the barn and see about George."

Maire went pale. "Oh, heavens, I forgot about him. Was he all right?"

"He will be. I'll be back in a few minutes." She ran toward the barn and stopped ten feet short of the door. The Indian was back, alone this time. When he gestured for her to play for him, she shook her head in refusal, and tried to show him she wasn't wearing her flute. When he didn't respond, she said helplessly, "Ye've picked a terrible time."

Her mind raced. *Lord, have mercy. What can I do? George is injured, Father's away, Maire's in bed with a new baby. I don't think the Indian means us hurt, but if I can't make him understand me, he may change his mind. What would Mr. Blaloch tell me to do?* She closed her eyes, chewing her lower lip. *He'd tell me to not show that I'm afraid.* Falon took a deep breath, made a low curtsy—it was the only gesture she could think of—and opened the barn door and slipped in.

"George," she called out. "I'm back. You have a new little sister."

The boy moaned, but he sat up on the hide. "Mother is all right?"

"They are both just fine. Come on, we've got to get you into the house and see to that arm." Again, he wouldn't let her touch him, but he managed to get to his feet. Falon gathered up the hide. "Let's go." Cradling his injured arm, whimpering with pain, he followed her out. The Indian remained, watching, but he had withdrawn toward the trees, and George didn't see him.

Falon opened the door of the house to let George in. When she looked back again, the Indian was gone. Was that a good thing, or no? Once inside, she brewed a pot of coffee and made a sling for George out of her much-used shawl. "I should leave now to go to the Eversons' and fetch Dad."

"He'll be back at dark," Maire told her. "That was what we agreed. You don't need to go after him."

"What about George's arm? I'm pretty sure it's broken." She paused as George let out a loud moan, "And I don't know how to set it. It needs to be done properly. Dad does know how." She couldn't tell them about the Indian, or her worry that he might come back with his friends. She hated not being honest with them, but she didn't need to heap worry on either one. But, she told herself, *if I leave, who'll be here for them? They'll be unprotected.* She chewed at the edge of her thumbnail.

While she was still considering, she heard a shout, "Hello the house!"

Her eyes met Maire's. "That's James," they said in unison.

Falon flung open the door, and as soon as James was in reach, she took his hand and pulled him in. "Thank the good Lord ye've come. But where's Will?"

His pale eyebrows shot up. "Well, this is quite a greeting. Your brother should be here in another hour or two. Is everything all right?"

"Perhaps not everything, but now that you're here, things are better."

His eyes took in the situation at once—Maire with her newborn in the bed, Young George hunched over the table, his face gray with pain. "What happened to you, George?"

"Cow kicked me."

"Anything broken?"

George's throat worked, as if he was trying not to cry. "My arm."

James whistled between his teeth. "A horse did that to me. Broke my wrist when I was just about your age. Let me have a look at it."

Suddenly realizing she'd had nothing to eat all day, Falon found a piece of leftover corn pone from the night before and gulped it down with coffee. James finished examining George's arm. "It needs a splint. I'm going to go out and find one."

Taking a final swallow from her cup, Falon followed him out, shutting the door behind her. "I need to tell thee something. There may be an Indian somewhere out here."

His eyes narrowed. "You saw an Indian?"

"I did, yes, but . . ."

He picked up his gun, which he had left leaning against the outside wall by the door. "Where did you see him?"

Falon swallowed. "Mr. Carson, I need you to listen to me. I don't think he means harm. He's been here several times before, and he's never done us any mischief." She took a deep breath and told him a quick version of the whole story, beginning with the river crossing, and described the Indian, down to the scar on his arm.

He regarded her for a long moment. "Miss Macvail, you are a brave and intelligent young lady, but you have to know you can't safely make friends with Indians."

Mr. Blaloch has. She held her peace and waited.

"You were fortunate today." He sighed, "And you may be right. This one may mean you no harm, but trust me, there are plenty out there who do." He looked around him. "I presume Mrs. Macvail and the boy don't know about this."

"They don't know about him being here today."

He nodded. "That's probably wise. All right. You go back in the house. I won't be long."

Falon obeyed, unsure of whether she felt better or not for having told him. *Well, if he did intend to court me, he's probably changed his mind now.* She sighed. *And perhaps that's best. I like him. But how much does a person need to like someone to marry him?* Things were happening too fast for her taste, and that was the way it had been ever since they had been burned out of Sgall. They'd been forced to make quick decisions, decisions with far-reaching consequences. *This is no' so different, though Dad did say he'd back me up, whatever I wanted to do about Mr. Carson. Ah well, this business with the Indian may have decided for me.*

She busied herself tidying the cabin—not that there was much to do. About ten minutes later, James came in, carrying a straight tree limb he had split in half down the middle. "I saw your father and brother coming up the river," he told her. "They'll be here before long. Do you have a piece of cloth I can tear up?"

"There's one clean rag left. D'ye want me to rip it for you?"

"Not yet. George, you'll need to take your shirt off. I've got to get a good feel of that arm. Miss Macvail, you twist the rag. He will want something to bite down on."

The corn pone in Falon's stomach suddenly felt like a lump of lead. She glanced at Maire, who had gone wide-eyed. "Should we perhaps do this out in the barn?"

James shook his head as he helped George shrug off his shirt. "Light's better in here."

When Falon handed him the twisted rag he said, "All right, George, I'm going to feel your arm, and it will hurt. Bite down on this." He put the rag in the boy's mouth and began to probe the arm. When he got near the break, George squealed through the rag. His eyes rolled up in the back of his head, and he passed out. "Well, there's some luck for him," James murmured. "Now he won't feel a thing." He looked over at Maire, whose face was wet with tears. "Not a terrible break, Mrs. Macvail. The bone should mend just fine once it's splinted."

Falon worked the rag out from George's mouth and began to tear it into strips, which James used to bandage the arm to the splint he made. They had just finished when the door opened, and Father and Will came in. Will carried a rabbit in one hand and gave it to Falon."I've got us dinner."

"How is everything here?" Father asked, his gaze going first to Maire, then to George, who was still passed out at the table.

"You have a new little daughter," Falon told him. "George has broken his arm, but he'll be all right."

Father went to his wife and newborn daughter, leaning over the bed to kiss Maire's forehead. "Is all well wi' thee?"

"Aye." Maire pulled back the covers to show him the baby. "Here she is. I'd like to call her Janet."

Father's voice went a little hoarse as he stroked the infant's fuzzy head with the tip of one finger. "Janet, aye. What a bonny wee thing she is."

Falon noticed James and Will having a whispered conversation in one corner. Will ended it with a shrug, giving Falon a pointed look. *Mr. Carson's told Will about the Indian.* Falon turned her back. She didn't want to look at James now, didn't want to think about him, didn't want to talk to him. *I've had enough for one day,* she told herself.

Young George moaned, lifting his head from the table. He looked around, blinking with bleary eyes. "What happened?"

"Your arm is in a sling," James said. "We got you fixed up while you were . . . asleep. How do you feel?" George just shook his head.

Now that all the day's crises had been handled, Falon decided she had better begin putting a meal together, so she got the big kettle and started down to the river. After a few steps she heard movement behind her and, looking back over her shoulder, saw that James was following her, his rifle in one hand. He made no apology for being there. As he caught up with her at the water's edge, he said only, "It gets dark early this time of year."

"It does," she agreed, leaning to scoop up the water.

He caught her arm as she started back to the house. "Wait." Falon turned toward him, though she couldn't quite bring herself to look him in the eye. She concentrated, instead, on the neat line that cleft his chin down the middle. After a pause, he said, "About today . . ."

Here it comes, she thought. *He's going to chide me for behaving like a child with that Indian.*

"About today," he repeated. When she finally looked at him, she was amazed at how nervous he seemed. His face had gone red, and a tremor shook his voice. "I appreciate how difficult things were, and I just want you to know, Miss Macvail, you handled yourself with as much courage as I've ever seen in anyone."

Dumbstruck with shock, suddenly aware that she was staring agape at him, she snapped her mouth shut, then murmured, "Why, thank you, Mr. Carson."

"Please, call me James." And before she realized what he was about, he leaned down and kissed her lightly on the lips.

Falon's heart caught in her throat, and she dropped the kettle, spilling the water. James picked it up. "That was my fault. I'll refill it for you." She waited for him, frozen in the long moment, the tips of her fingers touching her lips lightly, as if they'd been burned. "Here you are," he said, handing her the kettle and peering at her in the gathering darkness. "Are you all right?"

"I . . . I've got to get supper on." She backed away from him and hurried up the path to the house.

Warm lamplight spilled out to greet her, but though her family's faces were familiar, she had the oddest feeling she had just stepped into the company of strangers. Impatiently, she shook it off. *Don't be daft*, she scolded herself. *Nothing has changed, and you have a job to do.*

But as she cut up the rabbit Will had brought in and started a stew, it occurred to her that something had changed. *I've changed.* Her back was turned, but she knew James was in the house. He had slipped in a few seconds after her, and though he hardly said a word, she was acutely aware of him—aware when he came in, aware when he checked on George, intensely aware when he pulled Father aside. ". . . a matter I'd like to discuss . . ." was all she heard of that whispered conversation, and the two men went outside.

They were gone a long time, and, anticipating their return, Falon jumped at every little sound. "What's the matter with thee?" Young George blinked owlishly at her. "Tha' think something's going to pounce? I've never seen thee so jumpy."

Maire intervened. "George, leave Falon alone. It's been a long day for you both. Be quiet and rest."

"Anything I can help you with?" Will, heaven bless him, was at her elbow.

"Aye, would you watch the stew? Give it a good stir now and again. I'm going to make a batch of pone to go with it."

Falon had just dipped a cup into the cornmeal when Father and James came back in the house. Neither of the men looked her way; in fact, her father seemed to be making a studious effort not to look at her, which she took as a bad sign. She added some dried wild onion to the cornmeal, wet the mixture with a bit of water, and shaped the dough into cakes. Falon kept her eyes on her hands and tried to keep her mind on what she was doing. The problem was, making corn pone wasn't exactly mentally engaging work.

Somebody had better say something soon. I hope they won't drag this out, or I won't get a lick of sleep tonight. She put the cakes into the pan, then set the pan on the fire. Another thought had her smiling, in spite of her agitation. *I may not get any sleep either way.* Her mouth still tingled where James had kissed her.

In less than an hour, dinner was ready, and Falon served up the stew in bowls and cups. She took a spoonful of her own. The stew was perfect—savory and hot. But after the first bite, she hardly tasted it.

The men talked while they ate. "Beason's Crossing started as just a ferry on the Colorado," James was saying, "but I hear they're planning to plat a full-fledged town. They're already talking about how it should be laid out, with the streets and houses and shops. It'll be as modern a town as you'd find anywhere in the States."

"The States, aye," Father said, taking another pone cake from the pan, "but this is Mexico, Mr. Carson."

"It is, but I'm thinking that's going to change, and sooner rather than later."

"What makes ye think so?"

"Stephen Austin's people are all Anglo, most from the United States. If he and other empresarios continue to bring folks in from the States, I'm thinking eventually Texas will leave Mexico."

"Mexico won't let go without a fight," Will noted.

"Probably not," James agreed.

A little shiver snaked up Falon's spine. *War talk.* She got up from the table and went to check on Maire, who had fallen asleep. Baby Janet had fallen asleep, too, and was still at Maire's breast. Smiling, Falon gently disengaged the baby, who continued to make sucking motions, and covered her stepmother.

When she turned around, Will said, "I'll fetch water for thee, for the washing up." Without waiting for her thanks, he took the little kettle and went out.

Father picked up Robbie. "Come on, lad," he motioned to George. "I need thy help in the byre."

George whined, "But my arm hurts."

"Nothing wrong with your eyes, is there, or your legs? Come on, now." Heaving the sigh of a condemned man, George heaved himself out of his chair and followed Father out.

Falon shook her head. One of these days, he was going to push Father past his endurance. And then she realized she was, for all intents, alone in the cabin with James. He spoke quietly, but it sounded like thunder in her ears. "Miss Macvail, will you come sit with me?"

Without a word, she lowered herself into a chair opposite him. He smiled and got up, and taking the chair beside hers, sat down again. "It's a long, long way from Georgia to Texas," he began.

"Is it?" Falon fisted her hands in her lap to keep from chewing on her nails.

He nodded. "I came here hoping to build a life for myself. Miss Macvail, I'm not very good with words. I've met a number of young ladies on my journey here, but none for whom I feel such . . . admiration and . . . and affection. What I told you earlier, that you are brave and smart, that's all true. I am wondering if you have any thought for me at all."

Falon bit her lip. *What to say?* "Mr. Carson, I appreciate everything you've done for us—for me." There she stopped. No more words came.

He looked stricken. "Did I offend you earlier when I kissed you? Please accept my apologies."

"Oh, no." She shook her head. "I wasn't offended."

His expression relaxed. He covered her hands with his. "I intend to propose marriage to you, but before I do, you should understand what you would be getting yourself into. You know what I do for my living."

"Aye."

"Well, sometimes I will have to be gone from home for long periods of time—weeks, or even months." He cleared his throat. "That can be hard on a woman. So when I was in Beason's Crossing, I made certain . . . arrangements."

"Arrangements?"

"There is a woman there whose husband recently died, leaving her alone. She doesn't want to stay in Texas. He had built her a nice house, so I offered to buy it from her. Austin was there, and he drew up the deed himself. So you wouldn't be living out in the wild by yourself while I'm away. You would be living in a settlement, with people around you. You'll have protection."

"You . . . you bought a house?" That anyone could have that kind of money staggered her.

"And it's furnished," he added with a smile. "Does that sound agreeable to you?"

"But the poor woman—where will she go?"

Now he grinned. "She isn't poor anymore, now that I've bought her house. She's going back east to her people. You don't need to worry on her behalf."

Falon sighed. "How will we do this? How will we marry? There's no church here."

"I spoke to Austin, and he offered to officiate the ceremony for us."

Falon managed to smile, though her heart beat so hard she felt sick and weak. "It sounds like you've thought of everything."

"Then will you consider—I mean . . ." He got out of his chair and went to one knee. "That is to say, Miss Macvail, I want to marry you. I would be honored if you would accept me."

"Mr. Carson . . ."

"James."

"James," she corrected herself, "I will accept you." And this time, it was she who surprised him as she lightly touched the cleft in his chin and leaned forward to give him a kiss.

★12

. . . It felt strange to leave, especially to go away from Father and from Robbie, but the morning after James proposed and Father gave us his blessing, we set off. I got my first hint of how challenging marriage might be, while riding behind James to Beason's Crossing . . .

"There's something I need to talk to you about," he began.

"What is it?" Falon was more interested in hanging on and watching the ground pass under the horse's feet than in talking.

"It's your given name. I'm wondering if you would object to altering it a bit."

As soon as he'd said it, she realized he had never called her by her given name. It had always been 'Miss Macvail,' and now that she'd accepted him, he had taken to calling her 'sweetheart.' "What's wrong with my name?"

"Well, it's just a little . . . *foreign.*"

For the merest instant, she thought he might be joking, but his silence told her he was in earnest. "You want me to change my name?"

"Just alter it a bit," he insisted. "How about Ellen? That's close. Or Helen, maybe."

She didn't answer for awhile. *What's wrong with Falon? 'Twas my grandmother's name.* She asked, "You want me to tell people that my name is Ellen or Helen?"

"If that's all right with you."

So I won't be Falon Carson. I'll be Ellen Carson. Or Helen Carson. I'll be someone else. Numb with disbelief, she murmured, "Ellen, then." Helen sounded a little too grand. *Maybe I should be like Missus and never tell anyone my given name.*

He turned back toward her with a smile, "I'll probably just call you 'sweetheart.'"

She tried to return his smile. "Aye, I think I'd like that better."

They reached Beason's Crossing late that afternoon, found Stephen Austin—as dapper and handsome as she remembered him—and he married them. *What a strange life this is turning out to be,* Falon told herself. *No church or clergyman, no friends or family, just the two of us and a land agent! I wish Betsy were here to see this. She'd never believe it otherwise.*

After the short ceremony, Mrs. Beason fed them all dinner. When they had finished, she said, "Here's a basket of food to take with you, dearie." She pressed the handle into Falon's hands. "That way you won't have to think about cooking for the next little while."

Falon thanked her, and she and James walked to their own place. James had the horse's reins in one hand, and offered his other hand to her. "I hope you like our house." His warm fingers wrapped around hers.

Our house. Her stomach was twisted in knots. *Have I done the right thing?* "I'm sure I will."

And she did. The cabin was about the same size as the one Father had built, but with a front porch and a wooden floor inside. The floor had been recently swept, and a fire burned merrily in the hearth. "Looks like our neighbors took care of us," James remarked.

Falon set the basket down on the table. "It's very nice."

He smiled. "Welcome home, Mrs. Carson." And he shut the door.

Falon's mother had often remarked, "Camran Macvail hasn't two cents to rub together." It wasn't a complaint, Falon knew; just a statement of fact. It was also something she figured she'd never have to say about James Carson. Apparently, slave trading was a lucrative business, and her James was generous—at least to her. Their first week in Beason's Crossing, he presented her with enough fabric for not one, but two dresses, and all the undergarments—he called them 'ladies' things'—that she needed. "I picked this fabric up in Perry's Point the last time I was there," he told her, "intending to sell it here, but I'd rather give it to you." He kissed her lightly on the nose and gave her a searching, knowing look that sent a thrill shooting through her.

The pleasure of making new clothes might have been unadulterated, if only he hadn't introduced her to their neighbors as 'Ellen Carson.' For some reason, the sound of the name jangled her nerves. *But I did give him permission to call me that.*

It was the same everywhere he took her. "Mrs. Tumlison, I'd like to introduce you to my wife, Ellen Carson." It seemed as if Falon Macvail had been erased. And who was this Ellen Carson? Would she be someone Falon could understand, let alone like? *You are just going to have to get used to it,* she scolded herself. Falon did her best to be charming and agreeable to her new neighbors, but inwardly she struggled with the new identity.

With one couple, however, she felt she could be herself. On their first Sunday afternoon, James took her calling. As they neared a cabin on the edge of the settlement, he said, "This is the Garrett place. He'll probably never be a customer of mine, but they seem nice enough."

He knocked on the door, and when it swung open, Falon gasped, "Kathleen!"

"Falon!" With a wide smile, Kathleen called over her shoulder, "Daniel, come see who's come to call!" She pulled Falon into her arms. "It's so good to see you again."

Falon returned the hug. "It's good to see you, too."

James' smile was perplexed. "You two know each other?"

Kathleen laughed. "We sailed on the same ship from Scotland, and our families traveled overland here together from the coast."

When Daniel Garrett appeared at the door, he shook hands with James, nodding to Falon. "You're looking well, Miss Macvail . . . that is, Mrs. Carson."

"Well, let's not stand here on the porch. You two come in." Kathleen took Falon's hand and led her in. "We had heard, Mr. Carson, that you married and moved into the Thomas place, but I had no idea who your new wife was."

Kathleen was clearly in her element acting as hostess. With the grace of a dancer she set out cups and a plate of dried fruit and started coffee brewing on the fire. Falon asked her, "How long have you and Mr. Garrett been married?"

"We married just a few weeks after coming here," Daniel said. "I had to do some fancy talking with her father."

"You did not," Kathleen disagreed with a laugh. "Dad thinks you hung the moon."

Daniel's pock-marked face spread into a grin. "Clearly it was my good looks that won him over."

After coffee, he said to James, "I just bought a new bull. Want to see him?"

"I'd like nothing better." The two of them donned their coats and hats and went out into the chill afternoon.

"How is your family?" Kathleen asked Falon when they were alone.

"All well, except that Young George got his arm broken. My older brother married my best friend, and he's getting ready to sail home to her in Ireland. Maire's just had a baby girl. She's named her Janet."

"Ah, that's sweet." A slow flush crept up her cheeks. "I didn't want to say anything with the men here, but Dan and I are expecting our first baby late in the spring, or maybe early summer."

Falon murmured congratulations and wondered how long it would be before she would be telling someone the same thing. *And how many children will we have?* She tried to imagine what she'd look like with a belly like Maire had. "I'm sorry," she said, realizing that Kathleen had spoken, "what did you ask me?"

"If you don't mind telling—what is it like for you?—with what your James does?"

"What he does? Oh, you mean trading slaves?" Falon shifted in her chair and took another sip of coffee. "Well, he makes a good living."

"That he does," Kathleen agreed. "But does he ever . . . I mean, do you ever see them?"

Falon shook her head. "We've only been married a week. He is leaving the day after tomorrow for the coast, but I don't know whether he'll bring . . . them . . . here." Falon's new dress suddenly didn't look quite as fine to her as it had that morning when she put it on.

Before James left Falon for his frist trip away from home, he said, "I have something for you." He handed her a punched metal sieve. "If you are looking for something to occupy your time while I'm gone, you can make some more paper."

She turned the sieve in her hands. "'Tis to drain the mash?"

He chucked her under her chin. "'Tis." Then he sobered. "I'll be gone at least a fortnight, but it may be closer to a month."

Falon nodded. "I understand, James. I'll be all right. You don't have to worry."

"All right, then." He gave her a kiss. "I'll see you in a few weeks." And he was gone.

She did her best to keep busy while he was away. She kept the house, made her second dress and three batches of paper. In the evenings she played her flute, relying on the sweetness of songs from home to soothe her loneliness.

About a week after James left, a peddler came through the settlement. His name was Señor Perez, an aging Tejano. Falon hadn't met many of the Texans of Spanish descent; Austin's settlement was decidedly Anglo. Señor Perez wore a battered coat of black broadcloth finely cut; it had once been a garment of refinement and gentility. No longer. The collar and cuffs were frayed, and a miscellany of holes peppered the fabric. Falon wondered why a man who traded in so many small luxuries couldn't afford better dress. But for all that, his black beard was neatly trimmed and groomed, and the tips of his mustache carefully waxed.

She showed her paper to him. "Oh, si, Señora. Very nice paper." He took the page she offered him and held it up to the sunlight. "You say you have made this?"

"Aye, that is, yes, Mr. Perez."

He cocked his head and grinned. A row of even, white teeth lit up his deeply tanned skin. "Our English does not match, Señora." She felt her cheeks redden as he chuckled, "No matter. We understand each other, si?" Now, you might be interested in this," he pulled a leather-bound ledger from his pack. Falon turned the book over in her hands and inspected the stitching. *I wonder if I could make something like this?* Now that she had become adept at producing paper, making a book seemed like a logical next step. When she said as much to the peddler, he answered, "That book cost me sixty cents. I'll probably sell it for a dollar. Books are . . . how do you say it? They are rare. If you want to make one, Señora Carson, I'll have a look the next time I'm here—provided your husband approves, of course."

So Falon spent the next day making as many batches of paper as she could. By the time she fell into bed that night, pale golden sheets were laid out drying on every horizontal surface in the house. Daniel

Garrett supplied her with leather and glue for the book's cover, and she used leftover thread from making her dresses to stitch the pages together. It took her more than a week, but before James came home, she had put together a workable book. "It's not the prettiest thing I've ever seen," she said to the peddler when he came through again on his way south, "but I learned a few things from my mistakes, and the next one will be better."

"It's a little crude," he admitted, "but serviceable. I can offer you thirty cents for it."

She took the book from him with a smile. "This one isn't for sale."

January 20, 1823—My name is Ellen (Falon) Carson. I made this book with my own hands, and I have decided to keep a record of our life here on the Colorado River. Whether anyone will ever find my thoughts of interest is doubtful . . .

Writing in her journal was something else to help pass the time. Falon still had the bottle of ink she had bought in Perry's Point, and when she told the peddler she would buy ink from him, he promised to bring some on his next trip to Beason's.

In the end, James was gone nearly three weeks. Late one afternoon she spotted him coming up the road on his horse, a pink-faced man walking beside him, wearing a broad-brimmed straw hat. Behind them marched a half dozen dark slaves, chained together at the ankles. Falon felt her stomach drop with horrified recognition. *They've been forced to leave their homes, too.*

As they neared the house, James said something to the man who walked beside him, and this one led the chained men and women away, around the side of the house and out of sight. Never once did any of them look up, or look toward her. Heads down, eyes down, they filed by, silent except for the dull clank of their chains. *We may have been forced to leave,* Falon thought, *but, thin as it was, we still had hope. These people have none.*

Her husband strode to the door, calling out, "And here is my sweetheart, right where I left her." He gave her a resounding kiss. "Is everything all right here?"

"Everything is fine," she assured him, though her mouth had gone dry.

"Now there's a forlorn look." He tipped her chin upward with one hand. "Don't worry, sweetheart. I'll have this bunch out of here this afternoon. No one's going to hurt you."

That thought had not occurred to her. What James did—it had a face. *He sells people.* Her teeth on edge, she followed him inside the house.

"I brought you something." He took off his hat and coat, dropping them on the table. "Actually, I brought us something—a servant." When she started to shake her head, he held up one hand. "Hear me out. I didn't bring a slave. When I spoke to your father about asking for your hand, he made me promise to never force you to keep a slave." He cocked one pale eyebrow. "Difficult for a man of my profession, but I keep my promises. No, I found an indentured man and bought his bond. He'll work for us for ten years, and then he's free."

"Is he the one who took the . . . the others around back?"

"He's the one," James nodded. "It'll help me when I'm gone to know there's a man looking after the place. Word is, the Cocos are stirred up, and he'll be some protection for you."

Coco. That's what my Indian was. I wonder if he's gotten mixed up in the trouble. She shook herself as she realized that James was still talking about the man he'd brought home. "Why was he indentured?" she wondered aloud.

James shrugged. "He's Irish. His family fell on hard times. It was the only way he could buy passage on the ship coming over. His name's Patrick." James sat down and had a bite to eat before he left again. "I'm going to deliver this bunch. I should be back before dark. You take a plate out to Patrick."

By the time Falon made it out to the barn, James had already left with the slaves. She pushed open the door, relieved that she wouldn't have to face those hopeless people. "Hello?"

"Mrs. Carson?" The servant came out from the horse stall, doffing his cap. "I'm Patrick." He nodded toward the plate in her hand. "Is that for me?"

"'Tis." She kept a smile on her face as she gave it to him, but inwardly she thought, *My goodness! The poor man!* Patrick had an unfortunate face, ruddy and puffy, with close-set eyes and teeth turned every which way. She had thought Dan Garrett homely, but Dan was a handsome man compared to this one.

Patrick took one bite of the piece of roasted chicken she gave him and smiled. "Thank you, ma'am. Mr. Carson said you would have some chores for me when I was finished eating."

"Oh well, I don't know." Falon couldn't think of a thing. "You've had a long walk. Why don't you just rest until he gets back?"

Patrick wagged his round head. "Oh no, Mrs. Carson. I couldn't do that. Your husband bought my bond. I have to work it off." He smiled around a mouthful of corn pone. "I'm sure you'll find something for me to do, won't you?"

So this is the way it's going to be—me stuck between two stubborn men. Falon drew herself up. "I'll think of something, Mister . . . what did you say your surname was?"

"It's O'Donnell, ma'am, but you should call me Patrick, or Pat, if you prefer."

"All right, Patrick. Just bring your plate to the back door when you're finished."

She went back inside, sat in a chair and buried her face in her hands. "Ah, Lord, what am I going to do with a *servant?* There's just enough to do to keep me busy. I can't give him all my work. I can't sit idle. It will drive me mad."

In the end, Falon remembered that she needed more firewood. "The axe is in the barn, just inside the door," she told him when he appeared with his empty plate.

Minutes later, the distinctive thunk of axe on wood reached her ears, followed by the most beautiful baritone voice she had ever heard. She moved a curtain aside and peeked out the window. Patrick had stripped off his coat, and was working in his shirt sleeves, splitting logs and stacking them near the house. And each time he had breath, he sang a line of "Greensleeves."

"Alas, my love, you do me wrong . . ." chop, split, pick up the pieces, "to cast me off so discourteously . . ." stack the wood, get a new log to split, "for I have loved you so long . . ." chop, split, pick up the pieces, "delighting in your company . . ."

His voice rang out, deep, mellow, melancholy, each lovely note perfect, in spite of his physical exertion. Falon could hardly breathe. All on their own, her fingers twitched, moved up and down the holes of her flute—though it wasn't in her hands. After a few minutes, she pulled away from the window. *How can such a voice exist behind that face?*

March 26, 1823—I have settled into a more or less comfortable routine, even with our bondservant Patrick. He seemed ugly to me at first, and indeed he is homely, but his voice seems to temper his rough appearance. He is always singing as he goes about his work. It is a welcome sound, particularly when James is away . . .

James continued to come and go, buying and selling slaves, and the Mexican government continued to assist his illegal activities by turning a blind eye. As for Falon, she had learned not to go out to meet her husband when he came in. Seeing the results of his labor, hearing the clanking chains, disturbed her deeply, though she never said anything to him.

And he seemed to have an endless string of justifying arguments for what he did. "They aren't slaves," she heard him say, "they're indentured." Then he smiled, "Of course, the term is for ninety-nine years." Other times, he invoked the Bible, speaking of the 'Curse of Ham.' "All of Ham's descendants are the African races, and the scriptures clearly say that they will be servants for the rest of us." He even claimed he was doing the slaves a service. "They would just die in their pagan ways if we left them alone. At least here they can become productive, Christian people."

On returning from one trip, James had, not a string of slaves, but more than a dozen head of longhorn cattle. When Falon saw this, she went out to meet him. "It never hurts a man to have a second source of income," he explained with a grin.

James made an agreement with Patrick. "You told me you know cattle. I want you to take care of these animals, build up the herd. When your service to me is over, I'll give you a quarter of whatever herd we have then so that you won't leave empty-handed. You'll have something to get yourself started."

Patrick removed his cap, his eyes brimming with tears. "It's more than generous you are, Mr. Carson. I'll be building you a fine herd."

When James had dismounted and gone inside, he asked Falon, "And how is everything here?"

"Everything is fine," she answered. "Nothing has changed." This was how she had become accustomed to letting him know she still wasn't pregnant. A shadow fell across his face, and she was tempted to remind him that his being gone for weeks at a time wasn't helping. They both wanted children, but month after month, were disappointed.

May 1, 1823—I got my flute out today. It seems like I play less all the time, as I can't play when James is home. It bothers him when he's trying to work. It seems a shame to play just for myself. Music should be shared . . .

She had played a dance tune, then switched to a hymn. She played it through once, feeling her spirits lift. The second time, her fingers felt surer—until she heard singing. She faltered and stopped, but the singing went on. "Jesus, thou art all compassion. Pure unbounded love thou art. Visit us with thy salvation. Enter every trembling heart." *Patrick*. She had thought he was elsewhere.

She put the flute down and went to the door. There he was, digging a new irrigation ditch for the vegetable garden. When he saw her, he stopped and removed his cap. "Mrs. Carson. Did my singing bother you? Only your playing was so fine, I couldn't help myself."

"No," she murmured. "No, it's all right. I just didn't know you were out there."

His anxious expression softened. "'Tis lovely, your music. I hope you won't ever give it up."

Falon felt her face grow hot, but she managed to answer, "Thank you, Patrick. Your singing is wonderful, too." After that, she didn't play unless she thought he might be near, and often as not, she heard his beautiful baritone singing along. He seemed to like the hymns and ballads best, so she played those. When she played, she remained hidden away inside the house, never again acknowledging that she was aware of him or his singing. He never again mentioned her flute. But there was the music—without and within.

May 17, 1823—I am having nightmares about Annie again . . .

Falon began dreading going to sleep at night, for each time she did, each time she saw her sister's head disappear below the hungry, lapping waters of Loch Naver, she woke with tears streaming down her face and George's accusing words ringing in her ears. Then one night, the dream took a turn.

As her little sister sinks into the water, Falon looks down at her feet and sees that they are shackled. Her skin is dark, too; on her feet and her hands, she has gone the color of strong tea. And there is James. He has her by the arm and is taking her to the barn. He is going to sell her with the others. "No, James, it's me! It's Falon!"

He hardly looks her way. "Falon? I don't know anyone by that name."

"No, you can't do this! Don't do this to me!"

She gasped as James shook her. "Ellen, wake up. You're having a bad dream."

Ah, Lord, she thought, w*ill these dreams plague me forever?* She told James the part about Annie. She couldn't bring herself to tell the rest. "In the end, I couldn't save her, and I've always felt like her dying was my fault."

"Sweetheart, I have a long trip ahead of me in the morning, and I have to get some sleep. What happened wasn't your fault, and you need to put it behind you. You have a new life now."

He turned his back to her, and within minutes, his light snoring told her he was asleep.

I do have a new life now, in a new country, with a husband who is good to me. Annie is in the past. I need to leave her there. But hard as she tried, she couldn't shake the memory, couldn't rid herself of the image of the water closing over her sister's head. She glanced over at James, his outline bathed in blue moonlight streaming through the window. She ached for him to hold her. And then there was the other part of the dream. *I wonder what he'd say if he knew about that. Would he stop selling slaves if I asked?* She sighed, touching the end of one of his straw-colored locks. *He needs a haircut.* Falon stayed awake the rest of the night, certain the nightmare would come back. She dreaded the thought, and didn't want to disturb her husband again.

The next day, after James had gone, Falon walked down to the bank of the Colorado River to fill her kettle. But once her task was complete, instead of starting back toward the house, she stopped and stood staring. The slow, murky current glided by, silent as a serpent. A few decaying leaves floated on the surface, and a handful of tiny minnows darted back and forth in a pool at her feet. Falon stared until she lost track of herself. The old stories of her childhood, stories about river sprites—dangerous, malevolent spirits that enticed and drowned unsuspecting people—seemed more real to her today than they ever had. Water gathered in her eyes, blurring the water that flowed by. *Is that what happened to you, Annie? Did they see your shimmering copper curls and become jealous? Did they pull you in?* This morning she didn't doubt it.

"Mrs. Carson?"

Angered by the intrusion, Falon took a hurried swipe at her eyes. Without turning around, she answered, "Yes, Patrick?"

"Are you all right? Is there aught I can do?"

Falon hauled in a deep breath, put on a smile and turned around. "It's nothing. Just old memories. Did you need something?"

He shook his head, dropping his gaze to the tin bucket he had set down beside him. "No, Missus. I was after some mud to repair a chink in the barn." After a moment's hesitation, he added, "Only you looked that sad . . ."

"My sister drowned when I was a girl, and I couldn't save her."

Patrick had pulled off his straw hat, and now he turned it around and around in his hands, as if to remake it in another image. "Well, then. That is very sad. I am sorry for your loss."

Simple words, and he meant them. Falon turned away again, crossing her arms over her chest. She didn't reply, didn't trust herself to speak.

Patrick stepped around her and scooped three hands full of mud into the bucket. He stood to leave, but stopped. "Mrs. Carson, may I bother you with a question?"

Falon nodded once. "You may."

"Your given name—it isn't really Ellen, is it?" When she didn't reply, he added, "I thought not. Good day to you, Mrs. Carson."

Months turned into years. James and Falon went to see Father and Maire every Christmas, and the third year, the Macvails had another new baby in the house, a boy this time. Falon received annual letters from Betsy. In 1829, Betsy's letter read:

Dear Falon,

I was so happy to get your letter this summer. The paper you make is just beautiful, with the rose petals scattered in it. We are all doing well. I just had our fifth baby, a boy we have named Camran after your father. Sadly, our second-oldest took a fever and died early in the year. We miss her terribly.

Will says he's thinking about coming back to Texas for another visit. If he does, I will send another letter with him. I am keeping you and your James in my prayers, and I believe the Lord will bless you with children one day.

Mother sends you her love.
Your sister, Betsy

Meanwhile, in the larger world outside the Carson household, ominous stirrings reached them from Mexico City. Settlers and adventurers continued to pour across the border from the United States, so many that Anglos now outnumbered Mexicans about four to one. Alarmed that they might be losing their grip on yet another territory, in 1830 the Mexican government tried stricter measures. Falon found out about it one afternoon when James came in clutching an announcement in his fist. "Will you look at this? No more immigrants. Do they really think they can do that? Do they think they can stop people from coming over?"

April 22, 1830—We have been told that on the sixth of this month, Mexico passed a new law prohibiting further immigration from the United States. It probably will not last, just like most of their laws. They will turn around in a year or two and change their minds, or they will ignore the law they have made. Either way, it will be meaningless . . .

As it turned out, she was right. The new law did little to stem the tide. What it did accomplish was a strengthening of distrust and ill will from Anglo settlers toward the government to which they were supposed to be loyal. Two years later, the Texans seized a Mexican fort in Galveston bay. Shortly after that, most Mexican garrisons departed Texas and marched south into friendlier territory.

"Good riddance to them," James remarked. "Now maybe we can have some peace and quiet." Falon knew he said that for her benefit. He understood all too well that Mexico was not about to give up its northernmost territory, but like most of the men she knew, he was doing his best to protect "the little woman" from unpleasant news.

That Christmas, they loaded up the wagon and set out for Father's place. "Is it ever going to be winter this year?" Falon asked. "Look, the grass is still green."

James nodded. "This is the warmest I've ever seen it."

She sighed. It just didn't seem like Christmas. No snow on the ground, not even a light frost. It was warm enough that she couldn't even see her breath.

"I hope we get a freeze soon," James said, "or we'll be overrun with grasshoppers this summer."

Falon made a face. "And mosquitoes and chiggers." She clicked her tongue to encourage the horse. She drove, with James riding beside her, shotgun in his lap. There had been a number of Comanche raids earlier that year, most of them to the north, but James wasn't taking any chances.

They had just pulled up at the back of the barn when a shot rang out, clear and sharp in the bright afternoon. With one motion, James jumped down from the wagon and brought his rifle up. "Stay here." He started toward the corner of the barn.

"I'm coming with you," Falon retorted. When he glared at her disobedience, she said, "I'm no safer here by myself."

James peered around the corner of the barn—and lowered his gun. Falon followed him and saw Robbie, George, and her father standing over something in the bushes. George was holding his gun. *He must have shot a snake*, Falon told herself, her head swimming with relief.

Robbie, now a sturdy eleven-year-old, spotted them and came tearing over to meet them. "Falon! James! Guess what?"

"My goodness!" Falon laughed, "I think you've grown a head taller this year." She gave him a barely tolerated kiss.

"Guess what, Uncle James!" Robbie hopped up and down in his excitement.

"What, Rob?" James asked with a grin.

"George shot an Indian!" Her little brother was dancing and whooping. "Shot him dead, right over there."

Falon felt the blood drain from her face. James had gone still, and she knew he was watching her. "I guess you better show me, Robbie."

Falon didn't want to follow them. She didn't want to look. But her willful feet carried her, and somehow there she was, standing over the dead man in the grass. Blue circles adorned his cheeks. His black eyes stared, unseeing, at the tree branches overhead, as if mesmerized by their rustling and scraping in the evening breeze. A long scar that looked like lightening gleamed dully on his right arm, and a hole on the left side of his chest—a hole hardly the size of a pebble—oozed crimson onto the fallen leaves.

The hole filled her vision. *'Tis such a small hole. A tiny thing, really. One little lead ball stops a beating heart.*

"This is no place for thee, lass," her father told her. "Go on inside. We men will bury him."

Maire met her just inside the door, the newest baby—her third with Father—perched on her hip. She gave Falon a one-armed hug. "'Tis good to see thee, lass." She glanced toward Falon's midsection, and her eyes became sad, but she kept her smile steady and her tone light. "You're just in time to help me dish up dinner." Little Janet peeked out from behind her mother's skirts and gave Falon a shy, gap-toothed smile.

Falon's limbs felt heavy, as if she was trying to move through water. She started setting the table, feeling Maire's eyes on her. Finally her stepmother said, "George shot an Indian."

Falon nodded, unable to speak. Maire sighed. "So much fighting. 'Tis a shame, really. There's plenty of room for all of us. We should have peace."

Father came in a little later. "Your James and George are giving him a burial. He should have known better than to come around here. Poor rascal didn't stand a chance. Our George has become quite the shot."

Falon found her voice. "Have you had a lot of problems with Indians?"

Father peered at her in the lamplight. "We haven't, but some folks upriver have been attacked by Comanche." He shook his head. "They have to be driven out."

"Indians, you mean, or Comanche?"

"They're all the same," George announced, striding in the door with James just behind him. "Comanche, Coco, Karankawa. The only good Indian is a dead Indian." He turned toward James with a grin. "We got us a real good Indian out there."

Falon managed to get through the evening, even playing a few Christmas songs on her flute after dinner. But when she and James bedded down in the barn, she couldn't hold the tears any longer. She sank down onto a pile of hay and wept. "I can't believe George shot him. That Indian never harmed any of us. He never took anything."

"Are you really surprised by this?" her husband asked. "It was bound to happen sooner or later."

Falon wiped at her eyes. "I . . . I didn't think he'd keep coming after I was gone. I haven't lived here for six years, James."

He shrugged. "Who knows why he chose today to come around? Maybe he figured out that you're here this time every year. But I told you, didn't I, that you couldn't safely make friends with an Indian. Not safe for you, certainly not safe for him."

"It still doesn't make sense . . ."

"Ellen," he interrupted her, "it makes perfect sense. If you saw a wolf near the house, you wouldn't feed it, would you?"

"No, of course not."

"Not under any circumstances? Not even if it was starving?"

"No. I'd try to scare it away." She began to see his line of reasoning, and she hated the analogy. It was too apt.

"And why wouldn't you feed it?" When she didn't answer, he answered for her. "You wouldn't feed it because you wouldn't want it to keep coming back. The next time it came, it might want more than a little handout. Wolves are wild. They're dangerous." He sighed. "And so are Indians, it seems. You encouraged this one. Now he's dead."

She remained silent. His argument was impossible to refute, but at the same time, she wondered how she could be guilty for the taking of a man's life. Her intentions had certainly been otherwise.

As if he read her thoughts, James added, "I'm not saying you pulled the trigger, Ellen. Your stepbrother did that."

He did. Falon hadn't been able to look at George all evening. *He's always hated me. I wouldn't miss him if I never saw him or spoke to him again.* She curled up on the hay and stared into the darkness. *I wish he had died instead of the Indian.*

★13

June 12, 1835—What a hot summer this is turning out to be! I have never seen it so dry. My corn and beans are languishing. The cotton withers in the fields, and I fear the plants will die before the bolls can fully develop. Even the cattle are looking thin and bothered. James is due home any day now . . .

Falon started up to the house from the river, hauling a kettle of water. Every step was laborious in the heat. It was time to do the laundry, and she dreaded it. Even building the fire outside to heat the water seemed like too hot a job. The day was utterly still. No hint of breeze stirred in the trees overhead, and her dress clung to her skin, damp and clammy. Ever-persistent cicadas kept up a dull throb in the sultry morning.

As she came around the corner, she saw a small hay wagon tied in front of the house, its horse standing patiently, its head drooped as though exhausted. A man stood at the door, but the sun in her eyes blinded her so that she couldn't tell who it was. When he saw her, the man called out, "Mrs. Carson? Falon Carson?"

Falon frowned. Who in Beason's Crossing knew her true name, besides Dan and Kathleen? "Do I know you, sir?" Her visitor stepped out into the sunlight, revealing a head of red-blond hair and the robes of a priest. He extended his hand, "You may remember me. You stayed a night with my sister when you first landed."

"Father Vincente?" Falon took his hand and curtsied. "I never expected to see you here. What brings you to Beason's Crossing?"

His smile faded—just slightly, just enough to warn her. "Is there some place we can sit and talk?"

"I can pull a couple of chairs out onto the porch," she answered. "Would you like something to drink?"

"A bit of cool water would be welcome."

Why is he here? Did he somehow find out that I was never baptized? Even as she thought it, Falon scolded herself. *Don't be ridiculous. He wouldn't come all this way for that.* She set the chairs out and poured a cup of water for each of them. As they sat, Father Vincente pulled out a handkerchief and mopped his brow. Falon noticed then the generous sweep of gray at his temples. "How is Miss Mattie?" she asked.

The corners of his eyes crinkled. "She is well. Just as contrary as ever."

Falon smiled. "I think of her often—every time I water my roses."

"Ah," the priest chuckled. "She sent you off with cuttings, did she? I think her plan is to spread her flowers to every corner of the country."

An awkward silence fell between them. Falon took a sip of her water. "But you didn't come here to talk about roses."

"I didn't, no." He sat back in the chair and wiped his face again. "I am here on behalf of your brother."

Confused, she frowned. "Robbie?"

"No, Mrs. Carson. Your older brother, William."

Falon gasped, "Will? You're here from Will?"

"He asked me to come find you." He reached into his robe, pulling out a folded piece of cloth. "He said to give you this."

Falon took the cloth, a simple square of white linen. When she unfolded it, she found tucked inside a curling brown lock of hair, tied at each end with a length of coarse gray wool thread. "My hair," she murmured. She looked up. "Is Will all right?"

"Your brother has been hurt," the priest answered. When she exclaimed in dismay, he laid one hand on her arm. "The wound is not grievous. I am confident that he will recover. However, he wants to see you."

"Well, of course." She stood up, hardly giving a thought to the long journey, or to the fact that James was gone. "I will put some things together . . ."

"That won't be necessary, Mrs. Carson." The priest also stood. "I have brought him to you. He is in your barn."

"In the barn? Why in the world . . . ?" Falon gathered her skirts, jumped down from the porch, and ran around to the barn. "Will? Are you in here?"

"Falon," came the answer. "Over here."

She found him in a corner behind a pile of hay. His left leg was stretched out; a white bandage circled his thigh. Falon knelt and kissed him. "Will, I am so glad to see you, but what has happened?"

"There was some trouble in Perry's Point—or Anahuac, rather. They've renamed the city." He grimaced as he struggled to sit up straighter. "I didn't mean to get caught up in it."

"Let's get you into the house, and you can tell me."

Will shook his head. "Too dangerous for you. It's bad enough that I'm in your barn."

"Nonsense. You're my brother. Whatever concerns you, concerns me." She looked over her shoulder. "Father Vincente, please help me get him into the house."

They hauled Will to his feet. With one arm around the priest's neck, the other around his sister's, Will hobbled out of the barn and across the yard to the house. "Shut the door," he told her between gritted teeth once they were inside.

"You lie down on the bed," she told him as she pushed the door shut. Crossing to the table, she dipped a cup of water and handed it to him. "Now, tell me what is going on."

Will emptied the cup in one long swallow. "More?" He held the cup out to her, his expression hopeful, almost teasing.

Falon planted her hands on her hips. "William Macvail, you aren't getting any more water until you talk to me."

He sighed. "All right." He glanced once at the priest, who nodded. "I came in from Ireland two weeks ago, on a different ship this time, not the *White Arrow*. Anyway, we landed some people, and I was helping a Mr. Harris, a relative of my captain's, to pick up cargo. We planned to take on cotton, hides, and tobacco from a Mr. Briscoe. We were getting ready to load the hold, but the Mexican commander there—his name was Tenorio—he stopped us. Apparently, Mr. Briscoe had not paid the duties on his goods."

Will's throat worked as he swallowed, and when he held out his cup again, Falon took it without comment and refilled it. Will took a sip before continuing, "They fired on us—Tenorio's soldiers. The man beside me was hit in the chest. I was hit in the leg."

Falon sat on the edge of the bed and took her brother's hand. "But Will, why are you here? I am so happy to see you, but why did you come all this way when you were hurt?"

Will licked his lips, glancing at Father Vincente again. "Briscoe and Harris ordered their men to shoot back. One of Tenorio's men was hit. Looked pretty bad. I don't know whether he lived."

Father Vincente picked up the story. "A witness told Captain Tenorio that it was your brother who fired the shot that wounded his man. Tenorio arrested Briscoe and Harris, and he's looking for Will."

"I went to Father Vincente for help," Will explained, "but I couldn't stay in Anahuac. Too dangerous. If that soldier dies, and they think I did it, they'll stretch my neck. Briscoe and Harris are locked up in a brick kiln, and the Mexicans are already holding Stephen Austin under arrest down in Saltillo for something else."

"We've heard about that," Falon said. "Austin's a good man. They had no reason to arrest him. Will, do you really think they'd hang you?"

His gray eyes went hard as stone. "I have no doubt at all."

"I would have kept Will in the mission with me," Father Vincente interjected, "but he refused sanctuary."

"I'm not about to put your orphans in harm's way," Will told him. The two men stared at each other until Father Vincente lowered his eyes. Falon guessed they had argued about this at length.

She sighed. "So you're here. Does Dad know?"

Will shook his head. "I didn't stop there for the same reason I didn't want to stay in the mission. Dad and Maire have all those little ones . . ." His voice trailed off. "I'm sorry, lass. I didn't mean it that way."

"But Dad should know you're here."

"No, Falon. The fewer people who know, the better."

"Will." It was all she had to say.

"All right. If I can, I'll go see him just before I leave."

A nagging pain began pulsing in Falon's forehead. She stood up. "I have to open the door, or we'll suffocate. And Will, you will stay here in the house. I will not have you crouching out in the barn like a . . ." *Like a slave?* ". . . like an animal." She chocked the door open with her flatiron. "I suspect you'd both like something more than water." She unwrapped a loaf on the table. "I have some real wheat bread here, and cold beef left from last night."

"Just a quick meal for me," Father Vincente told her. "I have to get back before I am missed."

"Does this Tenorio suspect you?" Falon sliced the bread onto a plate.

"Probably not yet," the priest answered. "But if I tarry, he'll think I've had something to do with Will's disappearance. I'm going to head down to Goliad. I have a friend there who's been wanting me to come and perform a wedding. It's a short trip to Victoria from there, and I can catch a ship back to Anahuac. If Tenorio asks, I can in good conscience say that I was away doing a wedding." He refilled his water cup. "Actually, I think all this intrigue may be for nothing. The incident may well have blown over by the time I get back. As for your brother, he should stay put for a couple of months, and then take the same road south. He'll have no problem catching a ship out of Texas in Victoria, and once he's away, Tenorio will forget about him."

The priest left after eating, but before he drove off, he pulled a packet from his wagon. "Mattie told me to give you this for your brother. It's a poultice for his leg, to keep the inflammation down."

Falon accepted the brown-wrapped packet from him. "Wait just a minute. I have something for her." She hurried into the house and came out holding a leather-bound book. "Please give this to your sister with my thanks and tell her I remember her fondly."

He opened the cover. "A journal. Well, this is a handsome gift. Are you sure you can spare it? Books like these are costly."

Falon smiled. "I made that." She dipped into the pocket of her apron and handed him a small pouch of coins. "And this is for you—that is, for your orphans."

"Ah now. This is very generous, Mrs. Carson." He peered into the bag. "May the Lord bless you richly for this gift." He said a final goodbye and drove away.

Falon went back in and unwrapped Mattie's packet. Inside was a generous helping of dried herbs. "Goodness!" she exclaimed. "This stuff stinks!" She turned to Will with a grin. "It must be powerful."

"At least I don't have to drink it," he murmured. He was lying on his back with one arm flung over his face.

Falon swatted at a fly buzzing in a lazy orbit around her head. "I'll have to build a fire to heat these herbs. How are Betsy and the children?" No answer came from the bed. "Will?" She went to check on him, and found him snoring lightly. "Worn out, then." She sat on the edge of the bed to have a closer look at him. His black hair was now salted with gray all through, and years of sun and sea had weathered and lined his skin. "We're not getting any younger, laddie," she murmured.

To Falon's dismay, Señor Perez came by the house less than an hour after Father Vincente left. "Do you have paper for me, Señora, or perhaps a book?" the peddler asked.

Was that a flash of suspicion Falon saw in his eyes, or was she imagining things? She had given her only book to the priest. Did Señor Perez know? Had he seen the priest here? Did he have ties to this Tenorio? "Not this time," she answered, trying all the while not to glance over her shoulder toward the house where her brother slept.

"Then, can I interest you in this calico?" He pulled a bolt of blue cloth from his wagon. "Very beautiful, yes? This color is good. Very pretty. You will like it."

Falon's throat had gone dry. She coughed and said, "I am sorry, Señor Perez. I can't buy anything today." She backed away from him. "Please, another time."

With a puzzled smile, he nodded, "Another time, then, Señora." He led his horse away, and Falon watched until he was out of sight before she ducked back into the cabin. She dipped her handkerchief into the water bucket and wiped her face. *What will I do if he comes back? Oh, James, please hurry home! I can't do this by myself.*

James came home the following day. He had only two slaves with him this time, a woman and a young boy, neither of them chained. The absence of irons on their legs meant nothing, Falon had learned. The growing network of trackers and hunters made escape difficult, and the presence of Indians, particularly to the north, made it dangerous. The one thing that never changed over the years was the hopelessness in their eyes. Falon tried not to look, she tried not to see it, but somehow it never missed her.

James waved to her before taking the pair to the barn. She waited for him at the door, and he greeted her as he came back around the corner. "Good afternoon, sweetheart."

She stepped down to give him his kiss. "Good afternoon, James. Did you have a good trip?"

He removed his horse's bridle. "Good enough. I brought you a surprise." He opened his saddle bag and pulled out two books. "A Bible, and a book of poetry," he announced.

"Books!" She accepted them as carefully as she might have taken a newborn. "What a lovely Bible, and oh . . . you got me Bobbie Burns!"

"Bobbie Burns?" He gave her a puzzled smile. "You mean Robert Burns?"

"This book, 'tis all Bobbie Burns' work?"

He grinned. "'Tis. I wasn't aware that you were familiar with his poetry."

"How could I not be?" she laughed. "He's Scotland's son. I've heard him quoted all my life. My grandfather used to brag that he met the man." She stared off into the trees, but it was hills and loch she was seeing. "I think he counted it the proudest moment of his life."

"Well then, I am glad I chose the right poet for you." James chucked her under her chin and started inside.

"James, wait." She caught his arm. "Will is here."

"Will? Your brother Will?"

She nodded. "He got mixed up in some trouble down on the coast . . ."

"Anahuac." He grimaced, shaking his head. "I heard about that. He got mixed up in it? How?"

Falon sighed. "Best he tells you himself." With a grunt, James turned and went in. Falon remained in the yard awhile, running her hands over the leather covers of her new books. Of all the little gifts James had brought her over the years, these would be her greatest treasure, she knew. She opened the book of poems, and a line caught her eye. "The best laid schemes o' Mice an' Men, Gang aft agley." She closed the book, thinking about Will's troubles, thinking how often her own plans had gone awry. *And intentions don't count, do they? The best of intentions don't make it better.* Slowly, she started toward the house.

That evening, after they had eaten, Falon asked, "Should I take a plate of food out to the barn, or are you planning to deliver the slaves tonight?"

James didn't answer right away. He toyed with his cup a moment. "I've been meaning to talk to you about them." He glanced at Will, then back at his cup. "I bought the woman and her son from Harrison down the river, and I intend to keep them." He raised his eyes to meet hers.

His stare was a challenge, but Falon knew better than to argue with him in front of her brother. She raised her chin. "I'll take a plate of food out." When a light of triumph glimmered in his eyes, she quenched it by adding, "You and I will discuss this later."

The woman and her son were sitting in the same corner where Will had lain earlier. Falon held out the plate and a cup. "Here is some dinner for you." When the woman took it without comment, she asked, "What is your name?"

"My name is Maggie, missus. My boy here is Eli." The woman looked young, probably younger than Falon herself. Her child appeared to be about ten, the same age as Kathleen and Dan's oldest boy.

"All right, Maggie. I don't think you two are going anywhere tonight. There's a hide rolled up in that stall, and you can spread it out on this pile of hay to sleep. It's so warm, you won't need a blanket. There's a bucket on a nail over there, and you passed the well on the way in. If you need more water, you can draw it."

The slave woman nodded. "Yes, missus."

Falon sighed. "Is there anything else you need?"

"No, missus."

"All right then, good night." Falon was fuming by the time she reached her door. *I could strangle the man, truly I could. Those books weren't a gift. They were a lump of sugar to make a bitter pill easier to swallow. Well, books or no books, I'm not giving in without a fight.*

The only problem was, she couldn't fight him with Will sitting there. Her parents had always kept their arguments "within the walls," as her father used to say. She wasn't about to expose the conflict to an outsider, even if he was her brother. So she bided her time.

"I couldn't say whether the duties Mexico expects Texas merchants to pay is unfair or not," Will said later, as they spoke of the growing unrest between Texas and the government in Mexico City, "but it does seem to me that shooting people isn't the best way to collect it."

That reminds me, Falon thought, *I need to check the poultice on his leg.* "Let me have a look at that wound, Will." She unwrapped the bandage. The wound was still seeping, but it ran clear, and the area around it didn't appear to be inflamed. "Looks clean," she announced, wrapping it up again. Later that evening as she put away the dishes, she noticed that the pungent, astringent odor of the herbs had transferred to her hands. She tried to get rid of it with a vigorous scrubbing and lye soap, but afterward, she sniffed at her hands and wrinkled her nose. The odor lingered. *I guess it'll just have to wear off. In the meantime, I smell like an apothecary.*

Not a wonderful way to welcome her husband home, but that night he didn't even reach for her. *He must be exhausted,* she told herself. *Either that, or he's reluctant, with Will in the house with us.* James' back turned to her seemed to add to the night's swelter. She stared at the broad-beamed ceiling for what seemed hours, breathing the warm, soupy air, breathing in and out.

"James." Falon had to trot to keep up with her husband. "We need to talk about the woman you brought in yesterday."

It was the next morning, and James was on his way down to the ferry, saying he had to meet with one of his slave buyers on the other side. He could move quickly when he wanted to, and apparently he wanted to now. "James!" she called out. "Stop and talk to me!"

With a heavy sigh, he halted and turned, hands on his hips. "Ellen, I am in a hurry. What is there to talk about?"

"You know good and well." Her face flushed from anger and exertion. "You promised when we married that you wouldn't force me to accept a slave in my house. I didn't want to keep slaves then, and I don't want to now."

"Are you sure?" He took off his hat, swatting at a circling wasp. "Do you have any idea how much work it will save you to have some help?"

"I don't want to keep slaves," she repeated stubbornly.

"I understand that. No, truly I do," he insisted when she gave him a glare. "But I need you to understand—you can't possibly keep up with the crops and the housework and the garden by yourself."

I have till now. She wanted to say it—oh, how she wanted to!—but it wasn't true. Patrick bore the biggest part of the farm work when James was gone, and now that Patrick had finished serving his bond, he was a free man. He had built himself a little cabin just upriver and was busy seeing after his cattle.

"Maggie can help you with the heavier chores," her husband was saying, "and the boy is a good worker. He can manage most of the field work." When she started to protest again, he said, "You know, it's hard to sell two family members to one buyer. If I sell Maggie and her son, they'll almost certainly be separated. You wouldn't want that, would you, for that mother to go to one place and her boy to another? If they stay here, they'll at least be together."

After one stunned moment, Falon realized she was gaping at him like a landed fish. She closed her mouth. But James had one more bullet in his arsenal. "If we had children, they could help out, but as it is, sweetheart . . ." He shrugged, as if to say, what else can we do? "I have to get going. I'll be back in a few hours." He left her standing on a ridge overlooking the river.

She started back to the house in a daze. *How did this happen? How did I let this happen? And what can I do about it?* She took a deep breath, but the still, warm dampness didn't get all the way down to the bottom of her lungs. She still felt starved for air. Something will come to me, she promised herself. *Right now I have Will to think about.*

She would have been dismayed, if she had stopped to think about it, at the ease over the next few days at which she adjusted to having Maggie and Eli. The weeds were chopped, the dishes washed, the laundry done, the garden watered—all this leaving her with more time to spend with her brother.

I'll think of something later, Falon kept telling herself. *Only now, I want to be with Will. This is probably the last time I will ever see him.*

"George spilled the beans about Annie," she remarked the day before he planned to leave. "He told me she drowned." She sat down at the table and started shelling a lapful of peas.

Will rubbed at the scruff on his chin. He preferred to be clean-shaven, but had decided a beard might be a good idea to disguise himself. "Let me guess," he growled. "George used what he knew to shame you."

Falon's face went hot. "He did, yes, but it doesn't matter now. At least I know what happened, and it explains so much."

"Like what?"

She snapped the end of a pod, and inserting her thumbnail, split open the seam and dropped the peas into the bowl. "Well, like the way Mother was. The last couple of years she lived, she seemed angry all the time."

Will stood and hobbled from the bed, where he had been sitting, to the table. He pulled out a chair and dropped into it. "Do you remember what she was like—before?"

"Only just," Falon answered. Still considering Will's question, she popped a pea into her mouth. The green, earthy taste pleased her. "Mother had a beautiful smile, and she was always singing, humming little tunes under her breath. After Annie died, she stopped."

Will nodded, rolled a pea between his thumb and forefinger. "She never got over it. I remember somebody—at Annie's funeral, I think—saying that time would heal all wounds. But it didn't. Mother's wounds festered. The grieving poisoned her."

A sudden thickness closed Falon's throat. "And we weren't enough, were we?" *Where did these tears come from, after all this time?*

"We weren't enough?" Will sighed and shook his head. "I hadn't thought of it that way, but I guess you're right. With Annie gone, nothing we did or said could ever make her happy again."

At that moment, a loud banging shook the door frame. Will quickly limped over to the bed, lay down on the floor, and scooted beneath it. Falon waited until he was hidden, then started for the door, just as she heard a voice call out, "Falon, open up. It's me, George."

"Speak of the devil!" Falon muttered.

"Did you tell them I was here?" Will hissed at her.

"No," she whispered, shaking her head for emphasis, "but I still think Dad should know." She pulled the door open. "Hello, George," she said as he pushed past her into the house, "what brings you here?"

"Where is your husband?" he demanded by way of greeting, looking around him with a scowl. "Where is James?"

She folded her arms across her chest. "He's in a meeting over at the tavern. Why?"

"Word gets around, you know, Mrs. Carson." He narrowed his glare at her.

Confused, she shook her head. "Word gets around?"

"You don't play the innocent so well that I can't see through you," he declared. "I have heard—from more than one person—that there's been a strange man hanging around here while James was gone."

She bit her lip till it nearly bled so that she wouldn't laugh in his face. "And you believe this?"

George smirked, his eyes cold and hard. "Do I have a reason not to?"

Will interrupted in a loud voice. "That is enough, George." He crawled out from under the bed.

George's smirk faded to a look of stunned disbelief. "Will? What are you doing here?"

"Listening to you insult my sister." Will stood and charged at George with astounding speed, considering his injured leg. He grabbed the other man by the collar and shook him like a dog worrying a bone. "If you weren't my stepbrother, I'd beat you senseless," he rasped.

George, a full head shorter than Will, and far less muscular, whined. "I . . . I didn't say anything . . ."

"You said enough." Will gave him another shake. "Now apologize." When George hesitated, Will shook him again. "Do it! Or, by heaven, I'll . . ."

"Sorry!" George shouted in desperation, his face florid. "Sorry, Falon. I didn't mean anything by it."

Of course you did. But aloud she said, "I forgive you, George. Now go home."

But when Will released him and stepped back, George asked, "What are you doing here? And why doesn't your dad know you're here?" He paused, then pointed to Will's bandage. "What happened to your leg?"

"I got hurt, George. And Dad doesn't know I'm here yet because I don't want him to know." Will's voice quieted. "I have my reasons."

George's foolishness didn't make him stupid. After a few seconds, his eyes widened. "You're in some kind of trouble with the authorities, aren't you? Are the Mexicans after you?"

When Will didn't answer right away, he grinned. "How about that? My stepbrother, a fugitive!"

"George, go home," Falon repeated.

"Oh," he laughed, "I will. You bet I will. Wait till they hear this! Will Macvail, in trouble with the law. Not so high and mighty now, are you?" He backed out the door, still laughing, tripped on the porch step and landed hard on the path. Falon thought the wind would have been knocked out of him, but he didn't seem to feel the fall. "Always thinking you were better than the rest of us," George muttered, standing up and brushing himself off. "Well, we'll see about that." He turned and trotted off down the path.

The look Will gave Falon was bemused, quizzical. "What was that about?"

Falon shook her head. "I have no idea. George is a little . . . odd, unbalanced." She laid a hand on her brother's arm. "I don't doubt that he'll tattle. You're going to have to get away from here, sooner rather than later."

Will's voice was heavy with regret. "This means I won't be able to see Dad before I go."

James was home within the hour, and when they had told him what happened, he said, "We have to get you down to Victoria right away. Ellen, pack us some food. We still have several hours of daylight left. Will, can you ride?"

So Falon's goodbye to her brother had to be quick. "Here's a note I wrote for Betsy yesterday." She pressed the folded square into his hand. "And here's the lock of hair I gave you."

Will took the handkerchief and the note and tucked them into his pocket before embracing her. "Give Dad my love, will you? And explain why . . ."

"Don't worry, Will." She pressed her face briefly against his shoulder. "He'll understand." She stepped back with an awkward smile. "Though I'll probably have to keep him from killing George when he hears why you had to leave."

"If he wants to kill George, he'll have to get in line," James muttered, handing the reins of one of his horses to Will.

The two men mounted, and with a backward wave, Will rode away. Heartsick, Falon turned back toward the house just in time to see Maggie emerge from the cornfield with a basket on her arm. Falon stopped in her tracks, watching the slave woman's silhouette. *Why didn't I see it sooner?* she wondered.

Even from a distance, it was obvious that Maggie was pregnant.

★14

November 5, 1835—Maggie had her baby last night, a little boy she calls Jack. He's a beautiful child, and they both came through the birth just fine . . .

It was nearly two weeks after the birth that Falon, sweeping the last bit of dirt out of the house, paused to look down the street. Still no sign of James, or any of the other men. *What in the world can be taking them so long?* Twelve years she had lived in Beason's Crossing on the Colorado River, and only now was real change coming. The men were all in a meeting to decide the town's new name, and to give approval to the platted layout, which would determine where the streets, houses and shops would be situated. *They've been talking about this for months. It shouldn't take so long to vote and be done with it.*

She paused at her front door. Coming toward her was a familiar redhead, with two russet-haired boys in her wake. *Kathleen. Looks like that baby's due any minute.* Falon felt a twinge of envious pain, but quickly put it behind her as she returned Kathleen's greeting. "Do you have time to come in?"

"Of course." Kathleen gathered her skirt to climb the step up onto the porch. "It'd be a sad, sad day when I didn't have time to visit with you."

"Well, Kathleen Garrett, how courtly you are," Falon said with a laugh. "Good afternoon, boys. Come on in. I have some roasted pecans, and there's tea."

Kathleen sighed. "That sounds wonderful. I'll just be happy to be off my feet for a bit."

"So the men are still at it?" Falon took the kettle off the fire and set cups on the table.

Kathleen rolled her eyes. "You'd think they were deciding the fate of the world."

"Well, it is the fate of this little corner of it."

"True." Kathleen nibbled at a pecan. "But if we women had been invited, we would have been home by dinnertime."

Falon smiled. "Then they'd have no more to argue about, and they'd all have to go back to work. Where's the fun in that?"

Kathleen laughed. "Exactly, so they argue on."

"Is your Dan still planning to go to San Antonio?"

She nodded. "But he wants to stay until the baby's here. I'm hoping things will have calmed down by then."

Better cross your legs. It's going to be a while before things calm down. Falon bit her lip. She wondered how much Dan Garrett had told his wife. The situation with Mexico seemed to worsen by the day, and James had said he figured the Mexican generalissimo and president, Santa Anna, would be arriving with his troops in the spring. "I don't expect them before March," he told her, "and I doubt they'll get this far, but it's possible."

"How much longer do you think you have?" she asked Kathleen.

The other woman rubbed her belly. "Probably no more than a week. Mother is supposed to be here in two or three days."

They chatted about small things for awhile. Then Kathleen asked, "Do you have any paper you can spare?"

Falon stood up. "Of course. How much do you need?"

"Only a sheet or two. I'd like for Dan to be able to write while he's away."

Falon knew several of the men planned to leave for San Antonio and other garrisons. "I'd probably better make a couple of batches," she murmured.

Kathleen went silent, and when Falon turned around, she had ducked her head and was taking a swipe at her eyes. Falon glanced at the boys. Fortunately, they were absorbed in conversation and hadn't noticed their mother's distress. *So she does know.* Pulling two sheets of freshly made paper from a shelf, she brought them to the table. "You know where to find me if you need more."

Kathleen looked up and nodded. Falon knew she understood the unspoken offer. This was about far more than paper. As they were leaving after their visit, she added, "Call for me if you need help with the baby."

Kathleen smiled. "You know I will."

Falon closed the door behind them and leaned against it, surveying the contents of her little house. Everything she could ever want to make a comfortable home was there, except for the one thing she and James hadn't been able to furnish. Twelve years had come and gone, and Falon was finally accepting that there would probably never be children for them.

"I'm happy for Kathleen," she murmured to the empty room, mildly surprised to realize it was true.

November 18, 1835—The men came out of their long meeting today with a shout. When James came home, he told me they decided to rename Beason's Crossing and call it 'Columbus.' The plat for the town is drawn. 'Columbus' is not James' favorite. He has been hoping for 'Colorado City,'

but I think that is a little too grand. We are still a raw settlement with a tavern, a mill, and houses. It is hardly a city . . .

"Have you decided whether you're leaving next week?" she asked him over dinner.

"I think I will, but I won't stay long. I have no desire to hole up in the Bexar fortress once we've taken it back from General Cos. However, I do think it's a good idea to accompany them, find out whatever I can about further threats to this area from Mexico."

This is Mexico. Falon pressed her lips together to keep the words in. She didn't want to rile her husband.

"I won't be gone much more than a fortnight, if I can help it," he added. "I can take you and Maggie over to your father's first, if you want."

She shook her head. "We'll be staying. Kathleen's baby is due any day, and she may need my help."

James offered her an indulgent smile. "That's fine, sweetheart. After all this time, I have little doubt you can take care of yourself in just about any circumstance."

She returned the smile. "Thank you, Mr. Carson." But she hoped sometime between now and then James would change his mind about going. Something about this military venture left her feeling cold inside.

But he didn't change his mind, and the day before he was set to leave, a knock came at the door. Falon opened it to find her stepbrother standing on the porch. "George! What are you doing here? Is everything all right with Father and Maire?"

He colored, giving her a sidelong smile. "It's nice to see you, too, Falon. Everything's fine at home. I'm on my way to Bexar. I heard James was going, so I thought maybe we could travel together."

He didn't say a word about Will's visit, or if he had ever told anyone that Will had been hiding in her house. Falon figured, in the end, he was too big a coward, knowing he'd have to answer to her father for anything that happened to his oldest son. But if George was a coward with men, he certainly didn't mind throwing his weight around with her, and neither James nor Will was here now to defend her. She would have to be courteous, to tread with caution. She invited George in and poured him a cup of coffee. "James isn't going there to fight, George."

The young man shrugged. "Doesn't matter. There are enough of us already to drive the Mexicans out of there. We drove them out of Goliad with fewer than this."

"We?" Falon pretended ignorance. "I didn't know you went on that campaign."

His face went florid. "I would have, if . . . Well, never mind that. Can't expect a woman to understand."

Having gotten her barb in, Falon now refused to take offense. "But you're going to the Alamo. You must be excited."

Her calm, unruffled demeanor caused George to relax. He sat back in his chair. "Of course," he grinned, "It's San Antonio. I've never gotten to go there, and I want to see it. I'm ready for a change."

"Ah, I see." Rooting about for something else to say, she added, "I hear the Alamo was a church at first."

George nodded. "The Spanish did that a lot, built churches with forts around them to protect the priests from the Indians."

"So, is the place defensible—I mean, of course, if it comes to that?"

She was asking the right questions. George loved to pass on information he'd gotten elsewhere, as if he knew all about it. He stared off into space, as though considering, then nodded. "I'd say so. That's where the artillery is—the big guns. Old Santa Anna doesn't stand a chance if he decides to attack."

A Mexican force is already entrenched there, the Texians have besieged it since October, and you think you'll take it so easily? Those big guns can be used by anyone. Falon itched to say as much, but instead she noted, "I bet you had to tie Robbie down to keep him from coming with you."

George laughed. "He wasn't happy, that's for sure. But this isn't a campaign for boys."

Two weeks before, a big, nasty river rat had gotten into Falon's house; she found him chewing his way through a basket of corn. It had taken several minutes—and she had been disgusted by the look and the smell of the animal—but she had driven it out with a broom. It had been frightening, but she stood it better than now having to endure the company of her stepbrother. *I got rid of that rat. I can do this.* Determined to make his time in her house go as smoothly as possible, and then be rid of him, she murmured agreeably, "No, this is something you men will have to take care of."

What a relief it was when James walked in the door! Falon gave him a hearty kiss—for George's benefit—and excused herself, saying, "I should go over and check on Kathleen." Once outside, she took a long, deep breath of fresh air. Her lungs felt starved for it. George's accusations from his previous visit still stung, even though she was innocent. *I only have to abide him for one night*, she told herself, *and then he'll be gone.*

She started down the street and heard someone call, "Mrs. Carson!" She turned and saw Patrick trotting toward her.

"Good afternoon, Mr. O'Donnell. I haven't seen you in a while. Is anything amiss?"

"Oh, no, ma'am," he assured her. "I've been culling the herd. Getting ready to drive them down to the coast."

Falon frowned and gathered her cloak around her. "You're going now? The weather's already turning."

"'Tis cold, all right." He looked all around him, as if afraid someone might overhear. "But if we have trouble with Mexico, I want most of my cattle converted to coin, if you know what I mean."

She nodded. "I understand. Was there something you wanted?"

"Your barn and your silence. It has to do with Joe Everson."

Years before, the Eversons had moved from their Brazos homestead into Beason's Crossing after losing their entire herd of cattle to Indians. They had acquired a new herd, which their slave, Joe, looked after. He and Patrick had struck up a friendship. Now it was Falon who looked around. She couldn't help herself. "What are you up to, Patrick?"

"Walk with me." They started up the street together, and Patrick told her the rest, his voice low and urgent. "This is probably his best chance to get away, to get free. If I can get him down to Mexico, he'll be all right. He's going with me on the drive, acting as my servant. We plan to leave just after the men go to Bexar. They'll head west, and we'll be on our way south. Mr. Everson is going with the others, so it's perfect timing. He won't even know Joe's gone until he's across the border."

Falon chewed the edge of her thumbnail. "This is a very bad idea. You know what'll happen to you—and to him—if you're caught?"

"It's worth it to me." He wiped his broad, lumpy forehead with a handkerchief.

"All right. Let's say for the moment that I'm willing to help you." She held up one hand, "Not that I am, you understand. What do you want me to do?"

"Let him sleep in your barn tonight."

"Our barn?" Falon spluttered, dumfounded. "*Our barn?* Have you lost your mind?"

"'Tis possible," he admitted, "but I'm thinking, considering that Mr. Carson is a slave trader, no one will bother looking for Joe in your barn—if they go looking at all."

She could still see Joe yanking Robbie out of harm's way, grabbing his arm and slinging the child behind him all those years ago, the dark flash of the serpent as it struck thin air where her brother had been. She remembered Father's words. *This family owes you a debt we can never repay.* "All right, he can stay. One night only," she told Patrick. "I never want this mentioned again. And it goes without saying that if you are caught . . ."

"You knew nothing about it. I understand. It's on my head."

It's a good thing James built that little cabin for Maggie. How would I ever explain this to her?

November 19, 1835—I am concerned that Kathleen's mother has still not come. There must be some way to find out if Mrs. O'Connor is all right, and if she is on her way, but I can think of no one to send. The men are leaving in the morning. I might persuade Patrick to go, but that would be nearly a day's journey for him—in the wrong direction . . .

Kathleen seemed to understand Falon's dilemma. "There's no one to send. I told Dan to go on with the others. I'd feel better about him leaving if he's with a group. I'll be all right, but it may be you who has to help me when this baby comes."

"I am here for you," Falon assured her. "Just send one of your boys to get me."

Nothing would stop the men from leaving, neither impending babies nor bad weather. The next morning dawned cold and raw, a chilly drizzle glazing both the men and the horses as they pulled out of town and headed west down the old presidio road. "See you soon, sweetheart," James called out.

George waved goodbye, but said nothing. Falon stood under the shelter of the eave of her house and watched him ride off. *I can't say I'm sorry to see the back of him. One night with our George is about all I can stomach.*

And was Patrick gone? She doubted it. Driving a herd of cattle was not quiet business. She surely would have heard something. When the men had been gone the better part of an hour, she went out to the barn. "Patrick?" she called softly after she closed the door behind her. "Joe? Are you in here?" No sound answered. The barn was utterly quiet. And cold. Goosebumps teased the hairs on her arms. She pulled at her shawl, but it defied her hands and nearly fell to the dirt floor twice, as if to escape her grasp. Falon felt the silent stare of countless eyes, now long absent. How many men and women had

James brought in to spend a few hours or a night before they were sold? Dozens, maybe hundreds. She had never come out to see them. Did they cry, those black-eyed people? Or were they beyond tears by the time they got here?

She shuddered, whispering, "I'm sorry." The empty air was no fuller for her regret. "Lord, I hope Joe makes it. I hope he gets free. No one deserves this. Maggie and her children don't deserve it. I have to figure out a way we can make it without her."

By the time Falon left the barn, the drizzle had stopped. Feeling at loose ends, she wandered a wide circle around her house, stopping on the east side to inspect the two rosebushes planted there, offspring from the plant cuttings she'd nurtured all the way from the coast. The shrubs had done well, both those at Father's house and the newer ones here. They bloomed like crazy in the spring, and the red one bloomed in the fall as well. *They were naught but sticks. They should have died on the way, but here they are.*

She went inside and poured herself a cup of tea. *I could make more paper,* she thought as she sipped at the steaming liquid. She had distributed what she had to the men that morning. *I wonder how many of them will even use it?* A rueful smiled tugged at the corners of her mouth. *It's none of your business, Falon Carson, whether anyone uses your precious paper or not.* As Father sometimes said, "When tha' gives something away, don't be calling it back."

Late that afternoon, she heard a youthful shout, "Mrs. Carson, Mrs. Carson!" She pulled back her curtain. It was Sam Garrett. She opened the door for him. "Mama sent me. She needs you. The baby's coming!"

"All right, Sam." Falon pulled on her cloak then picked up a basket she had prepared. "Maggie, I'm going to tend to Mrs. Garrett. I'll probably be back before dinner tomorrow."

Maggie, who was nursing little Jack, nodded. "I'll take care of things, missus."

"I'm ready, Sam. Let's go." They reached the house just before sunset, and Falon sent the two boys to a neighbor's to wait.

The birth was easy enough. Baby Caroline entered the world about an hour after Falon arrived. "She's a little beauty," Falon crooned as she bundled her into her mother's arms. "She takes after her mother."

Kathleen laughed weakly. "Ah now, you have a gift for blarney. Are you sure you're not Irish after all?"

Falon put her hands on her hips. "I'll have you know, Kathleen Garrett, I'm as good a Scot as ever there was."

"That you are," Kathleen smiled, "and as good a friend."

Falon's face flushed hot. She wiped off her hands and perched on the edge of the bed. "You know, there was a time when I didn't think you and I ever could be friends."

Kathleen nodded. "I thought as much. Can you tell me why? Was it because my family was Irish?"

With a deep sigh, Falon answered, "Not that you were Irish, but that you were Catholic. My mother would never have approved, and when we started the voyage here, I was already in trouble with her." She paused. "Then there was the salt pork."

Kathleen's brows met in a puzzled frown. "Salt pork?"

"On the ship, remember? Your family had a bit of salt pork, and my dad bought some from you to feed me when I was recovering from the fever." When Kathleen closed her eyes, Falon asked, "What is it?"

"Your dad didn't buy that meat from us." Kathleen reached out for her hand. "Actually, I cut off a bit when my parents weren't looking and gave it to him."

Falon felt like the breath had been knocked from her. "You stole meat from your own family to give to a stranger?"

"'Twas a good investment," Kathleen smiled. "I lost a bit of meat and gained a friend." Then she sobered. "You thought your dad was forced to buy it from us. No wonder you didn't want to have anything to do with me."

"Oh, goodness, what a mess," Falon murmured. "If I'd had my way then, I'd never have spoken to you again."

"Yet here you are." Kathleen cocked her head. "God has His ways. He meant for us to be friends."

"Maybe." Falon examined Kathleen's hand in hers, noting the ragged cuticles and the calluses that marked her otherwise delicate fingers. "I'm not so sure God had much to do with it."

"What do you mean?"

"Well, we were forced to leave Scotland, and my mother died." She looked up. "You lost family, too—your grandfather and your sister. Did God do that?"

Kathleen sighed. "Granddad said something just before he passed that I've never forgotten. He knew he was dying." A tremor in Kathleen's voice made her pause, and Falon felt tears gathering. "Lizzie had just died, and he said, 'We're quick to blame God when things are hard, but how often do we credit Him when things go right?'" She looked up, green eyes swimming with tears. "Granddad trusted Him." When Falon didn't answer, she added, "Life is hard, and that's sure, but look where we are now. This is a good place, better than the one we left."

"In many ways it is," Falon agreed.

"We can prosper here as we'd never have done there. Our children can prosper."

Our children. Falon released Kathleen's hand.

"Oh my dear, I am so sorry." Kathleen had gone pale.

Falon stood up. "It's all right. I understand what you meant." She leaned over to kiss her friend's forehead, then frowned. "You're a little warm. How are you feeling?"

"I'm fine. Just tired, I suppose."

"Well, it's time for you to rest. You've done enough talking." She tucked the blankets around Kathleen. "I will stay tonight, so if you need anything, I'm right here."

Falon made a pallet for herself near the fire, but tired as she was, sleep refused to come. *I feel like I've taken a beating. Why does it still sting when anyone mentions children? Surely by now I should be used to the idea that I'll never have any.* She turned on one side and stared into the snapping fire. *I wonder if Patrick and Joe got away?* She pulled her blanket higher around her shoulders. *I should have done more for Joe. I should have offered him food to take along—or something. I just hope he makes it to Mexico before spring, before the fighting starts.* She closed her eyes. *Maybe there won't be any fighting. Maybe the men are wrong and Santa Anna will leave us alone.*

Falon never knew what it was that woke her that night. She started out of a dream where she was sitting in the hayloft of the barn. She couldn't move, and she was waiting for some approaching doom—what it was she didn't know, but the dread of it jolted her awake, and she sat up. It took her a second to remember where she was, and she rubbed her face with both hands, as if to scrub the shadows of the dream from her memory. *Well, I'm wide awake now.* She got to her feet and padded over to check on Kathleen.

In the dying firelight, she noticed something odd on the bed, a discoloration. She put her hand to it, and to her horrified dismay, it came away wet. Blood. "No," she whispered. "Oh, dear God in Heaven, no." She lit a candle and pulled the covers back. The bed was soaked.

She laid her trembling hand on Kathleen's shoulder, leaving a smudge of blood on her friend's shift. "Kathleen?" she called softly, now noting the deep, dark hollows around the other woman's eyes. "Kathleen, please wake up."

No response, and Falon called out more sharply, "Kathleen!"

The green eyes fluttered open, stared without focus at the ceiling, then turned toward her. "Falon?" She held up one hand. "My children . . ."

"No, no." Blinded with tears, Falon shook her head. "You can't do this. You can't die."

Kathleen's hand found hers, gripping it with surprising strength. "My children," she repeated. "Promise me."

"Kathleen . . ."

"Promise me."

Sobbing now, Falon agreed: "I promise."

"Tell Dan . . ." Kathleen's voice trailed off, and she was quiet.

Terrified that she was gone, Falon shook her. "Tell Dan? Tell him what?"

"Trust him . . ." A deep sigh followed, and there was no more.

Trust him? Tell Dan that she trusted him? Falon remembered what Kathleen had said earlier. Did she mean for Falon to tell Dan she had trusted God? Or that he should? Or that Falon should?

"What did you mean?" she cried. The sudden noise woke the baby, who began to wail.

She picked little Caroline up and rocked her until she quieted, then laid her in the cradle. *Kathleen's dead. She was my best friend.* Falon wanted to run screaming out of the cabin. She wanted to throw things. She wanted to shake her fists at Heaven. But there was work to do, it wouldn't wait—and she was the only one there to do it.

November 21, 1835—The hardest part was telling the Garretts' two sons . . .

When she broke the news to the boys, little Stephen sat down on the ground and wailed. Sam was more stoic. He stared at his feet with tears streaming down his face, but he didn't make a sound.

"Your mother wanted me to watch after you until your father gets back," Falon told them. "So I need for you to gather your things. We're going to my house to stay."

"Just till Pa gets home?" Sam took a swipe at his nose with his sleeve.

"Just till then," Falon agreed.

Sam hesitated. He seemed reluctant to enter the house. "Are you going to bury her?" He peered in the door at his mother's still form, covered now with a clean sheet.

"We will, probably this evening. Mr. Burnham is coming over to dig the grave."

She had to coax the boys inside to get the few things they wanted to bring with them. Sam studiously avoided looking toward the bed, but Stephen crept up to it and laid a hand on the cover. "Can I see her?" With a nod, Falon pulled back one corner of the sheet, revealing Kathleen's pale, waxy face. Stephen reached out with one finger and touched her cheek, then backed away. "That's not my Mama."

Of course it is. But Falon swallowed the words when it occurred to her that he was right. The form in his bed wasn't his mother. Kathleen was gone. This was just a shell. She put a hand on his shoulder and guided him away. "Come on, laddie." Her voice sounded rough in her ears. "Get your things. We need to go."

By the time she reached her own cabin, everyone in town had heard the news, and they had a steady stream of visitors offering help, food, and condolences. One neighbor even offered advice. "Cow's milk?" she scolded when Falon told her how she planned to feed Caroline. "You cannot feed cow's milk to that child. It'll give her colic. Get your slave to nurse her. She'll have plenty of milk for both babies."

Falon reluctantly agreed that this was the best plan, and within the hour Maggie was ensconced in the rocker with Caroline and Jack. She and the two babies made an odd, strangely comforting sight—one tiny, pink-skinned baby with copper ringlets suckling at one breast, and a brown-skinned baby with black ringlets at the other. As soon as she'd finished feeding them, Maggie changed their diapers and put them both down for a nap.

"I appreciate you helping me with Mrs. Garrett's baby," Falon said, immediately realizing how silly that must have sounded. Earlier, she had ordered Maggie to help.

But if the slave woman was offended, she didn't show it. "Thank you, missus."

Rooting around for a way to converse with her, Falon asked, "How is your baby coming along?"

"My boy, Jack, he gets fatter every day," Maggie answered, bending down to stroke his curls.

The baby's skin was several shades lighter than his mother's, and Falon wondered if that was unusual. "He's a handsome little lad," she noted with a smile.

Maggie didn't return the smile, but only said, "I need to get these diapers washed now." And she took the soiled cloths outside.

November 22, 1835—I think I am never going to be used to this, used to having a slave in my house. Why did James have to bring her here? Of course, for Caroline's sake, I am glad . . .

James came home just two days later. When Falon went out to meet him, her heart quailed at the grim set of his face. "What's happened?"

He didn't answer right away, but dismounted and tied his horse to the porch post. When he turned to her at last, the lines around his eyes were tight with anger. "A rider caught up with us last night, and I had to turn back. It seems the Eversons' man has gone missing." He took off his hat and slapped it against his leg. "Do you know anything about this, Ellen?"

"You . . . you mean Joe Everson?" she stammered.

His reply came dry and hard. "He's the only slave they have. The rumor is, he was seen at our place. Did you know he was here?"

"No." Falon gave her head an emphatic shake, reasoning, *If he really did come here, I didn't know about it.* "I never saw him."

James studied her through narrowed eyes for a long moment. "I didn't want to think you were involved. He did save your brother's life all those years ago, and I know how you feel obligated to people, but this is different. He's a slave." He touched her under her chin. "I hope you're telling me the truth, Ellen. If I find out otherwise . . ." He didn't finish that thought, but shook his head.

Falon was saved further protest when Sam emerged from the front door. "Mr. Carson, you're back! Is my dad with you?"

"No, son," James answered, "I came by myself." Sam nodded and went back inside, his head hanging with disappointment

"What is he doing here?" James asked.

Falon took a deep breath. "Kathleen had her baby the day you men left. She died that night. I promised her I would look after the children until Dan gets back."

James bowed his head, sighing. "I'm sorry, sweetheart." He laid one hand on her shoulder. "Well, can you fix me something to eat? I have to go after Joe and bring him back."

"I have a roasted duck that Mrs. Beason brought over," she answered as they started inside, deeply relieved for the moment to be off the hook. Maggie, in her usual place in the rocker, had been humming to the babies, but as soon as she saw James, she went quiet.

"Ginny White sent wheat bread. I'll slice a piece of that for you, too." Falon picked up the knife to carve a slice of the duck. James sat down while Falon added the bread and a spoonful of beans to a plate and put it in front of him. He bolted his food down with little comment. When he had finished, he reached for his hat, and without looking at her said, "I'll be back as soon as I can. You go to your father's if you need to. If you're not here, I'll look for you there."

This is my fault. I never should have let Patrick talk me into letting Joe use the barn. She stepped out onto the porch with James, and after she shut the door she reached up and traced the cleft in his chin with the tip of a finger. "I wish you didn't have to leave again." But she knew from the faraway look in his eyes that he was already gone.

He gave her a quick peck on the cheek. "I wish so too, sweetheart." Then, for no reason Falon could fathom, he put his arms around her and held her close. "See you soon." She breathed in the scent of him—of outdoors, of leather and sweat. He released her and untied his horse. "I know Joe must have headed south toward Mexico. Hopefully he hasn't gotten far."

She watched him ride away, feeling lower than she had in a long time. James had made a reputation for himself as a successful tracker. She had little doubt he would catch up with Joe Everson. She had lied to her husband, or at least she had deceived him, which amounted to the same thing. Now he was going after the man she wanted to protect with the lie, and he was going in the right direction.

★15

January 31, 1836—Christmas and the New Year have come and gone, but it was no calm, bright season. Our men have won Bexar, but the rattling of sabers increases with each passing day, along with grim rumors and dire predictions . . .

"What about what Santa Anna did at Zacatecas?" Kathleen's father shouted at a town meeting a few weeks after the year turned. His face was scarlet with anger and the effects of too much corn whiskey. "Are we going to stand idly by and let him do the same here?"

"Have a care, Mr. O'Connor," the alcalde advised, looking at him sternly over a pair of spectacles. "There are ladies present."

General Santa Anna's troops had attacked the city of Zacatecas the previous spring. Though it was far to the south, word spread quickly. Gossip and speculation abounded about the brutalities the Mexican army had visited on the city's people. The men whispered among themselves that invading troops had not only killed combatants, but had abused and defiled innocent women. They said these things with sidelong glances at their ladies, who stood at a distance and pretended not to overhear.

"My family stays!" another man roared. He was a newcomer, and Falon didn't know him. "This is my land. I paid for it, and I have the deed to prove it. The Mexicans can't force me out."

Oh, can't they? Falon held herself so tightly she could scarcely breathe. The tension building in her new home mirrored all too well that terrible spring when her family was evicted from Sgall. *Give a handful of men enough weapons and the authority of law—whether the law is right or not—and anyone can be forced to leave.*

But she had other, more personal problems to think about. James had been gone for nearly two months. December and January had passed with no sign of him. She didn't know whether his long absence was an ominous sign, or a hopeful one. *Did Joe Everson make it to Mexico? If James caught him, would Joe tell about spending the night in our barn? What will James do if he finds out I knew about it?*

Patrick is still gone, too. I miss him. She chewed at her thumbnail until it bled, and amended her wayward thoughts. *I miss his singing. But driving those cattle, he won't be back any time soon.*

"Mrs. Carson, when is my Pa coming back?" Stephen gazed up at her with his father's eyes.

Falon reached out and smoothed the boy's russet cowlick with one hand. "I don't know, Stevie. Soon, I hope." It was all she could tell him. The Texan force had driven the Mexicans out of the Alamo and occupied it. Some seemed to think this victory would be the end of the story, but Falon had her doubts. And she had heard nothing from Dan Garrett—whether he was determined to stay in San Antonio, or whether he would come home to his children. She wasn't even certain whether he'd gotten the message that Kathleen had borne their baby girl and died.

February 3, 1836—No word. No word from anyone . . .

One evening, both of the babies started crying to be fed at the same time. Maggie picked up Caroline, and Falon, raising her voice over the squalling, said, "Go ahead and sit down. I'll bring Jack to you." She picked up Maggie's son. "Goodness!" she laughed when Jack's wails went high-pitched with frustration. "Be patient, little man. Your mama's going to feed you." It was then that she saw it: a perfect, tiny cleft dividing the baby's chin. Without thinking, she touched it. And she knew.

One dreary, raw winter day followed another, each shrouded in gray, an unending funereal procession. Falon swept the floors, cooked and cleaned, washed clothes and children—and started over. All of this under Maggie's watchful eyes. *James brought her here, but sometime before that . . .* Falon couldn't finish that thought, couldn't bear to think of what he had done. *Does she despise me because I can't have a baby?* And then—*What is the matter with me? No one else would be bothered by this. She's just a slave. Why should I care what she thinks? Why should I care that my husband . . .*

"Mrs. Carson, you are going to run yourself ragged."

Maggie's remark, though softly spoken, set Falon's teeth on edge. She didn't reply, didn't trust herself to answer. Maggie sat in that rocker like a presiding judge, a judge with a baby attached to each breast. But Falon had to endure her. She needed her.

In the middle of February, Falon sat down and wrote a letter.

Dear Mr. Garrett,

I hope this letter finds you well, and all the men with you. Everything here is much the same as in my last message. Sam and Stephen are fine, growing fast, and little Caroline seems to get bigger every day. I know you are busy at the Alamo, but I should tell you that Kathleen's parents are not able to look after the boys. I still have them in my care. This is no great burden to me, indeed, I welcome having them. However, the children miss you. They ask about you, and wonder when you will be coming home.

I don't know whether you intend to remain in San Antonio, but I urge you to consider coming back for their sakes. It is a hard time for them since they lost their mother.

My best wishes to you.

Sincerely, F. Carson

Kathleen's mother had come to visit the week before, and Falon strongly hinted to her that the children might be better off in her care, since she was their grandmother. But Mrs. O'Conner demurred. "I would rather, Mrs. Carson, that they stay with you for the time being. Mr. O'Conner is often unwell, and our house wouldn't be a fit place for the little ones just now."

Mr. O'Conner is often drunk, you mean. It occurred to Falon that Kathleen had made her promise to look after the children for just this reason. She must have known about her father's predilection for strong drink. So Falon agreed to keep them.

But the walls of her house seemed to shrink a little each day. "Stephen, give the whistle back to your brother." When the boy pouted, she added, "I mean it, now."

"You're not my mama."

She closed her eyes and sighed. *Lord, give me patience.* The wet weather had them cooped up; the boys squabbled regularly, and Falon was ready to tear her hair out.

"When is my Pa coming back?"

"I don't know, Sam." How many times had she answered that question? Only now, her heart was beginning to close, to tighten like a fist each time they asked.

February 20, 1836—Word has reached us that Santa Anna and his troops have been seen preparing to cross the Rio Grande, that they will be headed toward the Alamo, and that they probably outnumber our men by at least ten to one. What possible chance does Dan Garrett have against those odds? I am glad James is not there. Though I do not know where my husband is, at least I know he is not trapped in San Antonio.

Are we going to have to leave? If we do, what should I take? I dread the thought of venturing out into this cold. Where will we go? San Antonio is west, and so we cannot go that way. Anahuac may be safe, but it is to the south, and Santa Anna's troops are coming up from there. North is out of the question. There are too many Indians. We will have to go east, probably all the way to the United States. We will have to cross three or four rivers, at least. The wagon may not be much use, then, unless there are ferries.

Falon looked up from her journal, took a deep breath and smoothed her curls back from her face, listening to the drone of rain on the roof. *Heaven be thanked. We don't have to leave today . . .*

Less than a week later, a rider came tearing into town, yelling at the top of his lungs. Falon couldn't make out what he was saying. "Maggie, I'm going to find out what the matter is. You stay here with the children."

"Don't worry, Mrs. Carson. I'll take care of things."

Falon threw her cloak around her shoulders and ran out the door. The rain, thankfully, had stopped, but the streets were nothing but great rivers and pools of mud and water. She picked her way along what little grass remained, but her skirts were wet to her knees by the time she reached Mr. Cook's tavern.

More than a dozen people had already gathered inside. Falon pushed her way in, thankful for once that she was so small. When she caught sight of the rider, her heart leapt. It was Dan Garrett. "The Mexican army is only a few days' march from Bexar," he was saying. "Colonel Travis is calling for men and supplies to come to him before it arrives."

"Who's commanding the army?" one of the men wanted to know.

Dan wiped his face with his sleeve. "Colonel Travis has joint command with Colonel Bowie."

"No, I meant, who is leading the Mexican army?"

The noise in the room fell to a hush when he answered. "Santa Anna himself."

"Is the army headed this way?"

Dan shook his head. "Not yet. It appears they're going to concentrate their strength on the Alamo first."

The room erupted into a confused din. Daniel Garrett spotted Falon and elbowed through the crowd to her. "I got your messages. My children, Mrs. Carson, are they well?"

"Oh, Mr. Garrett, I am so glad you're here," she answered. "The children are fine. The boys ask about you every day."

"I will stop in and see them before I leave."

"Leave?" she cried. "You've only just arrived."

He took her by the elbow and guided her out the door. "The situation in San Antonio is dire," he told her, "and by all accounts, it will get worse. If I can't round up more men for the Alamo, those inside are surely doomed."

Falon remembered her stepbrother's confident boasting that they could hold the fort, and felt her heart sink. "James didn't go back there, did he?"

"I haven't seen him since he left. I presume by your question you don't know where he is."

"I don't." Falon tried to comfort herself that James wasn't in the Bexar fortress, but not knowing where he was, or what was keeping him, seemed nearly as bad.

"Well," Dan sighed, "you had better take me to see my children."

"They're at my house." She started that way, then realized how hard it was going to be for him with Kathleen gone. "Daniel, I am so sorry . . ." She stopped, having run out of words.

His face tightened in a pained expression. "I shouldn't have left her."

"There was nothing you could have done," she answered. "I should tell you, the last thing she said . . ." Falon swallowed against the lump that had risen in her throat. "She said, 'Tell Dan,' and then she said, 'Trust him.'"

"Trust him," he repeated. "Yes." By the tone of his voice, Falon guessed that he understood what Kathleen had meant. After a few more steps, he asked, "Where did you bury her?"

"On the west side of your cabin, just within the shade of that big hickory tree."

"Yes," he repeated, "That's a good place."

"We marked the grave. We covered it with stones." To Falon's own ears, she sounded like she was babbling, so she snapped her mouth shut and said nothing more.

They walked the rest of the way in silence. When they were almost to the house, the front door burst open, and Sam and Stephen both bounded toward them shouting, "Pa! Pa, you're back!" Dan Garrett dropped to his knees in the muddy road and embraced his boys.

Sam stepped back first. "Mama died."

Dan nodded, and his voice wavered. "I know, son."

"Are we going home now?" Stephen wanted to know.

"Not yet," he answered, rising to his feet. "Where's your baby sister?"

Stephen grabbed his hand and pulled him toward the door. "She's in here. Her name is Caroline."

Falon followed them inside, arriving just in time to see Maggie hand little Caroline over to her father. Maggie's black eyes shone with unshed tears, and Falon looked away, but not before a ragged, black blade of envy twisted in her heart. Maggie understood what Dan felt when he held his baby. But Falon probably never would.

Dan sank into the rocker, and even though the boys still clamored, albeit quietly, for his attention, he had eyes only for his daughter. "She looks like her mother," he finally said.

"She does," Falon agreed.

He leaned his head back and closed his eyes. "I am loath to leave again."

"You're leaving, Pa?" Sam asked. "Why?" His face had gone red, and he looked like he might cry.

After a long pause, Dan answered, "I have to, son. There are men who will die if I don't help them."

Somehow Sam held onto himself, though his chin trembled. "How long will you be gone?"

"No longer than I have to be." Dan squarely met his son's gaze. "You have my word."

Can I come with you?"

"No, my boy. I need you to stay here and take care of Stephen and your baby sister. Can you do that?" Sam heaved a great sigh and nodded. Dan reached out and laid a hand on his shoulder, but looked up at Falon. "I have to go."

"Do you need food for your trip?"

"I have enough," he answered as he stood. "I must try to make Goliad before nightfall." He settled the baby in her cradle, stroking her cheek.

Falon followed him outside after Daniel said his farewells to the boys. "Will you be able to muster enough men?"

His jaw bunched with suppressed emotion. "I will try." He turned to her. "Thank you, Mrs. Carson, for all you've done for my family. I'm afraid I must impose on you awhile longer."

"It's no imposition. I'm glad to see that you're safe and well. Don't worry about your children. I'll look after them."

He nodded. "I can't think of anyone I'd rather leave them with." He stepped off the porch, then stopped. "If I see your husband, is there a message you'd like me to give him?"

Falon thought, *What message should I send? That I want him home?* "Tell him all is well here." She tried to smile, but the look Daniel gave her told her that he was unconvinced.

"All right. Well, I hope to be back before long." And he set off back down the road toward the tavern.

February 24, 1836—Another rider has brought more news. Santa Anna is in San Antonio now with his troops. He has ordered his men to

give no quarter. They will take no prisoners. He intends to kill every one of our men. After the rider gave us his news, he rode away east, scattering evil tidings like a farmer sowing seed. All our waiting and wondering, and now the waiting is over. Those few men in the Alamo cannot hold out long against Santa Anna's thousands . . .

Falon hurried home after receiving this news, but instead of going into the house, she went around to the barn and shut herself inside. The barn was cold and dark—and quiet. She needed to think. Falon paced in a circle and blew on her hands to keep herself warm.

"This isn't Sgall," she said to the emptiness. "I will not be caught unprepared this time. I have the children to think about—and Maggie, too." She paused, running one hand along the side of the wagon. "I hope we can take this with us so we can sleep up off the ground." The nearly incessant rain had left the ground impassable to wagons in places. "But maybe the rain will let up." Falon sighed, "I have that one hide. We can take that, and the large oilcloth." The hide was rolled up, standing in a corner. Falon carried it to the wagon and laid it in the bed. "This will be as good a spot as any to collect the things I need to take."

Over the next few days, she gathered provisions and stored them in the wagon. One rare, sunny morning, she announced, "Boys, today looks like a good day to go fishing." They jumped up from the kitchen table, and hurried outside to dig for worms. When Falon came out, she noticed that they had put their bait in a battered tin bucket. A smile pulled at the corners of her mouth. The nanny's bucket had come across the ocean from Sgall to her father's house on the Brazos, and from there, it had carried rose cuttings to this house on the Colorado.

She walked the children down to the river. "I want you two to stay right here between that dead tree and this big rock. Stay together, now, and if you see anybody—anybody, understand?—on the other side of the river, you run back up to the house."

"Yes ma'am," Sam said, and Stephen echoed, "Yes, ma'am." Normally, they would have been excited to get outside, but their manner this day was subdued, almost somber.

They know. Falon watched them baiting their lines. The two red heads, shining like new pennies in the sunlight, bent intently, as if they were sharing secrets. *I've been careful not to say anything in front of them, but somehow they know. Thank heaven Dan isn't in that Alamo.* He had sent word that he was leaving Goliad and going to look for General Sam Houston. Not that this put him out of danger.

The boys fished all morning and came in for lunch with three perch and a small catfish. "Are we going to eat these for dinner?" Stephen asked.

Falon sat down and pulled him to her, putting an arm around his waist. "Stevie, we aren't. I'm going to show you how to dry the fish so we can eat it later."

Sam frowned. "Why?"

Falon glanced at Maggie, who merely raised her eyebrows. "Well, we might be going on a trip."

Stephen squirmed under her arm. "A trip? Where?"

"The Mexicans are coming here, aren't they?" Sam demanded.

Falon sighed. "It's possible. No one knows for sure, but they might. And we need to be ready when they do. *If* they do."

Stephen's lower lip trembled. "Are the Mexicans gonna' get my Pa?"

"No, your Pa went the other way," Falon said, hoping, praying it was true. "Don't you worry about him. But we need to see to it that Maggie and baby Jack and your little sister are safe. Can you help me do that?" Stephen nodded, wiping at his eyes. "Eat your lunch now," she told him. "Sam, I want to show you something in the barn."

Falon marveled, when she was alone with him, how much the boy looked like his mother. Her throat knotted for a moment, and she cleared it and sat down on the mule's saddle. "Sam, you are a smart young man. I know it's been hard on you, waiting for your father to come back." *And your mother's gone.* She cleared her throat again.

"Your Pa told you to look after Stevie and the baby. Well, now is the time."

He had been studying his shoes. Now he raised his emerald eyes to meet hers. "What do you mean?"

"We will probably have to leave here because of the Mexicans. You know that. The trip won't be easy, but I am trying to get ready for it. Come and look at this." She stood, showing him the provisions in the wagon. "Can you help me drive the mule, do you think?" Sam nodded solemnly. "That's good. Now, I need you to do two things." She held up one finger. "First, I need you to be careful about what you say in front of Stephen. Do you understand?"

"Because he gets scared."

But it was Stevie who went into the house when your mother died, not you. Falon bit her lip. "That's right. He's younger than you, and he gets scared."

"What's the second thing?"

"You have a good head on your shoulders," she told him. "I want you to have a look at what I've gathered so far, and if you think of something else we need to take, tell me."

He climbed up into the wagon and inspected the food and provisions, nodding to himself. "Our fishing hooks and line," he finally said. "That way we can catch more if we run out. And I'll need my gun."

"Your squirrel gun?" When Sam nodded, she asked, "Do you have powder for it?"

"There's some back at my house. I could get it."

"Good thinking," Falon watched him jump down and patted his shoulder. "You can be in charge of the fishing and hunting provisions." She smiled. "Let's go eat lunch now."

March 5, 1836—I had thought the waiting was over, but as the week has worn on, I realize that I was mistaken. Rumors about the Alamo are

flying fast and thick. This afternoon, I witnessed an argument in the street in front of the tavern . . .

"Santa Anna is sure to win with his superior numbers," one man said. She didn't know his name, but thought he might be kin to the Alley family. "The Texians are being bombarded. They're almost out of food, and they're surrounded. It's just plain sense."

The other, a man Falon recognized as one of the Thompsons' grown sons, argued, "No, sir. The Texians have the advantage of the artillery and the stone walls of the fortress. Santa Anna is going to have to sit there forever before he gets the upper hand. The Texians were well supplied—Travis' last letter said so. And the roads are still open. They can get out if they need to."

The argument went on, getting louder when Mr. Thompson accused the other of doomsaying and jabbed him in the chest with one finger. "You are unpatriotic, sir, to suggest that the Mexican army will prevail over our men."

A third man joined them then. "Unpatriotic? Why, he's a downright traitor."

The argument erupted into a fistfight, and Falon hurried away, giving wide berth to a big, yellow dog that lay in front of Beason's inn, growling and chewing itself. Ever hopeful, Falon wanted to believe the Texians would win, that Santa Anna would be forced to slink back to Mexico and leave them alone. She considered abandoning her plans to pack and leave, but decided against it. *Better to hope for the best and prepare for the worst.*

And finally, real news. The next day another rider thundered through on his way east, crying, "The Alamo has fallen!"

Fallen. She sank down on her front porch, the breath gone out of her. Moments later, she heard a shriek from down the lane, followed by a heartrending wail. *Elizabeth Tumlison. Her son George was in the Alamo. Are they all dead, I wonder? How long will it take to find out who died and who survived? Did our George live through it? Or did Santa Anna make good on his threat to kill them all? Surely he didn't!*

Falon's heart felt like a lump of lead in her chest as she got up and started down the road. *Where is James? Why hasn't he come home?* She passed the Tumlison house, where the wailing continued unabated. She hesitated, debating whether to go in and comfort her neighbor. But what comfort did she have to offer? Poor Elizabeth. Her husband had been killed in an Indian attack the year the Macvails arrived from Scotland. And now her son was gone, too. Or was he? Falon picked up her steps and hurried to Cook's Tavern. Maybe there were survivors, after all.

The scene outside the tavern told her everything before she had to ask. The rider, a teenager from Gonzales, was surrounded by men, many of them weeping openly. "Every last one," the youngster said, his own eyes red-rimmed with tears. "You lie!" One of the men shouted into his face. "You're a stinking liar! It ain't possible!"

The boy drew himself up, facing his accuser. "My pa died in that place." His voice, breaking with youth and grief, fell on Falon's ears like shattered stone. The man who had accused him went to his knees in the street. "Oh, Jim," he moaned. "Oh, little brother."

An older man brushed by her, "Excuse me, ma'am."

"Mr. Alley," she touched his arm as he passed. "Is it true, then? Are they all dead?"

He paused, regarding her through bleary eyes, as though he couldn't focus on her face. At last he said, "Mrs. Carson. Yes, my dear, I am afraid it is true." He started to turn away, but stopped. "Your James—he wasn't part of that action, was he?"

"No, sir," she answered. "I don't know where he is, but I had news that he wasn't there."

Mr. Alley grunted, his gaze shifted from her, shifted off and away, and with a nod he said, "Well, that's something, at least. That's good."

March 10, 1836—The Mexican army has to be coming this way. Nearly half of the people here have already fled eastward. I should go, too.

I cannot think of anything I have left to prepare. All the food I can spare from our daily use is in the wagon. I have checked and double-checked the wagon countless times, making sure it is sound. I should leave, but I have still had no word from James, and I do not relish the thought of making such a journey without him . . .

That evening, just before dark, Falon heard a shout. An ox-drawn wagon was pulling up alongside the barn. The woman who drove the oxen climbed down from her seat, saying, "You three stay right there in the wagon, you hear?"

It was then that Falon saw the children in the back, their curious eyes gleaming over the wagon's rail. She called out, "Do you all need help?"

The woman came toward her, her gait stiff, as if she had been riding a long time. "I'm Louisa Jackson. We are from Gonzales. Can we maybe stay in your barn tonight?"

"I'm . . . Ellen. Ellen Carson." Even now, the name still stuck in her throat. "The barn is too cold. Bring your little ones up to the house. I'll help you get them inside." The two women headed to the wagon.

"Cold or not," Louisa told her, "if you have a mind to be hospitable, your barn and your house will be full tonight. Just about everybody from town is headed this way." She pulled down the gate, and the two older children handed her the youngest, barely a toddler, before climbing out themselves.

"Everybody?" Falon swallowed a bitter taste that had risen in her mouth. "You mean, everybody from Gonzales is coming here?"

"They'll probably all be here tonight," Louisa replied, "once they make it across the ferry. Children, we're going to this nice lady's house."

March 21, 1836—The Beasons were busy all night, ferrying families across the river. I am not very good at figuring numbers of people, but I think there must be more than a thousand altogether. I had no rest myself. My house and barn are full, and I never heard so much weeping in my life. The sound of it breaks my heart. The women have left most, if not all, of their possessions behind in their haste to escape the approaching army. They and their children fill every corner of every house and barn, while the men have taken to sleeping out under the stars. Even General Houston does not possess a tent . . .

Falon caught sight of him the next day, and thought, *Goodness, he's tall!* At more than six feet in height, the general towered over most of his men. She watched him moving among the troops, giving orders, and thought he looked like he might have felt more at home in buckskin than in the coat and shirt he wore. He set up a makeshift headquarters on the eastern bank of the river.

"I hear he plans to make his stand against Santa Anna right here," Louisa told her.

Little by little, Louisa told Falon what had happened. "Our men were under siege for thirteen days. My husband had gone with the other men from Gonzales." She bit her lip and shook her head, unable to go on. Falon, stricken by Louisa's loss and grief, didn't try to ask questions, but her guest seemed to want to talk about it. Later, she said, "We were told that Santa Anna's men took ours by surprise on the morning of the sixth. Once the Mexican army breached the walls, there was nothing our men could do to stop them from . . . from just pouring in." She took a long, ragged breath. "They're all dead. Santa Anna said he would kill them all. Well, he did."

Poor George! I wished him dead, maybe more than once. And now he is. I wonder—if I had tried, would he have let me talk him out of going there? But in her regret, Falon felt no real grief. She shook her head. George had been so confident they would win. "So, no one survived?

"The only survivors I know about are Susannah Dickinson, her baby girl, and Colonel Travis' servant, Joe. One of Houston's scouts found them walking toward Gonzales. I heard Santa Anna himself gave Mrs. Dickinson two silver dollars and a blanket and told her to come to us and tell us what happened." She looked up at Falon, her eyes blazing with anger. "I guess he wanted to scare us into surrendering."

Falon took one of the woman's hands in both her own. "Louisa, I am so sorry about your husband." Louisa's chin came up. "Thank you for that." Falon's heart hurt for her guest. *She's lost her husband and her home—she and all the others.*

Instead of waiting to surrender, the townspeople of Gonzales had fled, burning their homes to the ground first, so the Mexican army would have nothing to plunder.

★16

March 23, 1836—These past few days have been an odd mix of disorder and calm. Disorder is the rule of the day here at the house and barn. Nearly a dozen families are crowded together, trying to keep themselves warm and dry. I have never seen so many babies, and most of these are now orphans. I have been compelled to open my provisions to feed those who have none. Thirty-two men from Gonzales went to the Alamo to reinforce Travis' small army. They are all dead, many leaving wives and children behind. We are paying dearly for a chance at freedom. Thirty-two men were not enough. The men who were already there were not enough. How many would it have taken to win?

How many will it take now? I guess that General Houston has five or six hundred under his command, with handfuls of newcomers arriving every day. His military encampment is orderly and quiet. I went out this morning to watch the men drill. Houston does not bark at his men. He gives orders quietly, and the men obey. All of this without the use of drums or bugles. It has occurred to me that Houston does not want anyone across the river to hear what is going on. The thought of this makes the hairs on the back of my neck stand up. There may be spies on the western side of the river. There can be, and probably are, men with guns, watching us. After this morning, I will no longer allow the boys to go fishing . . .

It was a shame, too. The extra food would have been welcome. Falon had reached the bottom of her first bag of cornmeal just that morning. She had only two left. *Well, if we starve, I guess we'll starve together.*

Louisa had seen the empty bag, and no doubt the dismayed expression that must have been on Falon's face. She put a friendly arm around Falon's shoulders, saying, "I cannot thank you enough, Ellen, for opening your home to us—feeding us and all."

Falon gave her a one-armed hug. "It's the least I can do. You have been through a terrible time, and I fear it won't be better soon." Only one other woman expressed thanks for Falon's efforts. The rest, lost in grief and despair, huddled in the cold with their children, and over the ensuing days grew quieter and more lethargic, more sunken into themselves. *It's like watching someone being pulled into quicksand,* Falon thought. *But what can I do?* And suddenly she had an idea.

She dug into the trunk at the foot of her bed, and when she had found what she wanted, she stuffed it into her apron pocket and marched over to the men's encampment. There she found Mr. Alley warming his hands at one of the cook fires. "Mrs. Carson, what brings you here?" he asked, seeing her make her way toward him.

"I need to have a word with General Houston. Can you arrange it for me?"

He frowned. "Now why would you need to speak to him?"

"It concerns some of the women . . ."

He interrupted: "Mrs. Carson, the general is involved in matters of grave import. I do not believe we should disturb him with trivialities. You ladies will just have to stop your fussing . . ."

An apology died on the tip of her tongue as Miss Mattie's face surfaced in her memory. What was it she had said? *We women need to do what we can to help each other along.* She faced him squarely. "Mr. Alley, I am not a frivolous woman. I understand the general is busy with important matters. But this is important, too. I do not need him to settle arguments. I only want his permission for something."

"I am certain that whatever you have in mind will be fine." He turned away, dismissing her.

"I have your permission, then?" Falon smiled brightly. "Why, thank you, Mr. Alley. I'll be sure to mention your name if anyone asks." She started to walk away.

"Wait!" He fixed her with a glare. "Very well, then. I will take you to him, but you had better not be wasting my time—or his."

Falon nodded, gesturing for him to lead the way. When they found him, the general was sitting at a camp table, studying a well-worn map. He said to an aide standing beside him, "I'll make that decision when I hear from Fannin. He should have already left Goliad with his men. I expect them here any day."

Mr. Alley cleared his throat as they approached. "General Houston?"

Sam Houston looked up from his map, and when he saw Falon, he stood—up and up. He took her hand and bowed over it. "What can I do for you, Mrs. Carson?"

Falon felt her face go hot. She had no idea that the man towering over her knew who she was. "I wanted to ask your permission, sir." She took a deep breath. "The women are in a bad way, as I am sure you know. I wondered if it would be all right . . ." She pulled her flute from her apron pocket. "If I played quietly for them—some hymns, perhaps?—I think it would raise their spirits."

Houston pursed his lips and grunted. Then he said, "Mr. Alley, you are responsible for bringing Mrs. Carson here?"

The older man's face went scarlet. "Sir, I told her . . ."

"This is the best idea I've heard all day." Houston didn't smile, but humor radiated from his eyes. "Unfortunately, however, we have spies across the river. So, Mrs. Carson, I will have to ask you to play outside where they will be sure to hear you."

Falon frowned with confusion. "Sir?"

Now he did smile. "Over the years, I seem to have garnered a . . . reputation. No Mexican spy in his right mind will think I am anywhere in the neighborhood if he hears hymns." He added, "But you might throw a reel or two in there to liven things up."

She thanked him and hurried home. As soon as she got back to her cabin, Falon pulled a chair out onto the porch and sat down. *Right, then. Let's see if this helps.*

She hadn't played in months, not since Patrick left. Her fingers felt clumsy on the holes, but she struggled though. Falon had hardly finished playing the first half of the first hymn when they began gathering. Worn, hollow-eyed women crept out of the barn and drifted from the house with their little ones tagging behind. They came, singly and in pairs from down the lane, Gonzales women and Columbus women. A semicircle formed in front of Falon's porch, and by the time she had finished the first hymn, about half the crowd was singing along, memory being the only hymnal they had, the only one they needed. Some closed their eyes, some swayed gently, many rocking small children in their arms.

Another hymn followed, and another. More voices joined in.

"Lord, if Thou plantest me in Christ,
in bloom shall burst my withered tree,
Weighed down to earth its boughs shall be
With graces, as with fruits unpriced."

After about half an hour, Falon's fingers were done. She finished with the doxology.

"Praise God from Whom all blessings flow,
Praise Him all creatures here below,

Praise Him above, ye heavenly host,
Praise Father, Son, and Holy Ghost."

A familiar voice joined the last song—a man's golden baritone, soft, but unmistakable. The final "amen" drifted gently into the morning, and without looking up, Falon put her flute away. Into the ensuing silence, one of the women spoke. "The Lord is my shepherd, I shall not want . . ." Just as in song, many voices raised to recite the old psalm. Falon did glance up at this, marveling at the scene before her. Scottish Presbyterians joined with Anglicans, together with Methodists, alongside Catholics, among the unchurched. This morning the differences didn't matter. *We're all in the same boat, aren't we? I wish Kathleen could have been here. She would have loved to see this.* Falon bowed her head and closed her eyes. *Well, and maybe she can see it. I hope she can.*

She heard them leaving, heard quiet footsteps as the circle broke and scattered, heard murmured conversations, words of encouragement, words of hope, felt an occasional hand laid briefly on her shoulder, thanking her. By the time she looked up again, most had gone. Only a handful lingered, talking quietly.

"Mrs. Carson?"

She pocketed her flute as she stood. "Patrick. You're back."

His lips stretched in a smile over his crooked teeth. "That I am. You heard me, did you?" When she nodded, he gestured toward the army encampment. "I'm just in time, it seems."

"And how did things go?" Falon cupped her elbows in her hands, held herself still. "Did you manage to do what you wanted?"

His gaze dropped to his feet. "I don't rightly know. We were forced to separate."

Falon's heart thudded dully in her chest. "Did Mr. Carson find you?"

"Not before Joe and I had to part. I didn't see him."

"And your cattle—did you make it to market with them?"

"With about half." He shook his head. "I ran into the Mexican army, and had to lose some in order to get away myself."

Falon frowned. "But you went south, yes? I thought the Mexicans were in San Antonio."

"They're all over the place. There have been rumors of battles here and there. It's lucky I am to have made it back at all."

"Well, I'm glad you did." Suddenly feeling as though she'd said more than she meant to, she asked, "What will you do now?"

Patrick nodded toward the encampment. "I've signed up to fight. I have a rifle. Bought one when I reached the coast. This country is no place for an unarmed man."

"Have you been to your house yet? It's probably occupied."

"'Tis. Four women with all their little ones." Now he grinned. "I had been hoping for a feminine presence in my home, but this is a bit more than I had in mind." Falon laughed, and he added, "They can have the house. I'll be staying with the men." An awkward silence fell between them. "Well, I'm glad to see you're well," he said finally. "I'll be going. Call on me if you need anything."

"Thanks. I will." She watched him walk away, and turned back to go inside, feeling as if a burden had been lifted. *Nothing's really changed,* she told herself. *We're still here, and war is coming.*

War came quickly. A few days later, Sam tugged at Falon's sleeve. "Mrs. Carson, come see." Falon took one look at his face, his skin pale under the generous sprinkling of freckles, his green eyes wide and serious, and she put down the bowl and spoon she had been holding to follow him outside. "Down here," he told her in a whisper, leading her along the path to the river. When he crouched behind the fallen trunk of a dead tree, she did the same. "Over there." He pointed across the river. "See them?"

Falon's heart bunched in her throat. Mexican soldiers—three of them, trying to conceal themselves but still visible from her angle.

"Does General Houston know?" she whispered back. When Sam answered with a shrug, she said, "Run, Sam. Run and tell him." She took one more look after he left. *Ah, Lord, they are here, and what will we do now?* Crouching low so they wouldn't see her, she hurried back to the house.

As it turned out, General Houston did know about the soldiers. "He said it's a General Sesma," Sam told her when he returned. "And he's got a big army with him."

Falon gnawed at her thumbnail. "Is he going to fight them here?"

Just then, someone pounded at the door. Falon bit back a scream and, covering her mouth, took a deep breath to calm herself. The Mexicans, after all, wouldn't bother to knock. She went to answer the door. Patrick stood on the porch, his gun in one hand and his hat in the other. He stared at the hat as if he expected it to come alive. "Are you ready to leave, Mrs. Carson?"

"I just need to hitch up the mule," she answered, running a shaking hand through her hair. "It's come to that, then?"

"It has." His jaw bunched with suppressed emotion.

Falon threw a glance over her shoulder at the women inside, and eased out the door, closing it behind her. "Patrick, what is it? What are you not telling me?"

"Our men at Goliad . . ." he began. His face went scarlet.

She knew the Texians had a sizeable army there, and that General Houston was waiting for them to come and reinforce the troops he had collected on the Colorado. Something about Patrick's manner, his refusal to meet her eyes, filled her with dread. "What about them?"

"They're not coming, Mrs. Carson. They're under attack."

"Under attack?" Falon felt stupid for echoing him.

"The Mexicans have enough men to divide and conquer." Patrick finally raised his eyes to meet hers. "If you're planning to leave, now is the time. Whether we fight here—or not . . ." He paused, drawing in a long breath. "Your people are on the Brazos, yes?"

"My father." As soon as the words left her mouth, Falon was galvanized into action. With or without James, she could go to her father. "I'll hitch the mule." She turned, opening the door. "Sam?" The youngster came right out. "Go inside and quietly tell Maggie to get ready to leave with the babies. Tell no one else. Then find Eli and bring him here."

"What about Stephen?"

"Not yet," she answered.

When the boy had gone in, Patrick asked, "And what about the others?" Unable to meet the tacit accusation in his eyes, she said, "Don't look at me like that, Patrick. I'm going to tell them, but I want Maggie to get the babies out without being trampled."

He walked with her to the barn. "You won't be able to keep it secret, you know. They're all watching."

"It doesn't matter." Her manner was rougher than she intended. "My first responsibility is to the Garretts' young ones, and to Maggie and . . . and her baby. They're depending on me. I have to take care of them." Falon shouldered the barn door open and stepped over a pair of children sitting on the dirt floor. Three families had taken up residence. All their eyes were on her as she led the mule from his stall and she and Patrick eased him into the wagon's traces.

One woman, who had been sitting in a corner, stood up. "Mrs. Carson?" Falon glanced toward her. She didn't have to say anything. "Henry, come here," she heard her call out. "Go find your sister."

The others sprang to their feet. "It's time, isn't it? We have to go."

"What about the Goliad boys? Have they arrived?"

Falon didn't answer; she found she couldn't. The Goliad reinforcement wasn't coming. This latest news was somehow worse than the first. Hope was leaving them, one fallen man at a time. The Colorado River was flowing at flood stage, running deep and swift from the recent rain. But though it was a barrier, it wasn't insurmountable. Santa Anna's army would cross it one way or another, no doubt with the general himself cracking the whip. *And then what chance will we have?* She remembered that long ago day, when her father spoke of the United States as if it were next door. "We'd just have to cross a little river," he had said. *Well, Dad, I wish it were that easy. But easy or hard, the United States is the only safe place for us—if there is a safe place.*

Falon felt some relief when she led the mule and wagon out of the barn and found Maggie waiting in the yard between, a baby on each arm, and Stephen and Eli standing close by. "We're going to my father's house," she told them, looking around. "Where is Sam?"

"He said he had to go talk to someone," Maggie told her. "Made no sense to me, but he promised to be quick."

A small town is a poor harbor for secrets. By the time Falon brought the wagon around to the front of the house, the lane through the middle of town had erupted with frantic activity. Every woman who lived there, and every woman who had landed there on the flight east—each one was gathering children, gathering belongings, gathering courage. Falon looked up at the sky. Not raining at the moment, but the clouds hovered low and heavy. *If we leave now, we can probably make it to Dad's by nightfall.*

But where was Sam? *Maybe he's gone down to look across the river again.* Falon turned to Patrick. "I think I might know where Sam is. I'm going to run take a look, and I'll be right back."

Patrick nodded, "I'll get everyone loaded up."

Falon rounded the corner of her house at a run. As she raced toward the river path, she felt a tug on her skirt and heard a distinct ripping sound. She nearly tripped, but righted herself and saw with dismay that she had brushed against one of the rose shrubs. The thorns had torn a gash in her skirt. *I'll have to mend it later,* she thought. *Good thing I remembered to pack a needle and thread.* She didn't see Sam at first when she reached the dead tree, but she heard a rustle in the bushes to her left. "Sam?" she whispered.

"Mrs. Carson," came the low reply. "Stay down."

She crouched lower behind the trunk. "I can't see you. Where are you?"

One tentative hand raised from the brush. "Over here."

"What in the world are you doing?" Lifting her skirts, she inched in his direction.

"I'm gonna' get that . . . that . . ."

Falon heard a click, and spotted Sam aiming his squirrel rifle across the water. "No, Sam!" She reached out and pulled the barrel of the gun downward.

His green eyes flashed with anger as he turned toward her. "Why'd you do that?"

"What in the world do you think you're doing?" she hissed. "You'll get us both killed."

"I could have got him!" Sam wiped his reddened face off on his sleeve. "Pa said to take care of things around here. That bastard has been watching the house all day."

Her mouth fell open. "Samuel Garrett! Where did you hear that word?"

He shrugged and muttered something under his breath she couldn't quite make out.

"Sam, listen to me." Falon could hardly hear herself over the thundering of her heart. "It won't help us for you to take a shot at him. Your rifle doesn't have enough range."

He wiped at his face again before he answered, his voice full of determination. "It might." He looked at her. "I want to stay and fight. I don't want to run away. I'm not scared."

She inched closer. *Lord, give me the words to say to him.* "Sam, I know you're not scared, but this isn't about being brave. It's about being smart. If you shoot at him and miss, or if the ball falls short, he'll know where you are. He will start shooting back, and I think his gun has enough range to reach you." When the boy hesitated, she added, "Besides, you told me you know how to drive the mule. I need your help, and I need you with me on the road, to protect us from whatever or whoever might be out there."

Sam considered this then let out a long sigh. "All right. I'll come."

By the time they got back to the house, the distinct—and horribly reminiscent—odor of burning assaulted her nose. *What is going on?* She heard a shout, and one of Houston's men ran to her door with a torch. "That's my house!" she yelled. "What are you doing?"

"Sorry, ma'am. Houston's orders," he replied. "We're to leave nothing standing. Don't want to give comfort to the enemy."

It was the right thing to do. She covered her face with her hands and forced herself to breathe. *This is right. It's the right thing.* But her heart refused to play in tune with her brain. *My house. The house James bought us.* Moments later, instinct had her patting the front of her dress. Her flute was there, safely tucked on a string under her bodice. She had taken to wearing it again since she started playing hymns for the women. "Come on, Sam." She laid a hand on his shoulder to steer him away, all the while keeping her face averted. *I can't see this. I just can't watch.*

Houston's men set fire to every house and barn. Billowing clouds of choking black smoke drifted up from the burning town into the darkening spring sky. From where Falon stood, it looked like all the world was afire. The crackle and roar of the fire mixed with cries and shouts of her neighbors, and the screaming of terrified horses as they tried to outrun the inferno.

Patrick stood by the wagon, waiting. He had helped Maggie up, and was holding Caroline. Falon held out her hands. "Give her to me. Get Stephen and Eli up there next. Sam, are you going to ride?"

"I want to lead the mule." He had the animal's reins in hand.

"All right then, but once we're out of town, you get in the wagon and drive him."

The town emptied quickly. For all her preparations, Falon and her little troupe would be some of the last to leave. She turned for a final look, and had to back away from her house when Caroline started to cry and rub at her eyes—the poor wee thing. The house burned and smoldered in the damp air. The black smoke made Falon's eyes smart, too. But there was no more time. She adjusted the baby's weight on her hip and turned around, "Boys! Sam—that mule's about to get away from you. Stephen, have you got your pack? All right then, let's go."

They started down the road through the center of the burning town, falling into silent step behind their neighbors, Falon shaking her head in disbelief. *How can this be happening again?*

They weren't even out of town when the first cold drops of rain hit her face.

Five miles. Falon huddled under the old hide in the wagon bed with Maggie and the children. She shivered, her head swimming with exhaustion. *We've only gone five miles. At this rate, it'll take three more days to get to the Brazos.*

"Mrs. Carson?"

"Yes, Maggie?"

"We're gonna be all right, aren't we?"

Falon sighed. The boys were asleep, heaven be thanked, so she spoke frankly. "I can't promise you that, Maggie, but I will do my best to keep us all safe."

A long silence followed, punctuated by the patter of rain on the hide. "You scared?"

Am I scared? A trickle of rain had managed to get through their makeshift shelter, and the back of Falon's dress was getting wetter by the minute. "Right now, I'm too cold and wet to be scared."

Maggie chuckled, a deep, throaty sound Falon had never heard before. "I guess if we're not moving tonight, those Mexican soldiers won't be moving either." *Well, they could be.* But to pacify her, Falon answered, "I imagine not." She clenched her teeth to keep them from chattering.

March 27, 1836—I have never welcomed a sunrise more than I did this morning. For the moment, at least, the rain is over. The sky now shines a clean, brilliant blue. Today will surely be better . . .

As soon as they'd swallowed a quick bite of breakfast, the entire camp set off east again. Patrick joined them when they were underway. "Do you have any idea where General Houston is heading?" Falon asked him.

"San Felipe. He wants to make the east bank of the Brazos by nightfall."

"San Felipe is just a mile or two south of Dad's place." Falon, walking with Caroline in her arms, watched Sam driving the mule. He sat straight and tall on the buckboard, handling the reins as though born to it.

"Do you still intend to go to your father's?"

She frowned. "Why wouldn't I?"

"Mrs. Carson, they're probably gone. The house will likely be empty by the time you get there." *Gone. Well, of course.* Falon had been so bent on getting herself under her father's roof, she hadn't stopped to consider that they, too, would have headed east to escape the oncoming army. "But I still feel like I should stop in there. What if they haven't left? What if Maire is there alone with the children?"

"Would your father do that? Would he leave them alone and unprotected?"

"No!" Falon surprised herself with her adamant denial. "No," she repeated, more softly, "he wouldn't. But they still may not have left. And if they're still there, we can help each other along."

"All right." Patrick shifted his pack to his other shoulder and rolled his neck. "I'll go with you." She started to protest that he didn't have to, that she could get there without him, but she knew he would insist—and she knew that she really did need him.

They were barely out of the woods that ran along the Colorado when a shout erupted from the front of the line. Falon was ready to tell Sam to turn the wagon around and make a run for it back into the shelter of the trees, but then she heard the word handed back down the line, "Reinforcements!" along with cheers and whistles. One hundred and thirty men had ridden up the bank of the Brazos, all the way from the coast, to join Houston's army.

The appearance of the extra men, along with the warm spring sun on her face, put Falon's heart easier. The whole camp seemed to feel it, and despite the mud, despite the road being completely washed out in places, they managed to make it to the Brazos that day. By now, though, Falon was teetering on the brink of total exhaustion. She hadn't slept the night before, and had spent most of the day walking, to lighten the wagon's load. It hadn't helped much. She had lost count of how many times she'd been forced to put her shoulder to the back of the wagon to push it out of the sticky, sucking mud.

"Where is your father's place?" Patrick asked when they came in sight of the river.

"North." She pointed. "Not far."

"Tell you what, I'll walk up there with you. We'll leave the wagon here. The children will be safe enough in camp. And when we've checked on your family, we'll come back."

Late afternoon had well settled into dusk by the time they found the house. Falon shouted from the river bank as they walked up, but there was no answer, no light in the window, no smoke easing into the sky from the chimney. *They've gone.* The place was quiet as a graveyard. She pushed open the door. Just as she expected, the house was deserted, and Dad and Maire had taken—or hidden—everything of value. Well, almost everything. A white spot in the gloom of one corner caught her eye. When she went to it, she found a rag doll, abandoned in haste where one of the little girls had dropped it. She bent to pick it up, held it to her heart.

"They've been gone a while," Patrick said. "The hearth is stone cold. There's not an ember left." Falon nodded. The fear and frustration of the past few weeks boiled and welled up inside, and without warning, she burst into tears. *I want my dad. I just want to talk to him.* She clutched the rag doll to her, covering her face with her free hand.

In a short while, she became aware of a warmth on her shoulder. Patrick's hand. "Mrs. Carson, I think they must be all right. They've only gone on ahead. Perhaps we'll catch up with them."

Falon nodded again, then wiped her eyes on her sleeve. Still clutching the rag doll, she took in a long, shuddering breath, "You're right. It's getting dark. We should go."

★17

March 29, 1836—We continue to travel east, impelled by the rumor, widely spread and believed, that Santa Anna has sworn to kill every Anglo man, woman, and child in Texas. I believe it. Word has reached us that Fannin's garrison at Goliad has been massacred. Patrick has told me that they surrendered honorably, but Santa Anna ordered them all shot, even the wounded. We have lost between three and four hundred men in this latest action.

I had thought that we would pick up many more travelers on the way, but most of the houses we pass are already empty, and the evidence of a hasty flight is everywhere. Doors hang ajar, beds are left rumpled and unmade. Dishes, many of which still contain remnants of the last meal, are left scattered on tables, with chairs pulled out, and some turned over . . .

Falon drove the wagon for most of this leg of the journey, with Sam riding shotgun at her side, his squirrel rifle loaded and ready. Maggie sat in the wagon's bed just behind her, both babies at her side. Stephen had planted himself just behind his older brother, and Eli rode in the back corner opposite Stephen. Falon, glancing over her shoulder from time to time, noticed how Stephen stared at Eli, though neither boy spoke. She had the feeling Eli was trying to ignore the younger boy's scrutiny.

When Stephen couldn't control his curiosity any longer, he finally asked, "Are you a slave?" There was no audible answer from the back of the wagon, but Falon figured Eli must have nodded, because Stephen said, "My pa doesn't like slaves."

Falon cleared her throat. "That's not true, Stevie."

"But Pa said . . ."

"I know your Pa. It's not that he doesn't like slaves—it's that he doesn't want to own slaves."

"Oh." A long pause followed. "But you own slaves, right, Mrs. Carson?"

"I guess I do," she muttered.

Falon had to comfort Stephen the next afternoon. Rain had set in again, and when they stopped for a noon meal, he was crouched under the hide, moaning and sniffing. "What's wrong, Stevie? Are you sick?"

"No, ma'am." He shook his head, his expression one of doleful misery. "The dog is gone."

Falon frowned. "Dog? What dog?"

Sam broke in and explained. "There's this old dog that's been following us since we left your house. Stephen wanted to feed him, but I wouldn't let him. Now the dog is gone."

"It's your fault," Stephen spluttered at his brother. "He would have stayed. He wanted to stay."

"There isn't enough food," Sam insisted. "We hardly have enough to feed ourselves."

"Yes we do!" Stephen started crying again.

"No more fighting, boys," Falon said. "Now, listen to me." She pulled Stephen close and dried his eyes with the corner of her shawl. "That old dog is part wolf, did you know that?"

Stephen screwed up his face with disbelief. "Part wolf?"

"Well, sure. Didn't you know? All dogs are part wolf. If he left, it was because he got hungry and needed to hunt something to eat."

"Like what?" He still didn't sound like he believed her.

"Oh, like maybe a rabbit, or a squirrel."

"He can't catch a rabbit," Stephen said petulantly. "He's too old and slow."

"Oh, I think maybe he can if he's hungry enough." Falon smiled, praying that he would believe her and take comfort. "I'd bet, if he's hungry enough, he could even climb a tree and get himself a squirrel."

Now Stephen wiped at his eyes, giggling. "I'd like to see that."

"Wouldn't you, now? I would, too. I'd like to see that old dog scamper up a tree. Wouldn't the squirrel be surprised?"

Stephen and Sam both laughed. Even Eli, who was the quietest boy Falon had ever seen, cracked a grin. Sam said, "The squirrel would have to throw pecans at him!" The rest of that day, the boys entertained themselves by telling stories about the Old Hungry Dog and his exploits. Sam had him biting the head off a rattlesnake, and Stephen told one about the dog holding his breath and swimming to the bottom of the river to catch a fish.

Maggie and Eli had both listened intently. Falon, noting how ragged Eli's clothes had become, promised herself to make him some better ones when they got home—if they ever got home. "How about you, Eli? Why don't you tell us a story?"

The boy's dark eyes shifted from her to his mother. When Maggie nodded, he said, "Well . . ." He tipped his head back, and despite the rain, stared at the tree branches above their heads. "Well, the Old Hungry Dog looked up in the trees and he saw some old turkeys roosting up there. And he said to himself, 'I know how to climb trees now, and I'm awful hungry, but if they see me, those turkeys will fly away.' So he looked around and saw leaves on the ground. He stuck leaves all over himself so that they looked like feathers . . ."

Stephen interrupted: "How'd he stick 'em on?"

Eli scratched one ear absently. "With spit. He licked 'em and stuck 'em on."

Stephen giggled. "And then what?"

"And then he climbed up in the tree and sat real still. One old turkey looked at him and said, 'You are one funny-looking turkey.' And the old dog said, 'Not any funnier-looking than you.' And he pretended to fall asleep. He started snoring, real soft-like, and that put the turkey right to sleep. And when he was good and asleep, the Old Hungry Dog grabbed him, jumped down out of the tree, and had himself a turkey dinner."

They all laughed. Stephen clapped his hands with delight. "That's the best story ever!"

So Eli became their storyteller. They hardly heard a word out of him until, usually at dinnertime when they'd stopped for the day, he had a new tale ready. Falon welcomed the stories as a diversion for the boys, and as a chance to stop having to think about food—or the lack of it—or the rain, or finding her family, or whether she'd ever see James again.

From San Felipe, they headed north. Patrick, walking alongside Falon just ahead of the wagon, shook his head over this new direction. "I don't understand it. Most everyone wants Houston to stop somewhere and make a stand. San Felipe looked like as good a place as any to me."

"Do we have enough men?"

"Who can say? We don't know how many men Santa Anna has, or even where they all are. But if I were a betting man . . ." He glanced toward her, tipping his hat in apology. "I would like the odds that the Mexican troops are south."

March 31, 1836—It has taken two more days, but we have finally reached the next stopping place, a plantation owned by a man named Groce. One of the infants in the camp has died. Louisa Jackson brought me the sad

news. It was Eleanor Thompson's little girl. Eleanor slept in my barn that first night the people of Gonzales came. Even then, I worried that such a wee infant would have trouble on the long, cold road. The poor little thing starved when Eleanor's milk dried up.

I stood with the other women while the baby was buried. One of the men dug a tiny hole on a bit of a rise, and lowered the baby's swaddled body in. Sam found a good-sized rock to mark the grave, and Patrick said a prayer. It was strange to me that no one cried, not even the baby's mother, though she looked bruised around the eyes. It is as if the cold and wet has finally seeped into our souls and left us all numb. Since then I have made sure that Maggie has enough to eat, even when it means I go without . . .

Groce's plantation turned out to be a welcome respite from the long march. The cold and rain continued off and on, but Falon and Patrick managed to construct a shelter of sorts under the cover of a stand of large trees. In spite of the gnawing in her stomach, Falon found comfort in the shelter and the chance to have a fire. Provisions were not much better, but a small lake nearby offered the boys a chance to fish, and they could usually bring in one or two small catches. Houston had ordered all the cattle driven to the eastern bank of the Brazos so that the Mexican army could not get at them.

Falon and Louisa Jackson had camped next to each other. An easy friendship had sprung between them. They cooked what little they had together while the Garrett boys played with Louisa's children. "Is Patrick your brother?" Louisa asked Falon one afternoon. She was bent over a dress of her daughter's that had been torn, mending the hole with tiny, even stitches.

Falon shook her head. "No. Actually, he was our servant for a time. He came over from Ireland as an indentured man, and my James bought his bond. Patrick worked for us for ten years. He's free now." Peering into a bag, she added, "There's only enough corn for one more meal."

"I have a cupful or two in a bag in my wagon, but that's all. What sort of man is he?"

"Who? Patrick?" Falon smiled. "He's the best sort. He's been a true friend. I cannot tell you all the ways he's helped me. And have you ever heard him sing?"

She nodded, "One of the times you played hymns for us." After a long silence, Louisa added with a laugh, "Still, Patrick is Irish, and he's not much to look at, is he?"

"That he is not." Something made Falon look up, and there he stood. She couldn't keep the guilty look from her face, and Patrick's expression was stunned—and stung, as if she had slapped him.

"I just came to give you these, Mrs. Carson." He held up a pair of prairie chickens then set them down near her feet. Tipping his hat, he turned and walked away.

"Oh, dear," Louisa murmured. "He heard that."

Falon could only stare, open-mouthed, at his retreating back, her stomach feeling as if she'd swallowed a cannon ball. Me and my tongue. *Ah, Patrick, I would not have hurt you, not for the wide, wide world. But that's just what I've done.*

April 2, 1836—I hardly slept a wink last night, but had a wonderful surprise this morning . . .

Falon had just come up from the lake where she had been laundering diapers and trying to think of a way to apologize to Patrick, to make things right again. The rare sunny day had her hoping they might have dry clothes by evening. She knelt, spreading the diapers out on the sun-dappled grass.

"Falon!"

The familiar voice had her scrambling to her feet. "Dad!" she cried and ran to his arms. "Tha' art well?" She found herself slipping into her old speech, as she often did when she was with him. "Are Maire and the children with you?"

"I'm well, lass, and it's good to see thee safe." He held her tight, nearly crushing the breath from her. When he let her go, she saw bright tears standing in his eyes. "Maire and the children are already across the Sabine. I went with them that far and came back here."

She frowned. "You left them?"

"We have men there to protect the women and little ones," he explained. "Robbie and I came back in. We've joined Houston."

"But Dad, Robbie's only fourteen."

"Fourteen, aye. He's old enough to help fight for his place in this world. Dinna' worry, lass. I don't intend for him to go to battle. He'll be helping, don't ye see? He can help wi' the baggage, and he can be a camp guard."

"Where is he?"

"He's gone down to the lake with the other lads." Father shook his head. "All of us fishing that water, I'm thinking we're bound to fish it dry. And where is your James?"

Falon shook her head. "I don't know, Dad. He left in late November, and I haven't seen or heard from him since."

Her father's face went pale, "Ah, forgive me, lass. We left the house that quick, and I figured James would have you out of your place. If I had known tha' was alone, I would have turned back for thee."

She slipped a hand into his. "Never worry, Dad. I had plenty of company." *And Patrick was there.* "Oh, I did stop by the place, and I found a doll that one of the girls left behind."

He smiled. "Little Lizzie will be happy for it. She cried for two days about that doll."

Just then, Maggie called out, "Mrs. Carson, can you take Caroline for a while?"

"Of course." She lifted the baby from Maggie's lap. "Dad, this is Caroline."

He took off his cap, running his fingers through his hair. "Tha's had a baby? Why, that's wonderful. How is it we didn't know?"

"No, Dad, she's not mine. Do you remember Kathleen, the redhead? Her family came with us from Anahuac."

"The O'Connor girl?"

"That's right. This is her baby."

"And a right pretty little miss she is." When the baby reached out for his beard, he took her in his arms. "But where is her mother? Are the O'Connors with thee?"

"Kathleen married Mr. Garrett. This is their third child. Kathleen died after the baby was born." Her father's eyes went soft and sad. "That's a terrible loss, Falon. So you're looking after her little ones now?"

"For now, yes, until their father comes back."

"And where is he?"

Falon sighed. "I don't know, Dad. He wasn't in the Alamo, and he didn't say anything about staying in Goliad. I was hoping he'd be here, but I haven't seen him yet."

The baby began to fuss, and Camran handed her back to Falon. "I think I remember Garrett. If I see him, I'll tell him where he can find you." He bent, giving her a quick kiss. "I'd better get back to the men. Houston has us drilling; he's trying to whip us into some kind of army."

"Come see me when you can."

April 11, 1836—No sign of Patrick. I wonder if he is still in the camp. Apparently, General Houston finds Groce's plantation to his liking. We have remained here for the better part of two weeks, and Houston orders regular drills for the men. Scouting parties continually go in and out of the camp, reporting the position and movements of the Mexican army. I have heard that Santa Anna's army is divided, and that one general is in this place with so many men, and another general is elsewhere with so many more. What I know about military matters could dance with an angel on the head of a pin, with plenty of room to spare, but it seems to me that dividing an army and sending them all over the place is poor planning . . .

The following day, Falon found herself standing beside her younger brother—who was now a full head taller than herself—on the bank of the swollen Brazos river, staring in amazement at *The Yellowstone.* "That's a steamboat, you say?" she asked him. "How does it work?"

"I don't know, exactly. It burns wood or coal, and the steam from the fire is what makes the thing go." Robbie grinned at her. "I have heard of these, but I never expected to see one. Houston plans to use it to ferry us across."

It took all that day, and half of the next, but while the women and children were ferried across the river in boats and on broad rafts, Houston pressed *The Yellowstone* into service as a troop transport. No sooner had the army crossed the river, when another company of men arrived from the south. Falon had to smile at Sam and Stephen's excited chatter as the ox-drawn wagon lumbered past them. In the bed sat two brand-new iron cannons, a gift to Texas from the people of Cincinnati, Ohio. The men had dubbed them "The Twin Sisters," and they looked a formidable pair. *Surely,* Falon thought, s*urely we will win this.*

But soon, too soon, it was time to say goodbye. To her surprise, Patrick came to her tent at first light. "Looks like we're off at last." He doffed his hat. "I wish you well, Mrs. Carson. It was a pleasure knowing you."

She could hardly look at him. "Don't talk like that, Patrick. You'll come through this just fine."

"I expect I will," he answered with a nod. "But whichever way it goes, I won't be coming back. I'm thinking I'll go to New Orleans, may become a cattle agent." He put his hat on again, repeating, "I wish you well." He started away. She called after him: "Patrick O'Donnell, you are one of the finest men I've ever known."

He stopped for a long moment. When he finally turned, his expression had relaxed and his eyes were bright. "Thank you, Falon Carson." And he was gone.

Puzzled, she wondered, *How did he know my given name? I never told him what it was.* And then it hit her. Joe Everson had heard it on their journey to the Brazos. Patrick must have asked Joe.

Father came with Robbie a little later. "Houston is ordering us to meet at a place called Donoho's. From there, I suppose we'll head south. The government is in Harrisburg, and we need to go to them because Santa Anna's on his way there. You ladies are to go east until you're safely across the Sabine in the United States. He won't dare send his army over that river. He'd have a fight on his hands the likes of which he couldn't imagine."

The recent lack of food had left Falon feeling weak and ill. She protested, "Surely Houston isn't sending us on with no protection."

"You'll have some, but not a lot." Father shook his head, "Likely not enough. We need every able-bodied man we can get to go on this campaign." He reached out and smoothed a stray curl from her face. "It's now or never, I'm thinking."

Falon wanted to be strong. She needed to be strong for him, but the tears came anyway. He pulled her in for a last embrace. "Texas is ma' home, lass. I could na' fight for ma' home in Scotland. I canna' fail to fight for this one." He cupped her cheek with one hand and kissed her forehead. The bright morning sun sparkled her blur of tears as she watched him pick up his pack. "Ah, I nearly forgot." He dug into the pack, and pulling out a folded piece of paper, handed it to her. "This is a letter for you from our George. He got a last note out with one of the couriers before . . ." he cleared his throat, "well—before." He slung the pack over his shoulder, looking at Robbie. "We'd best be going."

Robbie gave Falon a quick, embarrassed hug. "Wish us luck, Sis."

They turned away, and with Robbie striding at his side, Father took the road leading south. She watched their backs for as long as she could see them, until they were swallowed up, just one more pair of soldiers in Houston's ragtag army.

Ah, Dad. She groaned and dropped, heedless, to her knees. Her tears mingled with countless others that watered the earth at this parting. "Lord, keep them safe. Keep them safe and bring them home."

April 14, 1836—With the men gone, there is no reason for us to remain here. Indeed, there is much cause to pack up and continue on our way toward the Sabine. We do not know where the Mexican troops are, though we have heard they are concentrated to our south. Surely Santa Anna has more important matters on his hands than chasing a pitiful band of women and children out of Texas. Nevertheless, out of Texas we must go, if for no other reason than to keep the little ones safe. I loathe the thought of making this journey . . .

The United States of America was a long, long way from Groce's plantation. Days later, after the third river crossing, this one in pouring rain, Falon was as near to giving up as she'd ever been in her life. They had been forced to wait the better part of a week for the ferry because of the stampede of people trying to get across to relative safety on the eastern shore.

And which river was this? Falon no longer remembered or cared. She was soaked to the skin, shivering with cold, and desperately hungry. On the few good days, they traveled maybe twenty miles. This was not going to be one of the good days. *If I don't get out of this cold soon, I'm going to catch a chill, and then I'll be no use to anyone.*

She spotted a line of trees ahead and climbed onto the seat of the wagon. The shelter of trees was better than none at all. She snapped the reins, and the wagon lurched forward uncertainly in the mud.

"Ma'am!" came a shout from behind her. "Ma'am! You there in the wagon—stop!"

Falon had been camped close enough to men for the past weeks to have learned a few choice words. She used one of these now, under her breath, as she reined in the mule. "Ma'am," a rider appeared at her side on a gray—and thoroughly miserable-looking—horse. "That's not our road. Don't be riding on ahead. We can't protect you if you do. Stay with the group." He rode off again.

A short laugh burst out of her. *Who do you think you are? My husband? My father?* Heedless of his warning, Falon snapped the reins, and the mule took off toward the tree line. There was no getting out of the rain; she knew it, yet the trees still represented shelter and safety. The wagon almost bogged down in the mud twice, but after the better part of half an hour, she drove in under the branches. Fat rain drops spattered the ground. Driving was a little easier on an open way that seemed to be a road through the woods. A thick bed of fallen leaves blanketed the mud. *Where does this lead, I wonder?*

The rain let up a little, and being under the cover of the trees helped. Falon pulled up, and the mule stopped. His breath steamed and the muscles on his back quivered. She pushed her dripping curls from her face and looked around. She was alone, as far as she could tell. The others were all still back at the river, or had taken another way. At the moment she didn't care. She leaned forward, resting her forehead on her knees. *How much farther? Another week? Can we survive another week of this?* One of the boys coughed underneath the hide – deep, hacking barks. *There has to be some way out of this rain.*

A quiet noise to her left made her raise her head. She found herself staring into a pair of black eyes. *Indians.* Too late, she remembered the warning. *Don't be riding on ahead.* The Indian nearest her, a man who looked about her father's age, glanced back over his shoulder and said something. He wasn't alone. A woman stood about ten feet behind him. They were both wrapped in deer skins and appeared to be drier than she felt. At the man's bidding, the woman came forward, and Falon saw that she carried a basket. As she approached the wagon, she held it up.

The gesture was unmistakable. "You want to give this to me?" Falon took the basket. It was heavy, and she had to support it with both hands. A beautifully tanned animal skin covered the top. When she lifted it, she found dried strips of meat and a good quantity of cornmeal. It was enough to feed them for three or four days. The wetness that sprang into Falon's eyes had nothing to do with the intermittent drops that splashed all around.

The man spoke. "My people will help your people." He pointed back toward the river. "My people will help your people."

"Who are you?" Falon asked.

"We are Coushatta. Your people have trouble. My people will help." He gestured to her. "Come, follow."

Cradling the basket in one arm, Falon climbed down from the seat. Taking the reins in her other hand, she followed the man and woman deeper into the trees.

April 19?, 1836—I have lost count of the days, and am unsure of the date, but I doubt that it much matters now. We have received help from a most unlikely place. The Coushatta aided me in constructing a temporary shelter in these woods, and we have a good fire going, in spite of the damp. This is the second time in my life I have been helped by an Indian. Others in our group have also received food and shelter from these good people. I have no way to repay them, or even to adequately thank them . . .

The woman also brought a handful of herbs and gave them to me, making signs that I needed to brew a tea for Sam's cough from them. He doesn't care for the taste, but has been obedient to drink it down. I think the heat of the drink helps him as much as anything.

I read my Bible some yesterday, and found a passage that might have been written just for me. It's in Isaiah's book. "Hast thou not known? Hast thou not heard, that the everlasting God, the LORD, the Creator of the ends of the earth, fainteth not, neither is weary? There is no searching of his understanding. He giveth power to the faint; and to them that have no might he increaseth strength. Even the youths shall faint and be weary, and the young men shall utterly fall: But they that wait upon the LORD shall renew their strength; they shall mount up with wings as eagles; they shall run, and not be weary; and they shall walk, and not faint."

Maybe there is hope . . .

They remained there for two days, resting and gathering strength for the next leg of the journey. The Coushatta man and his wife brought another basket of food before they left. Tears streamed down Falon's face as she accepted this second offering, but she didn't care if they saw her cry. She said to the man, "Our Good Book tells about people giving from their poverty. I don't remember exactly how it goes, but I believe you will somehow be rewarded for helping us. You have saved our lives."

The man replied, "Maybe our people have trouble. Your people help."

"I will remember," she answered. "I will teach these children, and they will remember." She turned to the woman. Words would not do; she would not understand them, so Falon leaned close and kissed her lightly on the cheek. The woman returned the kiss, smiling and nodding.

"You go on this road, this trace," the man said. "It is through our land. No one will hurt you." With that, he turned and walked away, and the woman followed with a final wave back at Falon. She watched until they disappeared into the trees.

It was with deep reluctance that she packed and prepared to leave. "You know, Mrs. Carson," Maggie murmured after she'd taken her seat in the bed of the wagon, "you would have been there by now if you didn't have to drag us all along."

"Oh, hush, Maggie." Falon double-checked the camp for anything they might have missed. She returned to the wagon. "Sam, do you want to drive a while?"

"Yes, ma'am." He climbed up onto the seat.

"All right. Remember what the Indian said? You follow that trace. See how it runs through the trees? If you aren't sure which way it's going, tell me, and we'll figure it out together."

She settled in beside Maggie, taking Caroline from her. "I don't think it much matters, as long as we're going east." They rode for a while in silence. Maggie's baby had rested his head against his mother's neck, and his beautiful brown eyes bored into Falon's, as if he could read her thoughts. When she finally tore her gaze from little Jack's face, she said, "I promised the mother of these children that I'd look after them. You are here because I need you to help me. I don't want you to fret. If it's possible to get us to safety, that is what I am bound to do." She couldn't quite bring herself to add, *because Jack is James' son.*

★18

April 21, 1836—Texas is behind us now, though we haven't quite left it. Will we ever, I wonder? One thing is sure, Texas will never leave us. Its marks will remain . . .

Two days later, they reached the banks of the Sabine. When Falon found out where they were, she raised her face to the sky in thanks. *We made it. We're all alive, and we made it.* The only major loss was Sam's shoes. The day before, the knee-deep mud had sucked them off his feet. He was still coughing, and Falon worried that being barefoot would make him sicker. So she had him ride in the wagon, saying, "You keep your feet covered, you hear?"

The last two days had not been so cold, and the rain had stopped. Still, when they came to the river, they were forced to wait. Hundreds and hundreds of families were trying to get across to safety. From where Falon stood, she could see a huge encampment on the other side. Tents and temporary shelters had sprung up along the river's eastern bank, appearing to stretch for miles in both directions. Toward evening, they reached the head of the line, and the raft touched the shore. "Just drive that mule right on here, ma'am," the ferryman called out cheerfully. "I'll have you on the other side in no time." They were about halfway across when the raft pitched and bucked in the swollen, rushing water. She heard a hoarse cry, and then a scream as Sam tumbled from the wagon, hit the raft on his side, and slid into the river.

"No!" Falon yelled. Without thinking, she jumped down and dove in after him. She had never learned how to swim, but instinct took over, and kicking and paddling in the frigid water she surfaced, gasping for breath, gasping at the cold. And there was Sam, just off to her right. She reached out and grabbed at him. She got a fingerhold on his hand, but it wasn't enough. The raging water pulled them apart.

Suddenly, something hit the top of her head, and she heard the ferryman yell, "Grab it!"

He had thrown her a rope. Falon clutched the line in one hand, and with a mighty kick, surged toward Sam again. This was her last chance. Her skirts were dragging her down. "Take my hand!" she screamed. Sam reached out for her, and this time, she managed to get a grip on his forearm. At the same time, she felt a tug on the rope; the ferryman was pulling her in. "Kick, Sam! Kick toward me."

He did, and she pulled on him until she could give him a handle on the rope. The next minutes seemed like forever before they were at the raft again. "Take him first," she pushed Sam ahead of her. The ferryman took hold of the boy's shirt at the collar and hauled him up. Once on board, Sam rolled onto his hands and knees, coughing and retching.

"Give me your hand, ma'am." Falon reached up, and the ferryman pulled at her, but her skirts dragged so heavy in the water that she slipped out of his grip. The water closed over her head, filled her ears, sound went dim. But the next thing she knew, he had her with both hands, and with a loud groan, he hefted her up onto the raft. She was still in the water from the waist down, but now she could breathe, and with one final push, she got her legs up. She turned on her side, coughing and gasping.

The ferryman bent over her, his hands on his knees, his face florid with effort. "Ma'am, I've seen a lot happen working this ferry, but that was the most dang-fool . . ." He paused and shook his head. "You could have drowned."

Falon pushed her dripping hair out of her eyes. "What's your name, sir?

"Spivey, ma'am."

She sat up and started wringing water out of her skirt. "Mr. Spivey," she said through chattering teeth, "no one is drowning here today." Still shaking his head, he went back to his place at the ropes. Falon found her balance on the lurching raft and stood. Her legs wobbled under her, as if her bones had dissolved in the water. She laid a hand on Sam's shoulder. "Are you all right?" When he nodded, she said, "Wring out your shirt the best you can and get back in the wagon. We'll get a fire going as soon as we find a place to camp."

Ignoring the wide-eyed stares of Maggie and the children, Falon staggered to the wagon and stopped a moment to lean her head against the mule's flank. *Breathe. Just breathe in and out.* The cold air felt so good in her lungs. She heard, rather than saw, Sam climb back up onto the seat, and she turned her face to the sky for the second time that day. *Thank you.*

Minutes later, they were across. She took the mule's reins and led him onto solid ground, the wagon creaking and groaning behind her. Before she climbed onto the seat, she called out, "Thank you, Mr. Spivey." He was already on his way back across the current, but he raised one hand to wave.

We made it. We're safe. Or as safe as we can be for now. Falon marveled at this hard, this peculiar grace that had carried her through. She shook the mule's reins, and he moved forward and up the bank. *Pastor was wrong all those years ago. Hard as it was, leaving Scotland wasn't punishment for our sins, but something else.* The beginnings of a smile tugged at the corners of her mouth. *A test maybe?* Falon took a deep breath, looking around her, startled. *Was grass always this green?* Everything around her stood out in sharp relief—the ruts in the path up from the river, the branches of the trees waving in the wind—it was all fresh to her newly baptized eyes. Even the shouts and laughter of the children in the camp rang sharp as crystal in her ears.

Now what? She turned to look up at Sam. "Help me look for a good place to camp." In the end, they chose a spot on a little rise, well away from the river.

"This looks good," Sam said, pointing. "Lots of wood lying around."

Falon nodded. "And if it rains, we won't be sitting in a puddle." She gave him a sidelong smile. "I don't know about you, but I've had enough water to last me a while."

Using the wagon and the hide, they set up a shelter, while Stephen gathered sticks for a fire. She got the one dry blanket they had from the wagon and held it up as a curtain for Sam. "Strip off all your things, Sam. I can't let you sit in the wet." When he was done, blushing and muttering under his breath all the while, she wrapped the blanket around him.

He frowned at her. "What about you?"

"I think I have a dry shift in here somewhere," she said, digging through their baggage. "That and my shawl will do for me." She glanced around. "I don't expect we'll be receiving many callers." Once they had a fire going, Falon looked in the basket. They had enough food for two more meals, and then they would have to forage in the forest. "Do you still have powder and shot for your squirrel gun?" she asked.

"Only a little. How long are we going to have to stay here?"

Falon glanced at the others, shook her head and lowered her voice. "I have no idea."

That evening after they had eaten, she remembered George's letter. She had stuffed it into her pack, along with her flute and journal and her two books, forgetting about it until now. She rummaged around in the pack and pulled out the folded square of light-golden paper. *I gave this paper to him just before he left.* Sitting as close to the fire as she could without getting singed, she smoothed the creases and held it up to the firelight. George's handwriting was surprisingly prissy and precise.

March 2, 1836

To my sister Falon,

By the time you read this, I will probably be dead. The Alamo is surrounded, and the Mexicans are closing in on the roads. I just hope the courier makes it out with this letter. Since I am about to meet my Maker, I wish to confess that your sister Annie died because of me. I saw you standing by the loch that day, and I sneaked up behind and pushed you. I didn't see Annie there. Your skirts hid her from my sight. When I pushed you, you stumbled over her, and you both went in the water. I ran and got your parents, but by then it was too late.

It was never your fault, but mine alone. I didn't mean for anyone to be hurt. I am sorry for what I did, and I am sorry for what I said to you about it. I hope you can forgive me.

Your brother, George Morgan

Falon lowered the letter and stared into the fire. She had no real memory of that day by the loch, only the bits she saw in her dreams. *So George pushed me. He meant only a boy's mischief, but Annie died, and he carried the guilt of it all this time. No one ever knew.*

Now, sitting by the fire with the letter glowing in the firelight, the hateful things he had said to her, the way he had acted around her made sense. But that was done now. He was gone. Slowly, almost reverently, she touched the paper to the fire until the flames caught it. The light flared as the paper burned. Smoke filled her nostrils as the page curled and browned, then quickly turned black. In less than a minute, George's letter was just another layer of ash. Falon bowed her head. *I forgive you, George. I hope you're at peace.*

She buried her face in her arms, took a deep breath, then slowly let it out. *I'm free.* She had been nailed to the wall of her past, and now the wall was gone, burned away. The future could be anything.

The next morning dawned warmer and clear. "We might actually dry out today," Falon remarked to Maggie as she picked up the cook pot and headed toward the river. They had camped about a third of a mile from the bank, and after she had filled the pot from the stream and started to lug it back, she began to question the wisdom of settling in so far from the water. She stopped and set the pot down, pulling a handkerchief out of her pocket, which she folded to make a cushion for the handle.

Suddenly, a ragged cheer erupted from behind her. Curious, she left the pot and ran toward the sound. Two women at the water's edge were hugging each other, laughing and crying at the same time. "What's happened?" she asked them.

"It's over!" one exclaimed. "The war is over, and we've won! Santa Anna has surrendered."

Falon felt as if the breath had been knocked out of her; her knees threatened to buckle. "Are you sure? How do you know this?"

"A rider came through," the other answered, pointing north. Go on up that way, if you don't believe us. He's still there. Wait—here he comes again."

The rider came thundering back downriver, on the opposite bank, waving his hat in the air and yelling. "Houston has won! The war is over, and Santa Anna is defeated!" Another cheer rose from the encampment along the Sabine. One of the women turned to her friend. "Millie, can we go home now, do you think?" The other shook her head. "I don't think I will. There's nothing left to go back to."

Falon turned away. *What am I going to do? My house has been destroyed. What is left for me?* She found her pot and picked it up. *I suppose I have to go back, if the children have any hope of finding their father. But how long should we stay here?* She started toward her camp, when a man stepped into her path, stopping her. "Hello, sweetheart."

Falon gasped, dropping the pot. "James!" He limped on a cane toward her and caught her with one arm as she ran to him and threw her arms around his neck. "You're all right!" She squeezed her eyes shut tight, half afraid that if she opened them, he would be gone again. "I was so worried."

"I worried about you, too," he answered, kissing her face. "I'm sorry I left you."

She opened her eyes again. Dan Garrett stood just behind him. He smiled, "Instead of delivering your message, I brought him to you."

Falon released her husband and stood back, studying him. A generous sprinkling of gray lightened his beard, and there was an edge of sadness around his eyes that hadn't been there before. "Where have you been all this time? What happened to you?"

"I got myself in the middle of a fight down at San Patricio," he told her. "One of the Mexican armies ambushed a company of our men who were rounding up horses. I just happened to be with them—I was planning to go on my way the next morning—and when the Mexicans attacked, I was caught up in it."

"How did you get away?"

James stared at the ground for a long moment. "I shouldn't have gotten away. A horse fell on me and broke my leg." He sighed and raised his eyes to meet hers. "But Joe Everson was there. I had found him, you see, and I was bringing him back. He pulled me out from under the horse and hid me until the troops were gone." He chewed his lip a moment. "He fed me, and when I got a fever, he nursed me. Joe could have left, could have gotten clean away, but he stayed."

Falon felt suddenly lightheaded. The trees around her seemed to sway as if in a windstorm. "You brought Joe back?"

"No, sweetheart. I was going to until . . . well, I let him go. I wrote out a paper saying he's a free man, signed it with Garrett here as a witness, and gave it to Joe. He's gone now. I don't know where."

Dan interrupted them, "Mrs. Carson, where are my children?"

"Oh, they're up that way," she pointed. "Bear to the right past that fallen tree and go about a quarter mile. Your children are fine," she added. "They will be happy to see you."

James pointed to the spilled pot on the ground with a grin. Now, this is the second time I've made you do that. Let me fill it up again." She walked with him to the river's edge. "How long will it take your leg to mend?" He shook his head. "There was no way to properly set the bone. This is as mended as it will ever be." He glanced at her, and away again. "I will always have this limp."

She knew by his manner that his injury went deeper than his bones. Casting about for something else to say, she remarked, "So, the war is over."

"It is." He grunted as he stooped to fill the pot. "I think, in another day or two we can go home." He straightened and faced her, studying her eyes for a long minute. "That is, if that's what you want." When she hesitated, he asked, "Do you want to go back with me?" Falon's heart hammered, hard and raw, in her chest. "I do, but with two conditions."

Her husband's voice went quiet, cautious. "And what would they be?"

She took a deep breath. "First, I want you to see to it that both of Maggie's sons go free as soon as they are grown." His face flushed scarlet, but he nodded once. "All right. I will do that. And the other?"

The sun shone on him in the little clearing between the trees, kindled his fair hair so that it shone pale gold. In a rush, she said, "I want you to stop selling slaves."

"And if I don't?" He looked away from her. "No, don't answer that." He stared at the ground where his cane pierced it. Finally, he said, "You know, I always thought at some point, you'd ask this of me.

And I asked myself what I'd do." He raised his eyes again. "Truth is, I still don't know."

Part of Falon wanted to go to him, to comfort him and tell him she'd stay with him no matter what, but the other part, this new and strange part of her, held on to herself. "You let me know when you decide."

Just then she heard a woman calling her. "Ellen! Ellen Carson!" She stepped back from him and turned. It was Louisa Jackson. "Ellen," Louisa came and took her hand. "I'm so glad I found you! I wondered where you were. I lost track of you in all the panic."

She held Louisa's hand in both her own, smiled and pulled herself up to her full height. "My name is Falon."

May 30, 1836—We have returned to what is left of Columbus. It is not much more than piles of ashes, though many of the kitchen gardens are still here, and have flourished in the rain. My rosebushes were trampled to the ground, and I thought they were dead, but yesterday I found new leaves on both of them. This time, life wins. It's one more small thing to be thankful for.

My monthly courses are very late, nearly eight weeks now, and with other signs, my female neighbors assure me that I am finally going to have a child. I haven't told James yet, but I know he'll be pleased, and since he is raising and trading cattle now, he will be home more, and that makes things easier for both of us.

He has started building us a new house right where the old one stood. The neighbors are helping, and we will turn around and help build theirs, until we all have shelter over our heads again.

On the way home from the Sabine, I found a fiddle that someone dropped on the flight east. It was half-covered with mud, but none had gotten inside, and it cleaned up nicely. I took it to Dad's when we stopped by. It had no bow, but Dad says he can make one, and he can restring the fiddle. I gave Lizzie her rag doll.

This is our home now, Texas is. Home is family and friends, as Dad once said, but I know now that home is also a place. This place is ours. By the grace of God, this is where we will stay.

★Author Notes

Most of the characters in this story are fictional, with a few exceptions. Sam Houston and Stephen F. Austin were, of course, real people. So were Elizabeth Tumlison and her son, George.

The Texas army, under the command of General Sam Houston, won the **Battle of San Jacinto** on April 21, 1836. The fighting officially lasted less than half an hour, although some of the Texans, enraged by the slaughter at the Alamo and the execution of prisoners of war at Goliad, continued to kill Mexican soldiers well after they were ordered to halt. Santa Anna himself was found the following day, wearing a private's uniform, trying to escape the vicinity. Escape was virtually impossible, since the field of battle was surrounded by bayous and swamps, and the only bridge out had been burned by Houston's orders.

Santa Anna surrendered and signed the Treaty of Velasco on May 14, which gave Texas her independence and made her a republic. This did not, however, stop Santa Anna from attempting, at a later date, to reclaim Texas as part of Mexico. Texas remained a republic from 1836 through 1845, at which time it was annexed into the United States. Mexico did not officially recognize Texas as part of the United States until the Treaty of Guadalupe Hidalgo was signed in 1848, at the end of the Mexican War. Santa Anna himself, the self-styled "Napoleon of the West," went in and out of power in Mexico and was finally exiled to various islands in the Caribbean. When he grew old and was no longer considered a threat to the Mexican government, he was allowed to return to Mexico City, where he died in 1876 at the age of 82.

Sam Houston became the first regularly elected president of the Republic of Texas, and served for two terms. When Texas was annexed, he became one of the U.S. senators to represent the new state. He was governor of Texas when the Civil War broke out. He opposed secession from the Union, but the Texas Legislature voted against him, and when he would not swear loyalty to the Confederate States, he was removed from office. Retiring from public life, Houston moved his family to Huntsville, Texas, where he died in 1863 at age 70.

After being detained in Mexico for twenty-eight months, **Stephen F. Austin** was finally released and allowed to return to Texas. He served as commissioner to the United States during the Texas Revolution. His task was to solicit money and volunteers for the cause, and to promote the annexation of Texas by the United States. After the war, he was appointed Secretary of State for the Republic of Texas in 1836, and was serving in that office when he died in December of that same year, at the age of 43.

Elizabeth Tumlison was one of Austin's original settlers, and it was on her land that the present-day city of Columbus was built. Her husband, James, had been the first alcalde (mayor) of the settlement, and was killed in an Indian attack in 1823. Their son, George (his last name is variously spelled "Tomlinson") was at Gonzales when the call came from the Alamo for reinforcements. He answered that call and was killed in the battle on March 6, 1836.

The **Coushatta** did offer help to the settlers running eastward trying to escape Santa Anna's army, by offering food and shelter. Years later, when other tribes were expelled from Texas, the Coushatta remained, and were granted reservation land in the Big Thicket, in what is now Polk County.

Though they are not named in the story, four sons of Scotland died in the Alamo. They were **Richard W. Ballentine**, age 22, **John McGregor**, age 28 (who had his bagpipe with him and played along with David Crockett on the fiddle), **Isaac Robinson**, age 28, and **David L. Wilson**, age 29.

It is said that the Texans might have won at the Alamo if they had only had one or two more Scots.

★About the Author

Kim Wiese is a Texas woman. Her roots in the Lone Star state go back several generations to men and women of courage and determination, to rugged pioneering families who worked hard and played hard. She is grateful for the legacies they left behind.

Kim lives in North Central Texas, where she writes, teaches, and enjoys her antique roses. She is married to Bob, and they have four grown children (who are in and out) and one big couch potato of a dog.